BIRTH OF FLAMES

BIRTH OF FLAMES

Flames of Eternal Struggles

Brice Nowacki

Commonwealth Books Inc.,

A Commonwealth Publications Trade
BIRTH OF FLAMES
This edition published 2022
by Commonwealth Books Inc.,
All rights reserved

Copyright © 2022 by James W Haddad
Published in the United States by Commonwealth Books Inc., New York.

Library of Congress Control Number: 2022938715

ISBN: 978-1-892986-38-2 (Trade)
ISBN: 978-1-892986-39-9(E-PUB)

This work is a novel and any similarity to actual persons or events is purely coincidental.

First Commonwealth Books Trade Edition: August 2022

PUBLISHED BY COMMONWEALTH BOOKS, INC.,
www.commonwealthbooks@aol.com
www.commonwealthbooksinc.com

Manufactured in the United States of America

PROLOGUE

Deep inside the Hilos Galaxy, nine planets circled a sun. The third planet from the sun, Cilos, was born, and a meteor collided with the planet, creating a large land mass. Over the eons, the mass split into five different kingdoms. North was the Celestial Nation, bearing the fire. To the east was the strong Terra Nation that had control of the elements of earth, making its residents amazing crafters and engineers. To the southeast was the dark and corrupt Chaos Nation, where a devastating plague ravaged the land, blocking it from the rest of the world. To the southwest was the Aura Nation, populated by a proud people who lived high in the mountains and mastered the elements in the sky. Last, in the west, was the Kai Nation, where its people mastered water and controlled it with ease.

After thousands of years of war, the nations agreed to peace and banded together to create the School for Flyers, a military school to monitor each nation's strength to make sure one didn't gain too much power over the others.

In the middle of the continent, Kit, a young man of seventeen, began a great journey.

Flames of Eternal Struggles

Yellow sunlight glared through the cracks in the hut. I buried my face into my pillow, doing best to ignore it.

"Kit, it's time to wake! We have a busy day!"

Shaking my head, I tried to ignore him, too. At the sound of water rushing in through the window, I peeked past the edge of the blanket and saw several gallons of water hovering over me. I looked for a way to escape but didn't see it and stared at the water.

"Last warning, Kit! You've slept away most of the day."

I jumped out of bed, but I wasn't fast enough. The water drenched me, as I walked to the door. When I stepped outside, I saw Master standing there, his black hair flowing in the breeze, his green eyes staring like daggers.

"So, my apprentice wakes and got himself drenched, I see."

I flicked my arms, splashing water to the ground. Fish leaped from the water to catch flies. Our village houses were made of straw that floated on the surface, with bamboo paths for walking.

"Yes, I did, Master. Care to get this water off me? It would be appreciated."

He chuckled. "I know it would, but it's the student's job to get himself out of such predicaments."

Rolling my eyes, I walked away from him a few feet and snapped my fingers. Red flames whirled around me, drying everything, then I dispersed the flames, feeling much better. Looking down, I saw I barely scorched the bamboo. I took another step forward and stared at the lush woodland just off the beach.

"Do we have plans today, Master, or is it one of your lazy days, and you just felt I needed to get up?"

He walked toward me. "Just call me Kilyon. I hate being called Master. As for plans, we need to visit the Aura Nation and speak with Brother Hindoros."

My eyes widened. Hindoros was the head of the whole Wilone family, one of the only major families left in that region. "Really? It's been ten years since we were there. What's the big deal? Why go there now?"

He walked past and patted my head. "He asked us to come and take care of a personal matter for him. I'm not sure what it is, so we have to be quick."

Nodding, I realized it meant we would travel through the Forest of Dreams to get there. "All right. When do we leave? I can't wait."

We walked down the bridge that led to the market.

"We'll leave pretty soon," Kilyon replied. "I need to make sure we're supplied for the trip, then we'll be off."

As we passed through a small group of people, someone's hand grasped my shoulder.

"Hey, there, Kiddo. It's good to see you again."

It was Kelos, Kilyon's older brother. Each nation had three large families. Kilyon was part of the Icealis family, meaning they were the only ones in the Kai Nation who controlled ice and water.

"How are you, Uncle?" I asked. "What can I help you with?"

He handed us two bags, his steely blue eyes studying us closely. "Kilyon asked me to meet you two here and bring supplies."

I slung the two bags over my back, as Kilyon shook his brother's hand.

"Thank you, Brother. I should be back in time for the registry. If I'm not, sign these three up from our family if you would." He handed Kelos a slip of paper.

Kelos read it and looked up. "What you ask is not only frowned upon but a national crime. If this were to get out, it would cause mass panic. Our family would be attacked."

Kilyon nodded, and Kelos sighed.

"All right. I'll make sure it's done if you don't get back in time. Just don't make me regret this, Brother." Kelos looked down at me. "I'm glad you joined our family, though I'm afraid of what you might be capable of."

He walked away. His stern demeanor always worried me, but I knew I was safe. He left so fast, I didn't have a chance to ask any questions. I'd do it next time.

"Why did he say that?" I asked.

Kilyon turned and began walking quickly. "Hurry up, or we'll be late!"

I caught up, dodging past people in the market until we reached a long causeway to the land. Looking over the side, I saw the water was crystal blue with green highlights that vanished into the distance.

"Why did you choose to live here?" I asked. "It's beautiful, but I feel strange here, like it's all foreign."

He took a few more steps before answering. "It's because your flame is a different color. Blue is the natural color of the Kai Nation. Your flame is red, for the Celestial Nation. It's easier when you live in your home nation, but I can't take you there. You'll have to get used to being here. You already know why I had to leave the monastery."

I looked up and saw his face turn pale with fear. He was hiding something. "It's all right, Master. I'll get used to it."

He glared at me, and I quickly raised my hands.

"Sorry. Kilyon."

We walked in silence for a while after reaching the golden sand that blanketed the rim surrounding the lush, green forest. Trees reached into the sky, spreading branches wider than most huts. Birds chirped around us.

"We'll walk for a while," he said, "until we reach a village close to the border with the Aura Nation. Then it'll take a day or two to reach their capital. Let's be off."

I followed him, as he entered the forest. It was like stepping into another world. Everything changed from the calm of the water to the unknown feeling of the land.

After several hours, we reached a small clearing.

"Let's rest here for a moment."

We set down our packs and sat there, staring up at the branches that allowed sunlight to shine down on us. I felt warmer after walking in the cool shade.

"Kit, I have a question for you," Kilyon said.

I looked at him. "Sure. What is it?"

A wicked smile came to his face. "Who would be faster to the idol, me or you?"

I gave him a similar wicked smile. "I'm not sure, but I know an old man like you would have a hard time getting through all of this."

He laughed. "Is that right? Young pups should know when to call something a losing battle."

We stared at each other.

"Make your wager," I said.

He raised a finger. "First, you have to admit I'm the best fighter in the whole world, then say that I'm the one with the best hair in the land. Second, you wash all our clothes for the coming week."

I almost freaked out, thinking how smelly his clothes got. I never knew how one man could smell so bad. His clothes were almost rancid at times, like he bathed in rotten fish.

"All right," I said slowly. "If that's on the table, why not add something to it? If I win, you have to go a week without sleeping on water."

He began sweating. "I accept."

We looked up at the sky.

"When do we start?" I asked, standing.

He stood, too, just as ice formed, snaring my feet to the ground. "I'll get there first, my student!" His hair turned white, and long blue beams lifted him off the ground, as he flew off.

I tried to snap my fingers, but couldn't, so I breathed carefully and looked down, forcing fire along my body until it melted the ice. I was furious.

"That was cheap, Old Man!" I shook my head to stay calm before I lost control.

I carefully raised power inside me. I wasn't able to fly yet, but I was great at running. The force of my power propelled me forward, zooming around trees. I kept my eyes focused ahead, while I leaned back to avoid branches hitting my head.

I did my best to avoid obstacles in my way. As I ran, I suddenly heard a woman screaming.

"Help! Help me! Anybody!"

I stopped, trying to locate the source, but there was nothing. An explosion sounded to my left. I used my power to zoom off and came to a small clearing and stopped as a water prowler began striking everything around him. I jumped back to stay out of reach. Water prowlers were four-legged creatures with bodies made of pure water and five barbed tails. All monsters were powered by flame crystals. To defeat one, I had to destroy the crystal.

Looking around, I saw a girl clinging to a tree above. When we made eye contact, she asked, "Is there something stopping you from killing that beast for me? Why haven't you? Are you scared?"

I wasn't sure what she was talking about, but while I concentrated on her, a tail impaled my arm. I felt water cut through my skin as if it were paper, and the bone felt almost crushed.

I sliced the tail off with my free arm and stepped back, while steam rose from the wound. I didn't have a sword, and I was weak against water, so how could I destroy it without killing everything around me?

The prowler rushed me, forcing me to jump back.

"Hey, don't run from it! Come back here!" the girl shouted.

The prowler and I carved a path through the forest. Two tentacles came at me. I dodged to the right, as they collided with a tree only to resolidify.

"I should have known this wasn't going to be easy," I muttered, heading back to the clearing through the line of trees the monster cut down. It seemed ready to destroy the entire forest just to get to me.

I felt the situation wasn't very fair and forced a fire wall to appear. Water boiled away. The monster raced forward and jumped at me. I put all my power into the wall and cut the monster in half, destroying the crystal in the process. The body fell apart, and my pants were soaked.

The girl dropped from the tree. I used my hands to dry out my pants and stop the flames, as she neared.

"How are you? Thank you for saving me. That was a big help."

She had white eyes with silver streaks running through them like beautiful clouds. She patted her pants, which were torn from climbing the tree.

"It's no big deal," I said. "I'm just glad I could help."

Realizing my master was far ahead of me, I panicked. I refused to wash his clothes for a week.

Looking at the girl, I said, "Sorry Miss. Don't hate me." I picked her up and forced flames to my feet. We rushed through the forest, as I did my best to hold her and keep track of oncoming trees and brush.

"Put me down! I didn't consent to this!"

I looked down at her blushing face. "Like I said, I'm sorry, but I refuse to let my master win this race. You don't appear to have anywhere safe to go."

She pressed her face against my chest. "You didn't say anything of the sort. Let me help you. I'll repay the favor."

She pointed down with one hand, and I felt myself becoming lighter. We quickly took flight. I shot through the branches into the sky, with sunlight all around us.

She giggled and said, "We're flying!"

I saw the idol and flew toward it. Once we were close enough to stop, I realized I wasn't in control of our flight.

"This will be a rough landing," I said.

She looked at the statue, then at me. "You're going to get us killed. You're insane."

I cut the power and fell to the top of the statue. I kept my grip on her, as we rolled to a stop. I looked around and laughed.

"I can't believe that worked."

She pushed me away. "You could've killed us!"

We stood, and I scratched my head. "Well, we're both alive, aren't we? I call this a win."

She started another angry outburst, her first raised to hit me, but Kilyon's laughter stopped her.

"Ah, Miss Razele. It's good to see you again. I'm surprised to find you here."

She ran over and hugged him. "It's been so long! Why are you with that buffoon?"

I gripped my chest as if stabbed. "That's cold!"

He laughed. "That buffoon is the boy who used to come to the temple to play with you."

Razele looked at me.

I waved.

"No way," she said. "He was much nicer then."

Kilyon nodded. "That's definitely true. I have tried to fix that."

Were they both going to talk crap about me? I glared at them.

"Why are you out here, Razele?" Kilyon asked. "Shouldn't you be near your father?"

"Oh, um, well, he had mission, and I was supposed to bring you back to the capital to see him," she said nervously.

Kilyon rubbed his beard. "Oh, is that true? That's certainly nice of your father. I must thank him for that."

I heard a loud crack, and fissures opened in the earth under the statue I was standing on. I tried to walk forward, but the stone toppled. Losing my balance, I fell backward with it.

Kilyon and Razele ran toward me, trying to help, but both missed. Razele jumped toward me.

Why is she doing something so stupid? I wondered.

I saw the ground coming up fast. I put power into my flame and held onto her tightly to keep her from touching the ground.

"I'm out of power, Kit," she said, smiling and blushing simultaneously. "Sorry. That was stupid."

"Well, I'm out, too. I used up the last bit to stop you. Hold on and don't let any part of your body touch the ground."

Her hands grasping my chest, she tucked into a ball to protect herself. My back hit the top branches of the trees. As we fell, I closed my eyes and waited for the impact.

I felt my spine turn to dust. Blood came from my mouth, and every organ exploded. I felt my body pull itself back together immediately. When I opened my eyes, steam filled the air. I was almost fully repaired. Looking around, I saw the impact created a small explosion, turning everything to rubble.

Razele's eyes opened. "Oh my gods! Kit, are you OK?"

Then I felt my lungs return to their proper place. My bones regenerated, and I slowly stood.

She was shocked. "What are you?"

I bent over and heard my back pop in three places. "I never fell that far before. That was something."

Razele's eyes filled with tears. She was mortified. I tried to tell her I was OK, but I blacked out. My eyes opened reveling myself in an open room water flowing below my feet, my throat constricted. It was getting hard to breathe. Smoke crawled from my mouth and took form in front of me. My body jolted and then I could breathe again.

"Kit," the smoky form said.

"What do you want?" I felt exhausted from my ordeal. Sweat dripped down my face, as a human figure emerged from the smoke.

When the smoke faded, a young woman stood there in a thin black dress to match her black hair. Her red eyes glowed like crimson in the night.

"It's nice to see you," she said. "Well, seeing is a little wrong, but we'll have to deal with it for now."

I tried to free myself, but something bound me tighter and tighter as she approached. "Yeah, well, I can't say I'm happy to see you. I'm a little tied up. Where am I?"

She turned, and the scene changed. Fire surrounded everything. Dead bodies covered the land, with crows feasting on the remains. The smell of burning corpses filled the air.

"You're in your own subconscious, deep in the further part where you pushed everything that was your destiny."

The terrain was unfamiliar. If I were in my subconscious, how could I see things I never saw before?

"Can I ask you a question?"

I tugged at my bonds without success. "I guess. There's not much I can do about it."

Her face took on an awkward smile. "Do you know your mother and father?"

I was shocked. "I'm Kit. My family was born in the Celestial Nation, but they were killed, so my godfather brought me to the Kai Nation."

She cocked her head to one side and walked closer, her right hand grazing my cheek. "Maybe. What if that's not true?"

I shook my head, trying to pull away from her touch. "I don't have time for this. I need to get back to the real world."

Soft, innocent laughter came from her. She held my head in both hands. "Monstrosities like you shouldn't exist in this world. They aren't what humans would call proper. Alas, I can't do anything about it, so I will oblige your request. Before I do, I should tell you that you aren't what you think you are. You're more a weapon than a shield."

I pulled away from her. "I don't care what you say. I'm not a bad person. Who are you? Tell me!" I fought the rising anger while she laughed, although her tone was darker, as if something evil lived inside her.

"I'm none other than the dark goddess Celnius, the one who gave you your powers. I bid you farewell, my child."

She dispersed into nothing. The bindings on my limbs faded, as the scene filled with intense light. I raised my hands to shield my eyes from it, but it wasn't possible.

2

When I opened my eyes, a cold breeze hit me. I saw stars in the sky, and the smell of a campfire came to me. I glanced right and saw a fire blazing. Razele sat beside it, stoking it and sending sparks into the sky that floated up with the smoke.

I lay on my back, looking up. That was the first time I ever had trouble with my power. I didn't want to go through that again.

As I sat up, the bandages on my arms and chest came off, revealing no scars or bruising. I had healed back to normal.

Razele saw me moving and ran over. "Don't take those off! You aren't healed yet."

Then she saw my skin was OK and stepped back. When she realized I wasn't wearing a shirt, she blushed and turned away.

"I'm sorry," she said. "Kit, how did you heal?"

I reached for my shirt and pulled it on. "I'm not sure. Luck is a good guess."

Rage filled her face. She turned and slapped me hard, catching me off guard. I rubbed my cheek, noting how fast the pain fled and knowing there wouldn't be a mark, either.

I stared at her. "What is it, Razele?" She looked ready to scream at me but couldn't. I gave a soft, awkward laugh

"What's so funny?"

I waved my hands to defend myself. "Nothing. I'm fine. I healed, so there's no reason to me mad."

She came closer and punched my chest several times, each blow getting softer as she tired. Finally, she hit me and let her fist push against my skin for a second before her arm fell to her side, and she almost collapsed and began crying. Her breathing grew heavy, as she fought her sadness.

"I'm sorry that I worried you," I said. "I didn't want you to die. I don't know what I am. I've had these powers since I was a kid. When I'm hurt, no matter how bad it is, I heal, although I still feel the pain that comes with it." I lifted my arms to hold her, but she slapped my hands away.

She remained there for a few seconds until she controlled herself. "Sorry. I've been holding it all in for a while now." She looked like the world shoved her off a cliff and never intended to save her from falling.

I extended my hand. "I'm Kit. It's a pleasure to meet you. If you accompany us on our mission, I hope we can become good friends."

She stared at my hand for a moment and then at my smile. Slowly, she shook my hand. "Hi. My name is Razele. Thank you for the opportunity to travel with you. I hope we can become good friends, too." She giggled, then she released my hand.

I felt Kilyon behind me.

"Hmmm," he said. "Aren't introductions for strangers? You two know each other already."

I turned and saw he carried two dead boars on his back. "What are those?"

He wore a ferociously happy smile. "They are the reason we can feast tonight. I hope you worked up an appetite."

Razele giggled again. "I'm sure we both have, Master Kilyon. Would you like some help with that?"

He nodded, and the two of them walked to the fire and prepared dinner. I turned to stare up at the sky filled with twinkling stars.

"I hope I find my parents and understand my past." Two shooting stars zipped by, and I felt hope.

"Kit, hurry up and come over here."

I turned and saw Kilyon with his arms into one of the boars. Jogging over, I helped gut the animal and disposed of the innards, while he started cooking it over the fire.

As I sat down, images of Razele crying and trying to hold everything back filled my mind. Kilyon tossed me a canteen.

"Drink, or you may pass out again."

He looked at the canteen, opened it, and sniffed. There was no scent, which I felt was ominous. When I drank, the liquid hit my tongue and tasted like sewage. In disgust, I spat it out and then ran to throw up into a bush while my guts grumbled. Eventually, I stopped dry heaving and tried to stand upright.

"What's that for, Boy? You need to drink your medicine."

I looked at him. "Are you trying to kill me? That tastes like sewage, you senile old man!"

His face grew red. "Good medicine tastes awful. Drink it."

I plugged my nose and drank as fast as I could while Razele laughed. Once I finished the horrible liquid, I tossed the canteen to Kilyon, who caught it and threw it over his back. It hit the ground before disappearing.

As I returned to the fire, Kilyon looked at Razele, "My dear, can you tell me something? I understand that your father sent you into an ally's territory, and no one in the Kai Nation would ever attack you, but there are still bandits and monsters, including traitors to both nations. Why would he risk sending you here? We may live in peaceful times, but there are always dangers."

She looked away. "Uh, well, you see...he was testing me. I had to prove I was strong enough to reach you, so he would let me join the School for Flyers under the Aura Nation."

He scratched his beard as if he didn't believe her. He only did that when he was thinking. "Oh. If that's the case, I shall leave the conversation there. We'll be back in the Aura Nation soon. I'm sure it'll be fine. Your father must miss you a lot. We must see him immediately."

She turned pale.

"What's the matter, My Dear? You didn't do anything to get yourself into trouble. You aren't running away to avoid punishment, are you?"

"No, of course not," she said quickly. "I'm just...." She took a deep breath. "Dad cast me out."

I swallowed down the wrong pipe and coughed so hard I landed on one side. They looked at me.

"Master, is that possible?" I asked once I caught my breath. "I thought no matter what someone did, the family would never cast anyone out."

He placed his hands in his lap. "They're supposed to stay with family if they're full blood. In this case, Razele isn't."

I looked at her. She seemed perfectly normal to me.

"I know," he said. "You're still young, Kit. You can't see the flame around people, but I can assure you there are three colors."

Confused, I studied her. She remained quiet and wouldn't look at me. Kilyon caught my eye.

"Listen to me," he said. "When a child is born, he or she has the flame of his nation. If the parents are from the same nation, it's the same. If you were to add a father from the Celestial Nation and the mother from Terra Nation, the child would carry two colors, red and green. If one of those families comes from the top three, there is a third color. In Razele's case, she has her main flame of air, with the outlines of silver and green. That means her mother comes from Terra Nation, correct?"

Razele stood as if to leave.

"Such trivial things have no consequence."

She froze in place, staring at him. He stared right back.

"What will you do with me now that you know?" she asked.

I looked at both of them, wondering what I was missing and why Master would have to do anything about it.

"Master," I said, "there isn't anything that needs to be done about it. She is who she is. Nothing will ever change that."

He chuckled and smiled. "That's right, my apprentice. She is who she is. Razele, you're safe with the two of us. There's nothing to worry about. Relax."

She acted as if someone lifted a heavy weight from her shoulders.

"Anyway, My Dear, I have my own problem to deal with in that regard."

Razele and I eyed each other, then we both looked at Kilyon.

"What are you talking about?" I asked. "What problem?"

He gave me a half-smile. "You, my boy."

I wondered if my dream was real, and the goddess was right. "What problem do you mean?"

He stoked the fire with a stick. "It's not a bad thing for me, but for your kind, it is. I'll try to explain the best I can. When a child is enveloped by three flames, the military calls that person a forsaken. It means someone with immeasurable power. A child born with three flames could destroy a nation. Someone with four could rule the world. Marriage and conception between the nations are completely outlawed. If that law was ever broken, the child and the parents would be put to death. If the child lives to adulthood, he or she is placed in a dark prison. The life of a forsaken is a hard one."

Razele stared at the ground, lost for words.

"I'm sorry, Razele and Kit. Mostly, I'm sorry for you, Kit. I never told you or anyone else."

Would he tell me about my parents after all that time? I was always an outcast when it came to friends, but I suddenly understood I should never have been born. I was a danger to the peace of the entire world, as was Razele.

"What do Razele and I do? If we're to be hunted down, what will happen?"

He waved one hand. "We trick them. In actuality, you aren't forsaken. You're just two normal flyers. My plan is to enroll you into the school to harness your abilities more than you already can."

She and I looked at each other in confusion.

"Yeah," I said slowly, "but if we go to school, won't some-one like you be able to tell we're forsaken, or do you have a plan for that, too?"

He grinned. "That's why we're going to the Aura Nation. A buddy owes me a favor, and I intend to collect."

He cut meat off the boar and handed it to us. We ate in silence for a while. As night wore on, we unrolled our blankets and lay down. I stared at the sky and the beautiful stars.

I realized with a start that Kilyon knew all along we'd run into Razele. He had it all planned from the start. What was the rest of the plan? Why didn't he tell me about myself until now? I could use fire, but what was my true flame? I wanted to figure that out. At the very least, I wanted to know who my parents were and why they weren't around. Kilyon was always like an uncle. He made sure I had what I needed, but he never discussed my parents. Why was he being so open at this point?

There was no use thinking about it anymore. I closed my eyes and let myself fall asleep.

"Come on, Kit. Wake up. It's time to go."

As Razele's voice cut through my dreams, I opened my eyes to see her kneeling beside me.

"Sorry," I said. "I'm awake. I'll get ready."

We packed and made ready, then we climbed from the hole and saw the statue's feet all the way.

"That's definitely a long way to fall," I said.

Razele looked at me angrily, while Kilyon creaked to his feet.

"Let's go before she throws you a hundred miles away," he said.

I scratched my head and followed him into the forest.

"Kit, I wanted to ask you something."

I looked at her. "Yeah? What is it?"

She slowed until we walked the same speed. "Your power. You heal faster than anybody is this world. No healer can match that, right?"

"I'm not really sure. I never met a healer. I know they exist, but I've never seen one."

She shook her head, as if I were toying with her. "Are you kidding? Every nation has a healer. It's not like they're super rare."

I glanced at Kilyon in front of us. "Like I said, I really don't know what makes a healer."

Her shoulders slumped. "OK. We have the flame that was bestowed on us. With it, we can summon power to release the flames in our hair. For me, I can use wind for many things. I can make it fast and extremely cutting. I can summon tornados, too. As for healers, they can summon power in their hands. They can't fly or use flames for offense. They use their powers to help someone's mind or body.

"If a healer came from the Aura Nation, they'd be able to tie tiny threads with the wind and stitch any wound no matter how severe as long as they were properly trained and had enough power."

I decided that was almost like my own power, although I didn't know if it was technically a power. No matter how badly I was hurt, everything always returned to normal as if it never happened, but the pain was excruciating.

"I understand," I said. "Thanks for that. What else is there? I never left the Kai Nation before."

She looked like she just realized what she'd gotten herself into. "Oh, that's not hard at all. OK. Like I said, for flyers, their offensive power is in their hair. They can transfer the flame to their feet or hands. For healers, it lives in their hands. They can transfer their flame through their life force. They're the only ones who can stop someone from dying, but it comes at the cost of another's life.

"There are two other kinds. Summoners have power in their eyes. They can form pacts with different creatures and spirits. They have the world's best eyesight to go with it. Lastly there are dragonkin, though it's more like something that's given to only a few."

I wondered about that. "What does dragonkin mean?"

Master looked sharply at me, staring into my eyes before looking ahead again. That was weird. He never looked at me like that.

"It's hard to describe," she said. "There hasn't been one in 300 years. Each nation is supposed to have one born every 100 years, but for some reason, there haven't been any. People in all the kingdoms have been searching, but they never found out why. From the stories, it seems that dragonkin can transform themselves into a half-dragon form. They keep their human shape with a few changes but have all the power of a dragon. Those are just stories, though."

The power of a dragon? I wondered. *It must be powerful. I wish I knew what one looked like.*

"All right, you two," Kilyon said. "We'll arrive soon at Scylean, the town closest to the Aura Nation border. We'll stay the night there and leave in the morning. Try not to cause any trouble, especially you, Kit."

I looked at him. "Come on. When did I ever cause a problem?"

He laughed without answering.

We walked to the edge of the forest and came to a wide clearing where a village overlooked a stream. Soon, we were on a dirt road. All the buildings were made of logs.

"Master, why not follow the road from the beginning?" I asked, instantly understanding why after I asked.

"It's because of our friend here," he replied.

"Then where are we supposed to stay? I'm sure you took care of that, too."

He smirked at me. "Maybe. You'll have to wait and see."

Razele and I looked at each other and walked until we came to a gate with two guards. They seemed uneasy about our arrival. On closer inspection, I saw they didn't have real armor, just leather chest coverings. Their pants were torn, and they drew their weapons when they first saw us, then they sheathed them again once we came closer.

"It's good to see you, Crimson Water," one guard said. "We didn't think you would return."

Kilyon looked nervous. "Please, just call me Kilyon."

Both men bowed without hesitation.

"Of course, Master Kilyon. Shall we escort you to the inn?"

He shook his head. "No, that's all right. Thank you. I hope we can chat later if you don't mind."

They agreed and shook his hand. We walked into town just as the sun set. The street was lively with merchants and kids running around.

"Kilyon, they called you Crimson Water," I said. "What did you do to receive such a title?"

He turned to face us, walking backward for a few steps. "That is very simple, my dear apprentice. I'm awesome. Maybe, when you're as awesome as me, you'll receive an amazing name, too."

He smiled. "Maybe the Magnificent Little Pup, or even the Pup's Calling."

My smile turned to a frown. I knew he was patronizing me. "Yeah, well, I'm not very old yet."

He laughed. "Yet? You mean even when you're my age, you'll never surpass me, Little Pup."

Razele giggled.

"Does that mean you believe him?" I asked her.

"Oh yes, Little Pup."

My eye twitched. "I'm not a pup!"

They laughed just as we reached the inn. The sign had two swords with a red rose and the words *Hero's Rest.*

Entering, we heard a bell jingle above the door.

"Of forgive me. One second!"

As I looked around at a desolate room, a crash came from a back room.

"Sorry! I'll be there in a moment!"

More crashes sounded.

"Do you need help?" I asked.

Pans clanged against the floor, and a small cloaked figure ran around the corner.

"Oh, Master Crimson Water! It's an honor to have you here again."

He stepped forward to the girl who knelt before him. "Miss Patrunice, it's wonderful to see you again. You haven't aged a day."

I wondered what he was talking about. She wore a cloak over her head. Black smoke whirled around her, as the cloak dispersed to reveal a girl with two furry ears and a long black tail. Her eyes were darker than an abyss, and a scar reached down toward her right eye.

"See? What did I tell you? Patrunice, you're as lovely as always."

She blushed. "You still remember how to sweet talk a gal. Why have you returned after such a long time, Kilyon?"

Once her eyes locked on me, she moved away from Kilyon to me in a flash and leaned closer to sniff me. "Chaos? But how is that possible? None of them could have escaped from prison. Why are you here?"

He stepped forward quickly. "I can discuss that with you later. Please don't say anything else to him about this matter."

She considered his words and stepped away from me. "It must be really important."

I stared at her. "How do you know Master, and what are you?"

She burst out laughing. "What an audacious little one. You're as nosy as a puppy. We can discuss that over dinner, Little Pup."

Her, too? I wondered. *Is it the way I smell? Do I resemble a puppy? Am I growing dog ears?* The name thing would drive me crazy.

She clapped her hands, and other people like her appeared with platters of food and drink, bringing them to a table where the four of us sat down. She clapped again, and the extra people vanished.

Trying to ignore what just happened, I said, "Thanks for the meal."

We ate for a long while, then Patrunice looked at me. "Little Pup."

"I'm not a pup. Call me Kit."

Her eyes grew wide. "What a troublesome name for yourself."

"I feel it's a great name."

She set down her fork and held her hands together. "In our language, it means *hope*. Your name is the definition of hope, but the last person to carry that name was a cruel warrior for the Chaos Nation."

"Patrunice...," Kilyon began.

"He was born into a special family. You know every nation has three major families. The Chaos Nation has only two. It's because one of the three families grew too careless in their desire for power, and they were wiped completely out. There was left behind no home or knowledge about them. Nothing more than memories in the air."

"Patrunice, that's enough!" Kilyon said.

She looked at him. "The boy deserves to know. His future is so gloomy with such a past, and now a ruined future? What a shame."

Kilyon slammed both fists against the table, startling Razele and me. "You know better than I do that people can change the future. You're a shining example of that!" His voice was steady and firm.

She sighed. "You may be right, but do you believe this boy has what it takes to fix the travesties of the past?"

Kilyon nodded.

"All right, my partner. I shall step back and allow you do with him what you wish."

I looked around and saw swords flying in the air around us. Why hadn't I seen those before?

Patrunice snapped her fingers, and the swords vanished. "Well, Kit, I expect great things from you. I hope you can meet my expectations."

I gulped the food still in my mouth. Razele looked ready to cry. She looked at Patrunice and asked, "How do you know Master?"

Her eyes widened. "Oh, that's right. I'm not sure where to begin."

"You could start with the day we met and why," he said.

She snapped her fingers. "Ah, that's a glorious place! I'm sure you know the wars we had suddenly stopped thirty years ago?"

Razele and I nodded.

"Right," she continued. 'The school was started to help relieve the tensions."

I nodded.

"Good. Maybe you're more than just bronze. Forty years ago, the nations tried a peace treaty, but it failed miserably. The wars continued. Me and this great, magnificent Kilyon joined forces. We were two rival nation's best warriors."

He hid his face and shook his head. "You know that's not true."

She pouted. "Oh, come on. Don't be mean. Alas, he's right. The treaty failed, but the five great warriors came together and formed an alliance to force the nations to stop the fighting, or we would attack them and bring all nations under our rule. It was awesome. They were cowards and decided to stop fighting, but not before a few amazing battles." She looked at Kilyon.

"You're right," he said. "We had some amazing battles. Have you talked with Quantum lately?"

Patrunice clapped her hands. "Oh, yes! She's doing fine and has a pupil, too, though that's illegal. Magnus, Mullium, Masstine.... I can't remember his name. She's still in the Celestial Nation. I've been meaning to ask you, how is Hindoros? I see you have his child with you."

Razele's eyes grew wide. "You knew my father? Did you also know my mother?"

Patrunice was shocked. "Of course, Dear. Did your father never mention me?"

She shook her head.

"Well, that's rude. Yes. I helped bring you into this world and bring your mother back to her nation."

Razele was even more determined. "Do you know her name or what she looks like? Anything would help, please."

Patrunice laughed and patted Razele's hand. "Her name is Slicia Querom. She has beautiful green hair. Her eyes are the same as yours. She's a little shorter than you. She has a soft voice and is delicate like a rose petal, but her fists are as strong as boulders. We weren't very good friends, but I can tell you she was delivered to the Terra Nation safely. I'm afraid going there from here is almost impossible. You'd have to go through the school. Unless you have strict permission, you'd be killed on sight. You could traverse the walls into the Chaos Nation, but then you'd die of the sickness. I'd just stop there."

Razele slumped into her seat, as if the thing she most wanted had been moved even further out of reach.

"Or you could become one of the most-talented warriors and force yourself there," Patrunice added.

Razele looked shocked. "Wouldn't I start a war with the rest of the nations if I did that?"

Kilyon shrugged. "How would they know unless they caught you?"

Patrunice looked at him with a smile. "Reminds me of a careless wolf I know," she added in a loving tone.

When we eventually finished eating, Patrunice clapped her hands, and the food disappeared. We stood.

"For the time being," she said, "there are three rooms upstairs. Kit, yours is all the way at the end of the hall. Razele, yours is the first one up the stairs. There is a bathhouse down the main corridor. Help yourself. If you need anything, let me know."

We both bowed and chorused, "Thank you very much."

Walking away from the table, I went alone down the main corridor and saw a door labeled *Male,* and another labeled *Female.* I went into the male's room and undressed, setting my clothes in a basket before walking into the bathroom.

Steam filled the room, not enough to obscure all visibility but enough to notice. As I walked, the tile floor changed to wood. I stepped into the warm water and felt heat melt away the tension. I sat on a stone slab and rested my arms on the edge of the pool with my head back.

"This is nice," I said. "I should've done this a long time ago."

"Yes, you should have."

I lifted my head but saw no one.

"Down here, Human."

I looked at the water and saw a Nyix, something between a cat and a spirit. They were insanely rare, or so Kilyon said.

"You can talk?" I asked. "I was told Nyix can't talk in this world. You're part cat and part spirit, correct?"

The Nyix swam in circles. "That is correct, but technically, we aren't in the human realm. Our dimension is outside the realm of anything else."

I tried to think about that but failed. "What did you say?"

The Nyix laughed and continued swimming. "What you heard is correct. My master is one who can bend the fabric of space. She's the last of her kind, I'm afraid. Such a shame."

I stared, expecting the Nyix to laugh at telling such a joke, but I began to believe he was correct. If that was the case, what was she? Her power would be that of a god.

"There is no god," the Nyix said. "In human terms, faith is nothing more than something to help people feel better about death. There is reincarnation, if you believe in it. I would classify it as more part of the nature of life. When one dies, they move on. That path continues for eternity."

I scratched my head. "That sounds more like a curse than something worth praising. By the way, what's your name? Do you have one?"

The Nyix stopped and cocked its head at me. "Yes. Don't all beings of life have a name? Grass is grass. Tree are trees. Rocks are rocks."

I rubbed my temples harder. "That's not what I meant. My name is Kit."

The Nyix rolled over. "Oh! I misunderstood. My name is Enestal, the beautiful Nyix of meaning."

What is she talking about? I wondered. "I'm sorry, but I don't understand. Are you saying you're the Nyix of meaning?"

She floated. "Yes. There are five great spirits. I'm the spirit of meaning."

I closed my eyes and tried to comprehend it, but I couldn't.

"He means he's the meaning of life. He's the spirit of Terra. Sorry about that."

I nodded slowly, recognizing the voice as Patrunice. I opened my eyes and saw her standing fully naked over me.

"What is it?" she asked. "Haven't you seen a naked woman before?"

I took a deep breath and tried to control my rage. "No, I just didn't want the first woman I saw naked as the one who wants me dead."

She laughed. "I apologize. I'm a wild card, but I trust Kilyon a lot, so I won't harm you. If he gives me the order, I'd hunt you down like a scared rat." Her voice held more pleasure than expected.

At least you're on my side for the time being. I heard the water splashing, as she got in beside me.

"What are you doing?" I saw her hands slide down her sides.

"Nothing, just enjoying my bathhouse. I'm supposed to apologize to you and offer some advice, too."

I looked at her carefully, but my gaze went to her breasts before I could look away. "Sorry."

She laughed. "That's fine. I know that's just how it is. We'll call that the apology. As for the advice, be careful. I mean that wholeheartedly. You're in dangerous waters, and there's no one who can swim after you. I don't envy you or the power you have. I still can't believe your father went as far as he did to attain such power, but that's in the past. At least, I hope it is."

I looked at her. She spoke as if she and my father were good friends, but if that were the case, that would've made him one of the best flyers in the world. "What was he like before he went after the power he wanted so bad?"

She giggled. "That's a long story, but I'll shorten it. He was a sweetheart, always caring and putting others first. I believe he sought what was out of reach for the ones he loved. It consumed him and changed him once he received the power. I think he saw how far he sank, but I'm not sure. I haven't seen him in a very long time. I want to believe he's still alive.

She looked ready to cry, as she stared at the steam above the water.

"I've wanted to meet my parents for some time now, but I don't think the chance will come easily or at all."

Snapping out of her thoughts, she patted my head. "Maybe, but I wouldn't seek something that's the root of all problems. Just keep moving forward. Your master is a good man when he wants to be. Nevertheless, he'll always be in your corner. I wouldn't worry too much.

I smiled at the thought. She was right. He'd been amazing to teach me for years and give me somewhere to live. "Patrunice, what is the School for Flyers?"

She looked at me in confusion. "Well, it's broken into different sections, one for each nation, to teach the students equally. There's an army run by the school. All students who go there must be part of the army."

If we both have to join the army, will it be beneficial? I wondered. "OK. What happens?"

She raised her hand. "Maybe if you'd wait instead of interrupting people.... Anyway, once you're there, you're put into different classrooms with other flyers from the other nations. You're trained for war. The better you are, the higher up the ranks you go until you reach the top. All students are sent out on missions, but only the top ones are allowed to take S-class missions. SS is the toughest. Those could be a range of things. Do you understand?"

I nodded.

"Good. Now get some rest. Something tells me tomorrow will be a handful for the two of you, and I don't want to miss it."

I was surprised, as she stood to go. "Does that mean you're coming with us?"

She smiled. "Yes and no. I look forward to the expedition you'll be on. Sleep well."

"Wait. You said you'd tell me what race you are."

Her black tail swished back and forth. "I'm a Catherian, one of the last ones. Sleep well, my little pup."

Patrunice left the room, as the Nyix continued swimming.

"Are you going to bed, Human?"

"Yes. I should get some rest. Thanks for the company."

It disappeared. I walked away from the tub and went into the changing room. Once I was dressed, I walked back into the main corridor and saw Razele leaving the women's room.

"Kit, that water is amazing, isn't it?"

I nodded. "Yeah, it was stupendous. It left me tired, though. I'll get some sleep now."

We walked down the corridor, then went upstairs to our rooms.

"Thanks for walking me to my room," Razele said. "Have a good night."

She walked in with a smile and closed her door. I went to the end of the hall and the room on the left. When I opened the door, I saw a plain room with a single bed and no windows. A simple light hung on the wall. I closed the door and sat on the bed. When I lay down, I sank into it like I was lying on air and was immediately asleep.

3

Rain sounded all around me. I opened my eyes and saw I was in the village from the last vision. No one stood nearby. All the houses were demolished as if an attack just transpired.

I looked up, rain passing through me without touching my skin. Was I dreaming? I walked toward one house that was missing all four walls and the roof. I walked over the door that lay on the ground and saw dead flowers littering the grass. Two corpses lay together, holding hands. Their bodies were severely decomposed, and I had no idea who they were.

"They're close to you, my little monster." Celnius stood behind me with her arms crossed.

"I'm assuming they're my parents, is that it?"

She didn't speak.

"That's a bummer. I wanted to meet them and ask them what they did to cause so much trouble."

She walked past me and raised her hand. A pile of debris was swept aside to reveal a hatchway. "Go and seek the answers if you wish, but I warn you, Little Monster, there are answers I wouldn't want to find."

I gulped and walked toward the hatchway. Leaning over, I took the handle. The weight of the hatch handle seemed to grow heavier, as if it didn't want me learning what was down there.

Celnius walked closer and placed a hand on my shoulder. The sensation of weight disappeared, as I opened the hatch and stared down into the abyss.

"How far is it?" I asked.

She stared down. "Farther than I would care to travel. I may be the goddess of Chaos, but what your father did is something I would never consider doing."

I grabbed the ladder and started my descent.

"Don't hate your father for the future he set out for you," she warned me. "I must tell you that your life is in danger."

I nodded and kept climbing down. The hatch closed over me, and nothing was visible anymore. I climbed down, feeling my way, then the ladder broke.

I lost my grip and fell for what seemed like an eternity until I struck water hard enough to break one of my legs. I lay back to absorb the pain without crying too much. The bones moved back into place, and the pain vanished.

A red orb illuminated a cavern around me. The walls were moist with something unknown. I got to my feet, and the orb floated away. I followed it deeper into the cavern, trudging through muck and water that glowed red. Bones floated on the surface.

The red glow illuminated some of the cavern but not much. The walls looked dark, with a thin trickle of water coming down them. Droplets struck the water, the echoes filling my ears until the sound grew louder.

The red orb stopped moving, then it disappeared into the darkness. I flicked my wrist, but nothing happened. I couldn't summon my power. Maybe that was part of the dream.

A bright beam of light landed in front of me, and a figure emerged from it. It was hard to tell his age or hair color, but his presence was strong with death.

"Hello, my son. I'm sorry. If you're seeing this, then the goddess has done what I asked her to do. For starters, I'm sorry that neither of us were there for you. I hope you've had a nice life."

A smile emerged on my face, as if I heard something I always wanted.

"I'm sure you have many questions, probably more than I have answers. I have a limited time to record this, so I have two things I must say. First, if you wish for more answers, you'll have to come home yourself. Second, I'm sorry for what I did. I never could have imagined the repercussions would have tossed so many into this pit just for the power of immortality. It went straight for you. No matter. Kilyon should have raised you well. I'm sure he'll throw you into the school. Go along with it. When the day comes, you'll need to come home. Maybe then we can have a good conversation."

The beam of light dispersed, and the scene changed back to the ruined house.

"How was it, Kit?" Celnius asked.

I was confused. "I don't know. There wasn't anything that devastating or bad. He said if I want the truth, I have to go home to receive it."

She bit her lip hard enough to make it bleed. "Of course he did. He didn't have the guts to show you anything, I'm sure. What a lowlife."

I looked at her. "What is it?"

She shook her head and snapped her fingers.

I awoke in my room and looked around. Everything seemed normal. I heard two knocks on the door and looked toward it. "Come in."

Razele opened the door. "We're leaving soon. I wanted to make sure you were up."

I nodded, as she walked closer toward me.

"Are you OK? You look tense."

I thought about my dream and rubbed my temples. I hated going there. It was always so gloomy.

"Kit."

I looked up and saw her in front of me with her hand on my head.

"Are you OK?" she asked.

I removed her hand and stood. "I'm fine. I'm ready."

I walked out the door and saw Patrunice at the end of the hall, smiling at me.

"Did you sleep well, Kit?" she asked.

"Of course. Sorry. Where is Kilyon right now?"

She pointed down the stairs. The master sat at a table, drinking something.

I walked down and sat across from him. "Kilyon, may I ask you something?"

He looked up and slowly set down his glass. "Yes. What is it?"

I didn't know how to explain what was happening to me. "Who's the goddess of chaos?"

His eyes widened. "Every nation has a god or goddess who's in charge of looking over their nation. Celnius is the goddess of Chaos and she is, well.... I don't really know. I never met her. If you don't hail from Chaos, you can't see her. Why? Have you met her?"

I realized my dreams were real. "I think so."

He moved his glass to the side and placed his hands on the table. "What did she say?"

I recounted the two dreams.

"I see. That makes sense, considering how close your father was to her. He really did do it."

I had no idea what he meant.

"What are you two talking about?"

We looked over at Patrunice and Razele standing at the base of the stairs.

"Tell him, Kilyon," Patrunice said, leading the way to the table. Both of them sat down.

"As Patrunice was saying yesterday," Kilyon began, "your father was named Tellium Exporoc. That family name carries more weight than any family in any nation. They were ruthless and never left any witnesses behind. They were skilled at offensive attacks, and their defense was better than most. They were scary. The children were trained from an insanely early age. By the age of five, they had to kill their first target. Your father destroyed the whole family, leaving none alive. He feared their power. He also destroyed the other family, Lunusmal, the greatest support summoners in the world.

"The Chaos Nation then held almost all the power, but they fought among themselves and killed themselves off. That's why there are huge walls blocking off the border. A deadly disease runs rampant in there, corrupting everything it touches.

"Your father used his knowledge to create a new kind of miracle—immortality—which was given to you."

That explained why I always healed, especially from supposedly fatal accidents. I should have thanked my father for what he did, but I couldn't imagine his cruelty in reaching for such power.

"Thank you for telling me."

Razele slammed both hands on the table with tears running down her cheeks. "You aren't taking this seriously. That's taboo!"

I looked at her. "I'm not sure. I wasn't taught the ins and outs. I was taught to live a normal life. I know how to fight thanks to Master, but as for the laws of this world, I have little to no knowledge of them."

Razele calmed herself and lowered her head. "That's so sad. You can never die. You'll live forever."

I stared at the table, not knowing what to say.

Patrunice coughed. "Well, my dear, it may be sad, but in the end, he'll have more influence over the world. He can be a hero who can bring all together, perhaps even take his father's place."

That made Kilyon smack the table with his fist. "No. He doesn't need that. You know that's true, Patrunice!"

She raised her hands. "It was just a thought. You know he won't let him pass, not by himself. He's too big of a threat."

Kilyon stood quickly. "We're leaving. Thank you, Patrunice, for a safe place to rest."

I followed him to the door, as Razele followed. Kilyon opened the door just as a strong breeze hit us. Walking into the sunlight I let my eyes adjust.

We were no longer in a town. We were on a mountain overlooking the valley of the Kai Nation. Behind me were walls that must have been the border of the Chaos Nation. The air was very cold.

"Stay close, you two," Kilyon said. "They're here."

As Razele closed the inn door, the building disappeared. Three plumes of smoke landed on the rocks a few feet away. Once the smoke dissipated, it revealed three flyers holding spears, looking down at us.

Kilyon walked toward them. "Tell your master that Crimson Water has come to say hello."

One disappeared. Tension grew between us. When the guy returned, the others relaxed and walked down to us. Thunder crackled overhead, and a bolt of lightning struck in front of Kilyon, kicking up dust.

I coughed and stepped back, taking Razele's arm. "Are you OK?"

She coughed, too. "I'm fine. What happened?"

She waved the dust away. Wind cut through it, and I saw Kilyon holding his sword to Hindoros' neck, while Hindoros held two daggers near Master's neck. Hindoros wore a full white cloak with bluebirds stitched over the back.

"So you're still a capable man," Hindoros said. "It's been years since you came here."

Kilyon's blade didn't move. "It has, indeed. I've come to collect on that favor."

They sheathed their weapons and stood a foot apart, staring at each other, until they began laughing and clasping hands.

I slowly released Razele's arm. "I thought we were dead."

"Yeah, me, too."

Hindoros looked at me. "Ah, Master Kit. It's good to see you again. If he brought you, then you've gotten yourself into some bad trouble, is that right?"

What did he think of me? "When do I ever get myself into trouble?"

He laughed. "There was the time you sneaked into the women's bath when you were younger. I can only presume your bad habits have continued."

Razele giggled, and he looked at her. She quieted instantly.

"Why are you here?" he demanded. "You were banished from this place."

She stared at the ground.

"She's with us," I said. "I'm not sure what Master wants to ask of you, but she's under our protection."

Razele's hand clutched the back of my shirt.

"Do you think you can beat me? I know your master is the Crimson Water, but you wouldn't be so lucky." He smiled, and the air between us almost sparked with challenge.

"You can knock me down as much as you want. I won't stop. I'll always get up to protect her."

He smiled for a split second, then it vanished. "So be it, but she has to be at your side at all times. If she's alone, I can't stop my guards from doing their duty."

He looked at her. Tears came from her eyes, before he turned back to me.

"That's fine," I said. "I'll stand by her."

Kilyon and Hindoros turned their attention from us.

"All right," Hindoros said. "Follow me, then, if you can fly."

I watched them activate their flames and take flight, then I looked at Razele. "I'll need your help with this."

She smiled. I lifted her in my arms and activated my flames. She used her power to give me flight, and we caught up with them. Hindoros looked over his shoulder at us, then looked forward again.

Looking down, I saw the creatures on the mountains. Birds flew below us. The feeling of wind in my hair was unmatched.

Razele gripped my cloak, not wanting to look down. "Still scared of flying? That's bizarre. You lived high in the mountains."

She chuckled and slapped my chest. "I've never been one for heights."

"Sorry. I never heard a flyer said she was afraid of heights. It's a new experience for me. Ever since I was little, I wanted to fly. You gave me that chance. Hopefully one day I'll be able to fly on my own."

I felt her grasp tighten a bit. "I'm glad I was able to do that for you. I hope you can fly on your own someday, too."

I looked ahead. Kilyon looked at us and gave a thumbs-up. I shook my head.

4

We flew over a peak and started our descent. A monastery appeared, and a large town came into view on the mountainside. Snow fell softly, covering it all.

"We're here," Kilyon said. "Follow my lead."

We moved up close behind him and flew toward the monastery with its red bamboo walls and large bell at the top. Stone walls surrounded the building, with guards posted at each entrance to the courtyard.

"All right, Razele, you can cut the power," I said.

My body grew heavy. I landed hard on the stone floor and almost lost my balance, although I caught myself in time. Master and Hindoros landed beside me.

"I see you two have become quite close," Hindoros said.

We blushed, as I released her and stepped away from her.

"I could never master, not her," he continued. "She's too forward for my liking."

"Yeah," she said. "He's too stupid for me. He gets himself hurt for no reason."

"You would've died," I said. "Whose fault was it for falling, anyway?" I crossed my arms, and we glared at each other.

Hindoros laughed. "Ah, young love. How I envy them."

Kilyon laughed with him. They walked ahead, leaving Razele and me to blush, then look quickly away from each other and follow their lead.

We walked up a few wooden steps, where Guards were posted at the door. One opened it for us. The monastery was older than I thought. The floors creaked, as we stepped inside.

The guards closed the door from behind us, and a long hall with several doors greeted us.

"Razele and Kit, your room is at the very end," Hindoros said. "Kilyon, come with me."

We started to protest, but they didn't bother looking at us. We stared at each other, then walked forward.

"Looks like we're stuck together, Kit. I couldn't imagine a crueler fate."

We opened the door to the last room and saw it was spacious enough, but there were no beds, just a floor with a door leading outside.

"What are the people like here?" I asked.

She sat on the floor, and I sat beside her.

"They're normal people, but our culture is different," she said.

That wasn't very helpful. If she were to ask me the same thing, I wouldn't know how to answer. Every culture is different. None are worse than any of the others, but their differences are a fact. Not all people are the same. If everyone was, what fun would that be?

"I get it," I said. "Thanks."

Her smile filled my heart, but I didn't know if that was worth mentioning. "What do you do on days like this?"

She had a wicked smile. "We train relentlessly. Want to spar?"

I gulped down my fear. "Sure. I'd love that." I didn't know why I replied like that. I never fought against anyone from the Aura Nation. I had the feeling she'd wipe the floor with me.

Razele stood, and I followed her while trying to keep my face calm, so she wouldn't think I might be scared. She opened the door leading outside, and I followed her out and around the house to a square with a few people already sparring, though not with their flames. They used their fists.

Standing near them, a lot of monks watched the fight. Their forms were impressive, almost like a mystical dance between two people. As the fight continued, both of them remained calm, without fear or anger. All their feelings were contained deep inside.

One of them rushed his opponent, who made no move to dodge. In a split second, he threw his palm into the guy's chest, and he fell over without a sound.

"What did he do?" I asked.

Razele giggled and turned toward me. "That's a family secret. Most of the subfamilies don't share it, but since I'm feeling generous, it's called Wall of Despair. It strikes the body and causes such a massive disturbance, it sends the brain into a false sense of panic, then knocks them out. It takes a tremendous amount of practice. If you're off by even the tiniest bit in the power of the shot, it will ricochet and shatter your hand."

Two men walked up to remove the body.

"What about your family, if you don't mind my asking?"

She grasped my hand and pulled me into the fighting area. "That's a secret. I promise to go easy on you."

We stopped with Razele a couple feet away.

"All right, Kit. It's really simple. Don't use your powers to attack or defend. Just use your own strength. That's it."

A crowd gathered, many looking intrigued.

"Hey, Brother," one monk whispered, "isn't that our master's daughter?"

"Yes, and the boy is Kilyon's apprentice. This should be good."

I took a deep breath and blocked out the others. I'd never fought without using my flame before. It sounded difficult.

"All right," I said. "How do we start this?"

She circled me with a happy gleam in her eye. The monks clapped and whistled. I glanced behind me and saw Kilyon and Hindoros watching from the steps. When I looked back, Razele was almost on top of me. I immediately tried to step back.

Her right foot struck my side with tremendous force. I felt ribs crack, as I fell and rolled, getting up and ready to activate my flame, then I stopped myself. I took a deep breath and winced at the pain.

"Did I break your ribs?" she asked. "We can stop if you want."

I shook my head and felt the ribs healing. "No. I can do this all day. I wonder which one of us will tire first."

I ran toward her and felt how slow I was without my flame. I raised my right leg for a kick, but she grabbed my ankle with one hand. We stood there a second, our eyes locked on each other. She knew I was completely outmatched and flung me backward.

I landed hard and jumped to my feet. "I guess this is the difference in our abilities." I felt like a frightened forest animal running from a predator.

"Come on. You have to be better than this. I feel like I'm beating you up."

I ran at her. Her left leg came up slower than her previous attacks. I ducked under it and leaned back while I punched. She moved slightly to the right. Her fist came into view and hit my face like a hammer. Rattled, I stepped back, feeling my vision swim.

Once I recovered, Razele bowed. "We should stop. Kilyon didn't train you very well in hand-to-hand. He...."

I called on flame. Waves of heat extended from my hair, and ripples went through the ground like shockwaves. Rubble and dirt flew in all directions. The monks chattered in excitement.

"Wanna up the power?" I asked.

She looked at me. "Oh, yeah? Don't come crying to me if you lose."

The monks jumped away as quickly as they could. Razele ignited her own flame, and her hair turned white. Gusts of wind rippled the ground, and our two flames collided, neither one able to push the other back.

"You can't fly by yourself, can you?" she asked.

I shook my head and watched her lift off the ground. "That's not fair, but fighting an enemy isn't fair, either."

I looked up, as she flew toward me. I glided to the right with immense speed. She might be able to fly, but she wasn't as fast as I was.

"Come on, Razele. Let's see what you can do." As I moved aside, scorch marks appeared on the stones underfoot.

She flew toward me. I jumped up, kicking her side. She flew off sideways and lost control, slamming into the ground hard enough to send an explosion of debris everywhere. I rushed her before she could recover.

I was within a foot of her when she twirled up to kick my face. Blood and teeth shot from my mouth. I was slammed sideways into a wall so hard I sank into it until I was nearly encased.

Breaking free of the stones, I wiped blood from my mouth, watching it steam away.

"That was good, Kit, but I feel like you're holding back," she said.

I was slowing down. Just because I was immortal didn't mean I was free of exhaustion. I took a deep breath. "Maybe I am. Who knows?"

She laughed, her power subsiding. "We can call that a tie." As she straightened her posture, she noticed I was tiring.

"Yeah, that's fine. I'll have to beat you the next time."

The crowd applauded. Hindoros walked through them, followed by Kilyon, who slapped my back.

"That was good, Pup, but you're worthless without your flame," Kilyon said. "We have to fix that."

I shook my head. He was the one who told me to work on fighting with my flame in the first place.

Hindoros came up to his daughter, his eyes piercing her soul until she looked away. "I can't accept you back in the family. I can't allow you to ever live here again, nor will you be my successor."

Her shoulders slumped in distress.

"But I am proud of you. throughout your life, you worked hard to master the techniques of our people and the elders. There will never be a more-talented fighter from this nation. I hope you will carry that with you the rest of your life, Razele. It's the best I can do."

He turned to Kilyon. "You'll have what you want. I'd like to see what these two will do even if they're both forsaken calamities." His soft voice held a hint of anger.

I wondered if I was the only one who heard it. "Master, what's he talking about?"

"That's a matter we will discuss later. For that to happen, you have a little quest to do."

Razele and I looked at each other.

"What quest?"

Hindoros tossed me a pendant. "If you're in trouble, there's enough holy water in there to save you. It's not like you'll need it." He walked off with the rest of the monks.

"I'm sorry," Kilyon said. "I won't be able to assist you with this. It's something you two have to do. As for the target, well, I guess it's OK to tell you. It's a basilisk. There's a wild one on the mountainside that's been causing trouble with the villagers and farmers. Would you be a good pup and kill it?"

I stared at him. His gaze was totally innocent. "You want us to kill a basilisk on the mountainside?"

He nodded. "Oh, yes. It would be best if Razele didn't die. That would be bad."

My right eye twitched, meaning I was at the end of my patience. "We'll do it." My anger subsided, and I looked at Razele. "You understand what you just agreed to, right?"

She looked at me with a smile. With a slow exhalation, she said, "Fine. We'll do it."

Kilyon laid his hand on my shoulder. "I believe in you. I will accept the head as proof. Have fun." He walked away.

I bit my lip and watched him go.

"Do you think we can win?" Razele asked worriedly.

I walked past her and found a gate that exited the monastery. Outside, I walked over rocks and dirt with almost no grass until we overlooked the landscape. I peered down the mountain at the meadows below where some villages sat.

"Is it wrong to think that this world is corrupt?" I asked, when she stood beside me.

"I don't think so, but I believe that it's not the whole world. Just a large part of it."

I studied the clouds moving in the sky and saw my breath in the fresh, cold air. "Will you always be at my side no matter what?"

She turned and looked at me, but I stared at the landscape. "I will. I'm happy to be by your side, even if you're dumb sometimes."

I chuckled. She had a light heart. I hoped it would stay that way. I didn't know how to tell her my feelings. I wanted to explain how much I cared for her, but such things were hard for me. "Thank you. Shall we get going before it's too late?"

I felt her hand touch mine.

"I don't know if we can win, but if you're in trouble down there, I'll do my best to protect you." I handed her the pendant, and we looked at each other.

"Why give this to me?" she asked, hanging it around her neck. The red jewel hung on her chest, with liquid gently moving inside.

"I'm immortal. All I have to do is smash part of my body that's petrified. You can't. It would take weeks to mend a missing limb."

She chuckled at the thought. "Yeah. How long would it take if you were completely made of stone?"

I thought about that. If I cut off a limb, it would grow back, but if I were turned into stone, I had to guess I'd still be alive. What if I were destroyed? I didn't know the answer to that.

"I'm not sure," I said. "I really don't want to figure that out. Do you know where the beast lives? Saying it lives on the side of a mountain isn't much help."

She grabbed my arm and jumped off the cliff, taking me with her. With a laugh, she said, "This is amazing!"

Cold air rushed past my face, A I saw the hillside quickly approaching. I took her hand to pull her close, sending all the power I could muster to my feet to break our fall. Once we slowed, we hit the ground gently.

"You're insane," I said. "You realize that, right?"

She let go of me. "I'm aware of that, but that's why you're here, to make sure I don't go overboard."

I shook my head and looked behind us. A large tunnel went into the mountain. Touching the sides, I saw it wasn't natural. Something made that tunnel.

"Did the basilisk do this?" I asked.

She nodded. "It's an ancient beast. We've sent several people to fight it, but no one has ever returned. It grows more dangerous with every passing day. Is there anything else you'd like to know?"

I stared up. The tunnel was twelve feet tall and at least fifteen feet wide. We had no idea how deep it was. What did it eat to make it grow so huge?

"No, I'm good. We should get going."

We began our descent into the tunnel. Darkness took over quickly. We were barely able to see anything in front of us. I held out a hand and kindled flame. Looking around, I saw the sides were rough and black. When I walked to one wall and ran a finger over it, it came back covered in soot.

"What is this monster?" I asked. "Can it breathe fire?"

Razele came over to look. "It shouldn't be able to. Basilisks are known for petrification and poison, nothing more."

We looked and saw the walls were burned to a crisp, as was the floor.

"Let's keep going before we find the monster that did this," I said.

We followed the tunnel, as it turned occasionally. When we reached an intersection, we stopped.

"Which way?" I wondered.

Both the right and left tunnels were charred. Either might lead us to the beast, but sticking together meant we'd spend a long time finding it. We had to split up.

"I'll go left," I said. "You head right. Try not to die."

"Don't you die, either. It would be a shame if I lost someone I liked."

I smiled at her comment and listened as her footsteps receded and stopped echoing. *If we're descending into a mountain, how long until we reach its base?* I wondered.

As my fire flickered, I quickly looked around without seeing anything. I stopped when another breeze grazed me and disappeared. It smelled foul, as if something was rotting from the inside out.

I stepped forward slowly and tripped over something. I fell and inhaled soot, making me cough. My flame vanished.

I stood again and brushed dirt off me to re-ignite my flame. Statues were all around me, some broken in half, others missing their heads. I walked through them and saw little kids holding onto their parents.

"This doesn't make sense. If this beast lives down here, why would those families come in here?" I knelt to look into the little girl's eyes. There was nothing of her left. The petrification was complete.

It still didn't make sense, but there was nothing I could do but kill the beast. I walked through the maze of statues for at least ten minutes. When they didn't end, I looked around and saw I was back at the little girl with her mother. That was impossible.

I looked around. All I had to do was retrace my steps. Maybe I had gotten turned around without noticing.

I walked back toward the entrance but never reached it, even though I walked longer than I had the first time. I always returned to the same spot no matter what I did.

In irritation, I sent a blast of flame in the direction I was walking. It disappeared, but I immediately felt something warm on my back and turned in time to be smacked by the flame on my chest. I fell and patted out the fire.

"That may have been a bad idea," I muttered. "I'm not sure what's going on, but I don't like this."

I went back to the little girl, but she was alone that time. Her mother was missing. When I touched her, I felt immense power coming from the stone. I placed my flame against it and heated it up until it exploded, sending dust and debris everywhere.

I stepped back and coughed, gasping for fresh air.

"Are you stupid? Who places a hot flame on somebody? You're a monster! That's what you are!"

I heard the girl's voice and looked around without seeing her.

"Hey! Down here, Numbskull! Stupid human!"

I looked down and saw a girl about chest-height. "A kid? Wait. Are you the kid I saved from the stone?"

Anger washed over her face. "Did you just call me a kid?"

I felt confused. "Well, yeah. You're a kid, right? I mean, you're a young woman?"

Her fiery red hair floated off her scalp, and her purple eyes glowed. "I'm not a kid. I'm a vampire, you cretin!"

"OK. I'm sorry, Little One. I won't call you a kid anymore."

She punched my face and threw me against the stone wall. My spine shattered, along with my arms and legs.

"You're strong for a kid," I said, coughing up blood. My body was stuck in the wall.

She jumped into the air and flew toward me, kicking my gut hard enough to pulp my internal organs. My stomach split open and poured out blood.

"Now you can rot, you unpleasant buffoon!" She backed away.

I felt my organs return to my body, then I healed enough to break free of the wall. I stood in front of her and turned my neck to feel the bones go back into place.

"I have to admit, that was a hard punch. You turned my spin to dust."

She stared in awe. "Are you a vampire, too, Sir?"

I shook my head. "No, just a buffoon, if I remember correctly." I walked away from her. "Can I ask for your help? I seem to have landed in a predicament. I'd like to catch up with a friend of mine."

Her mouth remained open in shock, as she stared at me.

"Be careful, or a fly will nest in your mouth."

She closed her mouth. "Flies don't nest, you imbecile!" She chuckled and walked closer. "I don't know if I can help. I don't remember much. I've been waiting for someone to save me from that prison after that devious monster trapped me and brought me back here."

It seemed I was right. The people were brought in here. They weren't stupid enough to come down on their own, unlike me.

"No matter how far I go," I said, "I always return to the same spot, which was your statue."

She looked at me curiously. "Really? Why mine?"

I shrugged. "I'm not sure. That's just what happened. A friend and I were asked to hunt down the basilisk. Do you know where it nests?"

She nodded and pointed farther down the tunnel. "Just a little bit farther in there."

"Then I'd better get going. It would be wise if you returned home."

I took a few steps and felt her hand latch onto my cloak.

"I'd be crazy not to help an imbecile like you. Anyway, I want revenge." Her glowing eyes dimmed.

"As if a kid like you could help."

She punched her fist into my gut and removed it. Blood flowed for a moment, then stopped, as I healed.

"I couldn't help myself," I added.

She hit me again and stared at the steam of my healing. "You're strange. I enjoy using you as my personal punching bag, so I'll accompany you."

I smiled awkwardly. "Well, thanks. I guess I don't mind being your punching bag."

We walked farther down the tunnel. I looked back at the statues until they were lost in the gloom. I assumed she was the one who trapped me in that endless loop, but did she do it deliberately or by accident?

"Say, what's your name, Miss Vampire?"

She frowned, as she walked beside me. "It's...." she stopped and stared at the ceiling. "I can't remember who I am."

I looked at her. "That's OK. Your old name doesn't matter anymore. Why don't we give you a new one?"

She smiled. "I'll have to approve it, but you can give me a name."

I looked her over and tried to think of a name that wouldn't end with her tearing me apart. "How about Ruby?"

She looked at me. "Ruby?" she asked, confused.

"Yes. It's a precious stone. It's red like your hair and just as beautiful."

She blushed. "I like it."

We continued walking.

"What's your name, man who is impossible to kill?" she asked.

"It's Kit. I'm not entirely sure what it's supposed to mean. My master told me my mother fought my father to call me that."

"Kit, Kit, Kit," she mumbled softly.

"Are you OK, Ruby?"

She shook her head and slapped her own cheek. "Oh, yes. I'm fine. I'm just talking to myself. That's all."

We heard movement ahead.

"Be on guard, Ruby," I said softly. "It seems we have entered the nest."

She clutched my cloak in fright, and I gently placed a hand on her head.

"It's fine if you're too scared," I said. "You can hang back."

She didn't speak as I kept walking, forcing my fire to burn brighter until I saw basilisk scales. Ruby yelped. As we came closer, though, it was just a shed skin.

"It's fine," I said. "It's not the real thing."

She walked up and touched it. "That's revolting."

I noticed she still held onto my cloak. "How can I fight it with you holding onto me?"

She slapped my back. "I'm not holding on. I'm protecting you. Be quiet and keep walking."

I sighed and continued past the shed skin. It was very long. When we reached the end, I saw an enormous head. Killing the real thing wouldn't be easy.

As we walked past, I made sure it wasn't the real monster. I didn't want to be tricked again. Up ahead I saw a flame waving in the tunnel and waved mine back.

"Kit, is that you?" Razele called.

I smiled, glad she was all right. "Yeah, I'm fine. Come over here."

She ran up to me. "What took you so long? I feel like I've been down here forever."

She looked down and saw Ruby. "You found a child."

Ruby's fist went back in preparation for a punch. I stepped in front of her in time to feel her fist go through my stomach again. When I coughed up blood, it landed in Ruby's hair. Her red eyes looked up in surprise when she realized what she did.

"Ruby, I would appreciate it if you stop doing that every ten minutes," I said.

Her hand pulled away from my torso. I felt blood fill my lungs, then dissipate.

"Razele, she claims to be a vampire. Her name is Ruby."

I stepped aside, as Razele came closer. Ruby barely reached her chest.

"I apologize for being discourteous," Razele said.

"That's OK," Ruby said. "I got a man today, so I'm in the mood to forgive you."

Razele's eyes filled with confusion. "You're dating this vampire?"

I waved my hands. "Whoa! No, I'm not. I rescued her. That's all."

Ruby clung to me. "What will I do without you? I surely will become plagued with melancholy if you leave."

I wondered if she carried a dictionary. "I'm not dating you. Anyway, we have more-pressing matters than this conversation."

Ruby twirled a little dance around me. "I'll win your heart. It's just a matter of time."

Razele gave me a fierce look, then the ground trembled. I was glad. I would rather fight any number of mythical beasts than deal with this conversation.

"We'll finish this later," Razele said. "I'm not done with this."

She stormed away, forcing me to look toward the approaching beast. "I can't wait," I said.

Turning aside, I saw two large eyes in front of us. They were very large, as orange as the sunset, and didn't blink.

"Can either of you see the rest of its body?" I asked.

Both looked around. Ruby pointed to the left. "There's a tunnel system that way. I can see the end. If I had to guess, this basilisk is an old one, give or take a few hundred years. It's about 500 feet long, maybe more."

She apparently had good eyes in the dark, which was helpful for her but not for Razele and me.

"Razele, do you have any bright ideas for this darkness?" I asked.

She chuckled and raised her hand. Wind came from it to touch my flame, funneling air into it and making the room much brighter.

"That was a genius move," I said.

She looked happily at me. "Thank you so much. I'm glad I could contribute." Her gaze went to Ruby, who looked away from her.

I increased the flame, feeling my hair change, as flames whipped around me.

"As beautiful as a dancing firestorm," Ruby said, "but the color isn't right. How can you handle so much power? Isn't your heart burning?"

Her comment confused me. "I'm not sure what you mean, but I need to focus on this beast."

"Of course. I'll cover you. I'm sure you know this already, but basilisks have two main attacks. When their eyes start glowing faintly, they can use petrification. Some are also known to hold a heart of flame, so watch yourself."

That explained the charred tunnels. I raced toward the beast. It lunged at me just as I leaped over its head. The basilisk's head struck the ground, creating a large hole. I turned quickly and blasted heat toward the eyes. One was scorched, but the other glowed fiercely.

I tried to move my right leg, but it was too late. It was turning to stone. I hit the ground and turned my hand into a hot knife to cut off the leg at the knee. It grew back immediately.

I saw two boulders nearby and hid behind them as two explosions rattled the cave. I peeked over the top of the rocks to see purple flame erupt around the basilisk. It hissed and went wild, throwing its body toward the ceiling. The flames began to die down.

"Razele, patch the holes in the ceiling!"

She sent air up there to light up the area again. I took a deep breath and allowed flame back into my legs. I shot up over the rock to attack. I had to take out the other eye. Luckily, I was coming in front of its blind spot. I jumped onto its back, and it tried to throw me off. I ran down the spine toward the head.

When I reached it, I looked down and saw its eye on me just as I shoved my leg into it and forced flame to burst through my foot. Screams of pain filled the cave and rattled my brain. I forced the heat to burn even hotter. All my power surged into my foot. I felt the skull melting under me.

The screaming started to die down. The head came down to rest on the floor, then it stopped moving. I pulled my leg free and saw it was covered with gooey remains. I kicked some of it off and went to the tip of the nose. The head was as soft as mush.

I jumped down and walked to Ruby, who wrapped her arms around my neck.

"Release him, you vampire parasite!" Razele said.

Ruby's laughter filled my ears. "Never going to happen."

I looked up and saw Razele holding what was left of her arm. She must've cut it off at the elbow. "How'd that happen? I destroyed both eyes."

She walked closer. "Yeah, you did, but when you first jumped, its eyes were on me before it went for you. I was able to stop it before it went too far. I should be able to get this fixed when we get home, but it'll be a little while before it's finished healing."

I looked at her neck. The pendant was missing.

She glanced at Ruby. "I had to save the vampire."

Ruby scowled at the pendant and crooked a finger. I walked over. When Ruby pointed at the ground, I looked over at Razele, who shrugged in confusion. I knelt, and Ruby latched onto my shoulder to suck out blood.

"Ruby, stop!" Razele shouted. "You'll kill him!"

She held up her hand and kept sucking blood. Once she was done, it took all my strength just to sit down. I watched, as Ruby took Razele's arm and waved her hand along it. As her hand passed, the arm returned, just as it was, although the new skin was paler than the older skin above it.

"Whoa, Ruby," Razele said. "How'd you do that?"

Ruby walked back to me and sat in front of me. "I didn't want my lord to feel bad, so I helped. Don't worry about it."

Razele's eyes widened. "Your lord? Who said you were even worthy to be his student, you little child?"

A cold breeze came to us, as Razele raised her fist, but I didn't have the energy to save her that time.

Ruby gently punched my arm. "I'm not a child. My name is Ruby. Razele, please be a little more courteous."

Razele bowed. "Sorry about that, Ruby. It might take me a minute."

Ruby looked around and sighed. "What's the next step?"

5

I looked at the basilisk's head. Even if all three of us worked at it, rolling the head out of there would take days, and then we'd have to fly with it.

"We're supposed to take the head to the monastery at the top of the mountain," I said. "It's a lot bigger then they knew."

Ruby looked at the head of the snake. As she raised her hand, blood spurted, and the head separated from the body. She placed her hand on it, and it disappeared into her satchel.

Razele and I stared.

"What did you just do?" I asked.

Ruby smiled. "That was nothing. Now we don't have to worry about the head. Shall we go? It's been a long time since I breathed fresh air." She laughed.

"I can feel it. We haven't been down here that long, and I'd love some fresh air. Why don't we get out of here?"

We soon left the cave. Once we were out, Ruby knelt to touch the grass, then she stared into the sky and took a deep breath.

"I'm finally free from that prison. It's amazing out here," she said.

Razele and I stood beside her and took deep breaths.

"It's nice," I said. "That was awful down there, but we aren't done yet. We have to deliver the head."

Razele looked down at Ruby. "What's your goal after we do that, Ruby? Do you have a home or someone you can be with?"

Ruby stared at the vast, open world. "I'm not sure. It's been a very long time since I saw my family. We may live forever, but we aren't immortal. We can die like anyone else."

Razele placed a hand on the girl's shoulder. "You know, we could always use a friend like you."

Ruby looked up with tears in her eyes. "Does that mean you incompetent fighters need someone like me?"

I chuckled under my breath, while Razele rubbed her temple.

"We need to work on your people skills," Razele said.

Ruby turned away to wipe her face. "I am my lord's blade. I will follow. I appreciate the offer."

Razele gave me a sour look. "Lord Hugh Kit? What did you do to her when we were split up?" Her expression made me feel like I'd been dishonest, while all that happened was Ruby blew out my guts several times.

"Like I said last time, nothing. I saved her. That's it."

Ruby walked in front of me and knelt with her head bowed. "I wasn't able to do this in the tunnel, but now I know I want to serve you and help you in any endeavors that come your way. You saved my life, and I owe you mine forever."

I realized she was serious. She wanted to pledge her life and soul to me just because I saved her. "That isn't necessary...."

"Lord, it's the way of my people. Please accept my selfish request."

I looked at Razele, who sighed and nodded.

"OK, Ruby. From here on, you may be my sword. Vanquish any enemy who wishes to cause me harm. Remember this, though—if you are ever outnumbered, I want you to run."

She looked up, ready to protest.

"Those are my requirements. I won't let someone I care about die a needless death. If you wish to be my blade, you must accept."

Ruby's face was suddenly filled with happiness. "I accept your terms!"

I extended my hand. She took it and stood. Once she was up, she looked at the heights above.

"Can you fly, Ruby?"

"Yes. Why?"

I pointed to the top of the mountain. "That's where we're going. Are you ready?"

She floated without any obvious flame. Wondering where her power came from, I decided to ask later.

I lifted Razele in my arms, turned on my flame, and forced it all to my feet. Razele used her flame to help us soar into the air. Ruby studied us with jealousy before following.

We quickly reached the monastery grounds and touched down. A platoon of armed monks surrounded us, their weapons aimed at Ruby.

"My Lord," Ruby asked, holding onto my cloak and looking ready to pounce, "are they the enemy?" Hatred filled her eyes.

"I'm not sure yet."

I saw Hindoros and Kilyon flying toward us to land in the middle of the open space. Hindoros immediately raised his arms.

"Stand down," he called. "I'm sure there's a good reason for this monster to be here."

He stared at Ruby, who seemed very worried.

"Bring out the head," I said.

Kilyon looked surprised, as Ruby opened her satchel. The head formed in front of us, and the monks ran away when it struck the ground with a thud.

"Impressive, my little pup," Hindoros said. "You actually did it. I didn't think you'd be able to and expected you to return empty-handed."

I looked at him fiercely.

"Don't look at me like that. You've never hunted anything of this caliber before."

As he peered as the monster's head, I realized it wasn't a test the way I thought. Kilyon expected us to return with our tails between our legs. What did Hindoros gain?

"So, Kilyon, your pupil killed the beast," Hindoros said. "I will uphold our deal. They will receive the artifacts you requested. For some reason, you were right about their new friend, so I'll make it three artifacts."

Kilyon slapped his back. "Don't you miss gambling with me?"

Hindoros sighed. "No. I remember why I never bet against you. The gods must love you." He walked toward Ruby. "So they weren't extinct after all. We have much to discuss, young princess."

Ruby smiled. "You were able to tell. I thought all humans were imbeciles. It seems there are a few of your rank who are somewhat intelligent."

Hindoros laughed, waving his hand. "You're known to our people. We still have a sacred contract with you."

Ruby stepped closer to me. "I'm sorry, but call me Ruby. I am Kit's sword."

Hindoros almost reeled in shock. "Are you serious, princess to a human?"

Ruby giggled, while Kilyon smiled. "Yes. He might be human, but he's stronger than any other human in the world. That's why I follow him."

Hindoros covered his face with his hand, then he reached into a pocket and handed Kilyon gold coins. He accepted them willingly.

"Thank you, Buddy," Kilyon said.

"Before we continue this conversation," Hindoros said, "it would be best if we go inside. I don't need wandering ears hearing too much."

We followed him into the monastery. Once we were inside, we went down the main hall and then turned right to a long flight of stairs. Guards stood at every corner. Once we reached the top, we saw two wide doors. Hindoros opened them, and we funneled inside, as he closed them behind us.

Two tables with pillows were in the room, with maids standing beside them. The redwood walls had etchings of great battles of the past. Hindoros waved us to a table. Once I sat down, with Ruby and Razele on either side, Hindoros and Kilyon sat across from us. The maids brought out cups and poured tea for all of us. Hindoros excused them.

As the door closed behind the departing maids, Hindoros clasped his hands and leaned forward on the table. "Princess Marynis, the ultimate vampire."

Ruby sipped her tea and chuckled. "I haven't been called that in a very long time. What can I do for you?"

He glanced at me. "I don't know what happened down there or why you were there to begin with, but why him? In the end, he'll die of old age."

Ruby set down her cup slowly and looked at him with kindness, but behind her eyes was a tidal wave of destruction just waiting to be unleashed. "He can't age. I would guess he will stay the age he is now for all eternity."

Hindoros studied both of us. "That's not possible. Human lifespans are between fifty to one hundred years. How can he be different?'

"That's something I can help with," Kilyon said. "It's the real reason I'm here. Like your daughter, Kit is a calamity. You knew that, but what you didn't know was his father was one of the great warriors, Tellium Exporoc of the Chaos Nation."

Hindoros slapped the table in outrage. "You knew this the whole time and still brought his son into my home?"

Kilyon nodded. "I did. His parents are dead, but the boy survived. I took him from their home deep inside the Chaos Nation and brought him to the Kai Nation for protection, but I can't keep him caged like a bird forever."

That meant my parents were dead after all. Why had he waited so long to tell me? I wish I'd known.

"So the crazy, stupid fool was able to do it? Do you know how?"

Kilyon shook his head and looked at me. "I don't. All I know is he wasn't able to give it to himself, so he blessed his son with it."

"It's not a blessing, it's a curse, and you know it."

Ruby laughed. "It's neither. It makes him a hero of this land. Kit will be able to do more than anyone else in this world, but it also means he could plunge everything into a fierce battleground."

The room became quiet.

"I don't understand this completely," I said slowly. "I can understand I'm dangerous, but I have no interest in politics or fighting. All I want is to go to school and protect people. I'll worry about my future when it's time."

Hindoros sighed and tapped the table three times. A maid walked in with a small box and set it before him. She bowed and left quickly before he opened it.

Inside was a cloth, which he set on the table. Metal clanked softly, as he set the box on the floor. "Well, then, I will do it now, even though I still think this is a horrid idea, Kilyon."

He unwrapped the cloth and revealed three metal crosses. Each had wings with a red jewel in the middle.

"These were gifts from our goddess," he explained. "When worn, they hide your powers and abilities. They are mostly used in assassination quests. They will disguise you as normal people from other nations. Even though you have high talents, these will show only your original nation and nothing more. They'll help you get into the school if that's what you really want."

We nodded, and he set a cross in front of each of us.

"As long as you carry one of these on your person, no one will know what power you really have. These aren't just items, they are artifacts. Above all, never lose it. There won't be a second one for you."

We took up the crosses and stared at the gems. They were completely black with a red circle in the middle with a dragon's head inside that.

"Death is something to fear and respect," he continued. "It can come at any time, and it doesn't discriminate. The longer you live, the more envious death will be. I would advise you, Kit, to watch out for any lingering sense of depression and hatred. All three feelings can be wicked in this world."

"I will," I said, feeling the cross in my chest pocket. "Thanks for the warning. There's something I wanted to ask you, Ruby."

She looked at me. "What is it?"

Her skin was much paler than ours, as if she were a ghost. Two fangs protruded slightly from her lips.

"What is a vampire, and why were you down there?"

She thought about it for a moment. "It's difficult to tell you what a vampire is. I'm just myself in the sense of a being, but I can tell you how I became the last of my kind. Long ago, this land wasn't ruled by nations or divided in any way. It was open to all. Vampires and dragonkin were the most powerful after the lizards and demon beasts. Humans were there, too, and everyone could use magic, an essence that could be drawn into the soul for power.

"Humans, though, couldn't wield such a power. Their bodies proved too delicate for it. Then came a meteor that struck, causing massive destruction. The land we're so comfortable with now is actually a giant continent that floats on the seas.

"When the meteor hit, many species died off. Dragons, vampires, and humans were left, with small groups of demons and lizardmen, though they haven't been seen in a long time."

I glanced at Kilyon, who nodded.

"The war of the nations escalated. Once, an auspicious friendship with the dragonkin was no more than a dream. That bloody war ravaged the land until humans developed their own power, what you call the flame of prosperity. We called it calamity. With your newfound power, you had the numbers and the ability to cut the rest of us down.

"In my final hour, I remember running into a cave with my people, then I became frozen into stone. I waited there until the day you saved me."

I rubbed my temple and tried to comprehend what I just learned. "I see. That's awful. I'm sorry for that."

She laughed and held onto my arm. "I harbor no hatred of humankind. It was just the will of fate. Now I have you at my side."

Smiling awkwardly, I tried to pry my arm free, but it didn't budge. I finally gave up.

"What of the dragonkin? Do you know what happened to them?" I asked.

She shook her head. "No. when the humans began the war, I went into the cave. I'm not sure what happened to them, but I would guess they didn't last long, either."

Hindoros coughed. "It's said that five dragons were enslaved after the war. One was given to each nation, and their powers were passed to one human, making that person into a half-breed. Those powers, combined with the human strength of flame, were too danger-ous. They went insane and burned everything in their path. They were told never to bear children, and I always believed they died out. That was what my grandfather told us, although he never said what happened to ours. As for Chaos, it was said she was killed."

"With the Kai Nation," Kilyon said, "my brother told me they had to execute ours. The only two who should be alive are from the Celestial and Terra Nations, if they survived at all."

Razele looked around the table. "If they're dead or close to extinction, what about the other races? Is there any likelihood they are still alive?"

Ruby's fingernails clicked against the tabletop. "I'm not sure. Lizardmen keep their homes near water. They can't survive long with-out it. As for demonkind, they were different. They all had horns and great physical strength, but most were adept with magic, too. They didn't breed very much."

It seemed humans were the cause of the extinction of most of the other races, all for the sake of power. That didn't surprise me.

"OK, Kilyon," I said. "What's next?"

He scratched his beard. "We stay with Patrunice, then head back to the Kai Nation, then go to the school."

Ruby became excited. "Did you say Patrunice, the Queen of Time?"

Kilyon laughed. "You know of her?"

"Of course! She was one of the only humans who were allowed to enter our kingdom. She was a courageous, amazing person."

Kilyon laughed and slapped the table. "That old woman, courageous? She's scarier than I'd like to admit."

Hindoros nodded. "I concur. She's a beautiful woman with enough power to destroy anyone who crosses her."

Kilyon stood. "We'll head to her tomorrow night. All of you should rest tonight. It's a long journey back to the Kai Nation."

Hindoros stood, too. "All right. The room you had earlier is the one all three of you will share. I hope you have no problem with that, Kit?"

I almost groaned at the thought of sharing a room with two girls who might tear me apart just to get my attention. "Not at all. I look forward to it."

The two men walked to the door and opened it for the rest of us. We left the room, and they closed the door behind us.

Two guards were waiting, their spears aimed at Ruby.

"We should go to bed before we overstay our welcome, you two." I walked down the stairs and went straight to our room.

Inside, I saw another set of bedding. I lay on mine and stared up at the ceiling. Ruby got under the blankets on one side of me.

"What are you doing?" I asked.

"Sleeping. What about you?"

I rubbed my forehead. Razele came over and got on the other side of me.

"What's the deal with you two?" I asked.

Razele gave me an innocent look. "This place is dangerous. It would be best if we were close together. If something happens, we won't have to go far."

I gave up, realizing I wouldn't win. "Do what you want, but someone needs to turn off the lights."

Razele snapped her fingers, and the candles went out.

"Goodnight, you two," I said. "Try to rest." I closed my eyes and felt both of them latch onto my arms. I opened my eyes once and closed them again.

These two will be the death of me, I thought. *I just know it.*

I quickly fell asleep.

6 |

I stood in an unknown room with distorted paintings on the walls. As I walked forward, I saw two black chairs and sat in one. Looking down, I saw the monastery and tried to remember what Ki-lyon called this. He said it was an out-of-body experience, although he didn't explain why it got that name.

I heard a woman's laugh, then black smoke formed in the other chair. A moment later, Celnius sat there in a short dress with plunging cleavage. Crossing her legs, she looked at me.

"We see a lot of each other these days, don't we, son of the destroyer of life?"

I wasn't sure if she was friend or foe and doubted I could trust her, but I kept hoping that would be established soon.

"I have noticed," I replied. "It's not like I'm going out of my way to see you. It's more a one-sided interest."

She clutched her chest. "Ouch. That hurts. I thought we were getting to be good friends."

"I'm sorry, but I don't understand why I'm being called here."

She stood and walked toward me, then sat in my lap to stare at me. "It's because your father asked me to watch out for you, of course. You're something special, even to me."

Her eyes swirled with dark clouds that nothing could escape. "What's so special about being a cursed power?"

Her eyes filled with rage. The hand on my arm contracted until I felt I was being crushed. "Don't ever say it's cursed. You aren't cursed. I gave you those powers because of your father. Don't label them as a terrible curse."

I bit my lip to deal with the pain and nodded. Her grip relaxed.

"Sorry," she said. "Even though I'm a goddess, I still have a tendency to overreact. I can't blame you. You have lived with humans who are ignorant of the world and the problems that come with it."

Her body felt cold and lifeless against me. I wondered how long she'd been like that.

"I don't know what to say. I just know I can't die, and being a hero is the last option for me."

She smiled more honestly that time. "That's good. A hero is something to strive for, but do you know what a hero is?

"It's someone who never gives up even in the presence of great evil."

Her smile remained. "yes, but it's more then that. A hero is something to see above the rest its more then ideology but a factual way of life one must be willing to go the distance for the betterment of those who the hero wants to save even at the cost of ones own life if one always believes that there life is more important then others then they will never be able to make the decision to better those who the hero wishes to save do you understand kit a hero is one who sacrifices and forces the will of the universe to save people and better them. Killing and suffering come with that title as well just realize that.

She wanted me to be a hero, but I wondered if that was something my dad wanted me to be. Maybe he didn't plan that far. "Can I really not die?"

Her smile faded. "You can, but it's hard. Immortality is tricky. I'll allow that to be a secret for now, though I'll clue you in on one thing."

She looked softly into my eyes. I didn't know what she thought of me, but I felt on edge around her. Something about her words bothered me.

"It's you, Goddess, isn't it? You can kill me."

She laid her head on my shoulder and breathed softly. "That is correct. I hold your life in my hands. Whether you live or die, I can control it."

My heart beat faster.

"I can't kill you," she added. "I need your help."

My heart rate slowed, and the atmosphere slowly returned to almost normal.

"What could you possibly need from me?"

She laughed and licked my neck, moving closer. "In time, my dear. You still have more to do. It can wait, even if it's the end of time, it's just the two of us."

She sat up, as I prepared to speak again, and the room disappeared.

My eyes opened. Ruby and Razele slept on either side of me. I sat up and felt their hold on my arms relax as I stood. I covered both of them and left the room, walking toward the square.

When I stepped outside, the sun was still down, but morning was near. I hadn't woken up that early in years. I saw Kilyon on one of the walls overlooking the valley. A few guards stood at their stations.

I found the stone stairs leading up. Once at the top, Kilyon turned with a smoke in his mouth. "It's good to see you up. Did you sleep well last night, or did those girls get carried away?"

I blushed and walked past him to gaze over the darkened valley. "No. They went to sleep immediately. I swear, your imagination runs wild sometimes."

He took a metal case from his pocket and opened it to reveal more smokes. I put one in my mouth. The smokes of that country were made with rice paper and a plant known as *cothorn,* a plant with the ability to wash stress away for a short time.

It was the first time I tried it, and I wondered why he was offering it at that moment. I lit it with a finger and inhaled, only to cough hard. Once the coughing fit was over, I put it back in my mouth.

The smoke was easier to inhale the second time. It still burned, but not enough to trigger a coughing fit.

"You've never offered me one before, Kilyon. Why now?"

He stood there, the wind blowing through his hair. "I did it, because I can tell you're going through a lot. Masking pain with an addiction isn't good. It might even be the worst thing you can do, but everyone needs to deal with the pain in this world somehow. If that's through addiction, who am I to say it's wrong?

"Human beings are animals by their nature. That will never change no matter how advanced we get. We'll always be animals at the core, nothing but primitive animals."

His words stung. Did he see the human race as nothing more than a plague?

"What do you think of the human race, then?"

Gloom covered his expression. "We're capable of so much. We could have true peace, but people will never accept it. They thrive on combat and war. Peace is a useless word with them. Throughout the years, abduction, murder, racism, and intolerance run wild in humans. They never want to stop it. It doesn't matter how many people would like to change it or even try to. A select few always upset the situation."

He inhaled from his smoke and exhaled a cloud in front of both of us. "Humans are capable of greatness. When there is a major enemy, we band together to protect each other. When there's a deadly plague, we band together to fix the problem. Isn't that good?" He turned to me.

"Do you really think they'd do that out of the kindness of their hearts?" he asked. "A massive plague affects everyone, so it's in the country's best interests to stop it. When a major enemy appears, it's in the country's best interests to kill them. Right when the problem is taken care of, they go back to the battlefield. The only reason we have peace right now is that school. It's only a matter of time before one country tries to destroy it, then it's all-out war again."

Rays of sunlight peeked over the hills and touched the land. I watched the frost on the walls begin to melt. "You're right, Kilyon. I don't know how to stop that kind of thing. Not only that, but my new friends and I are nothing but criminals awaiting execution. I can't run from any of it, because we're trapped on this continent. What should I do?"

He walked past me and stopped at my shoulder. "You fight and never give up. You become a hero for this world and never let anyone stop you, then you make the world a better place, even if you have to conquer every nation."

He walked past, and I stared out at the valley. Conquering every nation would be impossible, but if I could, wouldn't that make me the overlord of the world?

I smiled at the idea of saving everyone and still being able to raise them up to prevent a tragedy. At the moment, I was weak. I needed to go to the school and get stronger.

Birds flew over the land below. The mountain was beautiful, but a feeling of unrest followed me everywhere I went.

Footsteps grew louder, and I saw Ruby and Razele come up on either side.

"It's a beautiful morning, My Lord," Ruby said. "What's the plan for today?"

I realized I had to speak with that evil woman again. I had the feeling she had solutions to my problems, but what would be the cost for that information?

Ruby looked into my eyes. "My Lord, are you all right?"

Her gaze broke my concentration. "Yes. Sorry. I believe Kilyon wants to see Patrunice again. My guess is she'll give us a free ride to the nearest village. From there, we'll head to our home and then be off to the school. Are you excited about going there?"

Ruby touched my forehead. "You're doing it again. Stop worrying so much. You'll stress yourself out. We're both here for you." She removed her finger.

"I'm sorry. I'm thankful for both of you, although I'm afraid of what might happen.

Razele came up beside Ruby to hug me and I rested my head against hers. I caught the scent of jasmine in her hair. She was perfect.

"Relax, Kit," she said. "It'll be OK."

Ruby leaned over the rail, as Razele stepped away. We walked over to Ruby and looked out at the valley.

"I'm not ready to see Patrunice," Ruby said. "It's been too long. I'm scared of the school, too."

I understood her concern. If they found out about her, we'd all be in trouble. "Then if they do that, Razele and I will fight to get you out of there and go somewhere we can relax in peace. Try not to suck anyone's blood just for fun."

Ruby crossed her arms and scowled. "Very funny. Are you blaming a vampire for wanting to feed?"

Razele giggled. "It's not that we blame you, we just want you to be fine. Kit can't solve everything himself."

Ruby sighed and lowered her head. "All right. Fine. I won't drink from humans, but I still need a source of blood." She looked at Razele.

"Oh, no. Not me. I'm human. If anyone should, it's Kit. He can't die."

I sighed. "All right. I'll let you, Ruby."

She squealed. "Sorry, but thank you, My Lord. It is a pleasure. Your blood is tasty and sweet."

I remembered when she drank my blood before. I felt like she'd suck every ounce from my veins.

Looking at Razele, I asked, "Is there a good place to eat? We don't have to meet with Kilyon until tonight."

She thought for a second before snapping her fingers. "Yes. There's a lovely place in the village. If you want to eat there, I'm sure it would be fun."

I looked down at Ruby. "What do you say? Want to come eat something?"

She nodded and stared at the valley.

"I know it's hard, but we're here if you want to talk about anything. I can't imagine what it's like to be the last of your kind."

She turned to hug me. "It's OK. I know you mean well, but I don't want to talk about it right now."

The three of us walked down the stairs leading to the square. As Razele led us from the monastery, I heard Kilyon's voice behind us.

"Hey, Little Pup, make sure you're back by tonight. There's still a lot to do."

I waved over my shoulder without turning. Up ahead, an arch stood between the walls, with a flight of stone steps. I noticed each side of the arch was a different color. The right side was red with the sun at the top, while the other side was blue with a white moon.

"What's that mean?" I asked.

Razele looked at it, as we walked through. "It symbolizes the way we train without our flames, making us ready no matter what happens. It's a sign of the future, or so the elders say."

I looked ahead at the small town. All the huts were made of the same red wood. Sentry posts stood at the corners of the town, with guards at each.

"Why is this place so fortified?" I asked. "You're so far up."

She pointed down the valley. "There are still beasts that attack us. There aren't many these days, but it's enough to have a force ready at all times. The village wouldn't be destroyed, because all of the people have had some training. Still, some fear the beasts."

Ruby hovered a little to look ahead.

"What are you doing? Are you tired of walking?"

She sighed. "Yes. It's exhausting. I don't know how you humans do it."

I patted my back. "I can carry you."

She immediately perked up and floated over to land on my back. I held her to keep her from falling off. Razele looked at me with a hint of jealousy.

"You're always falling for other women," she said.

I shook my head and replied, "No, I just wanted to be helpful. She's been trapped for a long time. It might be nice to have a piggy-back ride."

Razele giggled. "You're so cute."

I smiled, as we reached the bottom of the trail to where the ground was made of softer rock. The roads aligned perfectly between the houses and shops. Two children ran up to us, a boy and a girl.

"Razele, it's nice to see you today!" the boy said. "Why haven't we seen you around?"

They noticed me, and the boy winked. "Oh, I see. You found a man. Does he treat you nice?"

Razele shook her head. "He's not my boyfriend. We're just companions."

The young man didn't seem convinced and walked closer. I stopped walking and knelt down.

"Hi, you two," I said. "My name is Kit. The woman on my back is Ruby. We're friends of Razele's."

He smiled. "I'm Nina and my sister is Tina."

The little girl bowed. "It's nice to meet you, Sir."

I nodded to her. Nina looked at me for a moment, then walked up to whisper in my ear, "Take good care of Razele. She's like a big sister. I don't want to hear that you hurt her."

I patted his head. "I promise."

He smiled and backed away to look at Razele. "I'm sorry we can't talk more, but Father said we should help skin the goats. We must be off. Razele, be a good girl."

They ran off.

I stood, and Razele seemed a bit flustered. "What did he say?" she asked.

I shook my head.

"He said he'd hurt the lord if he made you cry," Ruby blurted.

I flicked Ruby's forehead.

"What's wrong? It's true."

Razele giggled. "It's OK, Kit. I'm not mad. Thank you for telling me. I'm sure Kit would never have said the whole thing."

She looked at me, and I said, "I would have told you at least part of it."

She shook her head.

While we walked through the streets, many residents waved to Razele, as if she were a queen.

"What's up with all the praise from them?" I asked her.

She looked at me. "Head families are usually the kings or queens of the land. They trust us like that. Isn't it the same where you come from?"

I slowly shook my head. "No. Well, I'm not sure. I'm part of the Icealis family, but they don't treat me that way, nor do they with Kelos, who is the head of the family right now. We don't expect people to lower themselves. We're all the same, even if we're the ones who run the whole nation."

Frowning in thought, she looked at the people around us. "I never thought about it like that. I didn't think they were lowering themselves. It was more that they had someone to look to for hope and guidance."

She was right. I shouldn't have said they were lowering themselves. It didn't look that way, but that was the best way I could think of to describe it.

Razele grabbed my arm, and we rushed up the street. "It's just up here. It's owned by an elderly woman and her husband. They're amazing, and you'll love them."

Ruby held on tightly as we ran through the town until we neared a small shack with a long sheet covering the inside. I pulled back the sheet and saw five seats and a table.

I glanced back at Ruby. "Ready to eat?"

She slid to the ground, and I took a chair beside hers. Razele, sitting on the other side of me, rang a small bell on the table.

"One second!" an older woman said. "I'll be right there!"

She sounded frail. I noticed a doorway with a white sheet over it. Through the doorway came an elderly woman with a pale face and pinched eyes.

Ruby looked at her and said, "She smells dead."

Razele glared at Ruby. "That's rude. Apologize to her. She's one of our elders."

Ruby looked away.

The woman came over to our table. "That's quite all right, my dear Razele. Vampires are a proud race. She's not wrong, either. I'm not long for this world."

Ruby looked at her. "Why do you run this shop if you're so close to death? What if you accidentally poison someone?"

The elder regarded Ruby with a faint smile. "Why do you ride on your lord's back instead of walking, even though vampires aren't a lazy species?"

Razele chuckled, and Ruby blushed and looked away.

"I was encased in stone for so long, I was tired," Ruby said.

The old woman chuckled and began preparing food on a stove.

"Tell me, Young Man, what are your intentions toward my Razele?"

"I'm friends with her. I want to protect her and make sure she has a good life."

The woman tossed noodles into a pot of water and added more ingredients. "Really? That's nice, but it doesn't sound like friendship. It's more like a relationship."

Her words became a little more cutting.

"I do like her, but we're friends."

The woman looked to Ruby. "How is it being back in the world?"

Ruby looked back at her. "It's weird. So much has changed. Even the land is different."

She nodded. "Yes, indeed, it has. I remember when these lands were full of trees."

"What happened? Why has the land changed so much?"

She continued cooking. "The pact was destroyed. At least, that's what we thought. Our people started cutting off the trees, then the land turned to meadows, and the trees refused to grow here."

Ruby was confused. "What is she talking about? What pact?"

"Long ago," the old woman said, "a young woman was in love with a vampire named Hellistafar. He was a lovely man and kind to all, even humans. When the nation found out, the vampire and human were put to death. After that, the war between the Aura Nation and the vampires began. It was a bloody war that lasted almost thirty years. Both sides were pushed to the brink.

"They agreed to a pact that in the coming years, a human male and a female vampire would be joined as one, and the lands of the vampires would remain theirs forever."

She stopped cooking for a moment. "Then the travesty of the flames became a realization, and war broke out in every nation save one. With the war against the vampires having just ended, we were vulnerable. We let our allies die to save ourselves."

Ruby stared down, as tears fell from her face to strike the table.

I placed a hand on her back, rubbing gently. "I'm sorry, Ruby."

Her head shaking, she leaned on me.

"I'm sorry, too," the old woman said. "We made the wrong decision, and we have regretted it ever since."

Ruby's hair suddenly flared red, then it subsided.

"What was that?" I asked.

She looked up and shrugged. "Nothing, Kit. Don't worry about it."

The smell of cooked food filled the room.

"Let's stop all this drab talk. You came here to eat, so dig in," the woman said, placing three bowls in front of us.

They held noodles with slices of meat. She gave us all two sticks for silverware. Ruby and I stared at ours, while Razele laughed.

"That's not how to do it," she said. "Watch me." She positioned the sticks carefully in her fingers and picked up some noodles to eat.

Ruby and I tried. She was able to get the hang of it, but I had trouble. Razele grabbed a piece from my bowl and said, "Open wide."

I opened my mouth, and she placed it on my tongue. I chewed, then said, "Thank you, Razele."

The woman smiled. "That was so cute."

We stayed there for hours, chatting and eating in peace. When we finished, I saw the sun descending and realized it was afternoon.

"We should head back before we get yelled at."

Ruby jumped onto my back. Razele opened a pouch to pay, but the old woman waved her off.

"You need the money for the food," Razele protested.

"Not today. I have received my payment. Ruby, Dear, stay close to them, OK?"

Ruby bowed her head in acknowledgement. "I will, Old Lady."

Razele was angry for a second, but the old woman just laughed, so she calmed down. As we walked out, the woman asked, "Can you stay a few minutes, Razele? Have the others wait outside."

Looking confused, Razele nodded. Ruby and I went outside to wait.

As we waited, I saw Nina running with Tina and waved to them. Nina ran over.

"Did you eat Elder Milinas' food? Isn't it good?" he asked.

"Milinas?" Ruby asked.

"Yes. Do you know that name?"

She thought for a second. "It must be a coincidence. Nothing to worry about."

I looked at Nina. "Yes, we did. It was very good."

Tina looked at Ruby. "You have very pretty hair, and your eyes are cute, too."

Ruby blushed and hid her face for a moment. "Thank you very much. That was very nice of you, stupid human."

Tina smiled, and Nina laughed.

"I told you, Sister, not to say anything to her. Anyway, Kit, thank you again. It's nice to see Razele with someone like you. We're off. Have a good day."

"What do you think of the town?" I asked.

She looked around. "It's nice, but I'm still mad at them and this nation for what happened to my people. It wasn't right."

I nodded, understanding her anger, although hating an entire nation wasn't good, either. "You know these aren't the people who did that to your people. They're new. Only a few even know what happened. Don't hate all of them."

She rested her cheek against the back of my neck. "I won't for long. I just need some time. I'm not mad at Razele, either. It's the opposite. I'm happy I met her. I just don't want to lose you to her. That's my biggest fear."

I placed my hand on her leg and rubbed gently. "I promise not to leave you for her, but I won't choose you, either. I like both of you, OK?"

She tightened her grip on me. "Thank you for saying that. It means a lot to me."

I saw Razele come out with a smile.

"I think it's sweet," she said. "I promise to make sure not to make you feel like I'll take him away from you."

They looked at each other for a moment. I glanced at the sky and saw birds flying overhead. We started back toward the monastery.

Eventually we climbed the stone steps and saw Hindoros and Kilyon talking. Once we came close enough, they turned toward us.

We stopped a few feet away. Hindoros looked at his daughter.

"It's time for you to go, Razele."

She managed to keep her composure, smiling and nodding to him, then he turned to me. "Make sure that those who follow you never have to die for something that isn't achievable."

I smiled, thinking he was a good father. "You have my word."

He shook my hand.

"The Path of Despair and Destruction was once known far and wide. Few now will ever walk it. I hope you're strong enough for that road."

Our hands separated.

"There's only one way to find out."

Kilyon shook his hand, and Ruby got off my back. We walked away, picking up Razele to fly back where we originally appeared. Small amounts of smoke rose into the air from below.

Once we reached Patrunice's house, we landed. I set Razele down, while Kilyon knocked three times.

I heard the locks unfasten themselves, then he opened the door and walked in as if nothing changed.

Patrunice sat at a table, reading. When we walked in, Ruby closed the door.

"I see you need my help again, Crimson," Patrunice said. "How was your adventure?"

We walked to the table and sat down. When Patrunice looked up and saw Ruby, a brief smile came to her face.

"It was fine," he replied. "We were able to get the artifacts and acquired a new friend."

Patrunice set down her paper. "I see the princess. It's a pleasure to have you in my home."

Ruby was very excited. " Patrunice, I'm so happy to see you. It's been too long."

Patrunice took out a long, silver pipe and stuffed flakes into the bowl. It didn't seem like *cothorn* to me. She lit the bowl, and purple smoke rose.

"Yes, my dear. It's been two hundred...no, three hundred...years—a long time."

Ruby was silent.

"I'm sorry I couldn't help you." Patrunice took a long puff and sent out two large rings that floated in the air. When they stopped, she sent out two smaller ones that floated through the big ones, then the smoke dispersed.

"Death is inevitable for mere mortals. I don't harbor any hatred toward you. I know the reason, and I'm aware of the oath that was broken. It's null and void now, so there's no reason to dwell on the past."

Patrunice glanced at me and smiled. "I see you have a master, though I remember when you were little, you swore day and night you'd never fall under a human's rule. I believe that's what you said, but it was long ago. Things change."

Ruby twiddled with her fingers. "I remember. Humans *are* cretins, but this one and his companion are different. I have no issue with them."

Patrunice exhaled smoke, and it formed a dragon before swirling around Ruby's face. "Remember that kindness is a weakness and a weapon. Make sure the blade is always sharp, or it may fail you."

Ruby nodded before looking at me. "I believe I chose correctly. I'll fight with him until the end."

Kilyon smiled and nodded, while Patrunice giggled softly.

"My dear Kit, you have the charisma to lead an army. I look forward to your future. I wonder who else will join your band of friends."

After glancing at the two girls, I looked at Patrunice. "I don't know, but I know there's a lot I have to do before I make any big plans."

She nodded to Kilyon in approval. 'Well, then. It's settled. I'll be watching closely." She took a coin from her pocket and tossed it to me.

I caught it and saw a snake with many heads on one side, with a warrior holding a sword upright as the sky rained down on him. "What is this?"

She blew out smoke. "It's an artifact. If you ever find yourself outnumbered or on the verge of death, toss that into water. It can be a pond or a puddle. It doesn't matter, as long as the water completely covers the coin. Be warned, though. The friend of mine who lives in that coin is hard to control. Be ready to fight for his trust."

I slipped the coin into my pocket. It seemed counterintuitive to summon another enemy to a lost battle. Shaking my head, I knew it didn't matter. It was a nice gift. "Thank you, Patrunice. May I ask who this friend is?"

She smiled. "He's more of a what, and no, I feel you should meet him yourself. It's more fun that way."

"Why do I get the feeling this friend of yours is an unholy beast who will want to tear me apart? I look forward to that moment. Thank you for allowing us to come in and for the trip home, but I want a bath."

I walked down the hallway but stopped when I heard her voice.

"Love is something special, stronger than any other emotion. It can cure diseases and make hearts that have stopped beating flicker to life. It's not wise to remain closed up."

I continued my walk. When I found the changing room, I put my possessions in a basket and walked into the room with the baths. Everything was the same. I wondered if she ever changed.

Stepping into the hot water, I felt I could become accustomed to such luxury. After sitting on the edge, I realized I hadn't relaxed in a while. I felt I deserved it after that serpent in the tunnels. That was hard work.

I sank into the tub and laid my head on the stone before closing my eyes. The future held many things for me, but I felt like I was missing something I needed to do. I had to visit the Chaos Nation and find my home, but I couldn't get there if it was always blocked off. If I could gain the trust of the school, I should be able to sneak in that way, then travel from there. It would take days, but at least I'd get there. When I did, my father would be waiting. He did something so terrible, the goddess granted me immortality. How horrible was it? What was strong enough to make a goddess make me immortal? How could anyone person gain such power over death?

I tried not to think about it, but that didn't help. I heard someone enter the water and saw Ruby and Razele standing there. I immediately looked away.

"Come now, Lord. Why look away when there are two beautiful women in the bath with you?"

First Patrunice, now these two, I thought. *What is it with the women around here?*

"Why are both of you in the men's bath?"

Ruby laughed and sat down to look into my eyes. "I'm your blade. I go where you go. It's the law."

I stared back. "That doesn't mean we have to bathe together."

I peeked down and heard her giggle.

"True, but I like it."

Razele sat on my other side. "I'm here, because Ruby said she needed help to protect you."

I did my best to remain calm.

"Is that what she really said, or did you want to join her, because it made you jealous?"

Ruby held onto my arm. "You already know she's in love with you, Lord, but her chest is so small, no man would come to her."

I tried not to laugh. Razele glared at Ruby. "We can't all have voluptuous melons like yours. I'm surprised you can stand up straight."

Ruby chuckled. "Men like big breasts better than a washboard."

I felt a fight brewing, and I knew I'd get the short end of it. "You're both beautiful."

They stopped quarreling and held onto my arms. All I wanted was to bathe in peace, but I wasn't even allowed that.

"Ruby, has Patrunice showed you to your room yet?" I asked.

She gave a quick smile. "She told me I'm supposed to sleep next to you—her exact words."

I smiled awkwardly and knew what that meant.

Razele quickly said, "Well, if you're going to sleep with him, then I shall, too."

She was right on cue.

"You couldn't protect my lord even if you tried."

Their gazes went to mine. "OK. I submit. We stay in the same room."

I swore I'd make Patrunice pay for that someday.

Patruncie and Kilyon both walked in and sat in the pool across from us. My eyes twitched, as I tried to avoid staring. Razele noticed and giggled at me.

How can this get any worse? I wondered. *This will never end.*

Patrunice's foot touched mine. "Oh, my apology, Kit. That was an accident."

Ruby and Razele looked at each other and clung to me even harder. I knew Patrunice was lying.

"Why are you two in here?" I asked.

Kilyon put his arm around Patrunice. "To be honest, it's because this is the men's bath. For the females, it appears to be to make each other jealous."

I couldn't tell if my face felt hot from the steam or embarrassment. Maybe it was both. How could I escape the situation before it got even more awkward?

"Kit, can I ask you something?"

I looked at Patrunice. "What is it?"

She brought out her pipe and lit it. "What does chaos feel like?"

I didn't know how to answer that. I might have been born there, but I didn't know how to activate it. "I'm not sure. Why?"

She inhaled and held her breath for a moment. "What about hatred?"

I had never hated anyone in my life. I was a normal kid who got angry but never to the point of hating someone. "I don't know. I've never had that feeling."

She continued smoking, as Kilyon looked away. "What about despair?" she asked.

"Same answer. I haven't felt it."

She sighed and looked at Kilyon. "Crimson, you mean to tell him you never trained him in the power of his birth but only of a second flame? Care to explain?"

He tried to get up, but she stopped him.

"I can explain," he said.

With her pipe in her mouth. she crossed her arms and didn't seem impressed.

"What does it matter if he wasn't trained in it?" Razele asked. "Is that bad?"

"It's a big deal," Ruby said. "With magic, if you're trained in a different element than your birth one, it can have devastating problems. That doesn't mean you can't learn more than one kind, but your major one should be your birth magic, isn't that right, Patrunice?"

She nodded. "Exactly, my dear little vampire. Magic, and what we call the heart of flame, is in essence the same thing. We just draw power differently. Of course, there are three groups of flames now for people who can use magic. They can learn everything, but for the flames, they can only learn what's in their family line.

"If your parents are both water, then the water element is all you can learn. The only way past that is if your parents were part of the three great families. If the parents come from different nations and are also from the great families, their offspring would be the deadliest flyer of all mankind. All those with such magic capabilities have nearly been wiped out."

Ruby stared down in the water. I placed my hand on her head and rubbed gently.

"OK, then," I said. "Why can't I fly? That's something I've been wondering about."

Patrunice removed her pipe with one hand and blew a cloud toward me. "It's because you're using the flame that isn't your main power. You're using celestial or fire when you should be using chaos. I'm impressed that you can use your celestial flame that well. Normally, people would never be able to run so fast. You, however, can reach a high speed and still fight. You've been training well, but when you unlock your chaos flames, your strength will double at least. The sooner you learn to do that, the better."

That sounded amazing. I decided to work really hard to do that. "What's the problem with that? I should be learning how."

Kilyon looked at me with a gloomy face. "Then you must walk to the edge of the abyss and back."

I frowned, wondering what he meant.

"You have to see despair and feel it. Hatred must flow into you. The only way to do that is to allow Patrunice to do what she does best." He glanced at her.

"What does he mean?" I asked.

When Patrunice stood and raised her hand, everything stopped moving. The steam remained in place without flowing. She looked at me and said, "I control time. I can show you what's it's like to feel despair and hatred toward others. All I have to do is flick my wrist, and you'll be transported into the worst hell you could ever imagine. Just give me the word."

She had to be joking. How could she possibly do such a thing, and what kind of hell did she mean?

"Why would you do that to me?" I asked. "I thought we were friends."

She walked toward me and knelt. "The fate of the world lies in your lap, my dear little pup. I don't wish to bring you pain or hatred, but if you can't control your home flame, there's no way you can save this world. It means I must break you and force the flame to emerge. I apologize. I wish there was another way."

I tried to smile, but my face refused to move. She was serious, without any hint of a lie, although I didn't think she'd ever lie to me.

"Can I ask you one thing before I go?"

She nodded.

"Ruby and Razele won't be hurt, will they?"

She looked away. "It's time for you to go, Little Pup."

I nodded. I realized I might have to kill the ones I loved even if I didn't have a chance to get to know them very well. I had strong feelings for both women. "All right. Send me there."

She flicked her wrist.

Everything turned dark, and I fell into an abyss. I saw the others fade away. Once all was gone, a small glimmer of light shone from below and enveloped me. Just as the light surrounded me, my back struck the ground.

I stood and looked around, seeing a large box nearby made of white flowers. I knelt to touch them, and they turned to dust. Stepping back, I looked up at a long, rectangular shaft rising into the sky. Was I still in Patrunice's house, or was it just my subconscious?

Four black chains emerged from the ground and attached themselves to my arms and legs. I tried to break free, but my flame wouldn't activate. It felt as if flame was no longer part of me.

The chains grew tighter, then I heard a whoosh and looked up to see a red cloak. Ruby fell on the ground in front of me. Her eyes were gouged out, leaving empty holes, and her clothes were drenched in blood.

"Lord, is that you? What's happening?"

I tried to reach her, but the chains tightened again. Muscles tore with my effort. I screamed at the pain, then I went limp and hung from the chains.

"Lord, I can't see."

Tears fell from my face to touch the wilted flowers. "Yeah, Ruby. I'm here."

She crawled toward me. I didn't see any injuries on her body, just her eyes. She touched my cloak and pulled herself up, then she fell to the ground again but retained her grip.

I looked away and saw blood splattered on the walls. My heart raced at the sight of blood on all the walls. When I looked down, there was blood on my cloak from Ruby's handprints. Panicking even more, I didn't want to look further, but my gaze went to Ruby.

Her body was sliced open. Blood flowed from her stomach flowing into the ground all of the flowers changed drastically taking on new characteristics illuminating ruby red. Ruby looked up, blood dripping from her mouth.

"My Lord, I'm sorry I failed you."

I felt a tidal wave of frustration and anger. I pulled my arms, hoping to snap the chains, but all I did was hurt myself. Crying, I shouted, but my voice became hoarse, and I could no longer make a sound.

I felt my arms break off, then the chains no longer held me. I landed on Ruby. Using my mouth, I bit the back of her cloak and pulled her head onto my chest. Her arms tried to wrap around me, as I lay my head on hers. When I tried to speak, my voice refused to work.

"I love you, Lord," she said. "I'm sorry for putting you through so much. I don't think you're a cretin. I just didn't know how to express the love I had for you."

I cried, wishing I could have stopped the situation. My arms grew back, and I wrapped them around her until my vocal cords returned to normal.

"Thank you, Ruby, so much," I said.

She used the last of her energy to sit up and smile at me, and then a loud rattle sounded. I looked around but didn't see anything until chains flew from the wall and went around Ruby's waist. As she lifted away, I reached for her, but the old chains returned and bound my arms again.

"Live for me, Master," she said. "Please don't blame yourself."

I pulled on the chains, trying to reach her. I watched as the chains around her wrapped tighter and tighter.

"No!" I shouted. "Stop this! She didn't do anything wrong! Stop!"

The chains pulled on her body until she was torn in half. Blood splattered and covered everything under in a shower of red. The chains released her. Her body fell in front of me, a smile on her face.

I prayed it was just a bad dream. It couldn't be true. As I stared into her empty eyes, my heart became a void, and I wept bitterly.

"I'm so sorry, Ruby. I just wanted to protect you, but I failed. I wasn't a good friend to you."

I lowered my eyes and stared at the bloody flowers under me. Suddenly, everything turned red.

"So that wasn't enough to break you? That just means you didn't care. You couldn't even tell her you loved her. That must suck."

It sounded like Patrunice, but much darker.

"Shut up."

"Isn't it true? She was just a filthy vampire, a dead species without friends or loved ones to grieve for her."

Anger boiled in me, and dark mist suddenly permeated the air. Dark particles floated past. "I said shut up!"

Her voice was behind me. I felt a hand on my shoulder, as she leaned in close to my ear. "How could you love filthy garbage like that, anyway? Life with someone like her would be impossible. You should know her life was nothing but a waste."

My anger became even stronger. "I told you to shut up!"

Something broke inside me. Black flames erupted, consuming everything. They flowed over Ruby and ignited the flowers, then the entire room was aflame. The chains snapped in the heat.

I turned and saw Patrunice standing behind me, smoking her pipe. "So this is the power of chaos?" she asked. "To tell the truth, I'm impressed. Your father never had this much power, so how could his son? Your hair is completely black, and your eyes aren't red but pitch black. It's like looking into nothing, being nothing, always running into nothing. It's amazing. Your appearance has changed. I never saw a flyer with flames over his entire body."

I grasped her wrist with one hand. "What can you do? You aren't strong enough to kill me, and you know it. You can't even touch these black flames."

I flicked my wrist and shot spikes of black fire at her. They pierced both of us, trapping us in a prison of sharp stakes. Her head went limp, as black ooze dribbled down from where the stakes went through her body.

Her body suddenly solidified and vanished. "Good resolve, but I'm done playing with you. It's time to end this."

Looking around, I saw the room was empty. There was no sign of anything but my flames. I turned them off and felt myself being pulled upward. I felt everything I loved melt away. I closed my eyes and saw images of Ruby's death. I fought back more tears, leaving behind the darkness for a glimmer of bright light far overhead. Soon, it blinded me until I had to cover my eyes with my arm.

I woke and lay in bed, staring up at a wooden ceiling. When I raised my hand to grasp at the air, someone's hand touched me.

I looked over at Ruby, who lay beside me. As tears fell from my eyes, she wiped them away.

"Why are you crying?" she asked. "Are you OK? You passed out in the bath, so we brought you back here."

I held her close.

"My Lord? What's the problem?"

I wanted to speak, but the happiness that went through me was so strong, all I wanted was to hold her.

"I don't know what's the matter, but I'm fine, My Lord. I'm not going anywhere."

I sat there crying, while she rubbed my head and back, trying to make me feel better. The warmth of her body flowed into mine.

"It's OK, My Lord. It's over."

I finally calmed enough to lie down on my back. I felt movement on my right and heard Razele moving around, then her eyes opened.

"Kit, you're OK!" She threw herself at me. I barely caught her in time, and Ruby prevented us from falling off the bed.

"Careful, you washboard. You could kill us with those things."

Razele glared at her. "Oh, yeah? I'm sure your breasts would have acted as safety cushions if we fell."

I didn't understand them at all. Ruby's weren't that big.

"Yeah? You could knock someone out with yours. They're basically a wall."

Razele crossed her arms under her breasts. "Take that back, you little air bag."

Ruby was angry. "Who are you calling little, you lamb prey?"

Feeling the rising tension, I looked for a way to escape. They locked their gazes on me, then Ruby held me.

"What do you think, Kit?"

"Haven't we been through this already? I want to see the master for a moment."

I flicked my wrist and felt my bed turn to mist and reappear at the end of the body. "That's cool. I didn't know I could do that."

They looked at me.

"That's cheating," they chorused, smiling and jumping off the bed.

I opened the door and stepped outside, closing it quickly before I incurred their wrath. When I stepped forward, I ran into something soft.

Arms went around me. I realized I was being pressed against Patrunice's chest. When I saw her face, anger filled me, and flames surrounded me without being summoned.

"Interesting," she said. "You didn't even need to activate it. That's good."

I bit my lip and was about to flick my wrist. Instead, the flames gathered together and disappeared..

In shock, I glanced over and saw Kilyon holding them.

"There's no need for that, Kit," he said. "It's over. It was nothing more than an illusion."

I yanked my hand away. "That was overdoing it, Patrunice, and you know it."

She giggled and leaned close enough that I could smell her flowery perfume. "It's not my fault. You agreed to it. I showed you the best way to do it."

Kilyon sighed and moved me back a foot. "Patrunice, he's right. You went overboard, but thank you for helping him."

She bowed to me. "I hope you accept my apology. It was never my intention to make you break that hard. I wanted to nudge you and went too far. I'm sorry."

My anger subsided. "Everyone is fine. Ruby is alive. I understand now. You're forgiven."

Kilyon, taking both of our arms, guided us toward the dining hall. "All right, then. We'll toast this occasion."

We sat down, and three drinks and a vase appeared. Kilyon took out his smokes box and set it on the table with an ashtray. I took one out, as he poured drinks. I lit the smoke and took it to my mouth, where I inhaled to calm myself. As I exhaled smoke, my worries went with it.

"What was the reason for all of that?" I asked. "I get that it's positive. I should be able to fly on my own now, but won't this be a bad thing overall?"

Kilyon drank from his ale. "No. It will work out better this way. The artifact you received is special. It allows everyone to see the color you choose. You'll appear to be normal flyers, not part of any particular family. For you, you're adept with fire, but your main nation is chaos. You learned fire first. It would have ruined everything to use it. You must use chaos only at the school, nothing more."

It seemed I would be labeled as something else if I used different elements.

"What about the immortality? That's pretty hard to hide."

Patrunice looked at me. "That's where I can come in handy. I'll give you my artifact to solve that problem."

I inhaled from my smoke again, as she reached into another dimension and placed something on the table in front of me. Kilyon studied it.

It was a circle of pitch-black metal with three jewels in it. I saw the metal actually had three shades of black, not one.

"What is that?" he asked.

She tossed it to me. I grabbed it, and she sliced through the air with her hand. A long cut split open on my arm. I felt it healing immediately, but what I saw was a large gap in the skin.

Kilyon reached over with his hand, as water healed me.

"It's an illusion," she explained. "It will show any wound on your body as long as it's not lethal. Be wary of that. No one will know the difference."

I placed it in my chest pocket. "Awesome. So there's nothing to worry about now, is there?"

They shook their heads.

Kilyon raised his mug. "May the three of you graduate from that school."

Patrunice and I raised ours and touched them before drinking. The taste of ginger overwhelmed my mouth before I set it down.

"What's the point of the school for the three of us?" I asked.

The two looked at each other and laughed.

"It's more to have the experience," Kilyon said. "We could train you every day, but it would suck. You'll have the chance to meet friends or make enemies. You should have fun, just don't burn down the school—at least, not yet."

I shook my head at the thought. "Can I ask you something?"

"Of course, Little Pup."

I wondered if it was the right time to ask. "Why is your nickname Crimson Water?"

Patrunice hiccupped, trying not to laugh. Kilyon shrugged.

"You're bound to find out someday," he said. "If you don't, the school will definitely tell you. We're all hated there."

That didn't make any sense.

"During the war, like we told you earlier, the five great nations fought. All of us came together and were invincible."

He paused, and Patrunice placed her hand on his. When Kilyon stopped speaking, she continued.

"It was during one of the great battles," she said. "The enemy refused to stop. They pushed forward even after we decimated half their army of 200,000. Kilyon had a short temper back then. When they refused, he summoned a power that is passed down in his family and wiped out the entire remaining army, along with nearby villages and civilians. After that, he was given that nickname."

I inhaled from my smoke and thought about it. I could see why he got the name after killing so many people in one go.

"Once the nations understood the immense power we held, they agreed to peace," Kilyon said. "We were forced never to meet again, but since Patrunice is in control of space and time, I can see her whenever I want. Hindoros is another matter. Many of his monks were killed just to preserve the secret."

I nodded and looked at Patrunice. "Did all of you get names?"

She smiled and nodded. "Mine was the Witch of Time. I sent an entire capital city to the void, never to return. Your father was known as the Wrath of Relentlessness. No matter how great the foe, he cut them down with his sword to reach his target. He was like a great spear launched at an army. He single-handedly rushed their line, killing all in his way, to reach the general."

I chuckled. It sounded like my father was a tenacious guy. "What of the other three?"

Kilyon laughed and sat up straight. "Hindoros was known as the Storm Cataclysm. He destroyed three cities with one huge storm. Tricile was a great Terra Nation warrior, but we called her...."

Patrunice covered his mouth with her hand. "A brute is the best way to put it," she said.

Kilyon shook his head and chuckled. "Yeah. She was known as the Almighty Boulder. That was the dumbest name of all of ours, but she lived up to it.

"We were storming a large castle. Rock golems and armored giants kept us from crossing the bridge. Flames didn't work too well on them, but she was so strong, she rammed her way through.

"The last was the Celestial Knight. She was a blessing in disguise, with lovely golden hair, and perfect blue eyes. Her fire was so brilliant, it could discern between friend and foe."

Patrunice pinched his arm.

"Sorry. Like I was saying, she was known as the Celestial Knight. She covered an entire capital in flames. They spread over the nation. She rarely was matched in combat. Your father fought with her a lot, seeing himself as the ultimate swordsman, but she was on a different level entirely."

"Sounds like Dad was a sore loser, too. What happened to her?"

They looked at her.

"I'm not sure," he said slowly. "Your father and she died at the same time."

How could two brilliant warriors die so easily? That didn't make sense. "Thanks for telling me about your old comrades."

"It was a pleasure."

I stood and stubbed out my smoke before finishing my drink.

"Are you off to bed, Little Pup?"

"I am, indeed. I've been dealing with your crap all day. It's best if I get some sleep."

He nodded. As I moved away from the table, Patrunice held onto my hand.

"It would be in your best interests if you don't go hunting for the Celestial Knight or your father," she said. "Just go to school and become more powerful."

She released my hand, then the two of them resumed their drinking. I realized she slowed time enough to give me that warning.

I walked upstairs to the bedroom feeling a bit wobbly. When I opened the door, the room was intact, and the two women were asleep. At least they hadn't killed each other.

I crawled into bed and lay between them.

Ruby held onto my arm. "You took long enough. You smell of booze and smokes. Are you OK?"

I stared up at the ceiling. "Sorry. I need to talk with them. Yes, I'm fine. I just needed to relax a bit."

Ruby slid closer. "What happened to you? You didn't just pass out, did you?"

I shook my head. I didn't want to recall those memories, although I knew I couldn't hide from them, either.

"Will you tell me what happened?"

I considered what to do. Finally, I said, "It's nothing to concern yourself with, Ruby. We should get some sleep. We have a big day tomorrow."

She didn't push me any further. Instead, she closed her eyes and went to sleep.

8

I awoke and looked around. Both girls were gone. My heart rate increased, and I tried to breathe, but it was difficult. After two loud knocks on the door, Ruby walked in.

"You're awake. Hurry up and get ready. We're leaving soon, My Lord."

She closed the door, and my heart rate slowed. Ever since the experience of opening my flames, I felt moments of anxiety. I felt Patrunice caused more problems than she knew.

I swung my legs over the edge of the bed and stood, dressing my new clothes. After slinging a blue cloak over my back, I grabbed my bag and left the room.

Downstairs, the others were waiting. Patrunice touched my face with her hand and looked into my eyes.

"Remember what I taught you," she said. "Use it. It will hurt for a while, but once you control it, your power will grow even stronger."

I nodded and saw the others smiling. "Ready to go? We need to see Kelos, then go to the school. Actually, it's more of a school trip."

I walked past Patrunice and said softly, "Slow time."

Her hand moved, and the room froze except for us.

"What is it, Kit?"

I looked at her. "I'll find out about my parents, and I'll find a way to make this world a better place, even if I have to take it as my own."

I heard swords and saw them appear in the air around me.

"Oh, will you, now? Those who tempt fate usually regret it. I've seen every single ending to this story. I know who you and your friends are. You'll die, too. I know why you'll never have children and when you'll lose it all, so why this path?"

Her eyes flickered with rage.

"Because I want it, and I will take it for myself."

She was shocked by my answer. "Well, then, Pup, show me a new way."

She smiled. I walked forward, and time returned to normal. Patrunice held my shoulder to make sure all were watching.

"Are you afraid, Kit? There's nothing to be afraid of. It's no more than a wisp in the wind. If you allow wind to become a full gust, that's when you'll lose all sense of reality."

I tried to pull away.

"You have been warned."

Ruby, Razele, and I walked outside. Sunlight struck, as our feet touched sand.

"We're already in the Kai Nation," I said. "I thought we'd be transported to town."

When I looked back, Kilyon left the shack. Patrunice was there, smiling. Looking up the stairs, I saw a woman in a shining white robe, her face covered with a shawl, her entire body radiating light. I quickly looked away. When I looked back, the woman was gone.

I saw Ruby and Razele staring at the river. Razele sighed happily.

"I'm glad of this," she said. "To be honest, I didn't want to walk through the forest again."

Ruby pointed a finger at her. "That's because you blend in with the rest of the wildlife."

Razele stepped back and kicked sand at Ruby. "At least I'd be able to live there. You'd be caught on a branch with those things."

Why do they always have to bring that up? I wondered. *I really don't want to hear this again. I got them to calm down once, but I don't have the energy to do it every time.*

They argued for a few minutes, then Kilyon slapped my back and laughed.

"All right, Everyone," he said. "We'll walk farther down the beach and go to my family's home. From there, we talk with my brother, and he'll transport you with the other kids heading to the school. Any questions?"

Razele ran up. "Does that mean you won't come with us to the school?"

He shook his head. "No, I'm not. I'm not liked very much around there, so I stay away. I wouldn't mention our names there. We're all hated equally."

She was confused.

"I can explain later, but for now, we must meet Kelos."

Black flames erupted all around me, as I lifted off the ground. The two women stared.

"So that's what you did!" Razele said.

They flew into the air, but Razele waited to look bad sadly.

"I was hoping you still couldn't fly, so you'd have to carry me," she said.

I laughed. "Who said I can't carry you anymore?"

Her eyes lit up. "I'll hold you to that."

As we laughed, Ruby became flustered.

"I'll carry you, too, when you want," I told Ruby.

She smiled. "Thank you, Lord. That would be amazing."

Kilyon floated up to meet us. "Since the pup has grown his wings, should we let him lead?"

They nodded. I looked at the beach and saw the monastery just over the hill.

"All right," I said. "If I lead, try not to fall behind."

I forced all my power into thrust and shot off. They followed. Feeling the wind in my face like that was amazing.

We passed over the hill and saw the monastery, then we descended into the central square. Soldiers stood around wagons. Kelos jogged over quickly in his blue cloak, followed by two guards.

"Ah, nephew and brother," he said. "It's good to see you. Everything is ready. We just need to bring the others here."

Kilyon shook Kelos' hand. "Good. Thank you for setting this up. Did you get the three like I asked?"

Kelos nodded and gave all three of us a document. I saw my last name was changed to Kilyon's family name.

"What's this?" I asked. "I thought you had to be born into a family to be part of it."

Kelos shook his head. "Technically, yes, but in your case, you're family. You might not be able to control the flames for water, but you're still one of us. As for your friends, they're family because of you. Be safe out there."

We folded the documents and slid them into our pockets.

"Thank you, Uncle, for all your help."

We shook hands. He pulled me into a hug. "I was against your being here at the beginning. I thought it was too dangerous for the family. I'm sorry. I never thought you'd turn into a man I could respect. Thank you for proving me wrong."

I held him close. "I learned my father did some stupid things, but I'm glad to be part of this family."

We held each other for a moment longer, then he released me.

"The three of you take the last carriage," he told us. "Keep a lookout and help them if there are any attacks. It'll take two days to reach the school. Good luck."

A red gleam appeared at the top of the monastery tower, and I saw a man dressed in red.

"Nephew Zonakis Icealis," Kelos said. It's been awhile since you saw him, hasn't it?"

I nodded. Zonakis was a rough guy who didn't have any friends, although he was kind enough to me. In the last few years, though, he distanced himself from me, so I wondered why he showed himself at that moment.

"I hope he's doing well, Kelos," I said. "We have to go. Say hi to him for me."

I turned and saw Kilyon holding a sword in a black scabbard with red gems on it. The hilt was encrusted with gold molded into two dragons on the sides. "This was supposed to be given to you on your eighteenth birthday, but this seems to be the right time for you to have it. Entrust your life to it, and it will never fail you."

I took the sword and pulled it from the scabbard. The metal made a soft sound as it was drawn. The blade was metallic blue with a black spine and a very sharp double edge.

"What's the sword's name?" I asked.

He stared at it intently. "Dark Nebula."

As I watched, a chaos flame wrapped itself around the sword and went to the dragons' eyes, illuminating them with black flame that spoke to me.

Those who draw upon me will never be the same.

I felt those words etch themselves into my brain.

Sheathing the sword, I strapped it to my back.

"Thank you. I always considered you a father, even though I'm just a loyal pup."

He hugged me hard. "I promised your father I'd raise you as my own. I'll never stop doing that. Trust me when I say you'll be a great warrior."

We stepped back from each other.

"Now take care of those girls of yours. They'll be a handful."

I shook my head and looked at them. They smiled and blushed.

"I will," I said. "I can promise that much."

I walked toward the last carriage. A soldier waved his hand, and the convoy began moving. We jumped into the carriage, while Kelos and Kilyon bowed to us. We bowed before sitting down.

Kelos walked up and leaned in through the window. "Hey, Kit. Telos is in the head carriage. I know how you feel about him, but do the right thing, OK?"

I looked at him and saw his eyes were damp with tears. "I'll do my best to keep him in line, Uncle."

He nodded. "Do what needs to be done."

As he walked away, Razele looked at me. With a jolt, the carriage began moving forward.

"What was that about?" Razele asked.

I looked at her. "It's a long story. I wonder what he meant by it."

I laid my head back against the carriage wall and felt Razele lean against my shoulder.

"Why does this feel like a farewell, where we'll never see them again?" she asked.

"It's not a farewell. It's more of a see-you-later."

We laughed, then Ruby rested her head in my lap.

"They love you a lot, Kit. Even though you weren't born part of them, you were made to be one of them."

I looked back as we crossed the bridge and headed into the forest. "Yeah, I was. I might want to know more about my parents, but even if I never understand why they gave me up, that would be all right. I still had a family who loved me."

Razele saw how comfortable Ruby was in my lap. Ruby saw her looking.

"Hey, Lamb Prey. I was here first. Get your own man."

Razele sniffed. "I had him first. You're just trying to take something that isn't yours."

I placed a hand on both of their heads. "I care for both of you the same. Now calm down before you destroy the carriage and maybe the whole convoy."

They calmed down and rested against me. I remembered seeing Ruby torn to pieces and hoped I never went through hell like that again. Patrunice showed me the path to depression and hatred. It was one I didn't like, and I hoped I could stay clear or it. I realized bad things were waiting in my future, but seeing that had been horrible.

Ruby noticed my change of mood. "Everything will be fine. We're on a grand journey. You worry too much, My Lord."

"Thank you. I needed to hear that. We have to look out for each other and make sure what we do is the best for all of us."

They nodded.

We rode quietly for a while. It was pretty boring in some ways.

We stopped near a village. I heard a rustle behind us and saw Ruby and Razele napping. As I watched, a baby boar walked from the brush.

I heard a loud crash and saw an adult boar had rammed a carriage up ahead. The girls woke quickly, watching me jump from the carriage. Flames came on, as I rushed the beast and unsheathed my sword. Flames ran down the blade, and I absorbed the power, slicing at the beast. A wave of chaos cut it in half, then several nearby trees toppled over.

I stared at my sword, then at the trees.

"Hey, My Lord," Ruby said. "It would be a good idea to use that only in emergencies."

I sheathed it quickly. "Yeah. That's a good idea."

I helped a warrior to his feet.

"Thank you, Sir," he said. "Sorry wasn't any help."

I shook my head. "It was my fault. I saw a young one but didn't think the mother would attack."

We looked at the damaged carriage.

"This will take a few minutes to fix, then we can be moving again."

I helped him lift it, as others ran over to work on the wheel.

"What's the holdup, you stupid carriage men? This will set us back."

I looked up to see Kelos' son walking to us in his aqua-blue cloak. His blond hair was shorter than usual, and his icy white eyes glared at me. Three chains at his belt led back to three slaves, all of whom looked away. Shackles were around their necks, and their clothes were ragged and torn.

I didn't recognize any of them, which meant he must have gotten tired of the old ones and bought new ones. "Hello, Cousin. I see you're still keeping slaves. What happened to the others?"

He gave me a wicked smile. "They stopped screaming and crying. I had to break in new ones."

Though Telos was the son of the head of the Icealis family. He had perfect control over ice, but learning it turned him into the arrogant man I saw in front of me.

"I see. What a shame. We'll be getting on our way soon, Cousin."

He yanked the chains, and all three girls fell to the ground. I fought to maintain my composure.

"See that they hurry up, then. It would be a shame if I became bored."

I heard footsteps run up behind me.

"My Lord, the wheel is fixed. We're ready to go."

He locked gazes with Ruby, as he dragged his slaves toward her. When he stopped walking, the slaves stopped and knelt.

The closest one had hair of pure yellow and eyes as blue as the ocean. I knelt and placed my hand on her head. "What's your name?"

She tried to speak, but her voice was too hoarse, so she quickly wrote in the dirt, *Valis.*

I nodded and stood before Talos could see us talking. Talos held Ruby's hand and kissed it, but she pulled away.

"I'm my Lord's," she said. "Nobody else's."

He bellowed with laugher and looked at me. "I thought you hated slaves, yet you have one."

I shook my head. "She is no slave. She chose to be my sword. That is all."

He scratched his chin. "That's too bad. I would have loved having a girl like you. What's your name?"

She backed away slowly. "It's Ruby. My Lord named me."

He stopped smiling and turned to me. "Just like with Mother. You were always her favorite. I can understand that."

He walked past me and kicked one of the slaves. I heard bones crack, but she didn't cry out. They crawled back to their carriage.

All the guards stared at him. Ruby came to my side.

"Master, who is that?" she asked softly.

"My cousin, Kelos' son."

He's a kind man, but that child is not."

I chuckled and walked back to our carriage. As I passed a guard, I overheard him muter, "I wish he wouldn't dishonor his father."

I stopped, and the guard froze.

"I'm sorry for any disrespect, Sir. That was wrong on my part. I will accept your punishment."

I placed my hand on his shoulder. "You're right. He dishonors the family and treats people like insects. I hope he learns his place soon."

I walked past him and got into our carriage. Soon, we were on our way again.

Razele looked at me. "Was that really Telos? I've heard of him. He's known as the true heir of ice and has been given the nickname King of Frost. He's supposed to be relentless and sadistic."

I nodded.

"Why does he always have slaves with him? I thought that wasn't considered proper."

She wasn't wrong, but the main families were allotted a number of slaves to help them, even though it was frowned upon.

"It's legal for the main families, so what he's doing is legal under the law and in the school, as far as I know. I'm not sure how much restraint he has. He can't harm them within the school walls, but we know it won't work out well."

Ruby angrily punched the carriage wall. The driver looked over his shoulder at us. I waved to him, and he turned to look forward again.

"I know it's legal," she snapped, "but it's one reason why you humans are such incompetent, disgusting people."

Her anger quickly fled, and she added, "I didn't mean you or Razele." She waved her hands to dismiss what she just said.

"I know how you meant it, but I think you're right," I said. "I may not agree with it now, but there's nothing I can do about it. I can't take them away from him. That would break our family law. Then we'd be forced to a duel to the death. If I won, it would cause a rift between Kelos and Kilyon. I don't want that. I also don't want to see those girls suffer. With the beatings he gives, they don't have much time to live."

Razele slumped back and placed her head on my lap. "What can we do? Is there a way to get them to leave him?"

I thought about it. "Yes, but I don't know if it'll work. They would have to break their contract and immediately swear loyalty to me. Would they want to serve someone else once they're free?"

"What if we free them into the Kai Nation?" Ruby asked.

I shook my head. "No. Slaves are bound with a particular stone. It keeps them together. Once freed, they would be hunted down unless they find a new master willing to take them in. Then the new master would have to deal with the repercussions. Either way, he will die or be kind enough to give them to someone who can care for them."

Ruby laid her head against my shoulder and closed her eyes. "Then the best thing we can do is wish them the best. Maybe we can help them later on."

I thought what Kelos said earlier and wondered if he wanted me to do something about his son.

9

We rested during the carriage ride. Since we were in the rear of the column, I kept watch while the others slept.

Hours passed. The sky became an orange hue brightened with sky-blue waves. We were still in the forest, but we should reach a village soon.

The carriages slowed, and the girls woke and yawned. I stood and walked to the driver.

"Do you know why we're stopping, Sir?" I asked.

"We're arriving at the edge of a village, Sir. We'll be setting up camp. If you want to stay at the inn, though, you'd better hurry."

I watched soldiers set up camp around us. "Don't you need people to protect the supplies?"

He shook his head. "No. We're fine. We have several monks from the monastery, so that's not a problem."

I looked back at the girls, who heard us talking. "What do you two think? Should we camp out or get a room for the night?"

They immediately stood and lifted their bags.

"This might be selfish," Ruby said, "but I'd like to sleep in a bed tonight."

Razele nodded.

"OK," I said. "We'll spend the night in the inn." I turned to pick up my cloak.

"Master Kit, I was told to give this to you." The driver held out a sack about the size of my palm.

"Thank you," I said. "Be safe." I slipped it into a pocket, and the three of us walked around the carriage while students and soldiers helped erect camp.

Reaching the front of the convoy, we saw the houses were built into the trees, with elevators leading up. Bridges crossed between them.

"This is amazing." I was in awe.

A merchant walked past, and I stopped him.

"Sir, do you know the name of this village?"

He laughed and patted my back. "It's called Scylean. It's known for its medicinal herbs."

We walked to one of the elevators and saw a villager manning it. We got on just in time. I shook his hand.

"Thanks for having us here," I said. "I hope to see more of your beautiful village."

"Thank you for your kind words. That means a lot coming from someone from one of the three great families."

It seemed the villagers knew of us. I hoped Telos didn't embarrass us like usual.

Screams sounded, and we were instantly on guard. Telos came up, dragging his slaves into the elevator and forcing them to kneel in front of him. All had bandages on their arms and legs, but they were so filthy, bandages wouldn't help.

The villager started the elevator and glanced at the girls. "Master Telos, this village is known for medicine. It might be wise to fix up your slaves before you take them to the school looking like that."

"It's no matter to a lowly peasant what I do with my slaves," he replied. "Be careful before I turn you into one."

The villager bowed. "I'm sorry for my comment, My Lord. Forgive my ignorance."

Telos harrumphed. "Shut up and get this stupid ride over with."

Ruby gave an angry smile, and I placed a hand on her shoulder. Her tension dissipated.

Soon, we reached the platform at the top, where merchants and stores waited. Telos dragged his slaves away and pushed through the crowd. People watched him in fear.

"I'm sorry, Sir, for his stupidity," I told the villager who ran the elevator. "He may be my cousin, but the two of us are completely different in that regard. I hope you have a good day."

The three of us stepped off and watched as the people around us slowly resumed their normal activities after Telos barged through. Most vendors sold herbs, but I saw clothing shops, too. I didn't see a single vendor for weapons or armor and wondered why. They lived in the forest and needed to protect themselves. I caught the smell of roast boar on the air, and Razele and Ruby moved through the crowd.

I followed them to a nearby stall.

"Hello, you three," the vendor said. "Would you like to try my boar chunks?"

He cooked small chunks of boar meat on a thin rod. "Yes. I'll take three, please."

He prepared three for us. "That'll be five silver."

I pulled out the sack I'd been handed and saw it was a small silver case with a note and some coins. I paid him five silver and replaced the sack in my pocket, wondering what the other items were.

We accepted our meat and walked off, biting into the chunks until juices flowed over my lips. It was one of the most-amazing things I ever ate. The girls enjoyed the food, too.

We shopped for a while, looking at everything we could. The girls wanted new clothes, which I bought. We stopped at the inn and walked in, where the smell of booze struck my face.

A fire blazed in the middle of the room, with tables sprawled around at random. The innkeeper was an older woman who seemed blind, judging by the strips of cloth around her eyes.

We walked up to her.

"We need a room for the night, Ma'am," I said.

She inhaled deeply and looked at us as if her eyes were fine. Without the cloth on her face, it would be impossible to know she was blind.

"Ah, the son of Kilyon. These girls are your comrades? I'm pleased. I thought you might be like that wretched cousin of yours."

A man walked in from the back room. "Mother, you can't talk of the next head of a house like that."

She waved her hands. "What do I care? I'm almost dead. What can anyone do to me?"

Her son studied me. He had soft brown hair and eyes. "I'm sorry, Kit, for her mouth. Please forgive her."

I bowed to the old woman, who smiled. "I'm sorry for my cousin's incompetence. I'm not ashamed to say he isn't someone I would willingly call family."

The room was so quiet, I heard a fork strike the floor. She laughed and slapped the table. "Now that's something the next head should say. I like you, Kid. Come. I'll show you to your room."

The others stared at us in confusion. It wasn't illegal to say bad things about the major families, but Telos had begun to cause a major rift between the people and the head families. The Kai Nation had three main families, but the other two were busy minding their own business, while the Icealis family spread its influence far and wide.

"Thank you, Ma'am," I said.

She walked around the table to lead me down a hall, then we walked up a set of stairs to another level, where she pointed down the hall. "It's all the way at the end. Do me a favor, son of Kilyon."

I looked at her.

"Purge those who aren't worthy."

Shocked, I watched her walk away, whistling softly.

Razele giggled. "It looks like even this nation's people are behind you."

I waved it off. We walked down the hall and opened the door to our room. It was beautiful, with plants everywhere. The bed had a light-green blanket with pillows stuffed with hay and flowers sewn in. We had one window, which Ruby opened to give a view of the village.

I sat on the bed to remove my shoes.

"Why aren't you the next head of the family?" Razele asked.

I'd never really thought about it. "Kilyon isn't part of the family anymore. He was exiled. We stayed in Typhsa, a small village near a monastery. Although he was exiled, Kelos never treated him like an outsider. He was the one who accepted me into the family. Kilyon is exalted, but I'm not. I chose to stay with Kilyon in the village.

"Although Telos is Kelos' son, the family doesn't operate under a merit system. The next head is the eldest son in the line, which makes Telos the next one. If he died, the job would pass to me."

Ruby jumped onto the bed. "What if he were to have an accident?"

I chuckled at the idea. "He would sacrifice everything around him to do what he wants. He has no honor. He's spoiled and cruel."

I remembered the day my stepmother disappeared from the monastery. I stood in a field, watching the animals, when I saw a small rabbit with a broken paw moving slowly through the grass. It was scared of me and tried to run away, but I patted its head, and it calmed. The paw looked easy enough to heal. I did, and it hopped away, then Telos ran up and stomped it to death. Blood splattered everywhere.

"Master, are you OK?" Ruby asked, snapping me back from my memory.

"Yes. Sorry. I was remembering something. Anyway, that's why Telos is the next head."

The two girls were concerned. "Master, you don't have to suffer alone. We're both here for you."

I smiled. "I'm not suffering, but I appreciate it a lot. Thank you."

The sun was down, and small bugs lit up the surroundings outside. Lanterns were lit on the posts along the street.

"It's time for bed, Girls. We've had a long day."

We lay down, and they clung to me as usual.

I woke to something soft hitting the wall. The girls were asleep. When I turned a shadow flew out the window. I looked out and saw a few guards there, so I flew down to them.

They immediately drew their weapons. I raised my hands.

"My apologies," I said. "I didn't mean to frighten you. My name is Kit."

They relaxed and sheathed their weapons. Both wore uniforms with silver caps, and they carried short swords on their hips.

One stepped forward. "We were told Telos is here tonight."

It seemed they weren't guards for the convoy. "He is. May I ask what's going on?"

They seemed spooked for some reason. "Oh, nothing. We just wanted to make sure he's being taken care of."

They refused to make eye contact. I knew they weren't here to check on Telos. They wanted to kill him.

"I understand why you're afraid of him. Doing it here and now would be bad, especially if they can't prove who did it. The entire village would suffer. I know my uncle. He may be kind, but he wouldn't let it go."

They backed away in fear.

"Accidents happen all the time, though," I added. "Maybe one of his slaves will kill him in his sleep."

They smiled at each other and walked away.

"We'll pray for her well-being."

I wondered if I could take my cousin's life. He wouldn't make it alive to the school at this rate. If he were sent back, the girls would be killed, and he'd find new ones.

What should I do? I opened the sack I was given and saw there was plenty of money. I took out the silver case and saw it filled with smokes just like Kilyon's. That made me smile. I put the sack in my pocket and looked at the note. I took out a smoke and lit it, walking to stand near a lamppost, so I could read the note.

Kit,

I want to tell you that family is a strong bond. Even if someone causes trouble, it wouldn't be enough to make us hate you.

Kelos

I wondered why he wanted it done. Telos was his own son, but maybe Kelos knew what kind of man he was and feared letting him become the head of the family. Killing him was a job easier given to someone else.

Uncle, I hope you're right, I thought. *This will cause a lot of problems for all of us.*

I inhaled from my smoke, then dropped it and rubbed it out with my toe. Smoke dissipated in the cold air, as I walked in the inn's main room.

The old lady smiled at the sound of my footsteps. They echoed in my head. Each step made my cousin's death closer, second by second.

I walked to the second floor and looked around. Two guards stood outside a door. What would they do about this? Did they want the same thing? Was the whole day predestined?

I walked over to them, as they waved to me. They looked at me with hope. They knew what was going to happen.

"It's a little late," I said softly. "Why don't you get yourselves a drink to make the watch go easier?"

They smiled and glanced at each other.

"That would be nice," one said. "We'll be gone for half an hour. Kit, watch your step."

They walked down the hall without turning.

Watch my step? I wondered. *Has something already happened? Am I walking into something even darker than I know? What have you done, Telos? Why did it have to come to this? You had your life in front of you, yet you fell from the heights to nothing more than a pig ready for slaughter. Is that what you wanted?*

I turned to mist and slipped under the door. When I reformed and took a step, my foot touched liquid. Looking down, I saw blood covering the floor. A quick look around the room showed two of the slaves had been gutted, their intestines strung across the room, with blood splattered on the walls. Their eyes were wide in disbelief, and tears still glistened on their faces.

I knelt to close their eyes with gentle fingers. "Rest in peace," I said softly. "May the goddess take you to a better place."

Their skin was still warm. I kept my hand on them for a few seconds, then clenched them into fists. If only I'd been faster! Neither of them would be dead. There was no reason to let these poor slaves go through such a thing. I should have done something about Telos a long time ago. I hoped the dead could forgive me, although I didn't say anything aloud, because I didn't feel I deserved forgiveness. I chose to wait, and those young women were dead because of it.

I bit back my anger and saw Valis' naked body in bed beside Telos, covered in bloody handprints. She cried softly, curled into a ball, as moonlight shone down on her pale skin. That poor girl had been through more than any woman should ever experience.

Telos slept peacefully in bed, like a child being read a night-time story by its mother. Black particles floated around me as I took another step.

Remembering the vision of Ruby being torn in half, I carefully held my anger back. As I looked at Valis, my foot pressed on a weak floorboard and creaked.

She turned over, and our eyes met. Moonlight floated between us. I felt she wanted to call out, but tears and fear plagued her.

I moved through the blood to the side of the bed and looked down at her, our eyes constantly on each other, as she cried silent tears that stained her soul. I knelt down to cover her, laying my hand on her head to rub it softly. Blood was in her yellow hair. Once I showed her even a taste of kindness, she seemed ready to fall apart. She had been destroyed mentally and physically. It wasn't right. She would be better off dead, because she'd never be able to forget what happened.

I slowly took my hand away, trying not to cause any more panic. Her eyes were black and blue, and her nose was broken. Bloodstains covered her lips and teeth. Her eyes begged for peace. Death would be an escape.

Could I give her a life worth living? Would she want it?

Telos moved. Valis squeaked in fear, and I grabbed her wrist and pulled her off the bed. She curled into a ball in a corner, cowering and crying hysterically. I didn't blame her.

Telos turned over and saw me. "Ah, Cousin, how do you like the scene. Jealous?"

His words infuriated me. A dozen ways to kill him flashed through my mind. I could gut him like an animal or cook him alive. My expression must have been fierce, because the color drained from his face, and he raised his hand.

Ice covered me to my neck, with spikes against my skin. The slave, seeing what happened, froze. Her eyes widened to show how bloodshot they were.

"Did you think you could kill me?" Telos asked, lazily. "Father will be pleased to know you're dead. You're a worthless flyer from another country, anyway."

Looking back at him, I heard Valis get up and try to run. Telos slapped her, sending her sprawling to the floor. She bounced up. I saw fresh blood trickling down the side of her face, but she peered at me with hope. That was all she could do.

I looked at Telos. "Tell me, is this the path you'll follow? Is this really the path for the family?"

He laughed. "Who cares? I'll lead the family. It's my choice. No one else matters. I was planning to kill Father, anyway. He's no match for me, just like you."

Two of the spikes pierced my neck. They penetrated my throat, and the cold froze my esophagus. Blood flowed down the spikes. Steam wafted off them, and Valis screamed. I had plenty of probable cause and a witness. It looked like I wouldn't have to kill the girl.

The room exploded in black flames that raced along the walls and filling everything in a void. The ice melted slowly. I watched Telos fall into despair. I wanted him to feel everything he did to those women. He had to know he was going to die, and there was nothing he could do to stop it.

"How are you still alive?" he shouted. "There's no way! I saw the spikes pierce your neck! I can still see the holes!"

I looked down at the blood and water mixing together to form crimson water and thought of my master. I wondered briefly if he had anything to do with the current situation. Would he kill a family member in cold blood? If he had to, he would.

I looked at Telos, who had backed against the wall, his hands up. Spikes of ice flew at me, but black flames broke them before they could reach me. I stepped forward, the black flames creating a prison no one could escape.

"Stop! Don't come any closer! I'm the next head of the house. You can't kill me. I'm important, like a god!"

I unsheathed my sword and saw chaos flow over it until it became a beautiful petal of death. "I know. Sorry, Cousin, but there's only one place for gods like you. There are many others just like you. You'll get along with them. Let me help you meet them!"

Before he could speak again, I decapitated him. His head rolled off his body and hit the floor with a thump. His eyes showed no remorse, just sadness and confusion. What was he confused about?

Valis tried to speak, but she was barely able to make a sound. I swung the blade at her. She closed her eyes, resigned to death, but all I did was slice off the collar. When I sheathed my blade, the flames in the room died.

The room suddenly returned to as normal as anything like this could be. I knelt to pick her up. Her eyes watched me intently. She was surprisingly light. I wondered when she had a decent meal.

She held onto me as if she would fall from a mountaintop if she let me go, and I was the only one who could save her.

I carried her to the door and lightly tapped it with one foot. It opened, and the two guards stared at the carnage inside. One turned around and vomited on the floor, while the other was speechless, staring at the dead bodies and blood.

I walked up and stopped by the guard who stared at a world filled with despair and hardship. "Sickness and cruelty are a scourge on humanity. It takes all of us to fix the problem."

He nodded and closed the door so no one could see what had been allowed to continue for too long. Valis stared at me the entire time until we reached the room.

Ruby and Razele were awake and stared at me when I carried Valis inside.

"My Lord, aren't we enough for you?" Ruby asked.

When they saw her appearance, they ran over to help. I let them take Valis.

"Lord, what has this girl been through?"

We all sat in the middle of the floor.

"I don't know," I answered her. "I want you to check her voice and see if you can fix it. Razele, can you clean her up?"

They set to work. I walked to the window and took out a smoke. When I lit it, I glanced outside and saw a small bird coming toward me. It landed on the window with something tied to its leg. I untied it, and the bird flew away. Something was in the note, perhaps a small stone.

I inhaled smoke and carefully unrolled the note, catching the stone with one hand. It was completely black. I opened the note.

Good job on the kill. Make sure to help the girl.

Kilyon

Smiling, I realized that was his plan from the start. I stuck the note in my pocket and placed the stone on the table while looking at Razele.

She had cleaned Valis by then, and Ruby kept working on healing her. I walked over and knelt beside her.

"How is it?" I asked.

She shook her head. "I can't heal her vocal cords. They're completely shattered. I don't think anyone could. This poor girl must've been screaming for help, but all that it did was silence her."

Valis reached up to wipe her tears away.

"Let's try something risky," I said.

Ruby looked up. "What are you...?

I retrieved the stone from the table and knelt back beside Ruby. She stared at it.

"What's that for?" Ruby asked.

Razele recognized it. "That's a slave stone for the Chaos Nation."

Ruby crossed her arms. "You won't enslave me, but you'll do it to this girl?"

I rubbed her head and exhaled smoke. "I care about you a lot, Ruby. You two mean the world to me, but if this girl doesn't remain a slave, she'll be hunted down and killed. If she's mine, no one can touch her."

Ruby and Razele sighed.

I looked at Valis. "I need to ask you some questions. You can nod for yes and shake your head for no. Understand?"

She nodded.

"Do you want to continue to be a slave?"

She shook her head.

"Do you want to die?"

She shook it again.

"Would you be willing to serve as my slave?"

She nodded quickly.

"Even if I become an enemy of the world? You'd still agree to that?"

She nodded quickly.

"Then I, Kit Icealis, take you, Valis, as my slave from hencc-forth. You will serve me, protect me, and always ensure my safety."

She nodded.

I crushed the stone in my fingers until it was dust and infused it with my flame. Razele opened Valis' mouth, and I sprinkled all the dust inside. When the last speck fell, Razele closed her mouth again and held on.

Valis' eyes turned black. Her body pulsed with black streaks under her skin. She shook violently. We all helped hold her down until she gradually stopped moving.

She opened her eyes, which had completely turned black with a yellow circle. Her hair had become black with red tips.

"Are you OK?" I asked.

She nodded slowly.

"I'll ask you one more question, but this one will be hard. Do you want to speak again?"

Tears flowed from her eyes, but she nodded and tried to say something. Ruby took out a dagger and handed it to me.

"Do you think this will work, My Lord, or will it kill her?"

I looked down at Valis, who continued to cry. "I don't know. I wish I could say it will work, but I'm not sure. We'll have to stay at her side the entire time."

Razele opened her mouth. Valis stopped crying, and I sliced my palm with the dagger. I dropped blood into Valis' mouth, then she closed it. A black aura glowed around her, then it dissipated.

Ruby seemed disappointed. "That was anticlimactic."

Chuckling, Valis sat up. Razele covered her with a sheet from the bed, so she wouldn't feel so exposed.

"Valis, I have cured you of every disease. Any problem you once had should be cured completely."

Her mouth opened slowly. "Tha...tha...thank you, Master." Her voice was as sweet as candy and as soft as the wind.

"You're welcome, Valis. Now you should get some sleep. Tomorrow will be a busy day."

Crying again, she lunged forward to hug me. As her arms went around my back, I held her and gently rubbed her back, as she sobbed.

"It's all right," I said softly. "You'll never go through anything like that again. You have my word."

I looked at Ruby, who pouted and tried to act calm, while Razele smiled without a hint of jealousy. Valis couldn't stop crying.

Eventually, Razele came over to hug both of us, then Ruby. I felt trapped but let them enjoy it.

Ruby stroked Valis' hair. "It's all right. You're with a new family. Nothing can hurt you now."

Valis' crying grew louder. Ruby's eyes twitched.

"What did I say? I thought that would help. You stupid humans are so emotional!"

I looked at Ruby, who was red with anger. "You didn't do anything wrong. Valis has been through the worst of despair and sadness. She's happy and doesn't know how to contain her excitement quietly."

Ruby calmed and studied Valis with newfound respect.

We stayed huddled together for a little longer. Valis finally tired, and the girls helped her into bed, then they went to sleep. Ruby looked over at me.

"Where will you sleep, My Lord?"

I pointed at the floor. "The bed isn't big enough. She needs a good night's sleep."

Valis was already out, although her face was red and puffy from crying. Razele was asleep, too.

"But Lord, it's not right for you to sleep on the floor."

I sat in the window ledge and lit a smoke. "As long as the three of you take care of me, I don't care where I sleep."

Ruby smiled. "That's why we follow and love you, My Lord. You always put us first. One day, we'll put you first."

I watched as she drifted off to sleep and began snoring softly.

"I love you, too." I stared up at the moon casting faint light on the world below. My life wasn't anything like what I expected it to be. Everyone had to learn how to adapt and change.

I finished my smoke, stubbed out the butt, and folded a small blanket into a pillow. I fell asleep the moment I closed my eyes.

I woke and opened my eyes to the ceiling. Rubbing my face, I was grateful the goddess hadn't visited me again. I sat up and looked over at the bed. All three were asleep. Outside, the sun rose, and the noise of the merchants slowly grew louder.

I heard a soft knock on the door and tossed my blanket and pillow at the foot of the bed. When I opened the door, Kilyon was outside.

"How are you, Little Pup?"

I almost expected him to kill me for what I did.

"Easy, Boy. You're my son. I won't ever turn my blade against you. Neither will Kelos. He's downstairs waiting for you. Will you come down?"

He peered at the girls on the bed. "I'm glad she's safe. It's a pity about the other two, but there isn't anything we can do but give them a proper burial."

He turned and walked away. I stepped into the hall and carefully closed the door. We walked side-by-side.

"Was it wrong?" I asked finally.

He scratched his beard. "Hmmm. I'm not sure I would say no, and I believe Kelos would agree, but the rest of the family might say otherwise. Since he's the head of the family, there isn't much they can do about it."

We rounded the corner and descended the stairs.

"At least I won't be hunted down as a traitor."

He laughed.

"Even if you were, something tells me all of you would be fine. You're getting to the point where Kelos won't be able to best you."

Shocked, I walked into the main room with him and reached into my pocket for the silver case of smokes. I lit one, as we approached a table where Kelos drank from a mug. Two monks stood near the entrance, with more at each corner of the room. The patrons seemed a bit distressed by the situation.

I sat across from Kelos, as Kilyon walked away.

"Family is supposed to be precious," Kelos said, "yet if a plague corrupts the land and the people, wouldn't it be prudent to take it out?" He held back the pain for his lost son, but I also heard relief.

"Plagues are just that, Uncle. You can do your best to halt one, maybe heal from it, but in the end, a plague is just a disease."

I inhaled from my smoke, as he drank from his tankard.

"I want to thank you for what you did. You could have tortured him, but you gave him a merciful death, even after what you saw in that room. He wasn't a loving person, but he was still my son."

I wondered what he was leading up to. "I understand, Uncle. I will accept any punishment you wish to bestow. All I ask is that you don't harm the girls."

He smiled, though a few tears rolled down his cheeks and landed in his mug. "Your punishment is to eradicate anyone in the family who would do such a thing. Your punishment is to take over as the head of this family and follow the path that is best for all."

Why is he doing this? I wondered. *Many others are far more qualified.* "Why?"

A smile crept over his face. "Because you're my nephew, and you just took a huge weight off my heart. I'm thankful for that, but also, you're the best choice. You'll be able to make the hard decisions. I've been waiting for someone in the family to do what you did. I couldn't, because he was my son. Kilyon couldn't, because he was an exile. None of the others could, because they feared him.

"You didn't. That's why I believe you'll be a great leader when I step down."

I flicked ash onto the table and nodded. "I have a lot of work to do. I'll arrive at the school soon. Once I'm trained and know what to do next, I'll come home and take over, although I may take the nation in a different direction. You realize that, right?"

He drank from his mug. "I'm aware of it. You'll have my support in the endeavor when the time comes."

He stood and tossed a gold coin onto the table. It spun for a few seconds before landing flat. "Please make sure that the evil living in this world doesn't live for long."

He walked from the room, and the monks followed. Once they were gone, Kilyon came over to place a hand on my shoulder.

"You're seen as a man who will change everything in this world," he said. "Always remember that."

I exhaled smoke. "I'm aware, but that doesn't make it easier. I feel like I'm surrounded by despair since our meeting with Patrunice."

I felt his hand lift, then I heard his footsteps move toward the door. "That's why I never wanted you to take this path, but it was no longer my choice. Make the best of it and keep those you love close."

The door shut behind me. The old innkeeper came to the table and took the empty mug and gold coin. She placed a fresh mug of ale in front of me.

"It might not mean much," she said, "but at least he can't make anyone else suffer. That's a good thing to drink to." Her voice held no sorrow. I enjoyed hearing a voice that knew the truth and how to fix it.

"Thank you, Ma'am. You're right. That's a wonderful thing to drink to."

She smiled and walked away. I heard the girls coming down the hall. When they saw me, they ran over. Valis walked with her head lowered. The girls must've loaned her some clothing. Her light-blue cloak swept the floor, but it fit her well.

Ruby sat near me and held my arm, while Razele quickly did the same on the other side. Valis took a seat and stared at the tabletop.

I heard a rumble. Valis quickly covered her stomach in embarrassment. The girls giggled.

"Innkeeper, would you be so kind as to bring us some food?" I asked.

She walked to the back room to tell her son.

"You don't have to do that, Master," Valis said quickly. "I don't need to eat."

Ruby yawned loudly. "You may not want to eat, but if you don't, you would slow down My Lord. That wouldn't be good, would it?"

Valis smiled and looked up at her. "No. You're right."

I shook my head. "Valis, you may be a slave in name, but I will never treat you as one. If you don't want to do something, you aren't obligated to. I'm heading into some terrible places. Are you sure you're OK with that?'

Valis looked down again but nodded before looking up and meeting my gaze. "Like I said last night, I will be yours, Master. I'll never leave your side."

Razele chuckled and nodded.

"All I ask is you do your best," I said.

The smell of food caught us off guard, as the innkeeper and her son brought out a plethora of things to eat. Soon, the table was filled with bowls of food, plates, and wooden forks.

"Please eat until you can't eat anymore."

I reached for my money, but the old woman shook her head. "Your stay here and the food is on me. Don't worry about it."

As she walked off, Ruby and Razele were quick to serve themselves. Valis sat and stared at the food. I finally prepared a plate and offered it to her. She stared at it even more.

"If you stare at it, it'll get cold. You might as well eat it."

She looked up in disbelief. "This is for me?"

I nodded.

"I can eat it?"

I nodded again.

"You won't stop me?"

She was beginning to drive me crazy.

"I won't stop you, but if you keep making me answer your questions, I'll lose my mind."

She grabbed her fork and started shoveling food into her mouth. The girls watched her for a moment, then Ruby nudged me.

"She's never eaten a good meal in her life," Ruby said softly.

Valis choked, and I moved the mug of mead closer to her. She drank deeply and stopped to breathe. "Sorry. It's just that I never had a hot meal or even a regular one. Moldy food and even insects were a luxury for me."

I knew Telos was a horrid guy, but that was inhumane. "That's a thing of the past. I would get used to eating like this. There may be days where we have to camp out, but we'll make sure we have something to eat."

The rest of the meal passed slowly. Once we finished, Valis placed her head on the table.

"Master, my stomach hurts."

We chuckled and stood, all but Valis.

"That's because you overdid it," I said. "You ate more than you could handle. That's what happens when you overindulge, but I'm not upset. You enjoyed yourself."

Ruby walked over to pat her head. "Lord, she ate a lot more than I thought she could. You should probably carry her to the carriage."

She was right. Valis wasn't moving anywhere in her condition.

"All right. Razele and Ruby, go ahead and make sure we're ready to go."

They left the inn, and I lifted Valis in my arms.

"Sorry for this, Master. You shouldn't have to deal with your slave in such a manner."

I walked up to the innkeeper. "Thank you, Ma'am. It was delicious. I hope to see you again someday."

She smiled wickedly. "You will, Dear, soon enough."

I left the inn and saw the street was busy again. It seemed like the place was always busy.

"You can set me down, Master. I can walk."

I moved through the crowd toward the elevator. "If I set you down, you'd probably wobble off the edge and fall to your death. It's OK. I don't mind."

She grew quiet and buried her face against my chest. I found the elevator attendant waiting for us. A few more people got on with us, and we slowly moved down. I studied the caravan from above. It was almost packed and ready to leave. I was glad I sent the girls up ahead.

At the bottom, someone shoved past me wearing a red shirt and bandages over his face. Valis became angry and was ready to shout at him.

"It's OK, Valis. He'll get what's coming to him in time."

I walked to the caravan, where Ruby stood near one of the carriages.

"We're over here!" she called. "It's good thing you got here. We're leaving in a few minutes. We were about to come get you."

Razele walked around the back of the same carriage. "We're apparently in the lead carriage. It belongs to the next head of the house, and that's you."

I nodded, and she jumped in delight.

"Really? Is it official?"

I smiled, and she squeaked with glee and rushed over to hug me, almost crushing Valis.

"That's so amazing!" Razele said. "Congratulations!"

Valis struggled to breathe. "Please, Razele. You're crushing me down here."

Razele backed away. "Sorry. I was just happy."

I set Valis in the carriage. She immediately lay down and clutched her stomach. I walked back to Ruby and Razele. "Thank you both for everything. You've been amazing."

They hugged me, and Ruby rubbed her face against my chest.

"I will never leave your side, My Lord. I'm always yours, even if that washboard follows us."

Razele's grip on me tightened.

"You helped me out and gave me somewhere to be safe and have a home. I'll never leave your side. Maybe we can become more than just friends."

Razele gasped. "Wait a second!"

"You're one to talk, Washboard. I'll bet you float during a flood." Ruby finally released me.

"At least I can stay above water."

A guard walked up and bowed. "Sir, we're ready if you are. Just let us know."

The girls smiled and turned to me.

"Let's get going," I said. "We have a little time before we reach the school, so we should hurry before they don't let us in."

We got into the carriage, and the caravan moved away. I looked out and saw a lot of beggars eyeing us curiously, but none of them showed fear. That was good.

Valis sat up and leaned against a box. "Is it possible to die from overeating?"

Ruby touched her forehead. "No, but you need to learn portion control for a while, until you gain some weight. You've been through a lot, so just get well."

Valis looked at her. "Are you his lover?"

A wicked smiled came to Ruby's face. She looked at Razele and said, "My Lord and I have spent some intimate nights together."

Razele turned red and looked at me. "Kit, is that true? Have you and Ruby...?"

I shook my head. "You should know better. I haven't done anything with any of you, so calm down."

Ruby sat beside Valis. "You need to be careful if you sleep next to the master. He's a little grabby when he's unconscious. I've woken up in the middle of the night with his hand on my breast."

Razele stood up angrily. "You did not! Kit's not that kind of man."

Ruby giggled, enjoying her teasing. "Oh, yeah? How would you know? Your chest is so thin, there's nothing for him to grab."

Razele's eyes narrowed. "So he loves something so big his entire hand can't squeeze it? Is that right?"

Ruby nodded.

Valis was confused. "So the master likes breasts. Doesn't every man?"

They looked at her.

"That's not the point," the said simultaneously.

Valis became very quiet.

I felt the situation was going on too long. "You two need to calm down. We've been through this more than I want to admit. You both have amazing breasts. Now get over it already."

Ruby smiled. "You're only saying that, because you don't want Razele to feel bad."

I crossed my arms and glanced at Valis, who squeezed her breasts. The other two girls laughed and sat down.

"Lord, what about mine?" Valis asked.

I rubbed my temple and saw a group of men standing up in the following carriage, trying to peek at us. I cut a rope and let the tarp fall down to cover our conversation.

"They're fine, but it would be best if don't fondle them when there are other people around."

She turned bright red. "Sorry, Master. I didn't mean to embarrass you."

We rode for several hours. Ruby and Razele taught Valis the power of a flyer. She was a natural. From what Razele said, she was also a summoner, which might be useful for long-range weapons or beasts. I had to make sure she was trained. We were starting to have a good team. At that rate, we might eventually surpass the five great warriors.

The caravan stopped, and I walked to the front. "What's the problem?"

The lead driver turned and said, "We need to let the horses rest for a bit and feed them. It takes an hour or so, but at this pace, we'll reach the capital easily. We'll rest there and pick up the last of the people before heading to the school."

I hopped out in front and saw a few soldiers in full plate armor. "Is there a problem?"

"Yes," one said. "We sent a scout ahead, but he didn't return. We sent another to track the first one, and the same thing happened. We need to send a few soldiers out to find them."

I waved to the carriage. "Razele and Valis, you watch over the rest of the convoy. Ruby and I will go ahead to see what's going on."

Ruby floated out and landed beside me. The guards cautiously stepped aside.

"The missing men might still be alive," I told Ruby. "If you find them, bring them back to us."

"I will if I can find them," she said, flying off. "Let's hope they were just held up."

I walked past a soldier and patted his shoulder before walking down the path. It was dirt with a few rocks, and the sun barely shone. Shade covered the area, and I didn't see any animals.

The forest seemed a little too quiet. Ruby flew ahead, keeping a lookout.

"Ruby, do you sense them at all?"

She floated higher and looked. "No, My Lord. It's like they disappeared. Usually I can track the scent of blood, but even that is missing."

That meant they had to be swallowed whole, which meant a very large predator. "What are the chances it got the best of two scouts?"

She shook her head. "It shouldn't. At least one would have sent up a flare to warn us. I don't think they were bested by an animal."

It dawned on me. "What if it's not an animal but some flyers?"

Ruby stopped. "I need to extend my search. Hold on."

As she floated in place for a few moments, listening carefully, I heard a branch break behind me.

"My Lord...."

"I know. Don't destroy the forest."

She landed softly beside me. "I wouldn't dare, but insects need to learn their place."

Rustling sounded all around us. A moment later, at least ten bandits came out of the brush and stood around us.

"Hey, Kid," one said. "Hand over the little girl, and we won't have a problem."

I looked at Ruby, who hid her face, although the amount of power she channeled into herself was extraordinary. "I'm sorry, Sir, but I wouldn't even know where to begin with a rebuttal to that comment. I can offer some advice, though."

They laughed.

"You misread me. I told you to give me the girl. We don't want your stupid advice."

A red aura surrounded Ruby, as waves of power radiated from her.

"I tried to warn you," I said. "It looks like you made a big mistake. Ruby, would you mind?"

All the brutes were terrified at the sight of her power. They froze in place. It looked like she put so much fear into them, they couldn't run. One fell over onto his face with blood coming from his mouth.

"Insects defile the words of my lord," she said. "Insects believe they could be in a class that could touch me with their filthy hands. Insects, I squish!"

She seemed ready to lose control, but I wanted to see how it played out, so I prepared to step in and said, "Go, Ruby."

She vanished. Three men were suddenly decapitated and slumped over. Two others collapsed in fear. Ruby took care of all of them but left one alive.

I walked up to the last one, a scrawny man with tears running down his cheeks. He wore a black shirt and pants and clutched a dagger in one hand, but he couldn't move.

"That's enough, Ruby."

She shook with rage. She stalked up to the last man and raised her hand, ready to squeeze his head. I touched her hand and realized her hand had vanished.

Looking down, I saw her arm was rammed through my heart. I felt my hand grow back and pulled her close in a hug. Her rage subsided, and she collapsed, but I caught her before she fell.

Ruby pulled back her arm and looked up at me. "What happened, My Lord?" She saw the hole in my chest. "Who did that?"

She noticed the blood on her arm and asked, "Did I attack you?"

I helped her stand. "You did, but it's OK. I was curious about your power. You apparently lost control, so I brought you back."

Ruby stepped back and bowed. "I'm sorry, My Lord. I'm so sorry."

I patted her head. "That's OK."

A knife plunged into my side, sending a wave of pain through me as a rib broke. I flinched from the pain, and Ruby was instantly furious again.

"Stay there," I told her. "You've done enough."

I turned and saw the man staring at me in shock. "I was going to let you live, Sir, after everything you just witnessed, but I changed my mind.

I grabbed his throat and lifted him off the ground. He gargled and tried to talk.

"You aren't human," he gasped. "You're a monster. How are you still alive?"

I pulled the dagger from my side and tossed it to the ground. "I'm just an ordinary human." I snapped his neck and tossed the body into the woods.

"Ruby, can you clean up this mess?"

She turned and clasped her hands. All the blood lifted off the ground, and the bodies floated into the sky to circle over her head. Suddenly, all the blood vanished.

"Their blood tastes absolutely foul, My Lord."

I smiled. "You can drink some of mine later for doing such a good job."

We looted the corpses for money and information. I found a note, which I slid into one pocket, then we tossed the bodies into the forest and walked back to the caravan.

Two soldiers arrived to stand with the others.

"Hey," one soldier said, "they're back! Did you find anything that way?"

Ruby and I looked at each other.

"No," I said. "It was pretty quiet. We must've gone the wrong way."

Ruby giggled and leaped into the carriage. Razele noticed the hole in my cloak.

"What happened?" Razele asked. "It looks like you were run through with a large weapon."

Valis came over and touched my chest. "There's no scratch or anything."

Ruby didn't like Valis touching me. "Hands off, you harpy. He's mine."

Valis stepped back but flicked Ruby on the nose.

"I'm not anybody's," I said. "I feel the same for all of you. Don't get jealous."

All blushed.

"Master, thank you," Ruby said, looking away. "I'm not against it, but I do love those two."

I wondered what she meant.

The caravan started up again.

"Kit, what happened?" Razele asked.

I looked ahead down the trail. "We had some fun with a few bandits. Ruby took most of them out. It was pretty cool."

Ruby almost squeaked with excitement. "Thank you, Lord, for your comment."

As we rolled ahead, the sun began sinking, and I hoped we would reach the capital soon.

11

We rode for several more hours, feeling exhausted by traveling despite not having any trouble along the way.

Finally, I saw a clearing open up ahead. I held onto a rail and looked at a long meadow that opened as far as I could see. A huge city enclosed in stone walls stood in the distance. Farms and houses filled the open landscape.

"So this is the capital?" I asked the driver.

"Yes, indeed. It's owned by one of the three major families, the Dowmaers, I believe. They're talented with healing and other things."

I never met anyone from another major family before, so that could be fun. I knew that none of the other family's wanted to rule so my family did.

"Thanks for the information." I jumped down from the carriage and walked alongside, studying the people, flowers, and trees. It was so different from the beach or the woods. Cherry blossoms circled in the air and wafted past us.

"Beautiful, isn't it?"

Razele stood beside me. "It is, indeed. I'm glad we decided to do this. I'm happy you joined me in this endeavor."

She held onto my arm, as we walked. "I wouldn't want to do this with anyone else, but you realize that from now on, everything will just get harder, right?"

She was right. I knew we faced a long, uphill battle. "We'll need a lot more friends to make sure we survive the long haul."

She laughed and kissed my cheek. "Just don't bring any more girls. I feel like you're trying to make me jealous."

I looked at her and blushed. "That wasn't the intention at all. Like I said, I like you all the same, but getting emotionally tied right now would cause a lot of trouble, especially in a battle."

She held my arm tighter. "It's hard knowing we'll die someday, and you'll be left alone. Don't let that hold you back from experiencing life."

I hated it when she was right, but still, it wasn't a pleasant prospect. "All right, but I won't promise anything."

She skipped a little. "Thank you. Now I just have to hide this from the other girls."

A dark presence formed behind me.

"Just what are you hiding, Washboard?"

We turned to see Ruby.

"You can't forget me," she said.

I patted her head. "I would never."

Valis popped her head out the window, as the carriage passed. "Me, too, master."

We walked to catch up with her.

"Same with you, Valis."

She smiled.

We were a lot closer to the capital. The sun had almost set, and darkness would fall soon. Reaching the gate quickly, we saw two guards in gold-plate armor with a red dragon engraved on the chest piece. Their helmets had a single red feather sticking up from the top.

"Stop there," one said.

With my cousin dead, I knew it was up to me to get us inside. I walked up to the guards.

"Greetings. My name is Kit Icealis, the next head of the Icealis family. We're staying here for the night before we gather your students and continue our journey to the school."

The guards bowed, and the gate rose to let us inside.

"Please go straight ahead, Sir, if you wish to stay within the castle walls. Please have a safe evening."

We went inside. I stared at the buildings made of fine wood. The roads were cobblestone, with lampposts placed at intervals along them. I saw dozens of stores and merchants.

We led the convoy up the street, the castle came into view. Two different towers hung off the castle, both covered in ice. Ice also spread to different parts of the castle, with spikes sticking up from the roof in a few places.

We reached the inner gate to the castle, but there were no guards on the ground, just above us on the walls. When the last carriage came through, the gate slammed shut.

I suddenly felt it wasn't a good idea to spend the night in the town. Several guards came out to escort someone in their midst. It was impossible to see the person through the throng.

Once the men reached us, they parted, and a young man came out with hair as white as snow. His robes were made of white fur, and he carried a large scythe.

"So this is the next head of the Icealis family," he said. "I heard there was a family squabble, and you're the one who came out of it alive."

I reached for my sword. The guards lowered their spears.

"If you think you can stop me with those twigs, we'll have a lot of fun," I said.

The young man slammed his hilt to the ground. "Enough! We aren't here to fight but to welcome them to the castle." He walked forward with his hand extended. "My name is Orlando Dowmaers."

I shook his hand. "Kit Icealis. It's a pleasure to meet you."

The three girls eyed him suspiciously. A guard moved his spear point toward Valis' neck. It burst into twigs that flew in all directions, and I stared him in the eye. The knight stepped back a few feet.

I looked at Valis. She was all right, although her eyes revealed fear. Looking back at the knight, I said, "If you want to live, I would never raise a weapon to any of them again. They're part of the Icealis family through me."

Orolando laughed and turned. He picked up a piece of the broken spear and shoved it into the knight's heart. "See what you did? You disrespected a major family, and now you're dead."

The knight fell over dead.

"I'm sorry for the disrespect one of our knights showed you," he said to me. "I hope his death was sufficient apology."

I nodded.

"Good. If you would follow me? I'm sure you're famished and would like to relax."

The soldiers helped unload the caravan, while we went into the castle. Beyond the large doors, a long, red carpet flowed down a hall lined with magnificent portraits and fine furnishings. Maids stood beside the door, bowing as we passed. Golden chandeliers hung from the ceiling, their flames casting light over everything.

The castle was more luxurious than the monastery. I guessed they wanted to show an image of wealth to their subjects, but it was still a lot.

We walked down the hall to a set of large stone stairs leading to the second floor. Orolando called to two maids, who hurried over.

"Please take Kit's companions to their room, then help the other flyers. Make sure all are fed and they know where the bath-house is."

The maids bowed and started up the stairs. The three girls were hesitant to follow.

"Go on," I said. "I'll join you in a little bit."

They looked ready to protest, then they followed the maids.

I looked to Orolando. "I would guess your king wishes to see me?"

He walked down the right hallway. "Correct. He has some questions and wishes to talk in private. Do your best."

We continued down the hall. I saw maids stationed at frequent intervals, but I doubted they were being paid anything. All the halls had red carpets, and the interior was well furnished.

We made a few turns, and the hall widened. Stone statues were set in little alcoves. There were hundreds of them.

Orolando stopped. To our left were two large wooden doors guarded by spearmen. They opened the doors for us, and Orolando waved me in.

"The king wishes to speak with you alone. I will wait for you out here."

I walked inside. The floor was so reflective, I saw myself when I looked down. Guards stood at every corner of the massive room. Stone columns held a ceiling far overhead. The king sat on a large, golden throne with armrests that seemed to be made of human heads.

I approached him and stopped thirty feet away. He was an older man with a long, gray beard. His golden crown was encrusted with jewels over a balding head. He held a large scepter of silver that resembled a serpent.

He stood, then he walked down a few steps toward me. "It's good to have the next head of the Icealis family here. It's an honor to have you among us today."

I didn't move for a moment, trying to make sure everything was all right in that room. It felt like someone was watching me with the intent to kill. "Thank you. I'm sorry. My name is Kit Icealis."

He laughed loudly. "It looks like we've both been caught up in pleasantries. My name is Agust Dowmaers, the King of Coylinya."

We shook hands, and the guards seemed a bit nervous with how friendly we were.

"I'm thankful to your family," he said. "Ours never wanted the job of running the country and being so formal, but we started this city not long ago, and it blossomed into what you see today. We still know you are the leaders of this nation."

I waved a hand. "I'm not here to pull rank or correct you. I came to make sure you have your students ready with all the supplies needed for the journey."

He snapped his fingers. A man dressed as a fool came over and bowed while offering a large scroll.

"That's the list of all the names and supplies that will be brought to the school," the king said. "I hope it meets your family's expectations."

As the new future head of the family, I wasn't sure what I was supposed to look for, so I had to trust my instincts and make sure the list was all right. "Thank you. I will go over this tonight and see if there are any problems. If so, I'll let you know."

He bowed to me, and the guards muttered angrily. He raised a hand to quiet them. "I know you think I'm the leader of this nation, but I'm not. I have control over this city, but in the end, if something must change, it's up to the Icealis family. All of you would be wise to remember that."

I took the scroll. "I appreciate your kind words, but I have no interest in interfering with your kingdom. Do what you must. If there's a problem, I'll talk to you about it."

He smiled. That was what he wanted. I realized the whole meeting was a ploy.

"Anyway, King, I have other matters to attend to. I will speak to you later after I look over the list."

I turned to leave, but the door opened before I got there, and two guards shoved their way inside and rushed past me.

"Your Highness," one said, "this is an emergency."

I noticed I had splotches of blood on my cloak. Turning, I saw the soldiers were covered in it.

The king looked ready to chastise them, but I said, "Agust, this must be important. We should hear them out."

He walked back to his throne and sat down. The two men went to their knees.

"Sire, please, there is a huge problem near the mines."

An advisor came up to the king and whispered into his ear. The king nodded a few times, then the advisor stepped back. "I see. So that's the problem. You need to evacuate the mine. We'll send a platoon of men to clear it out. You two should be taken care of and rest. Thank you for this information."

They stood and left the room. It seemed the king had the situation in hand and wasn't inclined to ask for my help, but I walked back to the steps below the throne.

"Is there something I can help with?" I asked.

Sitting straight, he waved the advisor closer. He wore a white suit with black gloves, and his face was hidden.

"My name is Malnius," he said. "I am His Majesty's head advisor. There have been reports of a creature in the depths of the mine that is attacking the miners. Since no bodies have been found, we chalked it up to rumors. Now we believe the stories are true. It is a type of monster unknown to us."

I realized that wasn't completely true. They must have known the monster was down there, but they kept working the mine, anyway. It must have been nesting in there for a while. Why would the king endanger his subjects like that? He knew I would be arriving today. Maybe he ignored the issue to deal with me first, but that seemed ridiculous.

"I see," I said. "It would be a shame for your men to be slaughtered any further. I will gladly take care of this for you."

He smiled. "Then it is decided. When you leave our walls, head north, and you'll see the tunnel system. There will be guards posted. Tell them who you are, and they'll let you through."

Assuming they knew the monster was there, the king and his advisor probably thought it was something that would kill me. I imagined his panic when I returned with the creature's head.

"Thank you, King. I will get my comrades and vanquish it."

He raised his hand. "There's no need to make them worry. I'd just go defeat it and let the girls be taken care of."

How did he know they were all women? The entire thing felt like a trap. I wondered why they were being so brazen about it.

"Thank you for your consideration for my comrades. I'll do as you advise and be back soon."

I walked out of the throne room and saw Orolando leaning against a pillar. "Ah, it's good to see you come out of there. Were there any problems?"

I shook my head. We walked toward the entrance together. "There seems to be a disturbance at the mines. I asked for permission to remedy the situation."

He patted my back. "It's called a Sesaquit. They are powerful creatures."

It was nice to know someone wasn't against me, but I felt my hunch was still true. "Thank you for the information. Is there anything else about them you can tell me?"

He thought for a moment. "Yes. They're difficult to fight with our flames. It's like their bodies are completely immune to them. Physical attacks, though, work fine."

We reached the entrance.

"Will you tell the girls what is happening, so they don't worry?"

He bowed and walked up the stairs. I went out the doorway thinking I could never catch a break.

Outside, the sun had set, and stars twinkled in the sky. It would have to be a quick job unless I wanted to spend all night in the mine.

The carriages had been resupplied, and a few monastery guards stood around, talking with knights from the castle. When I walked toward them, they turned to me and bowed.

"Sir, it's a pleasure to see you."

I raised one hand. "It's all right. Stand down. I'm heading to the mines. Would you men escort me?"

They readied a carriage. I hopped in the back, and a knight got in with me wearing a full suit of armor that hid his features.

"Thank you for going there," he said. "It's been a terrible couple of months. We've lost a lot of workers, but the king hasn't done a thing about it."

I must have misheard him. "My apologies. Did you say months?"

He nodded. "Indeed. The mine holds many precious minerals. One is a star stone. If properly enchanted, it can create a field around you that blocks most flames. They're nearly impossible to find, but the mine is littered with them."

That explained the secrecy. If news of the stones got out, the entire world would be coming to take them.

"All right. Can you tell me why they're worth risking people over? I understand the stones are rare, but why let so many people be killed?"

He took off his helmet and revealed blond hair above a flawless complexion. His eyes were as green as grass.

"Sorry. I'm the head knight of the kingdom. My name is Randle Oceilion. It's a pleasure to meet you."

Oceilion was the last great family of the Kai Nation.

"You're from one of the major families. It's a pleasure to meet you."

He smiled. "Our family has mastered the flame of teal. We have the ability to create body enhancements, and we're great warriors."

I offered my hand. "Thanks for the information. I had no idea your family would be the kingdom's strongest knights, but I just inherited my position, so I'm doing my best to learn everything."

He laughed and slapped his knee. "That's amazing. I'm meeting the next head. I knew you were part of the Icealis family, but I didn't know you were in line to lead it. I hope we can become friends. I'm the heir to the head of my family, too."

I hoped I could be friends with him. It would make many things easier.

"You aren't going to the school for flyers?"

He shook his head. "No, I won't, but my little brother and sister will be. They want to join the military there."

That meant I could find some friendly faces. I would keep an eye out for them. "Back to what we were saying."

He nodded and leaned back. "It's because the king wants to sell the stones to neighboring countries and make a handsome profit. He doesn't care for the people, just his pockets."

I scratched my chin, wondering why the head knight was being so frank with me.

"I must level with you, Kit. The king wants you to fail and die. I was asked to assassinate you once we were inside. Actually, all of us were asked to do it."

I reached for my blade, but he merely raised his hands. "I'm sorry. None of us are here to kill you. That would be a sign of disrespect for the Icealis family. They'd send an army against us and wipe us out. Then your family would be the only to rule, but as the next head, I want to serve your family. I don't want any more innocent people hurt, nor do I wish for the city I have sworn to protect burn to ash."

He took out a piece of parchment and handed it to me. "This is a letter from my father, the head of the Oceilion family. It's signed with his and my seals, along with one from your uncle, proving what I just told you."

I studied the parchment and saw the seals were correct. "All right. I accept. That means we have to deal with the king when we get back. How many men are on his side?"

He smiled wickedly. "That's a good question. If I had to guess, I'd say twenty. Their leader was killed by Agust when he disrespected you."

I chuckled. "I see this has been going on for a while. I'm assuming Kilyon talked with your family and Agust?"

He laughed. "Oh, man. Your father said you were perceptive. Yes. You're right. This has been a plan for a while. Will you help?"

I nodded. "I will. It looks like my father wants me to. It will also help build a bridge of friendship between us."

I looked out of the window. We'd been riding for a while, and I knew we had to be close to the mine.

"Almost there, Kit. The problem is that the king has a few of his men posted outside."

I crossed my arms. "So what? I doubt they're a problem for the two of us."

He kicked my foot. "Of course not, but we believe he also has a scout nearby. If we attack the king's men, the scout will tell the king, and there will be a big mess in the castle."

A guard outside spoke. "We're close. I see more than the usual number of guards posted. I'd be ready for anything."

Randle and I stood.

"We can't let our guest wait, can we?" I asked.

He shook his head. "No. That wouldn't be polite."

The carriage halted. Randle put on his helmet, and we hopped out the back. The land around us was mostly flat, but a tunnel burrowed into the ground at the beginning of the mine. Ten or more guards stood in front of it.

"My name is Kit," I said. "I'm here to take care of the monster problem."

They stepped aside to let us pass. I walked into the cave and found it wide enough for three to pass easily. Looking behind, I saw Randle following, with the king's guards right behind him. I saw one stay behind, which might present a problem. Lanterns hung from the walls at regular intervals to keep the place well lit. I wondered if there were anymore guards ahead of us.

After walking for a while, we reached a four-way intersection.

"It's on the right, Kit. That's where the last miners died."

I led the way, and I soon caught a foul stench in the air, meaning the monster didn't eat his victims completely as the king said. We turned a corner and saw a pile of corpses. Randle stopped and turned away. A couple of guards in the back threw up.

I stared at the rotting corpses, then moved closer. There were no slash marks or punctures in the bodies. It seemed as if all the blood was sucked through their skin, which seemed a gruesome way to die.

"Are we sure this was a beast?" I asked Randle.

He steadied himself before kneeling beside me. "Isn't this what a monster does?"

I shook my head. "The bodies are in good condition, apart from the rotting. That means they were left like this. There are no signs they were eaten or even bitten. All I can see is they've lost all their blood."

He looked closer. "You're right. I was told it was a monster, but this isn't the work of one."

The king's men drew their blades. Two of them pressed against Randle and my backs.

"Sorry, Randle," a guard said. "You're a worthy warrior, but we can't let you and this kid out of here alive."

They called me a kid? This sucks, I thought.

Randle stood. "What's this about? You're knights of the king. You should be protecting the people!"

The knights laughed softly. Randle's men backed away from the rest of the group.

"Oh, we're in it for the people, all right. We'll make them slaves. We've been promised plenty of land and slaves. We'll be filthy rich. All we have to do is bring your heads to the king."

I looked at Randle. "We knew this would happen. I guess we have to protect ourselves from a dire situation."

He looked at his own men, who drew their swords and impaled two knights in the back. Randle drew his own blade and cut down two of them. Rushing past him, I grabbed two men by their helmets and crushed their heads together before tossing them aside.

The remainder of the knights tried to run, but Randle's men cut them down.

"What are the chances there's a real monster down there?" I asked.

Randle sheathed his sword. "I doubt it. My guess it was just a story to get us riled up and volunteer to help them."

The cave shook, and bits of dirt rained down.

"What was that?"

A loud roar came from the hall behind us. With a few more stomps of heavy feet, a large monster turned the far corner and glared at us with blazing red eyes. It had the body of a large wolf with two heads, a wolf's and a snake's.

"I hate to say this," I said, "but you were wrong."

It lunged. We leaped apart, and it struck the knight behind us. The poison made him solidify instantly.

"Don't let it hit you, Kit!"

I dodged a second strike. "I can see that. Send your men back. They won't be much help against this."

Randle waved, and his remaining men ran back up the tunnel. The snake rushed us and lunged. I ducked under its strike as Randle jumped over. He severed the snake's head while I drew my sword and cut off the wolf's head. Blood spurted all over my chest. Pulling the blade free, I stepped back.

"Was that it?" I asked.

"I think so, but I never saw anything like it before."

The beast turned to black smoke and disappeared.

"I assume you don't know what that was, either."

He shook his head. "It could have been a summoned beast. There are many of those we've never seen, but it doesn't make sense. Summoners usually go straight into the military at the school."

Looking where the beast had been, I saw a few stones on the ground and picked them up. They were clear with all the elemental colors coursing through them.

"What are these?" I asked.

He knelt in surprise. "They're star stones, but way more refined. They look spectacular. I'd put them away before anyone sees them."

I handed one to him.

"What's this for?" he asked.

I stood. "For helping me with the kill. Now I can give these to the girls, which will give them better protection."

We walked back down the tunnel toward the surface.

"What are the chances there are more people in play here?" I asked.

The question made him curious. "It would explain a lot. The king wouldn't have set all this up. I understand he might fear for the mine, but that beast wasn't the one I was told about. It makes me think someone else came in here, killed the original, and placed their own beast here to kill us."

I nodded. That made sense. "All right. I'm sure the king has been notified by now. We have to hurry back to the castle."

We picked up our pace to the entrance. When we walked out into the night, I saw the remaining king's guard was dead from a slit throat.

I saw burn marks near his feet, too. "Do any of the king's knights have flyer abilities?"

Randle shook his head and stood. "We might have a problem."

We ran to the carriage and saw all the horses had been killed.

"Crap!" I said. "It was a trick!"

Glancing back at the city, I saw a large plume of smoke rising from the castle. Randle stood beside me and watched, as a large, purple lightning bolt struck the castle and sent a shockwave in all directions.

"Was that one of your teammates?" he asked.

I smiled. "I think so. There's only one person who could do that."

Flame ignited around me. "I'm heading to the castle."

Randle looked at his comrades. "I'm joining Kit. The rest of you head to the castle on the double."

Blue wings sprouted from the back of his armor and flapped, as he left the ground. "So, Master Kit, shall we proceed?"

We shot toward the castle and soon encountered pungent smoke. As we flew over the town walls, I saw monsters all over the place.

"It seems you were right, Kit," Randle said. "There's a third party involved."

Most of the beasts seemed weak enough that normal guards could have dealt with them, but they hadn't.

"Should we stop?" he asked.

"No. The guards can mop up what's left. They aren't a threat. My guess is the castle is the bigger problem."

We flew toward the castle. A large basilisk wrapped itself around the entire castle. Three more lightning bolts crashed down, knocking it off. I watched it hit the ground. Guards rushed up to cut it to pieces. More beasts were moving within the castle.

"We should touch down," I said. "Help your fellow guards. I'm going to the castle."

We separated. I landed in front of the main doors and ran inside. Several maids had been slaughtered in there, their corpses flung aside. I didn't see any beasts.

There was a large explosion at the top of the staircase, and a huge wolf rolled down the stairs minus its head.

"My Lord!" Ruby shouted. "You're safe! We were so worried!" She ran to me and jumped. I barely had time to catch her before she clung to me.

"I'm fine. Where are the others?"

She looked at me without speaking.

"Take me to them quickly."

I followed her, as she ran upstairs. We turned left down a long hall marred by claw marks on the walls. The rug was stained with blood, and monster corpses covered a large area.

"Did you hold them off yourself?" I asked.

"Yes, My Lord." She pointed to a door that was missing a handle.

As I kicked it open, a sword swung at me. I dodged and kicked the person against the nearest wall.

"Kit, don't!" Razele shouted. "He's friendly!"

She held Valis in her arms, and I ran to them.

"What happened?" I asked.

Valis was burning up sweat pouring from her with a strange green ooze on her arm corroding her flesh.

"A basilisk spit at her. I've been trying to heal her, but I'm not a healer, so there's only so much I can do."

I sliced my hand and fed her some of my blood. The wound healed, and her temperature dropped to normal. "She'll be fine now. Do you know where the king us?"

Ruby knelt beside me. "I had to kill him. He ordered his soldiers to kill us."

I raised my hand. "You may have inadvertently caused a war between the major families. Do you realize that?"

She pressed her blade against her neck. "I know, Master. I'll make up for it with my life."

Anger rose in me. "Stop!"

All three of them quieted, but Ruby kept the blade where it was, her eyes filled with tears.

"You made a mistake," I said, "so you plan to take your own life and leave the ones you love behind?"

Her hand shook. I walked closer and placed my hand on hers. She lowered her blade and hugged me.

"Everyone makes mistakes, even me. I'm not angry. I planned to kill him myself. I had no idea this was going to happen. Don't ever do that again, Ruby."

She held me and cried. "I killed the king, and I couldn't protect Valis. I'm worthless."

I brushed my hand down her hair. "You're mad because she was hurt, right?"

She nodded against me. "Then make it right. Next time, do your best to protect her."

We heard a knock at the door. I turned and saw Randle.

"Looks like our job is a hundred times easier now," he said.

I rubbed Ruby's back. "Yeah. At least we fixed things in here. How is it out there?"

Randle walked in. "It's safe now. The king was slaughtered in his throne room. It's a little hard to tell which pieces are him, so we made a big pile of the corpses."

I looked down at her. "I'm glad you didn't even hesitate. Thank you for doing your best. Make sure the girls are safe."

I released her and followed Randle from the room.

As we turned the corner, he said, "She must've slaughtered most of the guard. Their corpses are all over the castle. The monsters never reached the throne room."

I nodded. She'd done a good job. I just feared if it happened in another nation, it wouldn't end this well. "What's your plan?"

We rounded a corner and walked down the stairs. "We'll clean up this mess," he said. "Someone just arrived from your family. They wish to talk to you. After that, we'll see what happens."

We reached the bottom, where maids and soldiers worked to clean up the bodies and blood.

"Who is it, do you know?" I asked.

He shook his head.

"Hey, Pup," Kilyon called. "Getting into more trouble, I see."

I turned and saw him standing at the entrance. "It's good to see you, too. This wasn't my doing. I was just a bystander."

He walked toward me with a smile. "All you had to do was get to the school and learn, not leave a path of death in your wake." He placed one hand on my shoulder. "The good news is, you're doing a great job of cleaning up this nation. I'm proud of you. Because of you, we can stop the illegal sale of star stones and use them for our own military. Now that the city is without a ruler, we need to find a new one."

Orolando walked up. "That's where I come in."

I knew he was next in line, but I didn't know if he could be trusted.

Kilyon noticed my concern and said, "His family will be merging."

I looked at him in confusion. "They'll be absorbed into ours and take our name?"

He shook his head. "No, Pup. Their family will be absorbed, but they'll be directly under our authority. They'll have a head of family, but the only one who can make the rules is our family head. They won't be allowed to do anything but take our orders from now on. It's like having a child family."

Looking at Orolando, I knew that was a very cruel thing to do to a major family. "I'm sorry to hear that."

He shrugged and said, "It's all right. I was the one who asked for this to happen. If I didn't, none of the families would trust us again. It's best this way."

He sacrificed his family's power to save their lives. That was the work of a responsible man.

"All right, Master," I said. "When should I leave for the school, or should I just keep on dominating the world?"

He laughed and took out a coin, tossing it into the air. It struck the floor with a loud clang and landed on the carpet. "Looks like you're going to school," he said, studying the coin. "What a shame. We'll try to salvage as many flyers as we can. A lot of the students didn't survive the battle. We lost a fair amount of supplies, too. While that's being sorted out, why don't you and the girls get some rest?'

I took out the list the king gave me and handed it to him. "This was the list of things we were supposed to have, along with the flyers. I don't know if it'll be any use now."

He opened the list. "This will help a lot. Good job, Pup."

I bowed to him and turned toward the stairs.

"Pup, she fought hard and was ruthless. I watched from a distance. She killed the basilisk, the king, and many of his men, not to mention a ton of beasts. She needs to think better of herself."

I smiled. "You're right. I'm incredibly proud of her, but at the same time, I'm a bit worried."

He laughed. "That's true. She could be dangerous, but if you want my opinion, she's a very valuable friend, maybe even more."

I blushed. She was a beautiful young woman, and so were Razele and Valis. I couldn't choose among them. I held my head in my hands for a moment. Why was it so hard to pick one?

At the top of the stairs, I turned right. The carnage was almost gone. There were far fewer bodies, and the maids were working hard.

Walking into our room, I saw Valis sitting up, while Ruby held her and cried. Razele smiled at me and waved me in. Ruby and Valis finally noticed me. I looked around and saw the man who guarded them must have left.

"My Lord," Ruby said, "welcome back."

I knelt before the two of them and studied their faces. "How are you, Valis?"

She shook her head. "I'm fine, just weak right now. Master, don't be angry with Ruby. She did her best. It was my fault."

"No, Valis," Ruby said quickly. "It wasn't. You didn't do anything wrong."

I held up a hand to stop both of them.

"What happened?" I asked Valis.

Valis coughed slightly. "We were just talking, planning on going out into the city and buying you a gift, when the door was kicked open. Several guards ran in. Ruby and I fought them off. It was quiet for a moment, then a loud bang shook the whole castle. We didn't know what it was.

"Screams came from inside. We ran out and saw guards waiting in the hall, so we all fought them. We pushed on to the main entrance, where monsters were pouring in. After we beat off that attack, we were able to reach the outside and saw that enormous basilisk. We tried to fight it. It lunged at Ruby, who didn't have time to dodge, so I shoved her aside. The poison hit me instead.

"Razele brought me back to this room with the help of the knight who said he was a friend of yours, but I heard Ruby losing control. Her power washed over everything. Razele did her best to heal me."

I was glad they worked to protect each other.

"From what I've heard, none of you did anything wrong. You did what was necessary to protect yourselves and each other. There's no need to feel bad or apologize. Now we need some rest. We'll arrive at the school tomorrow, and I'm not sure how that will go. Be ready and diligent."

Valis and Ruby nodded. I walked to the window and looked out. Smoke rose into the sky, while the city resembled a battleground stripped of hope. Many buildings below were in ruins. It would take a lot of time to rebuild them all.

I wondered how the situation would affect the other nations. Would they move against us, or would they respect the treaty? The Aurora Nation wouldn't attack, but the Celestial Nation wouldn't hesitate if they saw an opening. War with them would be difficult. I hoped it wouldn't happen for a while, at least.

As Valis and Ruby fell asleep, I lit a smoke and flicked ash out the window.

Razele sat on the edge of the bed. "What happens now?"

I sat in the window seat, watching ash fall when I flicked my smoke again. "To be honest, there are a lot of things that might happen right now. Our best option is to go to school and learn everything we can, then we make our first move before anyone else. Something tells me this peace won't last, especially with the supply of star stones being cut off."

Razele got off the bed, her body flowing like a rose in the wind. Her eyes locked on mine, giving me butterflies in my stomach. "Well, then, we have to be diligent.

She stood only a foot away, her pale skin glistening in the light. Why did she have to be so magnificent? All three of them were.

"You're right. Maybe we can survive."

She grabbed my cloak with one hand and pulled me to close the distance between us without hesitation. Our lips locked, and love sparked so strongly I was left speechless. We stayed that way for a moment, then pulled away. She blushed.

"How was that?" she asked.

I touched my lips. When she pulled away, it felt like a dagger struck me. "It was amazing."

She turned. "At least I can say I was the first of us to kiss you."

I smiled and puffed on my cigarette, sending smoke out the window. "I'm happy with all three of you. I wouldn't get rid of any of you for anything in the world."

She came closer and leaned against me. "That's good. Even if you wanted to get rid of us, the chances of any of us going anywhere are slim."

I chuckled, knowing she was right. Even though I wouldn't be able to get rid of any of them, after chaos took over, I felt lonely. Having all three of them with me helped a lot.

She wrapped her arms around me, her scent of fresh rose wafting over me. "I know you love all of us. You won't say it, but deep down, you love us a lot and want to be with all of us, yet you're worried if you choose one, the others will leave, or you worry we won't feel the same about you."

She was as bad as Kilyon, but she was right. "Maybe I do, bet even if I love all of you a lot, there will be war soon. I see nothing but destruction and carnage ahead."

She sat in front of me on the ledge, our legs hanging out the window, and leaned back to rest against me. "I know. I've known that for a long time. I'm happy with this, but I'm not happy to be killing people, although I'll do it if it means I can continue being with you."

I tossed the smoke out and watched the ember fall into the darkness. "You're a ridiculous person, you know? What girl would want any of this?"

She pulled my arm around her. "There are three of us in this room."

I glanced at Ruby and Valis, still fast asleep. "Yeah. That's correct. Let's say I choose all three of you. If we all fall in love, what happens if one of us is in trouble?"

She giggled. "What are the chances of that? We're the best squad in the world, with an immortal who can get us out of any pinch we might fall into."

I gently rapped the side of her head. "I'm immortal, not indestructible. Don't do anything stupid."

She touched my arm with one hand. "I won't, but you never know. War is a dangerous thing. You never know what might happen."

We looked out the window until she fell asleep with her head against my chest. I leaned against the window frame and eventually slept, too.

12

Morning came all too quickly. The rising sun peered into my face. I opened my eyes and looked out. The fires were out, and the smoke stopped. People were already rebuilding. The sound of construction rang out.

I saw people harvesting the giant basilisk. Those scales made strong armor that only a few swords could pierce. If a flyer merged his flame with his sword, he could, in theory, cut down anything. The power of flames always surprised me.

I felt Razele move and looked down. She slept against me all night. Ruby and Valis were still asleep in the bed.

I yawned, covering my mouth, as Razele sat up slowly and rubbed her face.

"Morning," I said. "How'd you like sleeping in a window seat?"

She looked at the sunrise. "To be honest, I'd sleep in one more often if it was a bit more comfortable."

We smiled and lifted our legs back into the room.

"When will we have to leave?" she asked.

I heard footsteps, and Kilyon entered the room. "Good morning, you two lovebirds."

Razele, flustered, looked away.

"Morning," I said. "What's the problem?"

He tossed me an envelope. I opened it and took out a slip of paper.

Dear Kit,

Please try not to destroy the school. We can't fight their military. Kilyon will escort you to the school and then return.

There are rumors you're on the warpath, so the school is being overly cautious. You may be detained at the entry point. Kilyon is there to help with that.

I tossed the note on the bed. "So that's how it is?"

He nodded. When he walked closer, I saw signs of worry on his face, making him look like an old man.

"Yes, indeed. You've made a name for yourself, and not just at the school but with the other nations. The Celestial Nation has its eye on you. I'd be wary of them They have a powerful military. All the families are flyers of high caliber."

I knew I'd be a problem for some, but I was hoping that wouldn't become an issue until later in the game. "It looks like I'll have to play nice for a while."

Kilyon nodded.

Razele stepped closer to me and said, "We'll do our best with this information."

I sighed. The situation was heating up. What else would happen? "Should we be going, Kilyon?" I asked.

He nodded.

We woke Ruby and Valis, collected our belongings, and walked from the building. At the gate leading into the civilian district, there weren't many carriages, only ten, and some were in bad shape. Looking over the crowd of merchants and students, I saw we had only one-quarter of the original number, which wasn't good. If we ran into trouble at the school, we didn't have may reinforcements.

I heard someone land behind me and turned to see Randle.

"How are you, my friend?"

We clasped hands.

"Is that the infamous Randle?" Kilyon asked. "It's been too long, my friend."

The two began discussing their business. Someone tugged on my cloak.

"My Lord," Ruby said, "I won't fail you again."

I placed a hand on her shoulder. "No. You might. We *all* might fail one day, but we need to be there to pick each other up. We aren't gods, although some might think otherwise."

Razele laughed.

"What?" I asked.

She shook her head. "If there was a god, it would be you, the immortal king."

All three girls had wide eyes at that thought.

"The immortal king?" Valis asked. "I love that name, My Lord."

"Then when I rule, that's the name I will use."

Kilyon and Randle overheard. Kilyon snorted.

"The immortal king," he said, "known by the gods as nothing but a heretic."

Everyone laughed.

Randle walked toward me, and Ruby stared him down. He stopped and bowed.

"I have no interest in harming your lord. I'm a good friend of the family."

She didn't believe him, but she calmed down.

"She'll be a tough one."

A soldier came over. "Master Kit, the time is now. We must be going."

The girls were quick to get into our carriage, and I didn't blame them. The whole trip was getting worse all the time. I wanted it over, too.

"Kit, there's something I wanted to ask," Randle said in a worried tone.

"What is it?"

He scratched his chin and leaned in to ask, "Do you ever see a god?"

My eyes widened. He stood upright again and waved goodbye. How did he know? Did he know a god, too? Was he speaking with my goddess?

Kilyon looked at me. "What did he ask?"

"It's nothing. We should get going. How long will it take to reach the school?"

We walked toward the carriage. "At least until nightfall. I hope they don't overreact when they see me with you."

I hopped into the back, where the girls were resting again, trying to stay awake. "Then I assume they don't know you're coming."

He shook his head. "Nope. It'll be a nice trip for the two of us."

He walked away from the last carriage so he could lead the pack in the first one.

I sat down, and Ruby laid her head in my lap. Valis looked at me, her eyes shifting from Ruby to me.

"If you want to put your head in my lap, too, come here."

She quickly slid over and lay down. I patted them both.

Razele chuckled. "How much do you know of the school?"

Once she asked, I realized I didn't know much. "Nothing, really, just the basics."

She was surprised. "Let me educate you. The school is known as Escalrion. It's the size of a small nation, but it's one giant city. On the outskirts are farmlands. With the five nations, there are five different schools, one for each, but they aren't loyal to their original nations. When you graduate, you can choose to return to your nation or join the school's army. A lot of the students stay. It's a good situation with free housing and protection.

"There are five generals and one lord who presides over the whole school. No civilians are admitted to the school. Either you're there to learn combat, or you're thrown out."

If that was true, I didn't see why they didn't conquer the world. "Why do they stay there? Why not branch out?"

She thought for a moment. "I'm not entirely sure. There are mediators whenever two nations have a squabble. If there is a large presence of bandits or terrorists, there are people to take care of them."

That meant the other nations relied on the school for protection. It sounded very one-sided unless the school got something out of it.

"What about the major families?" I asked.

She shook her head. "None of the heads are allowed to enter. Their kids can enroll, but they're made into soldiers who never return home."

Was that something the master had already thought of? Did he know all this would happen? I couldn't see us being forced to join the army. Still, Kilyon always saw things ten steps ahead without even trying.

"Kit?"

I looked at her.

"You looked ready to pass out. Are you OK?"

I must've been in really deep thought. "I'm fine. I was just thinking. That's all."

We traveled in silence for a long time. The sun was setting when someone knocked on our carriage. I jumped out the back and found Kilyon waiting.

"I need you stick close to me. The girls will be fine. It's you I'm worried about right now."

I couldn't imagine why, since I couldn't be killed. "OK."

I matched pace with him.

"It's because these people might do anything, including destroy all the carriages. If they can see you, they should be more open to talking. At least, I hope so."

Looking around, I saw plenty of farms but no trees. The land was nearly flat. A large hill rose ahead of us, and we began walking up.

Once we reached the top, I saw breathtaking stone walls taller than anything I saw before. They were much taller than any tree I'd seen in the forest. They didn't form a complete circle, though.

Gates in the walls were just large enough for two carriages side-by-side. I looked around to study the plain and see if anyone was coming out to greet us.

"What's going on?" I asked.

Shaking his head, he looked even more worried. "I have a bad feeling, like we shouldn't be here."

He stopped, and the rest of the convoy halted behind us. He walked forward a few more paces, but there wasn't anything visible.

I extended an arm and felt something grab it. Then something went around my neck.

Kilyon noticed and turned.

"Hold it, Kilyon! Move, and the boy dies!"

Figures suddenly emerged from a gray mist that evaporated. At least 1,000 soldiers surrounded us, ready for a battle. Hundreds of flyers from all the nations hovered above, ready to pounce on us as if we were insects.

"Hold it, Alfitz," Kilyon said. "The boy wasn't doing anything. We came here to talk. That's it."

The arm tightened around my neck, cutting off my air.

"Alfitz, he wants to join, not fight."

He released me, and I went to my knees.

"What did you say? He wishes to join? You know what that entails, and you're willing to allow it?"

I looked up at Kilyon, whose eyes filled with distaste over the situation. "I'm aware, Alfitz, but there's no other way he can learn at this school. If we don't hand him over, the entire nation will suffer, wouldn't it?"

A boot struck my side, flipping me onto my back. I looked up and saw Alfitz with a black blade that glowed with an aura greener than a forest. His face was dark red, and two horns stuck up from his skull.

"It might, but this kid is dangerous. He could easily kill hundreds of us. If I weren't here, he might have killed everyone."

He smiled, then kicked my stomach with all his strength. I felt bones break, and I coughed up blood.

"You're going to kill him, Alfitz."

When his foot pulled away, my organs and bones returned to their normal places. I knew they saw it and hoped that would come in handy.

I heard a scream. When I looked, Razele was being hauled from the carriage by two flyers.

"General, it's the daughter of Hindoros. What should we do with her?"

He was about to reply when he looked back at me. Black flames surrounded me, turning the grass to mist.

"Let her go, Soldier."

He didn't release Razele, and she kept fighting. I shot off the ground and grabbed both flyers by their necks. I saw tears form in their eyes, as I crushed their throats and slammed their lifeless bodies to the ground.

They lay motionless, mangled beyond repair. I stood up straight and saw Ruby staring at me. Black flames moved around me erratically.

"Lord, it's OK. Everything is fine now. You need to calm down." Razele stood in front of me.

I felt distorted, as if another part of me wanted to be released from the depths of my soul.

"Kit, stop. I'm safe."

Her voice finally broke through. I collapsed and felt her catch me before I keeled over, as all my strength fled.

Kilyon and Alfitz looked at me.

"I'm sorry for that, Kit. Our plan was not to hurt your companions, but I can't let this pass without some sort of punishment. You killed two of my men, so by my word, you and your companions will join my platoon."

I didn't have the energy to reply, so Kilyon shook his hand and said, "I accept on his behalf."

Alfitz ended the handshake and looked at Razele and me. "I assume if anyone touches these girls, you'll go berserk."

I stared up at him.

"All right. I'll tell the others if anyone tries to harm them, he answers to me. I must ask, though, that you not kill my men, especially within the school. I would hate for the Kai Nation to become a battleground. You may be strong, but you can't protect everything."

He walked away. With a wave of his hand, all the soldiers turned and moved away with him.

I laid my head down and blacked out.

13

The sound of dripping water made me open my eyes. I lay in vast darkness, with drops of water hitting my forehead. When another one fell, I sat up.

"So the brilliant Kit is finally awake. You lost control. You called on so much power that your body shut down. Isn't it awful to have such a weak body that it can't even hold all your power?"

Celnius' finger touched my chest. I fell backward into the cold water and saw waves ripple away. She floated down and crossed her arms on my chest, then leaned her chin on them.

"Tell me, Kit. What is the flame?"

That confused me. "It's another side of magic, a sister to it. It's the source of our power. You can't use any other flame than the one you're born with."

She rolled onto her back and stretched her arms to cover my face. "Yes and no. Flames are like you said, a sister to magic itself. When the meteor struck our world, it caused major damage and also harmed the life force, or magic in your terms. With that damage, it desperately tried to heal itself, and the flame was born. There are beings that can be born of magic descendants, but that's rare. Most of the time, flames have taken over to protect magic. Think of it as a defense."

That meant the flyers were more powerful than magic, but that couldn't be right. Ruby was a phenomenal fighter, and her power easily rivaled mine.

"Then that means flames are supposed to be defensive, not offensive. Magic users are offensive. Without both of them, we're vulnerable."

Chuckling silently, she turned over again, uncovering my eyes. "That's correct. Without the two, there can't be one. If all the magic users were killed, the flames would fade. if flames fell so would magic. How would someone bridge that gap, my young man?"

"Were dragons able to use magic?"

That is a hard question to answer, if one of their kind was born with it, it was seen as weak and killed or cast out. There were no exceptions. That was their mistake.

"Life is interesting. Magic will generally find a way to bridge the gap between all the races. When they saw weakness, they didn't see the peace it could bring."

That sounded like the dragons were ignorant beings obsessed with their own power. "Are there any dragons left alive?"

She sat up and raised her hand with three fingers extended. "Who are they? Can they help? Will they be a problem?" She giggled to herself. "My dear boy, your future will be so amazing. I can't wait. It leaves me in so much suspense. What will you do next? Will you become a god, or will you fall and become a peasant? Your father was right. I owe him a favor for this opportunity."

A light shone into my face.

"Until next time, my little man. I look forward to seeing you once more."

The light intensified, surrounding everything.

I opened my eyes and stared up at a stone ceiling. I was in a room made of stone. When I moved my hands, I saw shackles attached to my arms. In panic, I lifted my head only to find I was completely bound to the bed. Dim lights hung around the room.

I looked ahead and saw bars with a door. A single guard sat in a chair, staring at me.

"You're in a maximum-security prison," he said. "Nobody leaves, and nobody can escape those chains. A special jewel is encrusted at the base to negate all flames. Unless you have a dragon's strength, you won't get out of them."

So much for a warm welcome, though I don't blame them for it. I carved a path of destruction al the way here, then killed two of their men. This seems fair.

"Where are my companions?"

He spat. "They should be hanged for their incompetence for joining a stupid man, but they're fine. They're with our general."

At least Alfitz was being honorable. The chains were strong but not terribly so. If I broke out and carved a path out of the prison, I assumed the girls would be harmed. They were leverage against me.

"Why are you so pissy with me? Are you having a bad day?"

He stood and kicked his stool across the room so hard it broke. "What did you say, Plebian?"

I lifted my head and saw his face full of rage, like he was ready to pounce. "I asked if you're having a bad day. I'm worried about you, stuck in a tower away from those who might help you. You must be insanely weak to be placed here. The general must not think much of you."

He punched a bar hard enough to make it creak, showing me they weren't very well set in the stone. "Shut up, Plebian!"

I smiled. "Oh? What would a weak man like you do if I don't? You can't kill me."

He drew his sword and grabbed the keys hanging at his waist.

"Marcus, stop!"

I heard footsteps approaching, and Alfitz came into view. Marcus went to his knees to bow.

"I see you're doing well, Kit," Alfitz said. "You nearly got this man killed."

Marcus looked up in anger. I broke all the chains in one motion and stood up to adjust my neck.

"Good to see you, General. I have to ask if you put me in here to stay forever as punishment, or did you want to see how I reacted?"

The general laughed and opened the door. "I was taking bets with the other generals. We decided you'd level the place, then I noted I had your companions, which meant you'd sit here until I came to get you."

He was right. I wouldn't put them in harm's way just so I could escape, but I wondered if the other generals would accept the arrangement.

"So, Alfitz, why did you demand I join you, and not the others?"

He studied me and waved me to walk forward. "Because, unlike the others, I liked your father and Kilyon. Many see what he and the others did as heresy, an affront to the school, but few know the wonderful things they did. They saved this land."

"You speak as if you fought alongside them."

He turned to look at Marcus, who looked away. "I did, long ago. So did Marcus' mother."

I looked at Marcus, who seemed even more furious.

"Shut it, General," Marcus said. "You know that's not to be discussed. It could land you in hot water."

Alfitz led me away. The prison was shaped in a large spiral, with only a few windows the size of small books in each cell. The other prisoners were chained to their beds. The place reeked of urine and feces.

"Who do you keep in here?" I asked. "I assume you don't have any of the great five."

I saw men and women try to move, but the chains held them securely. Did they deserve being in there, or was that what the school did to quell disorder.

"You're right. This place could never house them. This is a prison for Class-A criminals, like murderers, deserters, and robbers. It's all basically midlevel crime."

Murder is a midlevel crime? I wondered. "What would you do if you caught one of the great five?"

Marcus, who followed us, scuffed his foot. "They're killed on the spot. Why the general broke one of the most-important rules is beyond me. He had Kilyon, the war criminal called the Crimson Waters, in his hands, and he let him go."

I stopped and turned, grabbing Marcus' neck so I could stare into his face.

"Release him, Kit," Alfitz said. "There's no need for a brawl in this place. We don't want to rile the inmates."

I released Marcus and continued walking with the general. The spiral seemed endless.

"General, how many does this place hold?

He thought for a moment. "It's always being improved. If I had to guess, I'd say about thirty thousand. We have a large underground prison that can hold S-SS inmates, but they're judged differently. Their crimes don't place them, but their abilities and strengths do. S-SS are our strongest prisoners. We have about 15,000 of those."

Thirty thousand was the size of a small army. "How do you feed and care for them?"

He shook his head. "We don't have the manpower, so often they feast on each other. As for getting sick, if they die, they're burned in their cells. Nobody leaves this place, even for small crimes. They're here to die despicably."

If that was true, the school was nothing more than a dictatorship. "Then everyone in the school has to follow a strict line."

"If you're in a general's army, you're impervious to this place. You're punished by your general. Half the time, it isn't even punishment. You just have to lay low for a while. Students from other nations who slip up even once are put in here. That quells any trouble in the school and the nations. I'm sure you knew this, but heads of families are immediately drafted. That's how they bypass war. They don't care for their people over their family."

We were near the bottom of the spiral, or so it seemed.

"So I have to do your bidding while I'm here? What if I fail in a mission?"

He shrugged. "You'd be labeled as incompetent and given fewer missions. After a while, you'd be sent back home in disgrace."

That didn't sound like a bad idea, but to destroy the school, I needed all the information I could muster. I wasn't even sure it was possible to destroy the school. The prison would be a key target to hit first, but even if that succeeded, the prisoners were already dead inside. Getting them to convert back to society would be nearly impossible.

Still, it wasn't right to keep them in there. I had to set that problem aside for later. No need to worry about it right away.

"Kit, I wanted to ask why you followed in your father's footsteps."

I looked at him. "I don't understand. I never met him, nor have I ever spoken to him. How could I know what he did in his life?"

Alftiz' voice became softer, which was different from before. "Your father was a brilliant fighter, strong-willed and someone who never gave up no matter the foe. He and Kilyon were like brothers. It doesn't surprise me that you're with him, but what does surprise me is the amount of power you're controlling. If you really wanted to, you could have killed everyone when we met, and nothing could have stopped you. I have to admit it would take all three generals to stop you, and only to hold you back. They couldn't kill you. Like your father, you're a strong one."

We finally reached the bottom and entered a wide room of stone. Looking around, I saw no passageways out.

Alfitz walked to one wall and pushed open a door. "Welcome to our academy. It's a pleasure to have you."

Light struck my face, and I smelled a fresh breeze. Birds flew above tall buildings of stone and wood. It was larger than any capital I saw or heard of. Thousands of people walked around, all in the same uniform, black with an insignia on the back of a shield with the four flames surrounding it.

"This is amazing. Why are those buildings so tall?"

He laughed. "The engineers who built them called them skyscrapers because of their height. Most of the buildings here are that size. The schools are all rectangles. They're posted in each branch. The school is still separate from the nation, but there are no restrictions for people who want to learn anywhere.

"In the heart of the city is where the generals and our headmaster live. Our armies are in barracks over there, too. If there's a problem in the school or out, the nations are able to mobilize quickly."

It was astonishing to see all those skyscrapers and people moving so closely together. It looked more like a utopia, not a military school.

"So what happens now?" I asked.

He raised a hand, and a carriage arrived and stopped. "I will take you to your comrades before one of them burns down the building. I'm sure the other generals and the headmaster wish to see you, too. Let's be off."

We got into the carriage. Marcus stood just outside the door to the prison.

"Sir, I'll be leaving now. Have a safe trip." He bowed and turned around.

Alfitz closed the carriage door. "Don't think badly of him. He's had a hard life. Seeing you wasn't easy for him."

The carriage moved away.

"What do you mean? What have I done?"

He pointed out the window at the plethora of shops offering everything from food to clothing to armor to potions.

"This is a nation in its own right," he said. "For some time now, there's been a ripple moving through the people. It's subtle but there if you can see it. Poverty is rising. There are factions in the city who would like to gain more power. If we aren't careful, we could face civil war."

Why is he talking to me like this? I wondered. *He's treating me almost like a son.*

"Our mission will be to root out some of those organizations," I said. "Since we're in the city, that means you want it done timely and quietly."

He smiled. "Very good. Yes, the headmaster will undoubtedly give you and your companions that assignment. You may be part of my army, but he's in charge of everything. What he says, goes. I'm just letting you know in advance. The use of deadly force is an enviable thing. Don't feel bad for what must happen."

They clearly didn't care as long as they got the results they wanted. I sensed that the factions he was talking about had the potential to cause a disaster, but that would work nicely for me.

"Well, then, I'll have to do everything I can to make sure their horrible crimes end."

We rode along quietly. I peered out the window periodically. It was a beautiful city. There weren't many trees or grass. It seemed like a world unto itself, filled with marvelous inventions.

The carriage slowed.

"Here we are," he said. "I hope you enjoy your stay."

He got out, and I followed to a beautiful stone skyscraper taller than the rest. Fountains in front of the building added to its splendor. Cherry blossom trees sat fifty feet apart in the shape of a box around the courtyard. Several guards stood at the entrance.

"So this is where all the figureheads live," I said.

He chuckled. "Indeed, and now you and your companions."

As we walked, I saw people around the square staring at us as if we were unusual.

"What's with all the people staring? It's putting me off."

His hand slapped my back. "They want to see the son of the infamous Tellium."

I didn't look at him. "Well, maybe I should give them a show."

Chaos flames flew into the sky and exploded into cyclist flowers. The people cheered in excitement.

"That was a show, indeed. I didn't think you had a kind bone in your body."

I looked away for a moment.

When we reached the doorway, three guards stopped us.

"Sorry, General, but he must be detained before he can enter."

Alfitz turned red. "What did you say? You intend to cuff one of my men? On whose order?"

The soldier was clearly frightened. "Sorry, Sir, but the orders come from the headmaster himself."

Alfitz calmed himself. "Not that it matters. Sorry, Kit. Is this all right with you?"

I held out my hands. "Like you said, it doesn't make much difference. I could break them with a flick of my wrist."

The guards handcuffed me.

"OK," the guard said. "He's safe to see the headmaster."

Two guards opened the glass doors, and we walked into a large, open room with marble floors and the ceiling painted with images of the first war of the nations. Hundreds of people were in the reception area, all standing around in the same uniform and talking.

"Where do we go now, Alfitz?"

He pointed to doors leading into other parts of the building. When we walked toward them, people stared at us. A small panel sat on the wall, and Alfitz touched one of the stones with an arrow on it. I heard something moving, then the doors slid open sideways to reveal a small room big enough for only a few people at a time.

He walked in, and I followed. The doors closed behind us, and he pressed the top stone on a panel on the right that held at least sixty stones with numbers. He added some of his flame, and I felt the box we were in rising with enough pressure to force my knees to bend.

"What is this thing?" I asked.

He slapped the wall to demonstrate it was made of metal. "We call it a lift. A Terra Nation operator powers it. You add some of your power to one of those stones, and it transmits that to the operator room. They force the lift up to the desired floor."

It sounded very useful, and I wondered if it could be used without a Terra operator. "What's the headmaster like?"

He thought for a moment. "Well, in short, he's a little crazy."

I glanced at him. "Do you mean ha-ha crazy, or suck-on-his-thumb crazy?"

He shook his head. "More like I-killed-your-entire-family-and-made-you-dance-on-their-graves crazy."

That sounded like a psychopath, not a crazy person, but I didn't have time to worry about it. The lift stopped, and the doors opened.

Alfitz walked forward, between tanks of water as tall as the ceiling, filled with fish swimming around. We continued walking and stopped when we reached a large room surrounded by the heads of beasts hanging on the walls. Weapons ranging from swords to new items I didn't know hung with them.

The headmaster's chair was turned away from us, as he stared out the window at the city. "So this is the boy, Tellium's son? Do you know who the mother is?"

Alfitz shook his head.

"That's a shame. Nevertheless, he's now part of your army."

The chair turned around. "Welcome to my city. My name is Antilunis Calsyus, the ruler of all this land."

He wore a round hat with cloth that draped over the sides and back. His dark-red robes had the Celestial symbol on them.

"You're the head of the Celestial Nation?" I asked.

He chuckled. "Oh, heavens, no. I was, but my family was all but destroyed by someone unknown. I came here and made this my home with a new name."

He waved his hands, and the cuffs and chains fell off my wrists.

"You're a Terra nation descendant as well?"

He nodded and said, "Yes. I house four flames within my body. Very few can hold that much power, but I sense you know how that is."

We stared at each other. "I'm not sure what you mean. I simply wield the power of chaos, nothing else." I took out my smoke container and removed one. With a snap of my finger, I lit it with chaos flame and inhaled.

"I can see that. I hope you'll supply me with some enjoyment while you're here. Your companions have been antsy to see you. Make sure they stay in line while they're here. It would be awful if anything bad happened to them because of their insolence."

I smiled and flicked ash away. "I'm quite aware of that. I'll make sure they behave. If I'm not mistaken, though, I think there's something else on your mind."

He clapped twice. "Very good. I do, indeed, have a request, your first request to be honest. Alfitz has already told you there are some parasites within the city who are causing us some trouble. I want them dealt with. I take no prisoners, so make that apparent. If you find them, obliterate them all, even the women and children. If you can't follow orders, I'll be sure to punish your companions for your mistakes."

If he really was a quad flame, I could be facing the fight of my life. I was only a tri, and he had many more years of practice. He appeared to be in his late forties, like Kilyon. I would have to watch myself very carefully, much more than I originally thought.

"I assure you I won't fail you. What should I do now, Headmaster?"

He stood. "Alftiz, show him to his quarters. For God's sake, don't let him or his companions kill any more of my men. It's so hard to find replacements these days."

A shiver went down my back. I glanced back quickly but didn't see a threat, so why did I feel as if multiple people were watching?

"I will, Sir," Alfitz said. "He won't be a problem."

He turned, and I followed him. A quick peek back showed figures moving behind us. I was right. There *were* other people in the room, but how did they mask themselves? Hadn't Alfitz done that somehow?

He noticed my look and shook his head, as we entered the lift. He pressed the button for *30*, the door closed, and we descended.

"You can already tell I use magic, not flames. I'm demonkin."

I had an odd feeling about him since we met. Now it was obvious. "What does that have to do with invisibility?"

"It's not invisibility. It's more a temporal distortion. We aren't technically in this dimension, but we can still move around. It's a rare gift for our kind. We walk a very thin line between the dimensions."

It sounded insanely helpful. "What could hurt you in that situation? If you're just a temporal distortion, you can't be harmed."

He laughed. The lift door opened, and we walked into a long hallway with doors on both sides.

"Technically, that's true, but if I receive a fatal wound in this dimension, I would receive half the damage on the other side."

"How long does that last?"

We stopped before a door, and he turned toward me. "That's difficult to say. For myself, I can last about half an hour without combat. In combat, maybe half that, assuming I'm at full capacity that day. Some have trained themselves to last far longer and can managed combat for a full hour."

I reached for the silver handle on the door.

"Be careful, Kit. I can protect you only so much here. You have to gain other people's trust, although I doubt that will be a problem for you."

He started to walk away.

"What if I can't kill just in his name?" I asked. "Would he really punish me for that?"

He stopped with his back to me. "Indeed. Not only that, but I don't believe he should rule. Since no one opposes him, he stays, and because of that, his rule is law. Be careful."

He continued down the hall.

I looked at the door again and saw my name on a little plaque. Turning the knob, I opened the door and saw another long hall with dozens of paintings on blue walls. When I closed the door, I heard a clash farther in and rushed quickly toward the sound, drawing my sword.

I slid across the floor at the end and saw the girls in the kitchen with a huge mess everywhere. Flour was thrown all over, utensils and food lay everywhere, and all three seemed to be drenched in sauce.

"Which one of you wants to tell me what happened?" I asked.

They looked at each other, all pointing fingers at someone else.

I rubbed my forehead and took a step, but my foot hit something slick. I fell backward and hit the floor hard enough to drop my sword. "You three are so ridiculous.

They came to sit around me and smile.

"I'm glad you're safe, My Lord," Valis said.

"I'm happy you're safe, too, Master. It's been lonely," Ruby added.

I sat up slowly, and Razele hugged me. "Thank you for what you did in the planes, but you didn't have to be so foolish. We would have figured it out."

I wrapped an arm around her. "Maybe, but I like a more-direct approach, if you haven't noticed."

We shared a laugh. I saw Valis and Ruby looking jealous.

"Lord, why her?" Ruby latched onto my free side.

"Maybe it's because Kit doesn't want to be smothered to death."

Ruby's face went red. "Again, Lamb Prey, maybe you shouldn't have a washboard for a chest."

I chuckled, and they stopped to look at me.

"My Lord, are you all right? Did you hit your head hard?" Ruby asked.

I shook my head and kept laughing softly. "No, my dear. I didn't. I'm just happy to be back. It seems like it's been awhile since I saw you. That prison was gross, I might add."

They were furious.

"Prison?" Ruby snapped, standing up. "For what, Master? I'll kill him!"

I took her wrist and pulled her back to my lap, where her sauce-covered hair smacked my face.

"If you're talking about Alfitz, he's the one who got me out. Now we're part of his army, so refrain from killing anyone for now. Just enjoy yourself, and please don't cook anything."

They looked at the kitchen just as something crashed to the floor, shattering and making them wince.

"Yes, Master. That may be a wise choice. We'll leave that up to you."

They stood and helped me to my feet. Razele picked up my blade and handed it to me. "Here. You probably shouldn't leave it far from you."

I sheathed it. "Thank you, Razele. How is the house and the city?"

Ruby jumped in excitement. "It's amazing. I never saw any-thing like it. All the roads are smooth. There are lifts, and there are lights everywhere powered by Celestial flyers. They also have running water, showers, and toilets from the Kai flyers. We have everything for an easy life, and it's all because of the nations."

A utopia might be overselling it. "That's good to hear, as long as you're happy and safe. Do you know what happens next?"

"Yes," Razele said. "We have our classes and lessons. We have books and robes and everything we need, but there are no schedules for you, and your uniform is very different than ours."

I looked without seeing the items she mentioned. Razele and Ruby ran to a bedroom. I looked at the living room windows, which were open to allow moonlight to pour in. The walls didn't seem very strong, although I sensed they were powered by flames. The place was incredible.

I walked to a piece of furniture and sat, feeling my body become slowly absorbed. I spread my arms across the back just as Valis came over.

"Master, can I sit by you?"

When I nodded, she sat beside me and scooted closer. Ruby and Razele came from the bedroom, and Valis quickly scooted away. I stood, as Ruby brought over a package that had already been opened. Pulling back the paper, I saw a black robe. When I lifted it out, something fell to the floor.

It was a mask made of some hard material that was warm to the touch. There were holes for the eyes but nothing for the nose. It looked like it was cast for my face. Black flames were painted over it, with a sun and moon on opposite sides being smothered by chaos.

"This was in it, too, Lord." Ruby held a small card in her hands.

I set down the mask and studied the writing on the card.

You are now one of the order, an élite assassin squad. Don't mess up. You don't exist, so it doesn't matter if you die.

I tossed it aside, but Razele picked it up and read it with a smile. "I'm assuming he doesn't know your true power, Kit?"

I put on the robe and mask. "No, he doesn't. That will be useful. The new job he gave me will be of even greater use."

Walking to a mirror, I looked at myself. I was scary. A half moon was embroidered over my heart, and the black robes moved easily when I did. I felt many needles inserted along the inner lining of the sleeves. In the middle, I found small knives with an assortment of vials.

"It appears I'm carrying a lot of expensive things. Any idea what they are?"

They shook their heads. I turned and faced them. "How do I look?"

Valis seemed shaky. "You look really scary, Master."

Ruby waved that aside. "Oh, please. He looks tough and strong."

Razele shook her head. "He looks magnificent, like a shadow, one who's always watching over the ones he loves."

I nodded to her. "Indeed. I need all three of you to watch each other a lot more than before. We're in a totally different place now. We have no idea how many enemies are here. It would be easy to call all of them our enemy, but Alfitz is someone I can trust besides you three. Play nice."

They nodded.

"Well, we have a busy day ahead. Get some sleep. Do you all have a room?"

They looked at each other.

"We do, My Lord, but we decided we won't stay in them," Ruby said.

I removed the mask and asked, "Then where will you sleep?"

They pointed at me.

"I see. That settles it, then. Do you know where *our* room is, or should I guess?"

Razele took my hand and led me to the room they came out of earlier. When I walked in, I saw the floor was covered in blue carpet with a large bed, three different dressers, and another adjacent room.

"This is the bedroom," she said.

I saw gold trim around the walls, which were painted to resemble a forest. "It's nice. We should get some rest. Tomorrow will be a long day."

They cleaned up before bed, and we got in together. The mattress was as soft as a cloud. I lay on my back, while all three of them lay on or against me. I was so comfortable, I fell asleep in seconds.

14

A soft creak on the floor woke me. I summoned flames in a shield around all of us and sat up, drawing my sword.

A black shadow emerged from the wall. "I'm from the order, Kit. I'm here with location details and your first target. Do you accept?"

I sheathed my sword but kept the wall of flame surrounding the girls. "I do."

"My name is Eli." His mask was completely red with glowing purple eyes.

"Nice to meet you. Who is my target?"

He handed me a piece of paper. "A shopkeeper known as Dimitry Celinum. His crime is distributing weapons and armor to enemy factions. You will cut off his head and bring it to the headmaster."

I studied the paper, which informed me Dimitry sold the goods in bulk from his shop. "I understand. Which part of town is this?"

Eli waved me to follow. We walked into the living room, and I saw the mess in the kitchen had been totally cleaned up. He took out a map and placed it on the table.

"The city is broken up into many districts. The city is a circle connecting each nation, and each one has its own district that leads partway into the city. In the heart of the city is the headmaster's building. That's where we are. The Chaos district is south of here. It has become a deserted part of town after the collapse of the Chaos Nation. Many folk were driven out and forced back into the Chaos Nation, but some stayed. That's where we have the most trouble. A lot of gangs and pirates live there."

I looked at the map. "Why keep it like this? Why not destroy it all?"

Eli shook his head. "Many others would agree with you, but the fact is, there are many lines connecting everything in the city. If you destroy that area, you would also cause mass destruction across the rest of the city. We have to go in to remind them there's no place for their kind."

I looked at the window and saw dawn had begun. "I guess I should get to work. I'll start by asking around the area to see if I can find his store, then I'll bring back his head."

Eli vanished in black flames. It seemed like the only people left from my nation were being used as assassins. It could be worse.

I walked to the bedroom and made the flames vanish.

Razele was sitting up and looked at me. "What happened? Is everything OK? I woke up and saw your flames surrounding us."

I walked to the edge of the bed. "Yeah, it's OK. I have to leave, though, so make sure the others are set for the day."

She got out of bed and came to wrap her arms around my neck. "Out to protect us again?"

I placed my hands on her warm waist. "Yes, for a little bit. Hurry up with what you're doing before the others see, and I have to kiss them all."

I felt her arms pull my head down. I kissed her soft, refreshing lips.

As she released me, she said, "I don't mind if you kiss them once in a while, but I like having you to myself sometimes."

I held her close. "I know. Make sure you watch them, especially Ruby. She's got a quick temper. I don't want to start a war immediately because of her. Have her restrain herself."

She held me tighter.

"What's wrong?"

She shook her head. "Thank you for this. I'll watch them."

I rubbed her back, then I let go of her and walked to the other side of the bed to kiss Ruby.

She slowly opened her eyes. "What's going on, My Lord?"

"Nothing. I'm leaving for a little bit. Don't do anything stupid while I'm gone."

She smiled. "I'll try."

I walked into the living room and put on my robe and mask.

"Kit, is this the right thing to do? I know what you want in the end, but is this the best way to proceed?" Razele asked.

I checked the strap for my sword and touched the needles inside the robe to make sure I could reach them easily. "I'm not sure. We all need more training and understanding of the world. This job will give me a way to make friends, but whether they're the right ones is irrelevant for the operation I have planned. That's a very large undertaking. We'll have a lot of enemies, so we have to make sure we have some very good allies."

I pushed the window open and stood on the ledge.

"Make sure you pick good allies. It would be bad if you found a traitor right off the bat."

I chuckled and felt sunlight on my face. Looking down at the streets, I stepped out and fell. Cold air struck my face. The sense of falling filled me. I summoned chaos and flew toward the south. Birds flew above me.

I looked down and saw people starting their day. Soon, I saw the Chaos district ahead. No one moved on its streets, making it resemble a ghost town. It was cut off from the rest of the city.

I landed on a building and looked at a door on the far side. Walking over to it, I didn't see a knob, so I kicked it hard enough to break it off and send it flying against the concrete wall.

There was no sign of anyone inside. Dust floated everywhere. I was a long time since anyone used that door.

A stairwell led down into the building. I went down to the first floor, where the lights were still activated, but the building seemed completely deserted.

The floor had the same layout as the room I was living in. All the doors were missing, and, as I walked past the doorways, I didn't see anyone. Everything had been broken and torn apart.

As I walked past a room, I heard something creak. Looking down, I saw I was walking on bare concrete, where the carpet had been destroyed years earlier. What could have made that sound?

I walked into the room on the left. It was a lot smaller than my bedroom, and I touched the wall. My finger came away covered in dust. I destroyed it with a small flame and walked farther into the building.

Two doors on the right were open, exposing corpses without any skin left, just bones. I stared at them.

"So this is the future of my nation," I muttered. "They were murdered or left for dead, and for what?'

I stood and burned the bones with a flick of my hand. "Rest in peace."

I walked farther into the building into what I presumed was the living room. Something squeaked underfoot. I picked up a small plush toy dragon. Hearing the creak again, I slipped the toy into a pocket and quietly drew my sword, walking forward carefully.

The sound came from a room on the right. I slowly came closer, hearing small footsteps scurrying about. I rushed in and summoned flames to encircle the walls, cutting off anyone's escape.

All I saw was a broken bed. I walked closer and kicked it, sending it into the flames to be burned. A girl jumped up and rushed me, stabbing my stomach with a small knife.

Her eyes were completely black, and she cried, as she fought. I went to my knees and stopped the flames.

She looked at her hands covered in blood and fell onto her butt, crying and holding her face with bloody hands.

I took the makeshift knife from my stomach and let the blood steam away. She looked at her hands, then at my wound.

"Are you hurt?"

I stood and waved my hand over the closed injury. "I'm fine. No harm, no foul. Can you tell me what you're doing in here?"

She shook off her hood to exposé rose-red hair. "I was hiding from somebody."

That piqued my interest. "Who would that be, if you don't mind my asking?"

She stared at my mask. "You should know. You're here to kill me. You all wear those things. I've been running for days. Why are you asking me?"

Why would the order chase her down? Had she seen them at work, or did she know more than she led on? I raised my hands, and she flinched, but I merely removed the mask and allowed flames to cover everything around us, cutting off anyone who might be watching.

"You're from the Chaos Nation," she said.

I nodded. "I was born there, but I was moved to the Kai Nation. After that, I grew up under Kilyon Icealis. He was my mentor and a father to me."

She was surprised. "You're part of the Icealis family and the Chaos Nation? Doesn't that mean you're dangerous?"

I laughed. "I don't know. You tell me. Do I look dangerous?"

She studied me, then slowly walked closer to touch my face before sitting down. "No. You don't seem dangerous, but looks can be deceiving."

She was right. Drawing my sword, I placed it on the floor between us. "Pick it up."

She was reluctant, but she finally touched it, and black flames surrounded it.

"It seems there are still some companions from the Chaos Nation who are alive."

She dropped the sword and tried to run, but the flames held her. She fought hard, but it was hopeless.

"Monster! What will you do with me now that you know?"

Why was she being so erratic? "There must be some misinformation about what's going on here. Let me apologize for that. I may work for the order, but I have no interest in hunting down targets unless they're on my hit list. As of now, you aren't. I just want to talk peacefully."

She stopped fighting to escape and gave me a strange look, one filled with hope and worry. "OK. I'll give myself up."

She still felt I would take her somewhere. "First off, why are you running from the order? Before you ask, I don't know."

She nearly bit her tongue. "I witnessed the massacre of the chaos residents who were here a couple weeks ago. Everything was fine, then the order came in bringing death and destruction for no reason. Most of the people living here were just normal civilians, trying to survive. The order didn't care. My parents and I lived in this part of the building."

She had to be lying. The corpses I burned were years old, not weeks. "Do you know how long it takes a body to desiccate like that? It's a lot longer than two weeks."

She hesitated for a second time, then tried so speak only to stop herself.

"If you don't tell me, I can't help you."

She sighed. "It's because the headmaster isn't human. He's something I never saw before. He stared at them, and the bodies decayed until their bones were all that was left. That's why I hesitated to tell you. It doesn't make sense, but it's true. I swear it."

It seemed the headmaster was far more powerful than I thought. That might become an issue. "Do you know of a shopkeeper in these parts called Dimitry?"

Her eyes grew wide. "Of course. He's the one who has been feeding us. He sells to rebels and other factions to give us a better life. Why?"

I picked up the sword, and her eyes were still on it. "Because I need to talk to him. It's pretty important. I'm looking for some new weapons."

She nodded and stood. "I can take you to him if you like, but it'll cost you some coin."

I reached into the sack the master gave me and dumped out forty gold pieces. Her eyes lit up.

"Will that suffice?"

She nodded and grabbed all of them. "Yes! With this, I can live a normal life."

She stood, and I didn't think she'd live long enough to spend even half that much, the poor girl. "How old are you?"

"I'll be eighteen soon."

I chuckled.

"What's so funny? You can't be much older than me."

I realized I offended her and waved a hand. "It's just that you're so short, and you're nearly eighteen."

She turned red. "Well, I'm five-feet-two-inches tall. Leave me alone."

I laughed and stopped the flames around us. Sunlight peered into the room again.

"Good. Now please escort me." I walked to the hole in the wall."

"Sir, I'm afraid of flying."

I lifted her in my arms. "Then don't go."

I walked off the edge into the air. She screamed, even as I summoned flames to bring us softly to the ground.

"That was awesome!" she said. "Can we do that again?"

I looked at her and shook my head. Why was she thrown into such a life? It certainly didn't seem fair.

"Sir, are you all right?"

I shook my head and focused my thoughts. "Yes. Sorry. I was lost in thought. Lead the way." I pulled on the mask, and we walked side-by-side.

"Tell me, Little One, why'd you stay here and not enlist in the military when you had the chance?"

She was quiet for a few minutes. We rounded a street corner, and she led me across the street. "It's because I wasn't strong enough. I tried, but I couldn't summon anything. I had the power, but something in me didn't connect. I'm a flyer without any power. That's why I was so shocked when your sword showed my power. I didn't think that was possible."

We walked down a straight section of road. "The sword doesn't care whether you want to give it power. It takes it for itself. I have to be careful when I use it. My father wielded it in the war, and it must've liked large amounts of power, because it tries to drain me at times."

"So why did Kilyon train you? Is he a criminal?"

I scratched my chin and chuckled inwardly. "He and my father were brothers. I'm assuming my father asked him to watch over me and train me. To be honest, Kilyon did a good job, especially in sword combat."

She grabbed my sword arm. "Will you protect and train me?"

I stared ahead. "How close are we?"

She withdrew her arm. "Straight ahead. You'll find him in the shop. He rarely leaves."

I saw a makeshift building without any defenses, although the windows were boarded up. "Thank you. If I were you, I'd get as far from here as possible. Run fast."

"What about you?"

I drew my sword. "I don't want to kill you, but after this, I'm sure I'll be given the order to hunt you down. After this, we're enemies. Run, and for your kindness, I'll let you go this time."

She began crying and turned to run.

"I'm sorry," I said under my breath. "You don't deserve this foul world. It's not good enough for you."

I pushed open the shop door and heard a bell ring. It was an old shop of dinning but with a few differences. I saw a huge stockpile of weapons and stones. Where had he gotten all this, and why leave it out in the open?"

"I'm coming, Sir. Sorry for the wait."

He saw my mask and turned to run, but I jumped the counter and cut the tendon on the back of his leg. He dropped to the ground.

"You're going to kill me and stop me from helping people who need it?" he asked.

I saw I'd cut his leg deeper than intended. He didn't have much time. "That's not why I'm here. I need all your contacts so I can oppose the city and free the people. For that, someone must die. I must ask if you're willing to be murdered for this."

He lay on his back and smiled. "In the back is a safe with all the information you require. If what you say is true, I gladly accept my death."

I drove my sword into his neck and cut off his head. Blood ran across the tile floor as if trying to cover everything in sight.

I walked into the kitchen and saw a door in the back. Inside was a small room filled with cluttered paper. A safe sat in one corner. I walked over and touched it with one hand, melting the lock and hinge mechanism. The door fell open. A single notebook lay in there with a peculiar, heart-shaped crystal filled with chaos. It wasn't a slave crystal, though.

I stuck it into a pocket and placed the notebook in another pocket before grabbing a smoke, lighting it with red flames, and sheathing the sword. I walked out of the building, taking the head with me, and let chaos flames ignite everything inside.

"Sorry, Guy," I said. "I wish we could have met on better terms, but things happen for a reason."

Sunlight struck me once I was on the street. Two masked figures appeared on either side of me.

"So the order is quick," I said. "I have the head." I tossed it to the one on the right.

"Good. I'll report this on your behalf. Thank you for destroying their supplies, too. Nice touch. We have another mission for you. It should be easy for someone with your expertise."

I knew what they were going to ask and prayed the girl was far from me.

"We need a captured spy to give us some information. Like all spies, she's hard to crack. Would you mind helping us?"

It wasn't possible that they didn't know that I talked with the girl. "Of course. Where is she?"

They pointed. "In that tower on the top floor. There are five order agents already up there. She's giving them a hard time, so make it quick."

I nodded and summoned flame so I could fly up there. I came in through a broken window and walked down a hallway. Two agents saw me come in.

"Kit, she's in here."

I looked into a room where three agents surrounded someone with a bag over her head. Deep cuts showed on her arms, legs, and stomach.

Stepping forward, I asked, "What's her name?"

An agent holding a knife said, "No idea, Sir. She's been hard to control."

Her legs shook, and she wore different clothing than the other girl I met, so I was relieved I didn't have to torture that one. "Give me a few moments. If you hear screams, ignore them. I'll get your answers."

They bowed and left the room, closing the door behind them. I walked closer and unsheathed my sword, touching her neck with the tip. "Who are you?"

Wincing in fear, she shook her head.

"What's your name?" I demanded, growing impatient.

She shook her head again. I slammed her chest with the butt end of the sword her torso cracked on the inside and heard her gasp for air. She started crying, and I sheathed the sword. My fist struck her head twice then drew a needle from my sleeve.

"I could give you a reasonable death. We could end this now. There's no need for you to suffer anymore. If you give me the information I need, you can die easily."

She nodded and stopped crying. I straightened and smoothed out my robe. "Thank you for that. Now tell me."

I waited a few seconds, as she gulped for breath. When she spoke, her voice was raspy and frightened.

"My name is Entity. People call me En. I'm sorry, Kit."

My heart almost stopped. It couldn't be! The stool collapsed to the side, and the bag fell off her face. It was the girl with the black eyes. She was fading quickly.

I went to her and knelt. "I'm sorry. I knew this would happen."

She cried a bit more. "That's OK. I'm the last member of the Chaos Nation head family. With me gone, there's no one to protect our people. They'll completely finish us."

I cut through her restraints with my dagger. "Are you from the Exporoc family?"

She shook her head. "No, Sir. They were all killed after my family was murdered. I'm the sole survivor. I've been on the run for years. We were the Lunerworfs, a strong family, but the Exporoc head member slaughtered all of my family. His name was Tellium."

Her pulse grew weaker. She didn't have much time. What could I do? I was supposed to kill her, but I felt a strong urge to save her. Where could I hide her?

I punched the floor in frustration.

"It's OK if I die at your hands. I'm OK with that. Please finish the job, so I don't suffer anymore. I've been alone for so long, I just want to die."

I looked at her. "Those corpses in the room weren't your parents, were they?"

She shook her head and looked up at me. "No. they were like my parents, though, the closest thing I had to a mother and father."

I pulled out a needle from my cloak and reached for her throat. She gulped, but I suddenly felt something become heavy in my pocket, as if trying to drag me down.

"Why do you hesitate? Finish me off. It's painful."

I pulled my hand back and forced my eyes closed. I shoved the needle forward fast, before anything could stop me.

Something exploded. Opening my eyes, I saw the gem hovering over the two of us.

"I'm sorry, Kit, but I can't let you kill this one," Celnius said. "She's the last of the family. You must take responsibility for her."

"What took you so damn long? I could've used your help a while ago."

She laughed. "My apologies. I've been wiping her memory from all the others. She's nothing more than a ghost now. Let the stone do its job, and I'll be in contact soon."

The stone hovered at her chest, sending out black strings. Looking down at my own chest, I saw green strings come out to attach themselves to the black ones. All the strings turned green, and the stone shot into her chest. Her body glowed green, then the color vanished.

I lifted her in my arms. "Are you OK, En?"

Her eye color changed from pure black to silver with a faint ring of black. "What happened?"

I shrugged. "I don't know, but we need to get out of here." I pointed her toward the window and walked to the door.

When I opened it, all the agents held their heads in confusion. One looked at me.

"Sir, why are we here?"

It seemed Celnius really did erase their memories. "Just a simple high-value target assassination. Thanks to you it went effortlessly. Congratulations. I'll be back at my house."

They seemed confused but glad to hear the story I gave. I closed the door and walked to the window.

"What about me?" she asked. "Where do I go?"

I shoved her outside and heard her scream. I jumped out behind her and caught her. She looked up at me with a look that should have killed me, as I caught her in my arms. Turning on my flames, I flew toward my new home.

I stopped outside the window and touched it. When it opened, we hovered inside until our feet touched the floor.

"This is where you live? It's kind of big for one person, isn't it?"

I chuckled. "Yeah. Three others live with me. They might surprise you. When they come in, do your best not to start a fight. I don't need to clean you off the floor."

She walked over and punched my arm. "That was rude."

"What do you want me to call you, Entity or En?"

She looked up at me. "Well, we're friends, aren't we?"

I scratched my face in thought, and she punched me again. "OK, OK. I submit. We're friends."

She smiled and sat on the couch. "That's fine. En is my name."

"Ruby will be in soon. She's a vampire. Then there's Razele, who's from the Aurora Nation. Then there's Valis from the Kai Nation."

She looked at me oddly. "Why do you have so many women living with you? Are you a pervert?"

Smiling, I sat beside her, and she scooted away.

"Oh, come on. I won't do anything."

She stared at me.

"Would you like to know how I met them?"

She nodded cautiously. "You didn't enslave them, did you, Pervert?"

I smiled, realizing she wouldn't let go of the idea. "No, I didn't. On my journey here, Razele became my first companion when I saved her from the Aura Nation. I can't go into why just now. Ruby was found under a mountain when Razele and I were hunting a basilisk. She had been turned to stone. When I first found her, she punched her fist right through me.

"Then there's Valis. My older cousin had three slave girls. He was giving our family a bad name, but he was also the next head. It was obvious he was a horrible person, so I executed him. The only one of his slaves I could save was Valis."

En scooted back closer. "I'm sorry for calling you a pervert. That was rude of me before I knew the facts. I sense you intend to let me live in your home."

I patted her head. The lights went off, and all the windows became blocked. I felt a familiar presence coming.

I shielded En with my flames and stood. Celnius, once again dressed provocatively, appeared. I released the flames from around En, who saw the goddess.

"Kit, who is she? Am I going to die?" She slumped back.

"En, I'd like to introduce you to Celnius, the Goddess of Chaos."

En immediately jumped to her feet and bowed. Celnius looked over at me.

"Why don't you ever act like this when you see me?"

I waved her questions off, and she giggled.

"Rise, My Child. There's no need to put yourself in such a state for me."

En looked up, then slowly stood. "Goddess, you're the reason I'm here."

Celnius walked closer to her and placed one hand on her head. "No. You're alive because of Kit. He saved you and made you his little sister."

I choked and began coughing.

"What?" I asked, Celnius turning toward me. "There are many stones in this world kit. Some can block all low-level attacks, while some can bind slaves. There are even some that can bind two into a family with the same name. That makes her part of your family, which now houses four flames."

I laid back my head and rubbed my temples.

"I'm not sure I understand, Goddess," En said. "How can that be? I was born in the Chaos Nation, part of a head family."

Celnius waved her hand, taking a smoke from me and lighting it. "Kit is the head of the Exporoc family. He was also born in the Chaos Nation, but his mother was from a head family in the Celestial Nation. That gives him a large amount of power. Since you have merged into one family, you have the same powers. Well, not quite all, but a majority."

En stared at me. "You're the head of the Exporoc family? Why didn't you tell me?"

I flicked ash from my smoke into a cup. "Because I didn't want to make you angry. I know the horrible things my father did, and I didn't want to lose your trust."

She stood and glared at me. "Your father murdered my family! He slaughtered my parents!"

Celnius placed a hand on her shoulder. "He did it all for power, but Kit didn't kill them. Kit would never want the power that came with it."

En looked up at her. "What power, Goddess?"

I handed Celnius my blade and stood. She plunged it through my heart. Blood rushed up through my mouth. I coughed and fought the pain, as everything healed once the sword was pulled out.

En ran over to me in shock, placing one hand over my heart. "Please don't die, Kit!"

Blood streamed away from the wound, as it closed.

"You're all right! You aren't human."

I shook my head. "You're right in a sense. I'm human, but I can't die. My father passed that power to me thanks to the goddess."

En turned back to the goddess. "You let him kill my family?"

She shook her head. "I was strongly against it. I tried to stop him, but he didn't listen and committed the worst taboo of all. I was able to save only one person, and that, my dear, was you."

En slumped into a chair. I flicked more ash into the cup and inhaled before blowing smoke into the room.

"I can't fix what my father did," I said. "What I can do is give you a better life to make up for what he did. I understand that's not enough, but for now, it's something."

En looked at me, then at Celnius, who smiled.

"That's OK," En said. "Thank you. You've saved my life three times now, so I won't hate you, but I won't forgive Tellium."

I nodded in understanding. I wouldn't forgive someone who murdered my family, either, but the man she hated was already dead. "Good. For the time being, you have to stay here. There's plenty of food and everything else. You can choose your own room. The other girls chose not to have one."

She frowned and looked at me. "What do you mean?"

Celnius giggled. "It's because young Kit has them all falling for him."

I sighed and tried not to look at either of them.

"I knew you were a perv."

I smiled.

"Well, your brother is a perv," Celnius added, "but he's a nice one."

En lowered her head. "Brother? I...I never had one before."

"You have one now," I said. "I won't promise to be the best one in the world, but I'll protect you. That's the best I can do for now."

She looked at me with tears in her eyes, so I put an arm around her.

"Your troubles are over for now. No one in the world will hurt you if I'm around." I released her and walked toward Celnius. "You owe me for this. I don't know your plans, but I expect something for doing this."

She waved her hand. A black beam washed over En, who was immediately unconscious. "I gave her a parting gift, but I also knocked her out. The poor little girl doesn't need to hear this."

I smashed the smoke with both hands and felt them burn, then I dropped the butt into the cup before crossing my arms to look at her. "And what would that be?"

She walked around me slowly, trailing a finger across my chest. "Come now. Don't you wish you could take me after everything? You must be wanting something exotic, correct?"

I watched her circle me, then she stopped in front of me, her face filled with excitement and desire.

"I do, but I'm not after your body."

She ran her fingers down my face. Her skin was cold but inviting. I wanted her, but I made myself stop, knowing she was deliberately enticing me.

"Well, you do have those three girls for that. Maybe you'll allow a goddess to show you the real ways of pleasure." Her voice grew more seductive and tantalizing.

"Maybe someday, but not today. I need a favor from you."

She embraced me, talking softly against my neck. "Oh? What kind of favor would that be, My Dear? Do you wish for immortality for all of them, or maybe the power to give it to others? Do you wish for the power of a god?"

It was as if she could read my mind. "To be honest, I don't wish to make everyone immortal, just those who are close to me."

Her hair rubbed against my neck. "I can oblige two of them, but not all, at least not yet. It would be no fun if all of them had it at once. What do you say?"

Two was a gracious offer, but that would leave two others without it. I had to think it over carefully. Ruby healed faster than all the others combined. En didn't dare leave the building for a while. It had to be Valis and Razele.

"Valis and Razele will do for now, please."

She pulled back slowly. "Wise choice, but is it the right one? Only time will tell." She snapped her fingers. "It is done. They are no longer human."

I nodded. "Thank you."

"Next time, Kit, you will owe me instead. Remember that." She walked away from me. "Oh, yes. Kit, there's something else. Be careful gods are noticing you."

Black smoke swirled around her, as she faded into nothing. I wondered what made a god. Were they humans who became drunk on power, or were they born to watch over us? That had always bothered me.

The door opened, and the girls entered the hall. The door behind them closed quickly.

"Ah, that stupid boy. He's so revolting." Ruby was irritated.

"It's OK, Ruby. Ignore him. He isn't stupid enough to try anything."

They walked in and saw me.

"Hello, Girls. Did you have a bad day?"

Valis seemed nervous. "No, it's just that Ruby almost started a fight."

"No! It was that insolent maggot! How dare he touch me?" Ruby asked.

I chuckled and walked toward them. "So was it an accident, Ruby, or did he deliberately go out of his way to make you uncomfortable?"

Her eyes flushed with anger. "That boy did it on purpose. If I ever see him again, I'll cook him."

When I touched her head, her anger washed away. "What will happen if you go on a rampage? I'm not saying you're wrong. If it bothered you that much, he did something he wasn't supposed to, but I'm the one who will be punished for your actions."

She lowered her head. "I'm sorry. I forgot. I'm just feeling irritated."

I pulled my hand back and looked to Valis. "What about you? Did you have a hard day, too?"

She quickly shook her head. "No. I made some new friends and learned new things. I'm happy about that."

I looked at Razele, who gave Ruby a worried look. "And you?"

She looked at me. "The same. I made some new friends and have learned a lot. How was your day?"

I looked at the couch, and they suddenly noticed En. "I have all I need from you three, but she was left alone. I saved her from a death that would have come at a large cost to my nation."

Ruby walked over to study her. "My Lord, why do you two smell so familiar?"

Valis and Razele clenched their fists.

"Lord, did you do something with her?" Ruby asked.

I turned and waved my hands in the air. "No. You have the wrong idea. I swear."

Ruby and Razele shared a look, then shook their heads. Ruby's fist went through my gut. My organs tore, and blood rushed from my mouth and splattered on her.

Taking a slow breath, I said, "That was uncalled for. She's my sister."

Ruby immediately removed her fist. I dropped to my knees, as my organs healed. Once the pain subsided, I stood.

"I'm sorry, Lord. I was angry."

I patted her head. "You needed to blow off some steam. Remember what I told you when we met? I don't mind being your punching bag."

Ruby cried and held onto me. Razele remained where she was and stared at En.

"I didn't know you had a sister," Razele said.

I shook my head. "I didn't until today. I was an only child, but thanks to circumstances, she has become my blood sister."

Confusion filled Razele's face. "That doesn't make sense. You can't make someone a blood relative just because you want to, can you?"

"Well, no, but what if a goddess wants it? Then anything can happen."

Her eyes suddenly became bright. "Does that mean a goddess made her into your sister?"

When I nodded, the room became very quiet.

"Was it Celnius?" she asked, concerned.

Ruby became worried and looked at me. "Who's Celnius?

"She's the Goddess of Chaos. I've met her a few times. Apparently, my father knew her well."

Ruby was definitely unhappy about that. "So you're loving with a goddess? How rude is that?'

I shook my head. En stirred on her seat, and the three girls quickly surrounded her.

When En opened her eyes, she asked, "Kit, why am I surrounded by all these concubines?"

Ruby nearly pounced on her. I grabbed her waist and pulled her back.

"These are the girls I was telling you about," I said. "The one I'm holding back right now is Ruby, the vampire."

En looked at her. "She has beautiful eyes, like a field of flowers."

Ruby calmed down and blushed, looking away. "I'm good. I swear I won't attack."

I released her slowly, as Razele offered En her hand.

"Hello. I'm Razele. We're not concubines, though we feel the same way for Kit. It's nice to meet you."

En took her hand with a smile. "You're very pretty."

Ruby huffed. I patted her head to calm her.

Valis bowed. "I'm Kit's slave. The name is Valis."

En offered her hand. "From what Kit has told me, you're no slave. You're equal to all of us. It's nice to meet you, as well. I hope we can be good friends."

They shook hands.

"Thanks for saying that, Miss," Valis said.

I stood behind all of them. "Her name is Entity or En, which is what she likes to be called. Please be nice. Ruby, don't kill her."

Ruby bowed to En. "I'm sorry for losing my temper. I won't kill you."

En offered her hand. Ruby regarded it for a few moments, and I tensed, ready to intervene, but Ruby slowly took it and shook.

"I hope we can be friends, Ruby. It would be amazing."

Ruby looked at her. "Yeah, it would. Thank you."

The mood in the room slowly calmed.

"Girls, I need to talk to you. Something new has happened."

They all looked at me.

"Valis and Razele, I asked the goddess to give me something. She owed me a big favor."

They looked at each other, then Razele said, "When we were walking back to find Ruby, we were surrounded by black smoke that entered our bodies. We don't know what it was, but she assumed it was you protecting us. Now you're saying it was the goddess? What was it?"

I stood there and wondered, *Should I tell them or let them find out. If I tell them, they might think they're invincible, but that doesn't mean they can't be stopped.*

"You both are now immortal, like me. You've been given that gift. I'm sorry I didn't ask permission. I thought it would be a good thing."

They rushed forward and held me tightly.

"Neither of you are angry about it?" I asked.

They shook their heads. "No. We've been upset, because we couldn't be with you forever and would grow old. Now we don't have to."

Ruby became depressed.

"Ruby, I'll make sure you have the same power. I chose them first because of who you are. The situation is more dangerous for them."

She walked toward me. "I'm aware of that, and I'm glad they're immortal, but remember, you must make sure I can spend the rest of my life with you, too, or I'll never forgive you." She began to smile.

"Of course I will. I won't go anywhere without you at my side."

En stood. "What now? I'm curious."

The three girls and I glanced at the kitchen.

"What's the chances you three can cook without destroying the kitchen?" I asked.

Razele held up one hand with her forefinger and thumb only a tiny bit apart.

"I see."

En walked into the kitchen. "I'll need their help. I can cook. Maybe with my help, we can do it."

They followed.

"We can do this, Lord," Ruby said.

I nodded, and they started work. Behind me, I heard a door open and turned to see Alfitz. "Girls, I need to leave for a few minutes. Please don't destroy the kitchen."

I walked down the hall and heard En run after me, sliding to a stop. "You're coming back, right?"

"Of course I'll be back."

I walked off, as she walked back to the kitchen.

Alftiz looked at En. "I see you have a new girl. Who is she?"

We left the house. "A girl from the Kai Nation who was lost. I told her she could stay with me until she's settled."

He nodded and handed me a piece of paper. "That was kind of you. After all the stories I heard about you, I'm surprised at your kindness."

I studied the parchment.

Your first mission was an overwhelming success. We learned a lot from the head. Now I need you to hunt down this man and his family, if you will.

The parchment also explained that the man I was supposed to kill was from the Celestial Nation. In his mid-thirties, he came from a farming family. He recently came to the city to learn new things, but the information was rather vague. He and his wife had a little boy.

"What's the affiliation, then?" I asked.

Alfitz looked around before saying softly, "He's a suspected enhancer."

"A what? I don't know what this is. Sorry."

I studied the man's picture, trying to engrave his image in my mind. He had bright red spiky hair and crystal-white eyes. He was human, or seemed to be, although the skin on his arms was ragged all the way to his palms.

"An enhancer is someone who melds the body and enhancing stones together. He's half-human, half-catalyst. It's an unusual thing that's been cropping up lately. In hindsight, they're extremely dangerous. Even some of the order have been killed by this man, which is why you got the assignment."

I stuck the parchment into a pocket. "What kind of enhancement does he have?"

Alfitz took out another piece of paper. "This is what we know."

I saw a list of over thirty vitality stones, thirty defense, and forty momentum. "I don't understand about these stones. Care to explain?"

"Vitality stones mean that if you have an arm cut off and have one of those, the arm can grow back. If you sustain a stab wound to a vital organ, it takes at least five such stones to save you.

"Defense stones are tricky. Normally, ten defense stones are as effective as one star stone, but he has that many plus the addition of thirteen star stones. In theory, he can take on three SS-rated opponents and withstand a barrage of attacks for at least fifteen minutes before he runs out.

"As for momentum stones, as the name implies, they help with speed and balance. With one momentum stone, you can run a mile in two minutes. You could scale the castle in three. They're exceptionally useful for assassins. The problem is, they also have a negative side. It takes days to recover from using one. If you used five at one time, you would die. It's no wonder he was able to kill some of the order. We're stronger than SS rated, but if he killed them that easily, we don't know what that makes him."

"How widespread is the problem with enhancers?"

He shook his head. "We have no idea. It's been difficult enough to stop them. Some even take animal parts and exchange them for human ones for a better effect. As far as we know, your target hasn't gone that route, but we aren't sure how he can use as many stones as he has done without dying. It should be impossible."

I wondered how to use that information. "When does this need to be done?"

"In the dark. He's usually recharging at that time. Sometime within the next two nights would be best. Enhancers move around a lot and don't stay anywhere for long. It might take you two days just to locate him."

"I'll have to let the girls know. I'm sure it will be fine. Can you find a class for En?"

Confused for a moment, he nodded. "Of course. Do you know her attributes?"

I wasn't sure what to say. "She's chaos, so something along those lines sounds right. I'm aware you don't have many teachers, but anything would help."

He scratched his beard. "The only teacher we have is a generalist. I'd have to introduce En to her first. I can set up a meeting for tomorrow morning. I'll let you know how it turns out when you report back.

"Before I tell you anything else, the only proof we need is the son's head. The father must be completely destroyed. Don't leave anything behind. For the wife, make it a humane kill."

He started to walk away, then turned back. "Oh, and Kit? Good job. Maybe your dream will become a reality."

I watched him leave, then walked back through the door into the house and caught the smell of something delicious that made me drool. I quickly wiped my face. It didn't seem that long since I last ate, but it must have been. I could go a long time without food when necessary.

I walked through the hall and saw the girls cooking a feast. "I can see you're busy, so I'll go relax."

Before I could turn away, En tossed me an apron. "Oh, no. You help, too. There's no choice."

Sulking, I put on the apron, then walked to where they were working. "What would you like me to do?"

Ruby pointed to a bowl. "Your job is simple. You'll make sweet, delicious pancakes."

What was she talking about? I've never eaten pancakes, much less cooked them. "I'm not sure what those are. How do you know that?"

En looked at me. "I told her about them. They're very delicious. It's OK if you don't make them right. We can work with it. I wrote down the ingredients. If you follow that, you'll be golden."

I saw the list included three cups of flour, an egg, and some cinnamon. I did my best to follow the instructions and put it all into a bowl to mix. After adding water, it just looked like soup to me, so I shrugged and said, "What do I do now?'

En came over to check my work. "Good job. Now I'll take over from here. You're free to go. You just needed to help."

I flicked a finger against her forehead and walked to the living room to remove my sword and robe, laying them beside the couch.

The rest of the night passed quickly. We ate a splendid dinner. En fell asleep at the table the moment we finished eating. Razele and Valis put away the dishes while Ruby and I sat on the couch.

Ruby was also asleep, so I took out my metal case and lit a smoke. Grabbing a nearby ashtray, I dropped ashes into it and enjoyed a few quiet moments.

Razele and Valis finished their work and sat with us on the couch. As Razele leaned her head against Ruby, she asked, "What are your plans? My guess is you won't be spending the night here tonight."

I shook my head and looked out the window. It was late, and I had to leave soon. "You're correct. It'll be a few days this time. Can I count on you to watch them? I know you're immortal now, but you can still be captured and tortured, so be aware."

Her arms went around my shoulders. "I'm aware of the downfall with this. There's no need to worry. Everything will work out. Yes, I'll watch over them and your new sister."

I looked at En, who remained slumped at the table. "I wasn't expecting her. She was a curveball, but at least I can say my family's legacy isn't dead. Hers is. Once she joined my family, hers is no more."

Razele rubbed the back of my neck. "I know you did what you could, and she's alive, so that's something.'

I nodded and stubbed out my smoke in the ashtray. "I need to go. I'll carry En to her bed, then I must head out."

I stood carefully to avoid letting Ruby fall over. Walking up to En, I lifted her in my arms and went to the other side of the living room to the extra bedroom. After placing her on the bed, I covered her and walked away, but she grabbed my sleeve.

"Thank you for everything," she said.

I walked back to her and held her hand. "I just made sure you could have a better life. Don't screw that up."

She smiled. "You can act as hard as you like, but you love me and want me here."

I walked back. "You wish, Sis."

I closed the door and pulled on my robe before strapping the sword to my back and pulling on the mask.

"Where do you have to go, Master?" Valis asked.

"I'll be heading to the Celestial Nation. Maybe I'll make a few friends there. You never know."

Valis shook her head. "No more women. That would be bad."

I chuckled. "I'll try not to."

Stepping to the open window, I stood on the ledge and stared at the vast city, where small gleams of light came from other buildings, although it wasn't enough to illuminate everything.

Closing the window behind me, I extended my arms and fell forward. Wind whipped past me, as I ignited flames and zoomed away.

15

I hovered in midair, studying the districts. When I saw the one with the Celestial flags, I flew toward them and passed over the larger buildings. I went lower and saw myself reflected in the glass, as I came in to land on the street.

It was quiet and empty. As I walked down the street, lights slowly came into view from a building ahead, with a long line of people waiting to get in. I saw a man in red robes, so I walked up to him.

"Hello," I said. "I'm looking for a good night and information, if you'd care to let me in."

He looked at me. "Make sure there's no trouble. If there is, I can't guarantee your life will be spared."

I nodded, and he moved a red rope aside to let me pass. I walked in to the sound of music rattling my ears. Smoke permeated the air, and low lights of celestial flames lit the room. Chained women danced on stages.

I walked past a variety of men and women, seeing men toss money to the dancers. As I approached the bar, the bartender looked at me.

"How may I help you, Sir?"

I took out the image and slipped it onto the tabletop.

"No idea. I've never seen him."

I slipped it back into my pocket. "Give me a drink of something heavy."

He smiled. "We have an assortment of drinks. We call this one Dragon's Breath." He set a jug onto the glass countertop and poured dark-brown liquid into a glass before sliding it toward me.

"That's five gold."

I placed money down and pulled the mask aside to chug the liquid. A burning sensation enveloped my esophagus. I set the glass on the table and grabbed a smoke from one pocket and lit it, then tossed five more gold coins on the table.

"Are you sure you can handle another one?"

I added another five and set down my mask to blow smoke at him. He quickly poured two in a row, as a crowd gathered.

"If I drink both of these, you'll answer the question I asked earlier."

He slid the drinks toward me. "This is enough to kill a man. You sure you want to dance with your own life?"

I smiled and downed the second one, although I nearly lost my balance, as my right leg wavered. The room spun around me.

"It seems you're not such a good drinker after all."

I downed the third and slammed it on the table. People around me screamed in excitement.

"His brother is here," the bartender said. "He just went out back."

I grabbed my mask and felt pain in my stomach. I stumbled toward the rear exit and felt something rush up my throat. I puked blood on the floor. Someone grabbed me and carried me outside.

Once I was spent, I was tossed down on the ground.

"Stupid humans." The person went back inside.

I puked again, as a puddle of blood pooled around my face. I felt my stomach healing itself, but the alcohol had really wrecked it. I felt it heal and then tear apart more than once. I clutched my stomach and looked around at the dark alley.

"Hey," a snarly voice said. "We don't want your kind here."

I turned to see a man with strangely jagged skin. Two women with messed-up hair stood behind him holding pieces of wood as weapons.

"My apologies, Sir," I gasped. "I'm looking for someone. If you don't mind, I'll get back to my job."

I barely finished before I vomited more blood. I fell onto my back and grabbed a dagger from my waist. With one stroke, I sliced open my stomach and let all the poison out. As the wound healed, I felt my new innards being replaced by healthy tissue.

I stood slowly, as the man snarled, "I know who you are. You're the order, Dog! My brother will be so happy."

I shook my head and walked away.

"I'm not done talking to you! The order is nothing more than stupid hounds waiting to be put down!"

I turned around and placed one hand on my sword hilt. "I suppose you're the one who can do that? Unless you have information I want, I'd hold my tongue. Do you understand? Didn't you just see what I did? You can't hurt me."

The women laughed and walked forward, as the man raised his hands, then he stopped. "What kind of information are you looking for?"

I stepped closer to him and took out the wanted poster.

"You want Jurango. That's man's crazy, but he's one of the best enhancers."

"You know him?"

He nodded and stared at me intently. "Of course. It would be hard not to know him. As to where he is, I'm afraid I can't help with that. Like him, I'm an enhancer."

The women rushed me from either side. I stepped back, and the boards they swung at me missed. The redoubled their efforts and missed again. I kicked one and then side-kicked the other. She flew sideways a few feet and hit the ground hard.

"So you're a skilled fighter?" the man asked. "Maybe Jurango will have a good fight on his hands, or maybe you'll die because of the small amount of power you hold."

He touched one of his jagged parts with a soft crushing sound. His body glowed. "That's more like it." He crushed two more places. "Now I'm ready. What about you, Dog?"

He vanished from sight, then something ripped through my chest. Both lungs popped out at once. I looked down and saw his arm all the way through me. He pulled his arm back, and I coughed blood, lowering my head until I was back to normal. I smiled.

"That's one less dog to chase my brother," he said.

Lifting my head, I saw him shaking at the sight of me. His servant girls were on their feet. One held her side, probably because of a broken rib. She lifted her shirt sleeve and crushed a stone. Her wounds healed instantly.

"I didn't know the order had enhancers, too," the man said. "This should be fun, Girls. Stand back. This is my fight."

I was glad he thought of me as another enhancer, but I realized I was severely outmatched. If it weren't for the goddess' power, I would already be dead.

"It seems you're far more powerful than I thought. Perhaps I shouldn't have been so forward. Too late for that now. What's your name, Sir? I'd like to know."

He was in fighting stance, ready to pounce, then he straightened. "My name is Tamel. It's a pleasure to fight another strong warrior."

I bowed to him. "You may call me Kit. I'm afraid I have to kill you. My job doesn't allow for incompetence."

He laughed and prepared himself again. "Funny you should mention that. I'm not one to take prisoners, either."

We rushed each other. I dodged a right hook. I had to sever his arm. That would stop the flow of his power. Two knives showed in my peripheral vision. I dodged with a shoulder check and shoved him back a few feet.

I threw three poisoned needles at him. He blocked two, but one struck his neck. He took it out and wobbled on his feet.

"It's coated in a lethal poison," I said. "You won't be able to activate any power before you die."

He crushed a stone and healed instantly. "Oh, really? You're forgetting I'm an enhancer."

Those stones are cheating! I thought. *This is ridiculous.*

I drew my sword and let power flow into it. His hair turned red, as he summoned his own flame. That meant he was a Celestial flyer. At least he wasn't a summoner. That would have sucked.

We skated toward each other. I swung at his head and saw him pull out a dagger to block the strike. My power blew a hole into a building behind me. I used all my strength against him again, and we collided, sending a shockwave down the road.

"This could go on all night," he said, laughing before he pulled a second dagger and cut the tendons in my arm.

I stepped back, but he charged after me, cutting the tendons down both my arms. He jumped and kicked me so hard, the building I smashed into crumbled, and my bones shattered.

I realized my arms were taking too long to heal. *What's on his blade?* I wondered.

He stood in front of me. "So the rumors were right. I'm glad these worked against a monster like you."

He pulled out a pendant from his pocket that held the flame of the Celestial Nation. "You're not the only one loved by a god, Kit, my friend. I'm glad we could have this talk. I know I can't kill you, but I can capture you. That's what I intend. Have fun sleeping."

One of the women smashed a board over my head, knocking me out.

I sat in a dark void and heard Celnius giggling.

"It's good to see you here again," she said. "What took you so long this time?"

I stared down at the water. "There are weapons that can hurt me, stopping me from healing instantly."

She appeared and sat in my lap. "Of course, My Love. Just because you're immortal doesn't make you unstoppable. The universe requires balance. Another god created something to stop you. You won't die. Suffer becomes the key word."

I bit my lip and fought back anger. "Giving the girls those powers was a bad idea, especially knowing they aren't safe at all but in even more danger."

She laid her head on my shoulder. "My Dear, isn't this what you wanted? If you're afraid of another god, take him out."

I froze for a moment. "What did you just say?"

She came closer to my ear. "If another god is your enemy, take them out. That's what you do, isn't it? When something is an obstacle, you eliminate it. Can you do that, my dear little Kit?"

Was it possible to kill a god? If true, that meant Celnius could die, too. If she did, what would happen to me?

"Why should I do the killing? Why not you?" I asked.

"My Dear, we aren't allowed. I'm not sure why. When we transcended to gods, we were forced never to lay a hand on one another. It never said anything about one of our children doing it for us. They just have to be as powerful as a god. Do you understand? This human body won't be a permanent thing, at least in the way it is now."

I tried to move my arms, but even in a dream with her, I couldn't. Was it a dream? "Where am I? Why did you bring me here?"

She touched my slit wrists. I realized he must've slit those, too.

"My Dear, you're in my world. We aren't on your planet, nor are we in the universe. Think of it as a secret domain between reality and dream."

That explained why I couldn't move my arms. I was still partially in reality. "Why am I here? You didn't bring me here because you want me here."

She wrapped her arms around me. "You're right. I do enjoy your company at times, but this time, it's so I can give you some words of caution to use however you want.

"You aren't a god. Don't think with your blade. Use your mind. You're a smart kid, but you do reckless things, because you think nothing can stop you. In theory, you're right, but you have attracted the attention of the other gods. One day, they may create a weapon that can kill you or me. We need to work together and maybe become a bit more intimate."

I pushed her head away with mine. "You're better than that, Goddess, trying to force yourself on a man who can't even fight back."

She smiled. "Indeed, but one day, you may not get the choice. We'll see what happens then, and if you're strong enough to fight the urge. I told you what I wanted. Now I'll send you back. You're in a very bad situation. Your body may be immortal, but your mind isn't."

Bright light struck my face.

I woke and opened my eyes, but something covered them. I couldn't see much. From the sound, I felt I was in a small warehouse room.

"How does it feel to be a caged dog, you filthy mongrel?" a woman asked.

I smiled and felt my arms were still badly damaged. "A mongrel? You remind me of someone. I wonder if she'll kill all of you out of anger or just because she would enjoy seeing you suffer."

A fist struck the back of my head. Everything spun for a moment.

"Shut up, you filthy rat! Kaster will finish you off. Nothing in the world frightens him."

How long will my wounds be like this? If only one cut did this much damage, I don't dare take even one scratch. My sword is gone, but I can still feel some of the needles. They tried to clean me out. If I could cut off the arms, they'd just heal.

"I'll bet a little girl like you couldn't cut anything. You're nothing but a pawn."

She drew in an angry breath. "What did you say, Plebian? Say that again."

I laughed. "You heard me. You're nothing more than a pawn."

I hoped she didn't have one of those enchanted weapons, or it would turn into the worst idea of my life. I heard her unsheathe a blade.

Before she could do anything, Tamel said, "Trish, stop. The kid's trying to get you to strike. Think, Child. He's the stupid one."

I bit my lip and drew blood. Of course he would show up right when I had her ready to attack. Fine. I would figure out something else.

The bag was torn off my head, and I looked around. I was right. We were in a small storehouse room, and it felt like it was underground.

"Good evening, Kit. It's nice to have you with us."

He noticed the smoke rising from my lip. "I see you bit your lip. That could be a very bad habit. I suggest you stop that. You'll be in plenty of pain soon enough. Calm yourself."

I didn't know how I would get out of the situation. It was stupid of me not to kill the guy when I had the chance. If I had....

"I'm aware that when some people become stressed, they smoke. Others like to drink. I bite my lip."

His lips pulled back in a wide smile. "I like you, Kid. That's interesting and amusing. Now, though, I must insist you be a good runt and wait until my brother comes to work on you."

He stepped back and looked at Trish. "Don't be hasty, my girl. Wait and watch him suffer. It'll be worth it, I swear."

She looked away from him and stared at me. Tamel left the room, shutting the wooden door.

"What did I do to you that has you so mad at me?"

She scuffed the floor with one foot and looked away. "Shut up, Prisoner, or I'll cut out your tongue."

I stuck it out and bit it off, feeling blood rush into my mouth and onto my lap. Steam filled my face.

When it passed, she stared at me. I opened my mouth to show her my tongue again. "You could cut it off all day. It'll always come back."

Disbelief flowed over her. ""What are you, a monster or something worse?"

I chuckled and gazed into her eyes, filled with hatred. "Far worse. You have stepped into your own destruction. I may be trapped, but an army will soon knock this place down to find me. I wonder who'll die first?"

Fear came over her. Trish stepped back and bumped into a box. "No. I won't be swayed by your false words. You're nothing but a monster. My master will make sure you never hurt anyone again."

I heard the door open. Tamel came in followed by a man at least a foot shorter. His hair and blazing red eyes showed flames, which meant he was a summoner. His body was wrapped in a Celestial Nation robe, with my order mask over his face.

"So, Brother, I see you brought me a new toy," he said.

Tamel led him closer. "Yes, Brother. I promised I'd get you the boy, and here he is, just like the god said."

Tamel's brother lifted his hand. "What did I say about bringing him up now? Be quiet. Trisha, come here."

She came over quickly with her head held high. "Yes, Master?"

He stared at her for a moment. "Was he a good prisoner, or...?" He peered at me. "...a bad prisoner?" His voice became viler at the end.

"My Master, he's been a problem since he got here. He needs your righteous judgment. Please give it to him."

He laughed, then he rushed me. A second later, he gripped my neck harder and harder, lifting me and the chair I sat on before slamming me down again. At least the chair didn't break. When he released me, I took a ragged breath.

"My boy, you're in for such a treat. I'm happy you came to play. Every time I get a toy, they break halfway through, but the god tells me that when you break, you come back. I so wanted you for my own, and here you are!"

The situation seemed like a trap.

"I'm glad I could give you some entertainment, but I have to insist you let me go. If you don't, it won't go well for you."

He looked at Trish and Tamel, then back to me. "Oh? Why is that? Are you talking about your lovely harem? If you are, I wouldn't waste my breath. None of them is strong enough. In a few days, I'll have them here to play with, too, just to see you suffer even more. I saw the new little girl you got. I'm sure she's far more delectable than the rest, with such an innocent appearance. Do you think she'll scream herself to death?"

I fought to break free of my bonds and the chair. I wanted to smash his throat to keep him from saying another word, but my damn arms remained limp. "I'm not sure. I do know they're far stronger than you think. I'd be careful, you slime."

His laughter echoed around the room. "I'm shaking in my boots, Young Man. Just so you're aware before you die, my name is Pholyon. When you see your goddess, tell her I'm coming for her next."

He turned to his brother. "Go get the girls. I'd like to have the young one here first. Worry about the others later."

I fought against my restraints again, but he turned with a dagger and stabbed my lungs. I heard them pop. All the air vanished, and I began to suffocate. He held the knife inside me, twisting it to keep me from healing.

"I'm having so much fun," he said, "but you can't scream, can you, my little man?"

Gasping for air, I began to panic. My heart rate increased. He pulled out the knife, and my wound healed immediately, as I coughed up blood.

"Oh, my, that was delightful."

I stared at him, and he stared right back.

"You want to kill me? That's a bummer. Weak creatures like you can't do anything but talk big." I hated being unable to move or fight. I was truly trapped.

Pholyon took a deep breath, walked back, and crossed his arms. "You aren't as much fun as the last order agent. He wouldn't stop screaming. He kept at it until he destroyed his voice box. It was marvelous. You, though, don't scream. You just sit there and take the pain. Why?"

I smiled. "That's simple, Sir. It's because there's nothing you can do to me physically that will ever make me scream. I have destroyed my body countless times. Stabbing me in the lungs is like tickling me with a feather."

I hoped he believed it. Just because part of it was true didn't meant it didn't hurt. It did.

"Then I can't wait until we have that little girl in our clutches. It will be a joy to play with her in front of you."

He was a sick monster. I hoped Alfitz noticed something was wrong. If they caught En, I would destroy the entire sector.

The door opened. "Brother, we have a problem. There's a small force on its way here—just three, to be exact."

Could it be Alfitz?

"Are they from the order, you idiot, or are they with the bounty hunters?"

Tamel shook his head. "Neither, Sir. It seems to be three girls in Kai Nation uniforms."

Pholyon ran up and slapped his brother. "You're a moron! Those must be the magots frends. Stop them!"

Tamel and Trisha ran from the room, I heard explosions a moment later, and the room shook. Dust fell onto my shoulders.

"It seems I was right when I said you made a very grave mistake."

He stabbed my stomach multiple times, then withdrew the blade. All the puncture marks stung, but they closed quickly.

"So they came," he said. "It doesn't mean they can beat my brother or his apprentice."

I chuckled. "I would be more frightened if I were you. Those girls are on the warpath. Their target is me. Anything in their way is just an obstacle. I wouldn't be surprised if they leveled the city just to get here."

He began shaking slightly, then he grabbed his arm to stop it from moving. "Shut it, Brat, before I cut you with the other blade. You won't stop bleeding for days from that one."

We heard another explosion, followed by screams.

"They're getting closer. I'm just trying to help you. My target is your son and wife. You must die, and your body must be completely destroyed."

He turned slowly toward me. "What did you say?"

I glared at him. "You heard me. My target is your son. He's the one I must bring back dead."

He ran off without hesitation, slamming the door. I heard an explosion behind me. Rubble flew past, and heavy dust made me cough.

"Brother," En said, "were here to rescue you."

She cut off my arms. They grew back quickly, and soon, I could move them again.

"They won't be at one hundred percent, but you'll be able to fight for a little bit. We have to get out of here. Ruby is on the blood path. She killed a lot of people to get here."

I had the feeling she would soon be completely out of control, but I didn't dare miss my chance. "Go back to the girls and tell them I'm free. I have to go after Pholyon."

As I walked toward the door, she grabbed my robe. "Brother, you can't win like this. You're too weak."

I stared at the door, feeling how close he was. "Fine, you win, but I don't like it."

I turned and looked on the ground. They left my blade, so I picked it up and sheathed it on my back. I followed En out of the hole she blew in the wall. We soon entered sunlight. I jumped out of the hole she created and saw we were on the street. Behind me was a monastery with stone walls.

"How'd you know where I was?"

En stood at my side. "I could feel your presence. I didn't know I could tell until I was close enough, then I felt your pain and guessed. I was right."

Another explosion tore off the top of the monastery. It collapsed, revealing Ruby floating up there with her arms up. Lightning bolts struck the building, and more explosions shook the ground.

"Ruby!" I shouted. "Let's go home!"

I broke her concentration. She flew toward me, and something flew from the ground toward her. I kicked on my flames and launched myself to intercept it. It impaled me through the stomach hard enough to throw me into a wall. Crashing through it, I rolled down the street before finally stopping.

I looked down to see blood gushing out of me. When I tried to pull the thing out, I was too weak.

Ruby screamed, and storm clouds covered the sky.

"Brother!" En ran toward me and pulled out the pipe, while Razele flew in with Valis in her arms. They landed nearby.

"Kit, we need to leave," Razele said. "Ruby will demolish the monastery and the surrounding area. If we don't leave, we'll get hit, too."

I tried to stand without success. Razele took my left arm, while En took my right. They starting flying. Valis tossed a gem to the ground. A giant bird emerged made of water. She hopped on, and it flew behind us. When I took a look behind, I saw a golden dragon made of lightning fly down from the sky and crash into the monastery.

The dragon disappeared, and all was quiet, and then a large beam of power flew into the sky from the impact site. It expanded with great speed. We flew as fast as we could, trying to get out of its range. Once we did, the beam subsided and exploded.

The shockwave smashed us into the ground. A large wave of dust followed, covering everything in sight. I heard the girls coughing.

"Kit, are you OK?" Valis asked, concerned.

"Yeah. That's a lot of dust."

I waved my hand, but it didn't clear anything.

Razele seemed fed up. "This is ridiculous. One second!"

The dust moved away from us. We stopped coughing and looked up to see Razele had placed us in a protective bubble. Watching debris and dust fly past, we tried to catch our breath.

"Thanks to all of you for coming to help me. I'm sorry I let this get out of hand."

Razele kept her hands raised to shield us. "It's all right. We're a family. Of course we came to help. Sorry we couldn't stop Ruby from leveling half the sector, though."

We shared a laugh.

"Ruby is who she is. I'm glad she didn't' kill us, too," En said softly, looking around.

"We'll have a lot of explaining to do. What's the chance they're dead?"

The dust began to settle. As it died down, Razele lowered her hands. Looking back, we saw an entire kilometer had been destroyed in a large circle. Buildings were missing, and dead bodies lay everywhere.

"I'd say, Master, this is pretty bad," Valis said.

Staring at the destruction, I saw it was worse than I thought. The ground had caved in at least fifty feet down. Buildings on the edge of the sinkhole were barely holding on.

"Girls, I need all three of you to find any survivors you can. Help them."

En and Valis moved off quickly.

"Kit, what happens now?" Razele asked.

"This very well could start a war. There were many students from the Celestial Nation here. This won't be good. Ruby will either be put to death, or all of us will. I don't see how we can get out of this mess easily."

What do I do? I wondered. *The headmaster probably knows about this by now. I don't have enough power to fight him even with all of us working together. It would be a losing battle. Why'd this have to happen now?*

I heard the echo of dice rolling on the ground. When they stopped, a woman's voice said, "The dice of fate are always unknown to those who can't see, but the ones who roll the dice are the masters of the unknown."

Everything fell silent. Bright-red light suddenly appeared over the headmaster's building.

"Razele, get all the girls and run! Get out of the city as quickly as you can. I have to find Ruby. We need to leave right now!"

Panic filled her eyes. "OK, Kit!"

She ran off.

I kicked off my flames and flew close to the ground, looking for Ruby. I found her in the center of the crater, lying on her back in the midst of all the destruction. As I flew down to pick her up, the red light brightened in the sky.

"That isn't good. Why'd you have to lose control now, Ruby, of all times?"

I held her tightly and flew toward the Celestial border. The girls were atop the wall, waving frantically at me. There was no time to escape. I threw Ruby and saw Razele and En catch her.

"Kit, let's go!" Razele shouted.

I shook my head. "You need to escape. I can hold him off. Get to the Kai Nation and wait for me there, all right?'

En ran toward me, but Valis caught her and brought her back.

"Of course, Master," Valis said. "I'll see you there."

Razele looked at me with tears in her eyes. She opened her mouth and silently said words I could feel in my heart.

"I love all of you!" I shouted.

They ran off.

I turned and saw wings wider than any I'd ever seen. They resembled Orlando's wings but were much bigger. With a loud roar, Antilunis burst into flame, making him look like a large, flaming dragon.

I gripped my sword. My arms were still weak, and my flame wasn't much better. I wouldn't be able to fight for long, although I had to try. I flew out to meet him.

His tail flicked from the side, smacking my sword hand and sending my sword flying over the wall. Antilunis opened his mouth, and it filled with flames until it formed a large ball.

As it left his mouth, the flames surrounded me and boiled my skin. I saw my skin melting off me but wasn't able to feel anything. I was completely cut off from my body. My lungs burst from the heat, and my body turned to cinders, leaving no trace of my existence.

16

I opened my eyes and found myself floating among the stars. Looking down, I saw the blue planet Cilios, with one large continent that was our home. I stared at the perfect circle of the planet.

"Beautiful, isn't it, My Dear?"

I looked for the voice, but I was alone in space. "It is. I don't understand. I'm immortal, so why aren't I down there?"

A bright beam of light shone down to touch my skin. "Yes. Immortality is such a fickle thing, but you were killed by a dragon of time. You were removed from existence, as if you were never born, never died. You are nothing."

Panicking, I tried to move, but I remained where I was. "What of my friends, Valis, Razele, Ruby, and En?"

The light began to fade. "They will suffer horrible deaths due to the choice set in motion by the Goddess of White and the God of Black."

"How do I get out of this mess? Send me back now. I can't stay here if they're in danger. I have to help them, do something. I can't just wait for them to die."

The light faded. When I turned, I saw a woman in a gold cloak, her hair in a bun, with a golden aura surrounding her. I stared into her golden eyes, which had six vertical lines in each.

"My Dear, didn't you hear me? You were never there."

I looked down at the planet, glad to know they were still alive, but if I didn't do something, they wouldn't last long. "How to I rewrite myself into existence?"

The goddess floated off. I followed, although it wasn't my doing, and we traveled until a small portal appeared. The energy seemed like chaos. We passed through it into a large void.

"Where are we, Miss?"

She turned, although we continued traveling along our course. "We are nowhere and everywhere, among the living and the dead."

We traveled for what felt like forever. Finally, we stopped. She pointed down, and I saw a pond of gray water circling clockwise. A few people stood motionless around it, staring into the water.

"What's that?" I asked.

The goddess looked at me, then back down. "It's the tether from the dead to the living. The dead may never enter it, but if you are successful, then you have a chance to return to the real world. I must warn you that if you travel there, the next time you die, your soul becomes one with me. I assure you I'll never let you go again, no matter what. Do you understand, Kit?"

I nodded. My body was released, and I felt control of my movements again. "Why are you doing this if you don't like me?"

She stared at the pond for a moment, then looked up at me. "It's because I love you. That's why I won't let your go. Your father was the best thing that ever happened to me, and I don't want you to make the same mistake, but I promised that if I ever met you, I would send you back no matter what.

"You must pass the test that is before you. I can't aid you in this endeavor. I wish you good luck, Kit. Don't let those girls go. They're the reason you live."

I nodded and floated down to the ground. I landed softly and the people suddenly noticed me. They began walking toward me, moaning in pain. If they were dead, how could they sense me?

I reached for my sword, but it wasn't there. All my needles were gone, too. I couldn't activate my flames, either. I had to fight with my fists.

One of the undead came close. I punched its face and saw the head explode. The corpse fell over backward.

I stared at my hand. I knew I was strong, but not that strong. Seeing the other undead still coming, I rushed toward them and sent out a flurry of attacks. Making progress toward the water, I was almost there when I heard a creak underfoot.

I jumped backward just as a large hand broke through the concrete floor, pulling itself up. The body was completely red, though without flames. The skin looked as tough as metal, and it had a human face.

Shaking off my fear, I rushed toward it and jumped high into the air, hoping to land a punch to its head. I grabbed my hand, broke my wrist, and tossed me back. I hit the ground and rolled. When I stopped moving, I jumped to my feet and saw my wrist was ruined, and it wasn't healing. I was glad it was only my wrist. If it was my neck, I would have died.

I saw several undead with him, then I saw the hole he came through. There was no way to defeat them all. The chances of winning without weapons were so slim, the best thing I could do was aim for the water.

I rushed them with my broken wrist pressed against my stomach and made sure none of the undead could grab me. When I neared the giant, he turned left to keep his eyes on me. I kept my focus on where I was going, trying not to make a mistake. I moved farther to the left, keeping the distance between us.

He didn't move or try to stop me from reaching the water. When I was only ten feet away, he appeared in front of me. His fist came toward me, and I jumped. A loud concussion sounded, and all the undead in his path were destroyed.

I jumped back, gaining distance again. He didn't attack until I was close to the water, and his speed was greater than mine. His goons were no problem so far, but, if I became trapped in the middle of them, I'd lose my life.

How could I get closer? The undead came toward me. When one was close enough, I crushed her skull and watched her drop. All her blood flowed to me and dissolved into my skin. How had I missed that earlier?

I looked at her corpse, which disintegrated and flowed into me. Attacking the other undead, I felt their power flowing into me. Their strength added to mine until I killed thirty. I felt lighter than a feather and took a step, passing through a bunch of the undead. They dissipated and entered me.

I looked up at the giant. I still had only one hand and hoped it would be enough. I ran toward the water again.

He appeared in front of me. Our arms came up simultaneously. I blocked his first attack, jumped into the air, and kicked his right arm. It snapped in half, as I scooted back to watch.

He punched the ground with a shockwave that struck several undead. They flowed into him.

I need more undead, I realized.

I ran to the right and killed another forty of them. Suddenly, my wrist healed. I had my immortality back. I attacked the monster again. When our fists collided, a shockwave went all around us in a huge explosion.

My fist began to gain ground. I penetrated his arm and destroyed it. When he had no way to defend himself, I jumped up and kicked his stomach. The force of the blow left a huge hole.

The monster looked down and smiled at me before he dissipated into black smoke. All the undead disappeared, and I heard applause.

Looking up into the void, I saw a huge dome with twenty golden chairs around it. Beings wearing white masks and robes, all of them covered in golden auras, applauded my victory.

"Splendid, just splendid. He did it."

One of the people stepped down a flight of stairs to stand in front of me. his face covered in scars with a proud smile covering his expression his right eye was missing, but the socket held a golden crystal. The other eye was fiercely black, radiating chaos and four red stars.

"What a splendid showing from you, Kit. I'm proud."

His voice was familiar and comforting, and I bowed. "I'm pleased you enjoyed it, but I must return to help my friends and warn a family friend."

I turned toward the water.

"Kilyon did a splendid job turning you into the man you are. We were right to leave you with him."

I stopped and faced him. "What did you say?"

He laughed so hard, the ground shook. "I'm your father, Kit, Tellium Exporoc."

Shocked, I walked toward him and touched his face with my hand. When I lowered my hand, I found I was crying.

"My dear Kit, I'm amazed at you. I hope we wouldn't meet here, but fate is never certain."

Looking up t the goddess who brought me there, I saw her crying, too. "Is that Mom?"

He looked up. "Not your birth mother but my wife. When you were born, your birth mother had to leave. I'm sorry."

I wiped away tears. "Who's my real mother, then?"

He laughed. "In time, you'll find out. If I told you now, she'd kill me, so you must forgive me."

I hugged him fiercely. "Why did you leave? Why'd you kill everyone for power? Why couldn't you stay?"

His hand rested gently on my back. "Those are good questions, but I'm afraid there isn't enough time now. Your friends are in danger. It was selfish of me to speak with you. don't take offense at this, but I hope I never see you here again."

I laughed and pulled away. "Thank you, Father. What kind of trouble are they in?"

He raised a hand, and a small orb appeared. Looking into it, I saw Ruby and En on their backs, injured. Razele and Valis fended off a long-range attack, but they were pinned in a hole that looked like it was on the border between the Celestial Nation and the Terra Nation. It was hard to tell. Razele held my sword.

"She is a lovely young woman, and strong at that, to be holding that sword like a real warrior. It devours the soul if you aren't from the Chaos Nation. Since she is immortal, her soul will regenerate, but it could take some time. Your vampire is a mess, but the love and respect she has for you is astonishing. A king would envy you for that.

"Valis, a poor slave girl, is willing to protect everything and be its shield so save the ones she loves. She's very noble. Paladins could learn something from that woman.

"Lastly, my daughter, Entity, is a pretty girl who reminds me of her mother. Such a devastating woman, though she must hate me for what I did to all of them."

I looked at him. "How did you know about her?"

He laughed. "You think I haven't been watching you? Please. I watch every second, even the embarrassing times. I'm enjoying it."

I saw Razele deflect some flaming shots with the sword, though she was barely able to hang onto it. "Was it the right decision to make her part of our family, or was that a bad idea?"

He sighed and brought Entity into full view. "That's a tricky question, indeed. You're one of a kind to hold the power of immortality. It's no surprise you would think Entity could grow up to destroy the entire world, but so could you. Maybe she'll be the one to save it, maybe not. There's always a third option, but be warned, my son, you've started something that can never be fixed with words, I'd be ready for the mess you have to clean up due to your loved ones."

He studied Ruby next.

"I love them all very much. I'll protect them."

He waved his hand, and the image disappeared. "Then I suggest you hurry."

I walked to the water and stood at the edge, looking back at him. He nodded and looked at his wife.

"I'm sorry we met this way, Miss," I said. "I'm glad you married my father."

I walked into the water and felt it suck me in. Arms grabbed my leg and pulled me into a dark abyss that waited underwater. I saw a giant hole sucking everything down into it. When I reached the hole, I felt my soul being created into a new world.

Looking down, I saw the planet and began free falling toward it. When I reached the atmosphere, my skin turned red from the heat, but it didn't melt away like last time. I saw the continent below and realized I was falling toward the border between the Terra and Celestial Nations.

I told them to go to the Kai Nation. Why did they go the wrong way? I shook my head, as the ground came up toward me even faster.

Razele was almost out of energy. Valis pulled her back to safety. It appeared Valis was healing the others, but she wouldn't be able to much longer. I hoped she could keep them safe for the moment. I was sorry for what I put them all through.

Looking ahead, I saw a squad of Celestials, two flyers, a summoner, and what appeared to be a healer. The girls were outmatched from the beginning. All the attackers came from the order, which meant reinforcements would be on their way soon.

I reached down for the sword. It flew from the ground toward me, and Valis looked up, but I doubted she could see me, as I caught it.

I landed hard in front of them, sending a shockwave out in all directions. Valis coughed, as the dust settled.

"It's good to see you again," I said. "Valis, can you explain why you went the wrong way?"

She looked at me in shock, not believing I stood in front of her. A Celestial flame whooshed toward us. Chaos flames erupted and formed a barrier to block it. There was an explosion, then the chaos flames receded.

"Master, is that you?"

I knelt in front of her. "Does it look like it's me?"

She jumped into my arms and knocked me down. "We thought you were lost after the explosion. We felt your presence vanish completely!" She became hysterical.

I held her and patted her back. "This isn't the place to lose your composure. I'm really happy to see you alive, but we need to get them healed, then leave."

I saw Razele was exhausted. I could carry her, but Ruby and En had bad injuries, as if the tendons in their arms were cut. En was extremely pale.

"I've been trying to save them," Valis said, "but I haven't been able to. We were ambushed with those disgusting weapons. They obliterated Ruby almost instantly. We got here and have been trying to hold out as long as we could."

She sank to the ground. "I'm so tired."

I cut my wrist and let her drink some of my blood. She was immediately healed. I did the same to all of them, though Razele still was weak.

"It'll take Razele more time to heal," I said. "I'll carry her. Ruby, I need you to create a diversion. Valis and En can lead the group. We need to get somewhere secluded quickly."

Ruby and En wanted to jump me, but they knew it was the wrong time.

"Ruby, now!" I said

Thunderclouds rolled over us. "We don't have long. I'll aim for a spot between us. That'll slow them down while we escape."

As I watched, lightning formed into a dragon. Taking Razele's arm, I slung her over my shoulder and watched the dragon fly down with a roar. Thunder rang through the air, as the lightning crashed.

We jumped from the hole and began running. There weren't any hidden areas, just sand and a few rocks. En and Valis led us straight ahead, and I followed carrying Razele.

We ran for hours. Finally we saw a town ahead, with smoke rising from several chimneys.

"Girls, we need shelter for the night. Let's stop here."

En looked behind me. "Valis and I can scout it out."

I nodded, and they ran off quickly. Ruby came to my side.

"I'm sorry, Lord, for what I did, and for killing you."

I saw the pain in her heart was slowly eating away at her. "I'm not mad, Ruby, not in the slightest. I would have preferred gaining more allies and weapons before that incident, but things don't always work out as planned. We have to do our best now and get back to the Kai Nation."

She stared behind us. "I'm sorry. I'll do better."

I wanted to talk more, but it wasn't the time. We needed a safe haven.

Ruby looked back at me. "It looks like the distraction worked. We should be far ahead by now."

She might be right, but the problem we caused at the school meant that they'd be hunting us down no matter what. The order would be after us.

I saw En running back. "The town chief gave us permission to stay for the night, but we have to be gone by morning, no exception."

At least we had a safe place for the night. "Thank you, En. Let's get there quickly."

We arrived at a low wall made of thin, weak poles that surrounded the village. We walked in and saw houses made of clay and dirt. As we walked farther into the town, people came out to watch us, all looking confused.

At the center of the town, we met an elderly man who was three feet tall. White bandages covered his eyes. He stood with a young woman with long blonde hair and red eyes.

"It's a pleasure to meet you," the man said. "I'm Galnius, the chief of this town. This is my daughter, Raxel. We don't have much, but we will share what we have."

I bowed my head.

The man's head turned toward Razele. "I see the dilemma. Come."

En and I looked at each other, then we followed him to his house. We walked through the doorway that had no door into a house that was smaller than I thought, although it was big enough for all of us.

Galnius waved me to come closer. He led me to the far wall, which had a cot. "Lay her there. My daughter will take care of her."

I gently set Razele down and looked at her. She seemed well enough for the moment. I stepped back, and Raxel took over.

I turned to Galnius and saw him sitting at a low table. He waved us to sit with him. Ruby sat, although Valis and En remained standing.

"Brother, I'd like to go out to scout," En said.

"Me, too, Master," Valis said. "It seems like a wise idea."

Before I could respond, Galnius stood. "Before you go, I should warn you that your clothing is foreign here. It would be best if you changed into something from our land. Raxel, please fetch these girls some clothes."

Raxel stood and went back out the door.

"I'm sorry," I said. "I've lost my money and my equipment. I have nothing to repay your hospitality."

He raised a hand. "Pish-posh. There's no need. You shall help me in another way. That's all."

I bowed my head. Raxel came back in with some clothing. "You can change out back," she said. "It'll be private there."

They walked out.

Galnius looked at my sword. "The Dark Nebula. Such a devastating sword. Only one man was able to use it. It belonged to a very kind, formidable man. Do you know the warrior of whom I speak?"

If I told him the name, he might think I was his son. If I claimed to be Tellium's son, I was certain Galnius would turn on us.

"Tellium was his name."

Galnius smiled. "Indeed, it was. Such a kind man when he wanted to be." He removed the bandage over his eyes. They were cursed with chaos. I saw chaos remnants floating over them. "I made the mistake of crossing his path in my youth, and I can assure you I'll never make that mistake again."

I reached for my sword.

"Easy, Son. There's no need to be defensive. I harbor no hatred to the Chaos Nation or his kin. I was a soldier doing my job. He was a liberator doing his."

I looked into his eyes and saw he was at peace with his situation. He fought my father and lost. "I'm sorry for what happened to you. I should apologize on my father's account. If you like I should be able to help you, if you wish."

Galnius smiled. "His son has finally come to my village. I'm glad I was in a caring mood today."

I walked toward him and took a knife off the table. "I'm glad I met you, Sir. If you would please open your mouth enough to take a drink."

He opened his mouth, and I sliced across my wrist. As blood poured into a goblet, I guided it to his mouth. He drank from it, and his body glowed. Sitting aside the goblet, I sat to study his eyes.

The chaos remnants faded, and his eye color changed to pure red with a white dot in the middle.

"My boy, I can see again!"

I nodded, and he looked around the room, touching things and lifting them to his face.

"Are you a god?"

I chuckled. "No. I'm a normal person. I must ask you to keep my identity a secret, if you would."

He quickly agreed. Looking at the goblet, he noticed the blood inside. "I see you're a miracle of the gods. Thank you for sharing your strength with me, Young Man."

I pulled the goblet close to me. "Tell me about the day you met my father, if it's not a bother. I'm curious."

He laughed. "Of course. Before the nations were on more-peaceful terms, we were constantly at war. I'm sure you know the story of the six great liberators."

I nodded.

"They came here, and Tellium was tasked with killing the king. I was an honor guard for over fifteen years when the city was attacked. I watched him weave through the innocent people, ignoring them unless they attacked. He was magnificent.

"When he reached the throne room, he had already slain an entire platoon. Most of my men were ready to run. Two had already deserted when they saw him fight. I couldn't do anything about it.

"Your father stood before me with his long, black hair, and that sword in his right hand. I always remembered his words. 'Young Man, death isn't the only way to peace. You can rebuild.'

"I was dumbstruck, thinking it was just a trick. Being naïve wasn't a good idea, either, so I challenged him to a duel. If I won, he would leave. If he won, he wouldn't kill my men. He laughed and said, 'Even if I win, I swear I won't hurt any more of your men for your courage. That is their reward. The king is my only target.'"

I listened, noting the happiness in his voice.

"We agreed to his terms."

I glanced outside and saw the sun sinking below the hills.

"He lifted that chaos sword, and flames completely surrounded me. When I woke up, my eyes were like this, but the rest of my body wasn't damaged at all. The king was dead. Tellium never touched another soldier after our fight. He kept his promise."

At least my father was a man of his word. Maybe he didn't make as many enemies as I thought. "I'm glad I could save your sight. I wish I could have healed Razele the same way."

He walked toward Razele. "That's because her soul is damaged. Her body is in perfect condition, and her mind is stable, but her soul has a large tear in it. I assume she tried to use your weapon?"

I looked away. "Yes. I was away from them for a bit. She used my weapon."

He walked back toward me. "It may take some time, but I can promise she'll come out of this just fine. Don't lose faith in her. You three are probably the only reason she's still clinging to this world."

He placed his hand on my shoulder.

Valis ran in, breathing hard. "Master, we have a big problem. A platoon of men are coming this way."

I was about to stand up when Galnius looked me in the eye, and I stopped.

"I need you to stay here and hide. Watch over your friend. My dear, what's your name?"

She looked down at him. "I'm Valis, Sir."

He walked slowly toward her. "Good. You look like the women from our village. Make sure your comrades stay out of sight. You should return to them. Your master and friend are all right here."

She looked at me, and I nodded. "It's OK. Do as he says."

She bowed and ran off.

Galnius turned to me.

"I have no interest in letting them destroy your village. We can make our escape."

He shook his head. "There's nowhere you can go. If you ran, you'd have a platoon right behind you without any cover. No. You're my guests and will remain here."

He pointed his cane at a trunk. "In there is a uniform I suggest you put on. You look like a bum in those rags you have on."

He laughed and walked out. I went to the trunk and opened it, taking out a new silk short and cloth pants. After putting them on, I added a robe with the Celestial Nation emblem and flipped the hood up to cover my face.

Raxel walked in and blushed. "I'm sorry, Sir."

I shook my head. "Don't be. Would you watch her? I need to keep an eye on your father."

She bowed and went to Razele's side. "Of course. Make sure my father doesn't embarrass himself."

I walked out the door and moved into some cover. It looked like everyone in town was outside. Two men sat on weird, four-legged animals with three horns and small bodies. They looked extremely fast. One snarled to show rows of teeth in an oval mouth, ready to tear a man in half.

I walked closer, staying in the shadows, to find a good vantage point.

Galnius stood before the fierce beasts without any fear.

"Sir Galnius, it's a pleasure to see you once more."

Galnius looked up at him. "Of course, Knight Commander Flexile."

Flexil slid off his beast and walked to his comrade. "I wish I had better news, but there are some fugitives in the area. Their crime is terrorism in the Celestial district within the school. They're wanted. If you have any information, I urge you to tell me."

People muttered among themselves.

"My Friend, I know nothing of these vile people you speak of. If we had them, we'd turn them over to you."

He didn't seem convinced. "That's a shame. You do know the crime for harboring fugitives, don't you?'

"Of course, my old comrade. You don't need to remind me."

Flexil nodded and mounted his beast. "That's good. I'll be back tomorrow. There is much to discuss."

He turned his troops around. Galnius glanced toward me, then walked into the crowd to calm his people.

I saw Valis with Ruby on a nearby hill and raised a finger, pointing at the departing men. Valis nodded and moved out of sight. Hopefully, she could warn us if they decided to attack in the evening.

I walked back to Galnius' house and saw Razele stirring in the cot. I ran to her side, and Raxel moved aside for me.

As I took Razele's hand, she asked, "Kit? Is that you?"

I held her hand firmly. "It is. How do you feel, you stupid girl?"

She gave a soft chuckle. "Me, stupid? You're the one who died."

We smiled at each other. "Well, I'm back now. Get some rest. You'll need it."

Her hand left mine and touched my face. "Thank you for coming back. I knew you would. I never lost hope. Ruby blamed herself the entire time and did everything she could to keep us safe. You should give her some love."

Her hand lay down beside her on the cot, and I covered her up. "I'll speak with her."

Razele closed her eyes and went back to sleep. Raxel looked down at her.

"What kind of relationship do you all of you have? It's like you're more than family."

I gazed at Razele with pride. "I guess so. I love all of them, and I couldn't choose one, so in a way, yes, we're more than just family."

Raxel leaned over to check Razele's temperature. "It's good you have each other."

Galnius came in, his cane clicking on the stones. "They know you're here," he said. "They won't attack unless they have support from the king."

I looked at him. "Then we must leave if they attack. They would kill all of you, and that would be very bad. There is no...."

He raised a hand to stop me. "Indeed, it would be bad, but it's our way to help those in need, even when one disobeys. They are nothing more than what they hate. Let us do this in our own honor."

I wanted to protest, but it wasn't my place to tell him what to do. I had to respect their way, even if I didn't agree. "Then allow us to help you."

He shook his head. "If you raised a sword to them, the entire village would be taken prisoner and turned to slaves. We'd rather die. We'll send a party of all our young to friends in another village. They'll be fine, but the rest of us will stay."

Raxel walked forward. "Father, I'm staying with you."

He tapped his cane on the stone floor. "I forbid it."

En waited outside. I saw her there, listening.

"But Father, you need me. You can't see that well yet."

Laughing, he went to her. "Are you sure, My Dear? I see you have aged well these years, but I can also see the lines under your eyes from years of stress. It's time to let those fade with everything else."

She looked at him in confusion. "How could you know that? You've been blind since I was a little girl."

He tapped me with his cane. "Our friend here is the son of the man who did this to me. I'm grateful to have him here. He saved my sight. Even if it lasts for only a day, I'm grateful."

Raxel turned to me, then ran out, crying. En looked at me.

"Follow her and make sure she's safe and doesn't stray far from the town."

En nodded and left.

Galnius sighed. "I'm sorry for the trouble. I doubt she'll go far."

I shook my head and sat at the table. "Don't think anything of it. You've been a great help."

"She's not disobedient. She'll do what she's told."

I looked at him, realizing what he implied. "I can't guarantee her safety. I can barely keep my current comrades alive."

He nodded and walked to the door. "Indeed. I still have to ask. Please take her with you."

I looked at the table. "The course we're on will take us through the Terra Nation, then the Chaos Nation. There's plague in there. Even with me and my sister to help, it'll be dangerous for the others. I'm not certain we can get through. I assume the headmaster has stationed members of the order across the Aura and Celestial Border.

"We will soon head into war unless I can reach the Kai Nation fast. It could even be full-out war by the time I arrive. Is that what you want for your daughter?"

He came to me and went to his knees with bowed head. "Please take her with you. I know the risk is great, but you will be this world's savior."

I stared, wondering how he knew what I planned. "I'll talk it over with the others. If they agree, I'll take her, but if they disagree, she has to leave with the village children. Is that all right?'

He smiled up at me. "Thank you for this, Kit."

I wondered if Kilyon knew I would be traveling across the entire world.

"My Lord?"

I saw Ruby in the doorway wearing a dress from the Celestial Nation with a gray scarf for a mask.

"Yes? What's wrong?"

She walked in and looked at Galnius. "I support this. So do Valis and En."

"How could they know?"

She took out a small device. "It's a transmitter stone. I stole some from the headmaster when he was out of the building."

She tossed me one. It was pure white with little holes in it.

"How does it work?"

She took out her stone. "This way." A few seconds later, the stone in my hand repeated her words.

"That's amazing. Can it contact anyone in the world, like Kilyon?"

"Yes and no. I would need a few pieces of his hair and saliva to link with our stones."

I touched her face. "When did you...?"

She shook her head. "Don't worry about it."

I placed the stone in my pocket and looked at Galnius. "It looks like they already decided. We'll take her with us, but you know I'm not a savior. I have different plans for this world."

He laughed and tapped my leg with his cane. "You think I didn't know that already? Your eyes speak louder than your actions, My Boy. This world may as well belong to you."

Ruby gave him a cautious look.

"Calm yourself, Ruby. It's all right," I said.

She turned to me. "My Lord, you are far too trusting. He could kill us. For all you know, he's plotting something. He's been far too kind to strangers."

Her eyes flashed with rising hatred. "Galnius has done nothing to us. In fact, he's been extremely helpful. He's giving us his daughter, because he knows everyone in this village will die tomorrow."

"Yeah? What if he only wants her to join us to kill you?"

I became tense and angry. "The only one who did that is you."

Ruby turned and ran out crying. I punched the table with my fist, making the goblet of blood fall. I watched my blood steam away.

"Sorry about that," I said. "I lost control."

"You've had that building up for a while. You don't seem like someone who loses control easily. Did she actually kill you?"

I shook my head. "No. We were in the city. I was captured and injured. When Ruby found out, she went berserk. She attacked the building I was in but used magic that was so potent, it destroyed an area nearly a kilometer across. It wasn't her fault I died, just bad luck."

He bent over to pick up the goblet. "Then you made a mistake to say that, didn't you?"

I took a deep breath. "I did. That was out of character for me. Since I almost lost them all, I've been on edge. Maybe it's a side effect of being resurrected, or it's something mental. I'm not sure."

Galnius set the goblet on the table. "Or maybe it's the stress between all of you, or something more than you have noticed."

I looked down at him, as he nodded. "I'm not sure I should go find her."

He tapped my back with the cane. "I would if I were you. It's the smart thing to do."

I walked from the hut and looked around. Seeing a small dune behind the house, I walked toward it, crossing behind a few other huts. Kids running past one bumped into me.

"Sorry, Mister."

I patted his head. "That's all right. Get going before it's too late."

They ran off, and I continued the path up to the dune. A small, single tree stood there. I trudged through sand to reach the top and saw Ruby staring out at the landscape, tears running down her face.

"Can I sit beside you?"

She looked away but nodded. I sat down with her and looked over the village.

"It's a beautiful village with nice people."

She looked at them for a moment. "It is."

As I placed my hands on my knees, I asked, "Can I ask you something?"

She fought back tears. "What is it?"

We both watched birds fly down to land on the huts and chirp at each other.

"Is there anything you want to say?"

She broke down and placed her head on my shoulder, as she cried. "I hate feeling this way. Growing up, I always was the strong one, not needing anybody, always being cold-hearted. Since you saved me from that horrible place, I've been losing that. I care for people. I want to help them. I love my new friends so much, and as for you.... I hate how much I care for and love you."

I put an arm around her, but she swatted it away.

"I hate how trusting you are. Do you care about me? Do you, Love? Are you so willing to accept so many people to you? What about me? What about Razele?"

Her words stunned me for a moment. I made myself reply calmly. "I have always cared for the three of you from the day I met you. I wasn't sure how I felt at first, but I know I love you, Razele, and even Valis."

She continued crying. "I didn't want to lose you, and I did. You...."

I looked down at her. "How did you know I died?"

Ruby wiped her eyes. "When that explosion went off, flames came over the wall. We could barely see, but your presence from the world evaporated. We began to lose our memories of you, too. I fought my consciousness, trying to remember you, but the more I fought, the more I lost.

"Then when I awoke, it all came flooding back."

I looked at her. "I see. Did the others have the same problem?"

She nodded and looked away.

"When I died," I said slowly, "I was far from here. All I could think about was returning to all of you. I had to endure a lot just to get the chance. When I saw you wounded, I blamed myself for what happened. I know all of you did your best, but still, if I were there, it wouldn't have been that bad."

She burst into more tears. "I'm sorry. I didn't mean to kill you. It's all my fault."

I pulled her to my chest and held her, as she cried. "I don't blame you. I lost my temper in the hut. I should be the one apologizing. I'm sorry you had to go through all of that."

She held me tightly. "It's not fair."

"I know this life isn't fair, but I can say this. I will always find a way back to all of you. Nothing in this world or the next will stop me."

Her fingers tightened against my belt. "Kit?" Her grip loosened, and she pulled away.

I looked down at her. Her hands grabbed my cheeks and pulled me close for a kiss. Her lips were as sweet as cherries.

Time stopped. We stayed that way for a moment. When we separated, her face was bright red.

"Sorry for that," she said. "It's something I've been wanting to do. Then you died, and I was mad, and...."

I pulled her close again, kissing her once more.

"What was that for, My Lord?"

"I never say it, but I love all of you a lot. I should be more open about that. I'll work on it."

She giggled. "You'll have to. You absolutely suck at your emotions when it comes to us."

I held her close. "Shut up. I do a damn good job."

Laughing, we stared over the horizon.

"What's the future for us, Kit?"

I saw En walk toward the hut, then she noticed us and stopped.

"I believe we're facing a long war. We have to get to the Kai Nation to prepare for it. We have to hope we can come out victorious."

Ruby shook her head. "No. I meant for all of us. What will we do?"

I thought about that. "I'm not sure. Maybe we can have a nice house deep in the woods, living out our days in peace."

Her hand lay on mine, and our fingers intertwined. "I'd like that a lot."

En walked toward the dune and began climbing it.

"As long as you're leading us, I have no doubt we'll be victorious in every battle."

A moment later, En was at my side. "I see you two have gotten closer."

I chuckled. "Jealous, Sister?"

She quickly turned away. "Of course not, Perv. I'm happy for all of you."

I laughed, but her expression turned serious.

"A small squad of soldiers is coming."

I looked beyond the village and saw them. "Is that what you came to warn me about?"

She nodded. "They're members of the order. One asked to see you personally. He says his name is Eli, a brother."

Ruby stood and stared down at them. "Lord, it's a trap."

I stood and wiped off my robe. As I walked away, I pulled the scarf over my face. "En and Ruby, go to the house. We have visitors."

I walked to the side of the dune and half-slid to the bottom. Ruby quickly flew down after me.

"You won't go alone," she said. "I shall accompany you."

I nodded and made sure En was following orders. She walked to the hut, as I reached the middle of the village. Three members of the order stood there.

Eli and I regarded each other, then I waved to him before walking to the chief's hut.

"Don't cause a ruckus, Ruby," I said. "Stand and watch. Be mindful but be wary, understand?"

She sighed in protest. "OK."

Once all five of us were at the hut, Eli came in, then I followed. En walked in behind me with another order member.

Galnius saw us come in and waved us to the table. Eli and I sat across from each other with Ruby, and the order agent stood against opposite walls to watch.

"It's been a long time, Kit," Eli said. "How are you?" He removed his mask and set it on the table.

I removed my scarf and let it hang around my neck. "Indeed. Why are you here?"

He waved his hand. The order agent moved, and Ruby and En immediately summoned their powers. The agent became spooked and drew his weapon.

Eli and I raised our hands.

"Ruby and En, calm down. There's no need for hostility."

They reluctantly stood down, and the agent walked over to place a piece of parchment on the table.

"It was drawn up by Alfitz," Eli said. "He knows you're alive. Personally, I knew, too."

I picked it up and frowned. "I can't hide anything from you guys, can I?" I read the message.

Dear Kit,

Eli is my most-trusted friend within the wall. His men are loyal only to him. Your secret of being alive will remain, but war is coming. There's already talk within the Celestial head family to march on the capital of the Kai Nation within the week.

I implore you to hurry home before you miss out.

1. Eli has a gift for you.

I looked up at Eli, who handed me my scabbard.

"Thank you for returning this to me."

He bowed his head and waved off his agent, who left the hut quickly. "As it states, war is inevitable now. Your family is stalling for as long as possible, but they won't be able to hold them off for long."

I gave him the parchment back, and he made it disintegrate.

"I see," I said. "I have to pass through the Terra Nation, then the Chaos Nation. Lastly, I must cross the Aura Nation just to get home. If I backtrack, I'd be walking into a trap."

He nodded. "Indeed. There are fifty order agents that way, along with fifteen squads of soldiers and the headmaster's apprentice. Only a fool would choose that path. The one you're on now is dangerous, too. You have to pass through enemy territory, then through cursed territory. Our homeland is in bad shape, and no one knows how to fix it."

I recalled my time at the beginning of the whole situation. "I think I know how to fix it. If I do, it would take time, but I might be able to raise the Chaos Nation back to normal again."

He was confused. "That's impossible. No one knows the reason for the outbreak."

I shook my head. "That's not true. My father conducted experiments on a whole head family and several different towns, as I understand it. The sorrow and hatred filled the land, poisoning everything. If I can cleanse their souls and let them move on, I should be able to save the nation from complete ruin. Then we'd have the upper hand in the war when it started."

He pondered that for a few moments. "If you're right, there would still only be about ten thousand people from the Chaos Nation and Chaos district. It's a small army at best. Those within the nation would need immediate aid that would cost a lot of resources. They'd have to rely on another nation until they were back on their feet."

I knew the Aura Nation had barely enough fertile land to feed itself. The Kai Nation was too far and would soon face war on their border with the Celestial Nation.

"Eli, who is the Chaos Nation allied with?"

His eyes widened. "They've always been neutral, without hate for anyone. The Terra Nation wouldn't attack them. They'd give immediate aid."

I nodded. "Good. We would have to convince our people to deceive the Terra Nation for the time being. Then we could hit them with a secret attack. They'd never expect it. It seems like the best plan."

He nodded and stood. "I'll allow you to make the preparations when the time comes. For right now, I'm the headmaster's dog, but when war breaks out, I'll join with Chaos. Just so we all know, I recognize you as the true ruler of the Chaos Nation."

He bowed and walked out, as Galnius laughed softly.

"You have two nations supporting you. You're much further along than I would have guessed."

The sun set outside, turning the land dark.

"Maybe. I was hoping for a lot more, like arms and the like. It'll be difficult to fight the Terra Nation without good armor. They're the best smiths. I'd like to get a few of them on our side to help with that problem, but that's something I must look into at another time."

I looked at Razele, who tossed and turned on the cot. "How is she, Galnius?"

He walked over to check her temperature, then his hand hovered over her body. "She's damaged, but she's almost healed. She'll be fine soon."

Ruby crossed her arms. "How can we trust that man, Lord?"

I sat and looked out the door at the village. "Tell me, Ruby, when you were among your own people, what would you have done if you were nearly wiped off the face of the planet? Would you trust a brother, or would he keep him at arm's distance?"

She looked down. "I would welcome them in without hesitation. If I could find one of my own kind, I'd vouch for them to join us in an instant."

I nodded. "That would be the right thing to do. There aren't many Chaos users anymore. If I had to guess, maybe twenty thousand. Most are in hiding. The ones still in the Chaos Nation suffer every day. Eli is a chaos user forced into his present life. I may not know him very well, but I can trust he wants to help get our nation back on track. I know he won't betray us, because the headmaster wants to eradicate all of us as a threat to the balance of the world.

"The Celestial and Terra Nations are allies. Aura and Kai are allies. Even if the Aura said they're neutral, the fact is, if the Kai Nation was attacked, they would run to our aid. Chaos has always been neutral. We can turn the tide of any war in the favor of the side we choose."

En walked up and sat on a chair. "Is that why your father did what he did?"

I shrugged. "I don't know. I don't even know what he really did. It was something far worse than anyone should know. He made a deal with the Chaos goddess, then he slaughtered innocent people for his son to become immortal. Now that the goddess is linked to me, a wide array of possibilities has opened up."

En looked down in pain at my answer. "I hope my family's deaths and those from our nation weren't in vain."

I shook my head. "I'll make sure that never happens. I'll give their deaths purpose even if I must descend to the darkest parts of the abyss to do it."

Ruby came to stand at my side. "Yes, you will, and we'll be there every inch of the way you're dragged down. Just make sure we don't die."

I chuckled and felt they were far too good for me. "I can't promise, but, if need be, I'll sacrifice myself again to make sure you all live."

Galnius spoke up. "Now that's a man I could follow."

I turned toward him. "Even though we're from different nations and beliefs?"

He walked slowly toward me. "A king doesn't just lead, my dear boy. He must shoulder the pain and the burden even more than all those he protects. He must be willing to sacrifice himself for those who follow him. A king is the one who makes the right choice every time. If he's wrong, he must make it right."

His eyes raged with passionate respect. "I wish we could have met under better times, my friend. If you see my father up there, make sure you give him a good talking to."

He nodded and slapped my arm. "Your father would be proud, Young Man. You need to go before they arrive. They'll be here soon after seeing the order was here."

Valis and Raxel ran in.

"Father, a large army is coming!" Raxel said.

I ran past her to look outside. She was right. The army was at least 30,000 strong. Why so many?

"It seems they believe you and your friends are a large threat," Galnius said. "In the back of the hut is a carriage and a Rothlorn. Take them and get away from here fast, My Boy."

I ran back into the house and grabbed the scabbard to sheath my sword. "Valis, En, go prepare the carriage."

They ran off.

"Ruby, I need you to create a diversion."

A crooked smile came to her face. "All of them?" she asked in pleasure

"Yes, all of them. Make them realize the folly of their mistake."

Before she could leave, Galnius stopped her. "Young Lady, I wish to speak with you privately, if you don't mind."

She looked at me, and I nodded, so she waited.

"I want to give you a fighting chance to get all those you hope to save out of here," I told him. "Ruby can thin their numbers considerably, but I'm sure there are other forces standing by."

He looked surprised, as I walked toward Razele, strapping my sword on my back. "I'm well aware she'll become a hero here."

Lifting Razele into my arms, I replied, "Trust me. I will make sure I repay this village with the kindness you showed me today. You have my word."

I walked away with Razele in my arms, but he obstructed my path with his cane.

"All I ask is that you never let those who died here be forgotten. Tell stories about us for as long as you can."

I smiled. "Your village will prosper more than it ever has once the war is over, My Friend. Your story will never end."

Raxel went to her father, crying.

"My Dear," he said, "it's time for you to go with this man. I know you have your reservations, but trust in him. Do as he says and get stronger. Help Kit take back this nation for the betterment of its people."

Going to her knees, she held him tightly.

"It's all right, My Dear," he said. "I may die, but I'll always be in your heart. There's nothing in this world that could take me from there. Live—that's all a parent could ever ask for."

I didn't want to break them up, but we were running out of time. Thunder banged overhead, and echoes sounded all around.

"It's time to go. I'm sorry, Raxel."

Galnius pulled away from her, as she stood.

"Good-bye, Father."

She walked out the back door after me.

"Kit, before you leave," Galnius said, "there's a friend in the Terra Nation known as Elscabar, near the Chaos border. He's all the way southeast but not hard to find. He's my ally from long ago.

"Tell him these exact words, 'The spirits in the land have nothing more than ears of the Dukslore.' Say that, and he will aid you in whatever way he can."

Bowing my head to him, I walked out to the barn. Inside was a clutter of farm tools everywhere. I walked through them and set Razele in the rear of the carriage. En and Valis got her situated. Raxel sat against the far side, her head down, crying.

Once I had everything loaded and ready, I jumped up and took the reins. The beast growled and walked out. Taking the stone from my pocket, I said, "Ruby, you're clear. We're heading out."

I led the beast down a small dune to a trail before I heard words come from the crystal.

"OK, My Lord. I'll be with you soon enough. Master, I'm sorry."

I didn't know what she was talking about. "En? Take the reins."

I walked to the back and sat with Raxel, as we looked up at the sky. Two dragons came down, and I shook my head.

No, Ruby. That's too close to the village. What are you doing? I wondered.

Roaring filled the sky. We saw bright flashes and bangs, as the dragons circled down toward the ground. Once down, a loud explosion went up, sending a shockwave toward us. I ignited my flames to protect the carriage just before it hit, but it nearly broke through.

Once that stopped, I released the flames. The whole land behind us was engulfed in flames. The village was utterly destroyed, and the ground smoldered. Off in the distance, a large glass jewel reached into the sky.

Raxel ran to my side and stared in horror. "Father! Father!"

I bowed my head. There was no need for them to die, too. *Ruby, what have you done?* I asked sadly.

"It's just a trick, right?" Raxel asked. "They're fine, right? Kit, tell me they're fine!"

I looked at her and saw rage, sorrow, and many conflicting emotions. "No, they're dead. Everyone back there has died. None of them could of survived that."

Raxel, sobbing bitterly, fell to her knees. With so many dead, I knew sadness would stain the country for a long time.

Looking up, I saw Ruby flying down to land beside me.

"It's done, my Lord."

I nodded. "And the villagers?"

She bowed her head. "They're dead, Lord, all of them. There were no survivors."

Her voice filled with pain. She knew what she was, but I didn't understand why she chose to do what she did.

"You filthy monster!" Raxel shouted. "Why'd you kill them? Why couldn't you hold back? Did you get off on it, you fucking monster?"

Ruby, crying, looked away.

"Why'd you kill my father and all the rest of the villagers? There was no reason for that."

"It was your father's last wish," Ruby said through her tears. "He wanted the whole village destroyed. I protested. I tried to tell him no, but the only thing he said was, 'Tell my daughter that white flowers always flow beautifully.' He tried to make me promise not to tell anyone, including you, My Lord. It was the village's dying wish."

I stared out at the burned, scorched ground. They died before they had time to scream. It was the most-humane act Galnius could have asked for.

Oh, Galnius, I thought sadly, *why didn't you tell me?*

Raxel fell to the carriage floor, still crying.

I turned to Ruby. "You did a good job, Ruby. Mission accomplished. It's time to head toward the Terra Nation. Make sure we aren't followed."

She floated up and back behind the carriage. We made eye contact one last time, and I saw she was still crying, as she moved away.

"Raxel?" I asked.

"What?" she asked in a trembling voice.

"Never forget this day. Never wish it to be gone. When we retake this world and make it whole once more, things like this will never happen again."

She slowly stopped crying. "I will always remember this day, Kit. I can promise you that." Anger filled her voice. She burst into renewed tears, and I couldn't blame her. If the same thing happened to me, I would be hard pressed not to be angry.

It was over, though. We had an opportunity to make the future right, and I vowed I would.

18

When Valis tugged my cloak, I looked down at her. "What is it?"

She smiled, catching me off guard.

"Why are you smiling, My Dear?"

She wiped away a few tears. "If one doesn't smile and be happy for the ones who are lost, they'll never be able to pass on to the next life."

I stared out at the burnt landscape, trying to control my grief. "Where did you hear something like that?"

She stood and held my hand. "From my father long ago. He was like that when our mother died. He smiled and never showed his sadness, because he believed if you showed too much sadness, the soul of the loved one would be trapped in your depression forever."

I forgot she had a family. "Your father was a wise man. I wish I had met him."

Her hand tightened in mine. "I wish you could have. He would have loved you, too."

The more I looked at the destruction caused at my hand, the darker the hole in my heart grew. Was it right to kill 30,000 people, washing them away as if they were nothing? War is devastation. Young men and women went off to fight for something they didn't know. Those deaths plagued the land, so what was the point of it all? Was it right to say they fought for democracy, or did they fight for something far worse?

Valis pulled her hand free. "You're doing again, Master."

I looked at her. "What's that?"

She pointed at my head. "Every time you think deeply, you frown. One of these days, you'll look like an old man."

Chuckling softly I touched my temple. "That isn't my fault. Maybe people shouldn't make me think so hard."

I turned back and walked to the front of the carriage to sit down and take the reins back from En.

"Do you think Brother, this will be the last time we fight until we're home?" she asked.

I shook my head. "I doubt it. The headmaster has troops at every border, town, and village waiting for us. We have to be very quiet in our movements to make sure no one recognizes us. I'd like to reach Galnius' contact before we fight again, but we have to pass through at least one town and the capital before we can get there."

En crossed her arms and leaned against the seatback. "Then we'll have to be super sneaky."

Valis laughed behind us.

"What are you laughing at me for?" En asked angrily.

"It's the way you said super sneaky," Valis said. "It was very cute and funny."

En blushed. "I have no idea what you're talking about. It was not cute."

I looked at En. "It was, at least a little. I have to agree with Valis on this one."

En threw up her hands. "Oh, come on, Brother. Not you, too. This is ridiculous."

We laughed, then we stopped and looked at Raxel, who was still distraught.

"Raxel, tell me what your father was like when you were younger," I said.

She looked at me with red eyes. "Why do you want to know?" she asked in a raspy voice.

"I respected him a lot. I knew him for only a day, but he is someone I'll always remember and cherish in my heart. I want to know more about him."

She cleared her throat, then sat up straight and looked back down the road. "He was an honor guard when I was born. We lived in the capital city of Saolemes for a long time when he was protecting the king. When I saw him, he was always smiling. He was the shortest guard ever to have the job. Nobody knew why, but he was a demihuman called a Quarll.

"He never told me much about them, just that they were famous swordsmen in the old days. I didn't believe him. How could someone that small be that good against a larger opponent?'

She gave a small laugh. "I remember one day we fought over it, and he never gave ground. One day, he brought me to the royal tournament where he was pitted against five other honor guards, and he beat them all with only one scratch on his cheek. I was so envious and never understood.

"When I was older, I asked why I was normal sized, and he laughed, saying, 'Normal, My Dear? You're a giant to me.' I felt ashamed of myself for asking him. Then he calmly told me that my mother was human, so I'm a mix of human and Quarll."

I glanced at her. "Who was your mother?"

She shook he head sadly. "I never met her. She died in childbirth."

En turned and said, "I'm sorry to hear that."

Raxel smiled. "Don't worry about it. I never knew her, but Father told stories about her. They went on adventures. She apparently came from a gifted family of sword users from the Kai Nation."

Suddenly, her story hit me. "What did you say?"

Raxel looked at me in surprise. "She was from the Oceilion family. Father said they were very capable knights from the Kai Nation."

I turned to Valis, whose eyes widened, then I turned back to stare at the road. If that were true, then not only was Raxel possibly one of the world's best swordswomen, but she was more important than I realized.

"When we get to the Kai Nation," I said, "I want you to train under Randall Oceilion. He's a good friend. That would be wise."

She wiped her face. "I can. Father told me to follow you no matter what, so I'll always be at your side."

That crazy old man aided me more than I had known. I watched Ruby fly overhead and took out the white stone. "What is it, Ruby?"

"There's another army marching through the fires behind us. I'm flying ahead to scout the area. I'm worried we won't get away without fighting."

I placed the stone back into my pocket. En looked behind.

"What drives them to kill us?" she asked. "Why do they put so much harm in their path just for us?"

To be honest, I wondered the same thing, but it seemed the headmaster knew more than I thought.

"The headmaster knows we're a threat to the balance of the world. He'll do everything in his power to stop us and make sure we can't dethrone him. I believe he's far more powerful than we assumed. He must have a hand in every nation, including Kai."

Valis punched the carriage wall. "That shouldn't be possible. He isn't supposed to have jurisdiction anywhere other than the school."

I'd never seen her lose her temper before. "That's true. My guess is that during our time in the capital in the Kai nation is when it began for us. I assumed the king wasn't with the Celestial Nation, but he's been supporting the headmaster's armies. If that's true, I wonder how deep this really goes. It's probably best I didn't make more contacts at the school. If I'm right, everyone there must have ties to the headmaster, even if they're being hunted."

Did that mean Pholyon was part of the plot? Was he just a puppet? If so, why sacrifice order agents to hunt me down? I wondered. If they were going to die, anyway, why risk everything?

Ruby flew back, circled, and landed in the back of the carriage. "I didn't see anything out of the ordinary."

She sounded tired. I looked at the others and saw all were exhausted.

"All of you should get some rest," I said. "We have a long trip ahead. Don't push yourselves."

Raxel was nearly asleep. Valis leaned her head against Razele, but Ruby fought against her exhaustion.

"No," she said. "We're still in danger. I can...."

I sighed. "How can you fight an army if you're exhausted? It'll be fine. Just rest. If anything happens, I'll wake you."

She almost fell on her butt trying to sit down. A moment later, she was asleep.

"En, can you go back there and make sure they're all covered? I don't want anyone getting sick."

En went into the carriage and ruffled through the storage areas until she found some blankets. I stared at the desolate land. We would reach the Terra Nation soon, and from there, we had to find the contact. Then I could finally go home to the Chaos Nation and fix the problem that began many years earlier.

We traveled along without problems. It was quiet for a few hours.

The terrain slowly changed. Sand turned to dirt, then I saw trees. Soon, the trees were as plentiful as in the Kai Nation, but they were shorter with many needles on them. The Kai Nation didn't have that kind.

Moving a little bit farther, I saw a checkpoint ahead. That meant we were on the right track. There were two carriages ahead of us. We stopped behind one, and En looked up at me.

"Will this turn into a fight?" she asked.

I shook my head. "No. I'd like to get through this unscathed if possible. We'll say we're survivors from the destroyed village. They should let us pass."

One carriage moved through the checkpoint. I moved us up another spot.

"Well, Brother, what if that causes an alarm?"

She was right. I couldn't say we were slave traders, because none of the girls were bound or beaten up. We didn't have many provisions, which meant we weren't traders. We wore Celestial Nation garments.

"What if we are diplomats, En, looking to make a deal on new armor or weapons?"

She shook her head. "That's just as dangerous, if not more so. Who's to say there aren't such diplomats already here?"

The carriage ahead moved through, and then it was our turn.

"I don't hear anything coming from you," I said softly, moving up to the front spot.

She smiled and whispered, "Just follow my lead."

That made me instantly anxious. A Terra Nation warrior approached. His sleek metal helmet fit him well. The body plates were polished to a sheen, with the Terra emblem on the chest.

"Hello, you two," he said. "Sorry for the bother. We're looking for fugitives."

En looked at him confidently. "It's nice to have strong men protecting the border. I'm thankful. What in the heavens did the fugitives do?"

He smiled. "Oh, they're charged with five counts of mass murder of five politicians and a general within the city, then there was an incident in the village of Dalluf. It was a horrible thing. Over 30,000 civilian soldiers were killed."

My heart sank, and I nearly vomited.

"Did you say civilian soldiers, Sir?" En asked in a slightly shaky voice.

"Yes, Miss. Thirty thousand were being trained for an impending war. They were slaughtered. One of the survivors said it was a vampire girl, but no one has seen any of those in hundreds of years, so we can't confirm that."

I secretly ignited my flames and sent them to cover Ruby's face in the back.

"Sir, are you all right?" he asked.

I cleared my throat and looked at him. "Yes. Sorry about that, Soldier. Hearing about all those deaths upset my stomach. My apologies."

He shook his head. "No, that's quite all right. I was the same way when I heard about it. Anyway, what are you doing here?"

"We seek new armor and armaments," En said. "We heard from a family member this is the best place to get them. We've been afraid of being drafted, so we're here to shop."

He laughed. "Oh, well, then. You're in the right place, if I say so myself. There's a village just east of here that makes the best swords. In the capital, the heart of our nation, there are people who make excellent armor and sockets for stones in the armor plate."

My eyes widened, and I looked at him, making him laugh.

"My apologies. Civilians wouldn't know, but there are people called enhancers. To become one, they have to give their bodies to the stone, but with the special sockets, they can hold up to five stones in their armor." He extended his forearm and waved his hand over it. A small layer of metal washed away to reveal stones in their protective pockets.

"That's really cool. You don't have to sacrifice your body. Brilliant."

The sockets were covered by metal again. "Indeed. If the Kai Nation got their hands on that information, it would hurt the Celestial Nation a lot."

We shared a laugh.

"Let's hope those criminals never get their hands on that."

He stepped aside. "Indeed. Have a safe trip. Please watch out for those criminals."

I nodded to him and flicked the reins. We moved ahead slowly.

Once we were out of earshot, En said, "That would be a huge advantage for us. The Celestial Nation probably doesn't have that many. That's the first time I ever saw that."

I nodded, but I still had questions. "Why is that? Why would the Terra Nation have all of them and not help the Celestial Nation?"

She looked at me in surprise. "I'm not sure. They're allies, aren't they?"

They usually were. "Maybe they want to become a superpower, meaning they want to take over the continent for themselves, but they have to show they're still allies, so they let the Celestial Nation people move freely and sell only a limited number of them. They could claim it's impossible to make them without the right materials."

That didn't sound right, though. If they wanted to become a superpower, that meant they'd be fighting the headmaster.

"Brother, if that's true, then they'd have to fight the headmaster," she said, figuring it out quickly. "If they did, it means they must have people who are his equal in power. How could they amass such people without anyone knowing?"

I realized they wouldn't have to. They could manufacture them, but it would still take time and training. "All they have to do is kidnap members of the head family and breed them together, using the children and breeding them in turn. They'd have lots of people with the head family's powers, making them nearly unstoppable."

Seeing the look on her face, I knew she understood.

"How close could they be to achieving their goal?" she asked.

I did some mental math. "It depends when they started. We won't know unless we find more information. If the headmaster doesn't know, we could be looking at all-out war. No nation would be safe. The flames of war would purge everything.

"We need to get through the Terra Nation as fast as we can and report this to the Kai Nation and Aura Nation. It's going to be a huge problem for everyone."

I slapped the reins, and we traveled faster. The sun rose slowly, and Ruby began to wake up. I heard her yawning.

"Why did you two let me sleep this long?" she asked. "It's outrageous."

I chuckled. "Ruby, I need you to keep your face covered the whole time we're here. Don't take that off no matter what."

"Why should I? Don't you love my beautiful face?"

En giggled. "That's not the reason. The whole nation is looking for a vampire. Your teeth are a dead giveaway."

Ruby sighed. "Fine. I'll keep my face covered, but I don't like this one bit, My Lord."

I looked at En. "Can you take over for me? I don't want to stop unless we absolutely have to. I need some rest."

She took the reins. "Of course, Brother. We still have to get through the capital, though, don't we?"

I nodded. "If what Galnius said is true, that's right. Most likely, we'll stay there for the night before taking the road to Leafaston. I'm not sure how far it is to the Chaos Border."

I walked into the back and looked at Ruby, who regarded me sadly. "It will be fine, Ruby. No one will harm us."

She shook her head. "You can't promise that. You died the last time."

I smiled at her and sat down, resting my head against the back. A moment later, I was asleep.

19

I heard waves crashing and opened my eyes. Bright sunlight shone down on me. I was alone on an unfamiliar beach. Only the Kai Nation had beaches, but from the environment, I could tell I wasn't there.

Walking along the beach, I felt my shoes dig into the warm sand, leaving footprints behind me. A warm ocean breeze washed over my face, and the smell of saltwater came to my nostrils. I looked at the nearby trees and saw none had leaves or branches, as if they were stripped of life.

A wave came washed over my feet. I walked through it and continued down the beach. The setting sun gave the sky a light-red hue, and the blue water gleamed with the color of the sky.

I sat on a dry part of the beach to enjoy the scenery. "How can I be in a place mentally that I've never seen? I shouldn't complain. This is absolutely beautiful, but still...."

A strange bird flew down to snatch something from the water, then it flew back into the sky. Clouds moved past overhead.

"Beautiful, isn't it, My Son?"

A woman in a long golden dress, with red and blue hair that burned slowly with white flames, came to sit beside me.

"I'm sorry, Miss, but this is just a dream. You're just an imagination of my mother."

She giggled softly, her eyes going to the sea. "Is that so? Then tell me, My Son, if this is a dream, where are all the ones you love? If this exists only in your imagination, where are we?"

I tried to find a good answer. "I'm not sure. It doesn't look like the Kai Nation. As for the ones I love, I'm not sure about that, either."

I watched her stare at the water.

"Water is a dangerous thing for the Celestial Nation," she said. "It weakens their power and can even extinguish their flame if they're too weak. If the celestial flame is too strong, then the water evaporates. Such a fickle thing, the power between flames. I never truly understood it."

I looked at her in confusion. Why was she speaking like that? "I'm not sure. I haven't fought many from the Celestial Nation. The last one I fought, well, I was destroyed. For the flame itself, I don't see it as something weird. It makes sense to me. All the flames are connected. They're the same. They can save or kill anyone."

As our gazes connected, I saw a star etched in red in her eyes, with the rest of the eye black. "Indeed, My Boy. He destroyed you. Tell me, how is your father doing up there?"

We glanced upward. "He appeared to me from a golden throne with a lot of others. I met my stepmother."

She exhaled as if releasing a large amount of stress. "I'm glad he found someone else, especially after what happened."

I stared at her. "Who are you? What's your name, and why do you call me your son?"

I watched black wings emerge from her back. Red flames raced across them until they were the same as the headmaster's wings. "My name is Staliruis Calsyus. I'm sure you can surmise that Antilunis Calsyus is my younger brother and your uncle."

I ran away from her in shock. She looked at me with no change in expression, as she flapped her wings and took off, speeding after me easily. I reached for my sword, but it wasn't there. I dodged too late.

She pulled up to stop in front of me, and a violent force pushed past me. A loud boom made me look over my shoulder, where a long funnel at least a kilometer long scorched the sand all of the way inland.

She pulled me close, my arms pinned at my sides, and cried. "I'm sorry I wasn't there for you. I didn't have a choice. I had to leave the continent and get as far from you as possible. Even now, I have to stay away. If I don't, you'll be cursed with the powers I hold."

"I don't understand. You abandoned your family because of a curse?"

She shook her head. "No. I left, because you'll destroy this world. You'll be the reason everything is ruined, including friends and family. I got away, so you wouldn't have that much power, but no matter what I did to intervene, you got stronger. Now it's too late. You've started something that can't be undone. It's been foreseen by our family. My Son, I'm sorry I couldn't help."

I pushed her away, and she sagged to the ground, crying into her hands.

"You're wrong! I'll change the world and make it better!"

She looked up at me with tear-stained eyes. "No, My Son. You have no idea what you're doing. This will be the end of this world."

I shook my head and knelt down. "I won't allow those I love to die. I'll rule the world and bring my nation back from the brink of death. You'll see."

I heard a lightning storm coming. Clouds formed overhead, and there was a loud roar from inland.

"It's too late, My Son. The founders know your strength and will destroy you. There isn't time. Celnius, take him away from here quickly!"

Dark smoke funneled away from me, as I reached for her. "Staliruis, you still haven't answered my questions. Why'd you bring me here? Who are the founders?"

I heard several more loud bangs.

"Celnius, get him out now! There's no time!"

Three cloaked figures landed on the beach and rushed me. They wore dark black robes and had red eyes. One of their arms had sharp claws and dark black scales.

Before they could reach me, smoke enveloped me, and I was in the abyss. The smoke dissipated to reveal Celnius in front of me.

"Where was I?" I asked.

She shook her head. "I'm sorry, but I can't tell you."

I bit my lip. "Who was that woman?"

"Your birth mother."

I bit down harder and felt blood trickling down my chin. "Who are the founders?"

She shook her head. "I'm not allowed to know that information."

Anger filled me. "How do you not know? I thought you were a goddess!"

Her eyes flickered with anger. "I am, but there are even more powerful beings in this universe than I."

We both calmed down, and I tried to breathe evenly.

"I didn't mean to yell at you. What did you mean you aren't allowed to know that information?"

She waved her hand, and a galaxy appeared in front of me. "Gods and goddesses think of them as the first part of ascension. Only a select few can claim that title. When a god or goddess transcends into an alpha, they become the beings who rule over the natural laws of the universe. It happens when it happens, but no one knows why.

"After an alpha transcends, he or she turns into a Celterion, one of the beings who rule over all. To my knowledge, there's only one every billion years."

I tried to process the new information. "She was convinced I would be the end of this world. Do you know why?"

Celnius waved her hands, and we looked down at the continent. "War plants seeds of hate and distrust everywhere. No matter what you do, how well you rule, or what comes from it, there will always be those seeds of hate and distrust. When the time comes, you plant more seeds in this world that haven't been planted before. Not even the gods can see through the fog you've set upon the world. It can go either way. That's why many of them see you as a threat and want to destroy you."

As we floated, I felt a sharp pain in my chest and began breathing hard.

"What is it?" she asked.

I shook my head, and the pain faded. "Nothing, just stress. If all the other gods and goddesses are against me, why aren't you?"

She faced me. "It's because I have faith in you as a child of the Chaos Nation and someone I have ties with. Remember when your father implanted power in you, it came from me. No matter what, we're intertwined in this cruel world and will share the fate that goes with it. Remember that from here on, OK?"

I nodded. The world was cruel, and the nations were out of balance. Was it wrong for me to dream otherwise? "I have no intention of causing this world to die. I just think that my vision for the world will be best for all."

She placed a hand on my shoulder. "I'll follow you through all of this. Don't worry about a thing. You don't have to justify your actions to me. Just make sure you do the best you can, and I'll always be at your side."

I looked down at the Terra Nation, where I should be approaching the capital. "May I ask you something before I go back?"

Her hand left my shoulder, and I felt her essence fading. "What is it, my dear love?"

I smiled at that. "What if I control all the nations? What happens to the gods and goddesses?"

She chuckled and said with enthusiasm, "Then they have to kneel to you, bringing you one step closer to ruling over all."

I watched her fade.

When I opened my eyes, I saw the girls standing around Razele. I stood and stretched, and Ruby came over.

"Now you're awake. You're so rude. Razele's finally awake"

In shock, I walked over to her and looked into her eyes. "It's good to see you still alive."

She gave me her lovely smile, and my mood improved dramatically. "I'll never leave you or the others."

Valis jumped forward and held Razele, crying against her chest. I walked away to give the girls their time with her.

I got out of the carriage and looked at our surroundings. We were in a forested area without much flat land. A large city nearby had to be the capital, which was good. We could rest and eat, then we had to keep going to reach the contact before we crossed to the Chaos Nation.

It wasn't far. I hoped everything would work out. I needed to see Kilyon as quickly as possible.

Someone jumped down from the carriage behind me. I turned and saw En.

"I got us as close as I thought would be safe," she said. "Do you still want to go into the capital? It could be dangerous."

I nodded. "Indeed, it could be, but we need a good night's rest and some food. There are some things I need to figure out, so I'd like to stop there."

She crossed her arms, although she wanted to argue. "Don't get us killed, Brother. I'd hate to have to beat you up when we leave."

I laughed, and we stared at the distant city. It resembled the school, with skyscrapers behind tall walls. It was so secure, it made me think of a huge prison.

"Let's go."

We got into the carriage and covered our faces, then we rode toward the city. It sat on an island with a huge hole all around the edges. The only way in was via a long, stone bridge that led to the front gates.

En looked at me. "It's a fortress, Brother. I'm getting nervous."

I patted her head. "It'll be fine. We'll all be fine. I promise."

I managed to quell her anxiety. We reached the bridge. I still felt uneasy about the whole plan, although I hid it from the others. A few carriages were ahead of us in the line. None looked any different from ours.

Five Terra warriors waited at the gate. One carriage went into the city, and the one ahead of us moved forward. I saw the driver shaking and glancing at his cargo. The ones in the back were weak, sickly children.

I listened, as they stopped to talk to the guards.

"Please, Sir, my family and I need help from the church. This is our last hope."

The soldier punched the kid who was driving. "I told you, Scum, that if you're ill, the church can't help you. The Church of Terra doesn't aid those who can't help themselves. Now leave."

The driver cried softly. "Please. This is our last chance. I don't know what to do."

"I told you to move on!" the guard snapped.

The bridge suddenly trembled. A large hole appeared under the first carriage, and the man's screams echoed, as the entire carriage fell through.

The guard waved us forward. *Can I get us through this?* I wondered.

En flicked the reins, and the beast brought us level with the guards.

"Sorry about that, you two," the guard said. "How can we help you today?"

En looked at me, and I bowed my head to the man. "We came for weapons and armor for our village. It was attacked, and we want to better ourselves."

He laughed and stood straighter. "That's a good man to protect the ones he loves. Of course. We have plenty of weapon smiths and a few armor smiths. Weapons are cheap, but armor is costly. Just make sure you have enough coin. There's a toll of two gold pieces, but for your predicament, we will waive that.

"You should also be aware there is a small problem with abductions in the city. Stay clear of the lower districts."

We nodded to them, and the guards waved their hands. A giant stone door opened slowly, trailing dirt behind it. Inside was a huge city with hundreds of people walking around happily.

The roads were paved, just like those at the school. En brought us forward, and the gate lowered behind us.

I looked around in amazement at how different it was from the school. It wasn't all skyscrapers. There were short buildings, too, housing many kinds of things.

An older man waved at us, and En turned toward him.

"Hello, Visitors," he said. "It's a pleasure to have you in our wonderful city. I can watch over your belongings and beast if you want during your stay."

I nodded thoughtfully. "How much would that cost us?"

He smiled. "That would be five gold pieces a day."

En nearly threw herself at him in outrage.

"It's a fair deal, but I have to sell some of our wares first, if that's all right with you."

He shook his head. "Of course not. If I take your offer, I'd have to raise the price to seven gold a day for the inconvenience."

I bit back a sharp retort. "That's fine. We'll pay you before nightfall."

I jumped off, and En copied me.

"Thank you, Sir, for your patronage," the man said.

The girls came out of the back, and he studied me with a corrupt smile.

Ruby came up to me. "What do we do now?"

Razele followed her. "We need to earn some money for our stay here."

Valis looked in the back of the carriage. "There isn't a lot, but we should be able to sell what we have for the night and pay him."

I looked at Razele. "Take the girls and get it done quickly. I don't want him to raise the price any more than he already has."

Ruby took my arm. "And where do you think you're going? The last time you went off, you were captured."

I smiled at her. "I promise I'll be fine. I'm taking a look at the stores to see what things cost. I want to get some armor, too, but I'll need to find weapons for all of you. That would make close combat a lot easier."

Ruby looked back at the carriage and sighed. "All right. We need the money, and we could use armor and weapons, but don't do anything stupid this time."

I waved a hand and began walking backward. "I won't. If you need me, I have the stone. Contact me so we can meet later to discuss where we're staying."

I walked off and felt their uneasiness. I said I was looking for weapons and armor, but I really wanted to visit the lower city and see what the fuss was about. I walked down the street and saw stone platforms fly across the roads. There was a network of travel going on. To my right, the road led far down a hill. At the bottom it seemed more desolate, so I walked down and watched the buildings change dramatically, showing how the rich and the poor were separated.

At the end of the road, I saw fewer houses, and most were damaged. I felt eyes on me, too. When I looked carefully at the houses, I saw kids staring at me with eyes full of envy and pain.

I watched one kid disappear around a corner. Looking ahead, I saw a large church in shambles, with some of the stone roof collapsing on itself. All the windows were shattered.

I walked to the front doors and saw they'd been smashed in. Ducking under some collapsed stone pillars, I caught a foul stench in the air and held my hand over my mouth while taking short breaths.

All the pews were destroyed. An altar with an orb sat hovering above it, pure green with a brown aura. As I went forward, I saw corpses strewn on the floor How had I failed to notice them?

Stepping over one corpse, I heard a voice in my mind so loud it rattled my skull.

Who trespasses within my domain?

I shook my head. "My name is Kit. I'm a curious wanderer, nothing more."

The orb glowed, and strong grass and flowers appeared around the church. It changed to a garden with bright sunlight above.

Those with purity in their hearts may gaze upon my figure, but those with intent to cause harm will be struck down. Tell me, Brave Soul, which are you?

I watched birds and forest animals walk past. "I'm neither. I can't say I'm pure of heart, but I also have no intention of causing you harm."

A bird flew in front of my face. Its mouth opened, and it said, "Those with purity may seek me, but those with obscurity fall far from me. How is it that someone like you can walk in my domain, if you don't have purity of heart?"

The bird flew off. "I don't know. What of the ones I saw dead in the church? Did they have ill intent in their hearts?"

A small viper slithered down from a tree branch enough that we could look into each other's eyes. "No. they pleaded for help but were given deadly poison. The Church of Terra helps only those who help themselves."

Anger rose in me, and the snake hissed. I calmed myself, and the snake calmed, too.

"I don't understand. They did everything to come to you, but you let them die within your domain. They did what they could."

The viper shook its head. "No, they didn't. They suffered a terrible death, because they couldn't help themselves."

I walked away from the viper down a dirt pathway. Flowers bloomed with every step I took. "What would constitute someone helping themselves in your eyes?"

A smaller bird landed on my shoulder, as I traveled down an endless road.

"Those who sacrifice what is dear to them to pay for the help them want. That would constitute what you ask."

I swatted at the bird, but it merely hovered over me.

"So if they sacrificed their souls, you'd help, but you, in turn, would own them?"

Laughter came from all around, shaking the trees. "Of course, my small friend. It's no different than your owning the girls who travel with you."

I grabbed the bird out of the air. All the tree branches suddenly closed in around me and formed points in their ends.

"Careful with your hostility. In my domain, my creations don't take kindly to violence."

I released the bird, which landed on my shoulder again.

"I don't own any of them," I said. "If any might fall into that category, it would be Valis, but I did that only to save her life. If she wanted to break the contract, I would do it in a second."

The bird flew around to study me. "Oh? Would you allow her to die? You know the rules about slaves. She would die very soon afterward."

I forced myself to remain calm. "She's not a slave, you mangy bird."

I stopped when bright, flickering lights gathered to take Valis' shape.

"Really? She's nothing more than a slave from childhood. She lost everything. Have you even taken the time to learn about her? She's in love with you. She took the time to learn everything about you, but you haven't given any thought to learning about her, have you?"

I touched the flickering image and saw my hand pass through. "They know I love them. I haven't, and you're right, but I'm trying my best. We've been on the move, unable to stay in one place for long. It's not easy."

The image shifted to Ruby.

"What of the vampire? That sweet girl is far more powerful than she lets on. She's a monster capable of destroying this world. If she got out of control, would you try to stop her or let her destroy all in her way?"

I sighed. "I'd do everything in my power to stop her, but I'd never kill her. I'd allow her to run wild."

The image changed to Razele, smiling at me.

"This one is Razele, am I correct? She's a strong-willed girl from a troubled home, but it seems all of you have. Isn't that right?"

I nodded. "You could say that. I may have come from a troubled home, but I had someone who cared enough to raise me. Valis didn't. Her parents died. Razele, on the other hand, never met her mother, and her father kicked her out because others found out about her past. He was forced into it."

The bird disappeared, and Razele's mouth opened to speak. "That's true, but your father caused more problems for me than any human in his world, yet you hang in the balance. You can turn into him or become a new man. I wonder which you will choose. With all these girls madly in love with you, I wonder which one will burn a nation to get you."

I walked through the image and kept going. "None of them. As long as I get strong enough, no one will have the power to trap me again."

I sensed he was still following me. The trail continued without apparent end.

"This is just an observation, but to hold that much power would be selfish. What would you do with it?"

I looked up at the sky. "That's easy, my mangy friend. I'd make the nations one and let the people become one, and then I'd find a way to create more land for a growing race."

Vines wrapped around my feet, stopping me. A man stood before me with a vine-and-thorn crown. He wore red silk robes and had a mark on his right cheek that resembled a tree.

"What of the gods that protect these nations? Would you kill them?"

I tried to move my feet but realized it was useless. "No. I don't intend to kill them, but they would no longer have the nations. It would become one large nation. They would keep their people to protect and watch over."

The man scratched his long, dark-red beard. "That's a thought. It's something I would feel all right about."

The vines left my legs.

"You have my blessing, Kit. I shall support you and my sister, Celnius. I look forward to the path you create for this world."

Butterflies flew around me, and the man spoke again.

"Remember my name, Teralicion."

My vision faded, and I stood back in the church, but the orb above the altar was gone, as were the bodies I'd seen.

I shook my head, wondering if I just passed out, or was I actually in a forest filled with talking creatures?

I turned and saw a woman on her knees, bowing to me.

"Please, Sir. Save my daughter."

I looked down at her. "I'm sorry. I have no interest in risking my life. Have a good day, Miss."

I stepped past her, but she grasped my ankle with surprising strength. "Please! They took her and all the girls from around here. They always disappear. I just want my daughter back."

Her voice was drowned out by Ruby's voice.

"My Lord, we have enough money for a room at the inn called the Terra Hollow."

I took the stone from my pocket. "All right. I'll be there a little later. Make sure you all stay in that room."

I looked down at the woman who held my leg.

"OK, My Lord. We'll do as you say. Try not to cause trouble."

I slid the stone into my pocket, as the woman collapsed. With a sigh, I touched her neck and felt a pulse. Lifting her, I realized she was incredibly weak. Her hair was mangy and dirty, and her skin was so filthy, I couldn't tell its normal color.

"It looks like you'll come with me for the night until I can figure out how to help you."

I heard bird wings flapping behind me. When I turned, it flew off. "Of course you'd set this in motion for me. I wonder what you want me to find, God of Terra."

I walked out and saw the scavengers eyeing me. They must have waited to see if I'd come out alive or be left dead inside. I walked up the street, and more came from the shadows to watch me.

They began chanting, *"Ra li mo oll noll foll."*

As they repeated the phrase, I asked softly, "What does that mean?"

The woman in my arms stirred. "It means *peace of the savior.* It's an old saying from those who lived in the past."

I looked down at her. "Rest. Don't push yourself. I'm still irritated that you walked into a dangerous place like that to seek my help."

She gave a weak chuckle. "Terra helps those who help themselves."

She fainted again, and I shook my head. When I reached the main street, it was like entering another world. A civilian looked at me as she passed.

"Miss, do you know where the Terra Hollow is?" I asked.

She seemed shocked at the sight of the woman I carried, but she said, "Oh, yes. It's one block down. Take a left, and it's the first building on the right. It's a small establishment."

I nodded in thanks and walked down the street. Those who saw the woman in my eyes did their best not to smile, although I knew they assumed I would abuse or kill her. None looked at me. All their glares were directed toward the woman. Were the poor so despised here? Why? It wasn't their fault they were poor. Some people would give up, but others simply fell and weren't able to pick themselves up again.

Why would they cast such hate upon others when they could lend a hand and pull them to their feet? Even if they fell again, at least the helper would have tried. It seemed all they saw was a disgusting person who had nothing to offer.

I stopped in front of a building with a sign that read *Terra Hollow.* The interior had white marble walls and carpet on the floors. Some walls were made of red stone.

I looked toward the receptionist counter and saw people eyeing me. I walked toward them, and a blonde girl waved with a smile that was quite deceptive.

"Hello, Sir. How may I help you today?" She peered at the woman.

"My name is Kit. Did my friends tell you I was coming?"

She bowed her head. "Of course. They're on the sixth floor in room 402. When you step off the lift, turn left, and you'll be there."

I bowed my head in thanks and walked away.

"Sir, be careful of the kind of luggage you carry in the city," she said after me. "Many unsuspecting people have come to harm when they helped those who can't help themselves."

I continued walking to the lift door and channeled my energy into the stone, waiting until I heard the lift descending. The doors opened, and I walked in to channel my energy again. We rose to the sixth floor. Leaving the lift, I looked both ways.

It was like the building we stayed in at the school. Everything was very clean. Fancy rugs and furnishings were everywhere in the Terra Nation. Perhaps it was because we were in the capital.

I walked left and saw the door numbers changing until I reached ours. I knocked three times and heard footsteps running toward the door.

Valis stood there. "Master, you're back!" She saw the woman. "Master, what is it with you always bringing new women home? Are you a pervert?"

I chuckled and stepped inside.

"That's not supposed to be funny, Master."

I walked in and saw the layout was almost the same as our rooms at the school, only it was smaller and had only two bedrooms. I walked to the couch and set down the woman.

To my right, Razele and Ruby were trying to cook, while En held a spatula in her hand with a fiery expression. It seemed Razele and Ruby had been defeated gracefully.

"How are you three?" I asked. "Where is Raxel?"

Her voice came from behind.

"I'm sorry. I was checking the room where En and I will stay the night." She looked down at the woman. "Who's that?"

"I'm not sure. I was in the church. She was there, too, on her knees begging me to find her daughter. She collapsed, and I couldn't leave her there. I brought her back. I hoped you girls could care for her so we can find out what's going on."

Raxel stared at the woman, then knelt and placed her hand on the woman's head. "She's burning up. Razele, get me a cold washcloth. Ruby, can you come here to help?"

I looked at Raxel. "I could give her some of my blood."

Raxel shook her head. "No. You could kill her if she's just a normal human being and not from a major family. Your blood would be too strong for her body and would destroy her from the inside out."

I stepped back, as Razele and Ruby came near. "I'll leave this to you. Let me know when she wakes up."

Going to the window, I saw the sun setting. There were fewer people in the streets, and I opened the window to jump out, igniting my flames to fly to the roof. Once I landed, I took a deep breath and tried to relax.

"What a stupid thing to do. Why would I help her and endanger the rest of us, just because she asked for my help? I know I always help those in need, but there must be a line somewhere. We're deep in enemy territory, and I just helped one of the enemy."

I kicked a pebble, watching it bounce off a wall and roll. Taking a deep breath again, I walked to the edge.

"It as the right thing to do, Little Pup."

I jumped and turned to see Kilyon, apparently in a small shower of water trickling down. He smiled.

"It's been a long time," he said. "I was hoping when I saw you we'd both have better news, but that doesn't seem like it'll happen now, does it?"

I shook my head and went to my knees. "Everything has fallen apart. I've been trying to hard to mend it, but war has started. I'm gathering all the information I can, and now there are far more problems, aren't there?"

He kept smiling. "There will always be more problems, but I know you have the resolve to fix them. Right now, the Celestial Nation is trying to invade our border. We've been holding off their advances, but we've noticed they've got a special kind of armor."

I stood and ran a hand over my face. "Yes. The Terra Nation developed it. We planned to steal some and bring it back with us."

He shook his head. "No need. We have destroyed several convoys and taken some for ourselves. What of the others? How are they?"

I knew he would be angry with me. "Valis, Ruby, and Razele are fine."

His gaze pierced my soul. "Oh? That's good, but how are Entity and Raxel?"

I opened my mouth to ask how he knew, but I realized it would be a waste of time. He probably knew what would happen even before I met them.

"Both are fine. Raxel has been a lot of help. En, well, it's good to have someone else who can control chaos. That's been a plus."

Suddenly, Kelos stepped into the image, too. "There's my favorite nephew. Want to explain why we're at war, or should I pummel it out of you when you get home?"

I smiled. "Does that mean I'm allowed to come home? I assumed you'd kill me."

He laughed. "Of course you're allowed to come home. You're the next head, after all. Since we're on the subject, I won't hold back, since I know you can't die. Be prepared for your punishment."

He waved good-bye, and Kilyon came back with his palm against the side of his head. "Sorry about that. You should know you're always welcome back. This will always be your home. To be honest, we've been having a lot of trouble with the Celestial Nation. My brother was going to announce a war soon, anyway. It's not like you did much that was wrong, but tell me what happened."

As I recounted the story, he listened intently, and as I finished, he seemed weary.

"So you actually died?"

I nodded.

"I felt my memories of you slipping away. The harder I held onto them, the faster they went. Kelos had the same problem. At least we know why, but what you're saying about the gods and the alphas is troubling."

I nodded. It was bothering me, too.

"Did you see your mother up there?"

I shook my head. "No, just my stepmother and Tellium. That was it."

He scratched his beard and thought for a moment. "I'm not sure where she could be. I lost her presence some years back along with your father's. I always thought she passed. None of the others have seen her, either, and that worries me. If she's alive, I wonder where she could be."

I wanted to tell him, but I didn't know what it might mean to say that the founders were real and very dangerous. That would make the war more devastating than any war that came before.

The stone activated with Ruby's voice. "My Lord, the woman's awake. She's asking to see you. Could you come back?"

Kilyon looked at me. "Another woman? How many does that make now, six?"

I shook my head. "No. I met her in the Church of Terra. She asked for my help to find her daughter. Before I could refuse, she collapsed, so I brought her here. I intend to help her."

He gave me a pleased look. "You're just like your father and mother. They could never turn down a fellow human being even if the person was an enemy."

I bowed to him, and the mist faded. I felt better after talking to him. He always gave me a sense of relief, as if everything would turn out OK.

I stepped to the edge of the roof and fell forward. Air rushed past my hood and flapped in the wind, as I ignited my flames and stopped at our window. I landed and walked in to see Ruby sitting beside the woman, who lay on the couch.

Raxel had cleaned her face, revealing a different skin color. Black lines traced across her face, and she had stars under her eyes.

"Hello, Miss. My name is Kit. Have the others introduced themselves?"

Nodding, she tried to sit up, but she was too weak. Ruby gently helped her back down.

"What's your name?"

"I'm Serina. I'm one of the Tamletal species."

Ruby looked at her in surprise. "You're a precursor? I was under the impression all of you were killed by the gods."

Tears fell from her face. "We were, but the Terra Nation god spared us. He sheltered all of us in his domain. We've been hiding here ever since. We have to conceal our appearance, but with the rise of humans, the world has shifted, leaving most of us buried under the rich. Our race has fallen again."

I sat on the table to look at her. She was human, but she had pointed ears that were tighter than ours. Her eyes were more oval, and her skin seemed harder and more resistant.

"Serina, tell me where your daughter is now. Why'd you risk your life to find me in that church?"

Her gaze moved away from me for a moment, then returned. "She was taken by guards of the Terra Nation. I don't know where or why, but I need help getting her back."

Someone touched my back, and I saw Valis looking at me solemnly. I nodded, and she smiled.

"We'll help you, but what can you pay for our service?"

Valis slapped my back gently, though I didn't turn again.

"I can't pay anything now, but when you get her, I'll give you a rare stone only my race can create."

I scratched my face while I thought. "It sounds like we have a deal."

I offered my hand, and she took it. I turned to Razele. "Help her get cleaned up and find her something to wear. I'm sure she hasn't eaten in a while, either."

Looking at En, I asked, "Would you make her some real food?"

"Why me? The others can do it as well."

I shook my head. "No. The last time, they almost destroyed the kitchen. I don't want Serina to die."

Ruby crossed her arms and turned away from me. "You know, I'm not even mad about that."

I chuckled and looked at Serina. "Could you be a little more help. If I'm to find her, I need your daughter's name or the names of the soldiers and any idea you might have where she was taken."

Serina looked down. "A few weeks ago, a noble named Galinish was given complete authority over the poor district. Even though we're within the city limits, we're seen as outsiders. I'm sure you've noticed."

I nodded.

"Galinish takes an interest in young women for his experiments. The Terra Nation has been abducting them from all the other nations, even some from the Celestial Nation."

My eyes widened.

"Kit, isn't this what you were thinking?" Raxel exclaimed.

"Yes, it is. We weren't completely sure, though. They could have been doing something else, but if I'm right, we have a much-bigger problem on our hands than just a war."

Serina didn't want to look up.

"You already knew they've been creating stronger people for an ultimate army. How long have they been doing this?"

Serina looked away. "Twenty years. There should be at least five thousand of them right now, with another five thousand in the next two years. Most of the soldiers in this nation are just ordinary soldiers with one flame."

I rubbed my face, trying to calm myself.

"What is it?" Razele asked nervously.

"The Terra Nation is purposely creating soldiers like us, people with multiple flames who have enhanced gear and weapons. We'll be fighting an army where even just one of them could destroy an entire city."

Serina tried to rise but fell back down. "What will you do, Kit? My daughter needs your help. She shouldn't be forced into this."

I looked at Ruby. "I'm sorry for asking, but we're running out of time."

She smiled at me. "I know. It's OK. Just make sure you hurry."

Serina looked at both of us. "What are you talking about?"

Ruby removed her mask, and Serina's eyes grew huge.

"You're a vampire! You're the one who destroyed part of the school!"

Ruby turned to me. "I won't let you out of my sight. Once you're in the building, I need you to locate her daughter. We'll cause a big distraction, but that means we'll have to flee the city."

I looked at Serina. "All of us."

Ruby ran into my arms. "I owe you for this. Don't feel bad. I'll be fine."

I held her close. "You don't owe me anything. I don't want to do this, but it's the best way to get there and figure out what to do. I'm sorry."

She shook her head against my chest.

"I'm happy to do this."

I looked at Serina. "What's your daughter's name?"

"Felicity."

Lightning flashed outside, and thunder rippled across the sky.

"That should help, right, Lord?"

I nodded, as Ruby walked to the window.

"You promise to be right behind me, no matter what?" she asked, her eyes filled with hope.

"I won't let you out of my sight no matter what. You have my word."

She flew out. Lightning struck all around, but it caused minimal damage.

"En, you're with me. Razele and Raxel, protect Serina. Valis, I need you on standby."

Valis ran toward the window and jumped out, saluting me before she fell out of sight.

"I'll make sure she's taken care of," Razele said. "I promise not to kill her with my cooking. En taught us well."

Smiling cautiously, I looked at Serina. "If the food doesn't look like a human should consume it, don't eat it. We'll be back."

En and I ran to the window and ignited our flames once we were outside, making us hover. A lightning bolt crashed in front of us and landed on the street, where was Ruby fighting some of the Terra Nation guard.

We remained up high and out of sight.

Ruby saw us leaving and raised her hands. "All right. I surrender. Take me to your master. I promise not to kill anyone else."

Several soldiers walked up to her and held her arms. One kicked the back of her knees, forcing her down. They cuffed her and stopped the force of flames, although I didn't know what use that would be against a vampire. Maybe they didn't know what she was.

They formed a box around her and walked to a large stone platform sitting in the street. Once all there on it, a soldier activated his flame, and the contraption moved away quickly.

I glanced at En, and we followed carefully, making sure we didn't give ourselves away.

They went straight for a few blocks, then turned right. Suddenly, they stopped in the middle of the road. We waited and saw the ground open under them. The contraption moved down slowly until it disappeared.

20

En and I flew down to see what happened. Landing, we knelt to touch the road, but it was solid.

"Where did she go, Brother?"

I looked at her and unsheathed my sword. "I'm not sure. Want to find out?"

She chuckled, as I swung the sword, carving a hole big enough for us. En jumped in first. Darkness swallowed her, as I followed.

We fell for a few seconds. I felt En nearby.

"How deep is this, Brother?" she asked softly.

We ignited our flames and hovered. "I'm not sure. Give me a second."

I waved a hand, and three balls of Celestial fire appeared, illuminating our surroundings.

"That's better, Kit. What next?"

I looked at the walls and saw tracks leading down. "We follow those."

I waved one orb over us to make sure we could find each other easily. "Don't attack unless you absolutely have to. We need to find Ruby, then Felicity."

We flew close together and followed the tracks for five minutes. As the end finally came in sight, I extinguished the orb.

We saw dim lights below, and we slowed to a soft landing on a metal floor. Small crystal lights provided illumination. A single door was in front of us. We walked to it, but, when I turned the handle, it didn't budge.

"What's wrong, Brother? No upper-body strength?"

I offered her a chance at the door. She smirked and walked forward, placing a hand on the door. It melted into the ground, and she smiled.

"That was cheating, and you know it," I said.

She jumped over the molten metal, and I followed her into a hallway that was better lit but still made of metal.

"This is weird," I said. "This is a lot of metal to be wasted."

She looked both ways down the hall. "It is. I don't understand. Did they find a new manufacturing method to create this? Even their armor is thick. Most swords and arrows won't puncture it."

We heard footsteps ahead. I filled the hall with flames, so there was no escape for the enemy, then we ran and turned a corner to find two soldiers ready and armed.

I ducked under the first and drove my sword through his friend's gut. He fell backward, dead instantly. I turned toward the first one to see En had punctured his armor with her fist.

"What are you looking at?" she asked.

I shook my hand to release the flames, as En came toward me.

"What do we do with the bodies?" she asked. "We can't carry the armor or their weapons."

I snapped my fingers, and chaos flames enveloped the corpses. When the flames vanished, nothing was left.

"That's one way to do it, Brother."

I nodded, and we continued walking down the hall.

"What's the chance this base extends under the whole city?" she asked.

I didn't want to think about that. We came to another door.

"My guess is it can't be that big," I said. "It must be relatively small, so no one can accidentally stumble onto it. I'm not sure, though. This might be an old evacuation tunnel being used by extremists. We could be walking into a dark, unforgiving hole."

En placed her hand on the door. "If it is, we have to stick together. Make sure you don't lag behind. It would suck to have your baby sister rescue you."

The door melted away, and we entered the next room. "My baby sister is pretty amazing," I said sarcastically.

We walked into a break room, where guards sat at a table, drinking booze, and gambling. Others stood or sat around talking.

They froze when they saw us, then En and I looked at each other.

"Get them now!"

The table flew to one side. Gold pieces scattered across the floor with a series of loud dings. I sliced two guards in half, while another swung at my head. I barely had time to duck. En jumped over me and kicked the blade from his hands, as I stabbed him.

Another guard came up from behind. En jumped again, summoning flames. Black daggers flew and killed him.

A few seconds later, the room was cleared. We looked at the mess, then at each other.

"I killed four," I said.

She laughed. "I saved you. I admit you got three kills but not four."

One of the men coughed. I turned to see he was one of those who took a chaos dagger. He leaned against a wall, blood trickling from his mouth.

"Both of you are scum that should be eradicated."

I walked closer and knelt to make sure he could see my eyes. I raised my blade to his neck, but he didn't flinch or look away, maintaining eye contact.

"We're looking for two women," I said. "One is a vampire. The other is called Felicity. Do you know either of them?"

He coughed and spat blood into his lap. "Oh, yeah. I know both those whores. I won't tell you a thing."

I nodded.

The man cast his eyes toward the ceiling and said, "Please, Terra God, exterminate these fools and bring me into your grasp."

I slid my blade into his throat and watched him choke on his own blood as the sword withdrew. He slumped over and died.

"He was no help. En, it looks like we have to keep searching."

I walked away, wiping blood from my blade before sheathing it.

"Brother, why do those who have nothing pray to a god who won't help?"

We stood back-to-back.

"When someone is desperate or filled with fear of the unknown, they place there hope and belief into something greater than himself. They pray that there hopes will be realized. That's not to say that prayer is bad, or believing in a god is bad, but if you're going to, you must realize that the god you pray to doesn't grant protection or love. He offers curses and despair. That's what I've learned."

Looking cautiously around the room I saw a few doors. One stood on our right, and I walked toward it.

En followed. "That's terrible to think about."

I nodded, as we reached the door. "A lot of people can't handle that idea. Maybe I'm wrong. Maybe in the end, the gods cherish them all, and the gods have a special plan for everyone, but the likelihood of that is zero. The best thing we can do is help those we can and make sure the world isn't destroyed by stupidity."

En melted the door, and we stepped over it into another metal hallway. The strong scent of iron filled the air, and we covered our noses.

"That's awful, Brother. Where is it coming from?'

I saw no doors, and there was no rust on the walls. We continued and turned left. Without realizing it, I stepped into a puddle of blood. It covered the walls. Corpses had been recently torn apart, with pieces thrown everywhere.

"This is Ruby's handiwork."

I knew she might lose control at times, but the damage was far too extensive even for her. "I don't think so. It looks like we might not be the only predators down here."

A high scream ricocheted off the walls. We covered our ears and dropped to our knees, but the screams continued. They bounced inside my head.

I saw a tall, dark figure ten feet away, its arms as thin as swords. There were no eyes in the head, but it had a large mouth. The legs were as thin as the arms.

"Brother," En asked softly, "what's that?"

"It appears we're the prey in this scenario, En."

I watched the beast and took deep breaths to remain calm. As I stood, I placed my hand on my sword hilt. The beast growled. I released my grasp, and it calmed.

"En, I need you stay behind me, understand?"

I took a step forward, and En grabbed my arm.

"Are you crazy? What happens if it tries to kill you?"

I turned to her. "That won't be easy. I'm immortal."

She let go, and I kept walking slowly forward.

"Easy," I said gently. "We aren't enemies. I'm looking for a few people here, a vampire named Ruby, and a girl named Felicity."

When I said the second name, the beast howled.

"Easy, now. I mean her no harm."

It calmed for a moment. I felt something invade my mind and stopped walking.

Who are you?

The voice grew stronger and echoed in my skull. The rasping sound cut like daggers. I breathed hard, trying to stay calm.

"I'm Kit. I'm just seeking friends. That's all."

The invasion grew. *Oh, your friends. What's your goal here?*

The uncomfortable feeling faded.

"I want to take them and leave." I bowed my head to the creature.

It disappeared. En was as shocked as I was.

"What was that?" she asked.

I shook my head. "I'm not sure, but it's a good thing we didn't upset it."

I walked down a trail of corpses to a wrecked door. We walked through and found a dead end, just four walls of metal. As En and I walked into the room, we touched the walls, trying to figure out where we were. Stamping my foot, I heard a hollow sound.

En asked, "How far do you think this drop is?"

I activated my flame and cut a hole. "Only one way to find out."

En jumped in and saluted, as she passed. I shook my head and jumped after her. Darkness surrounded us. We activated our flames, and I flicked my wrist to summon red flames around us.

We fell slowly toward the bottom of the hole, but there were no tracks to follow, just a tunnel going farther into the secret base.

The bottom finally came. We touched down and stepped on something that crunched. The floor was littered with skeletons and corpses. Taking another small step, I heard a moist crunch and saw someone's intestines. I looked at the face and saw the tracks of tears.

"She didn't deserve this," I said. "This is the fate of the women who aren't compatible with their trials, or maybe it's a sick human joke."

En walked to me and bent over to close the girl's eyes. "This is barbaric. This is what nations do when people stop asking questions."

I lifted my foot, looking where to place it next, but there was nothing but bodies all around. "It appears to be that way. The Kai Nation is no exception. I'm sure my uncle has skeletons in his closet, but I know something like this would never be allowed there. At least, I hope not."

We walked on the bodies. There was no way to avoid them. We saw children all the way to grandmothers. The site was revolting.

It wasn't easy to see where we were going. I sent red flames up and looked again.

The room wasn't as open as I thought. Just a little farther ahead was a metal wall. I cut through with my chaos flame and saw a bright light coming out.

We stepped in, with En slowly following. Peering back at the scene, she asked, "Are we going to leave them there? Is there nothing we can do?"

I nodded. Turning back to the opening, as En moved aside, I knelt and allowed chaos flames to race through the room, consuming them all.

"At least this way, I hope their bodies and souls will be at peace."

The new room was completely lit by crystals and large columns of vats in endless lines.

En and I split up to investigate. Some of the vats held tiny fetuses swimming in green ooze. I touched the vat and found it icy cold, although the room temperature was normal. Large tubes reached into each vat.

Walking farther down the aisle, we saw the size of the fetuses increasing all the way to birth. At the end of the line, we saw a girl of about twelve, floating in the liquid. Her hair changed through the colors of the elements without stopping. Her flawless face held no dimples, cuts, or any other mark.

I touched the vat just as En's hand tapped my back.

"Kit, you have to see this right now."

Looking at her concerned expression, I followed. As I walked, the vats became very different.

"Look, Brother."

We stopped in front of a vat that held a man with short hair that changed through all the elemental colors. Long black streaks raced down his body to his stomach, where they formed a spiral.

"It's like the girl I saw," I said. "Are the others like this?"

En nodded. "There are at least a hundred aisles with different people in each vat. This is where they're breeding their army."

I stared at the man floating in front of us. "They are, but how do they transport the fetus to the vats? If they're doing that, why are there so many corpses. Did they just learn how to do this? If that's true, then why continue to abduct more women?"

Footsteps echoed. A sleek figure walked toward us from where we came in. His face was covered with a mask, making him look like an order agent, but something told me he wasn't.

I stepped past En. "Go ahead and look for our friends."

She hesitated. "Brother, who is that?"

The figure stopped and looked at me, then at the vats.

"I see that the unnatural king has found his way down here."

It was a woman's voice, speaking with clear distaste.

"Unnatural king? Where, pray tell, does a name like that come from?"

En's hand left mine, and I heard her walk backward softly.

"It's something people have started to call you. Your name is spreading like wildfire within the school. Now it's leaking out among the civilians like a plague. It's disgusting to see such rabble cling to a disposable figure."

"En, hurry," I whispered.

As she ran away, four daggers flew toward her, but I caught them and gave her a chance to escape.

"That wasn't very honorable, attacking when someone's back is turned," I said.

The woman chuckled and disappeared, leaving only a small amount of dust. I brought up my defenses and looked around. When something whooshed behind me, I turned and saw her, but I was too late. Two daggers plunged into my arm.

I jumped away and pulled them out, realizing they were made by a god to incapacitate someone like me. "Funny, a woman with such ability and precision is rare. What if you were to join me?"

She grabbed her mask. Dark-blue hair waved to the sides of her face, while her gold eyes sparkled on red skin. "I'm sorry, but my master doesn't believe in siding with unnatural gods. I'll have to decline. If you'd like to beg for mercy, this is the perfect time. I won't hold it against you. No one would. The weak should die."

Looking at my arm, I realized there was no way it would heal quickly. I had to cut it off and let it regenerate, but that would take time. I was up against a very perceptive enemy who would do anything to keep me from having enough time.

We watched each other for a moment. "If I'm an unnatural king, what are you, Miss?"

She bit her lip hard enough to make blood trickle across her lips. She smeared it across them. "That's easy. I'm the queen of despair. Her king has gone too far this time."

She charged at me and swung. I moved toward her enough to let her sword cut off my left arm and jumped back, feeling it grow again.

I drew my sword with my right hand. She closed with me, and I swung, blocking her daggers. The force of the impact made us bounce apart.

"Not bad, Kid. I wonder, though, if you're really a king or just a fool with good luck. Only time will tell, I suppose. Until the next time I see you."

I charged, but she disappeared in red flame. I stared, dumbstruck, trying to understand what just happened. If she wanted to protect the place, why did she leave?

I shook my head, walking backward and heading where En went. As I took one last look at the vats with all those human creations in them, I wondered if I should destroy them. If I didn't, they could cause problems down the line, but was it right to kill those who couldn't protect themselves? They didn't want that, nor did they ask for it.

I stared at the girl in the vat. Her eyes opened slowly, and she looked at me in confusion.

"You didn't want this life," I said, "but nonetheless, you could destroy the world. I'm sorry, Little One."

I raised my sword, letting chaos surge into it. She looked at me innocently, without a hint of hatred or worry. She closed her eyes and smiled. Did she know what I planned to do, or was she happy to know someone saw her?

I prepared to swing my sword when a familiar presence appeared behind me.

"Hello, Little Pup."

I looked up, freezing at the sound.

"What is it, Kilyon?"

He looked around. "So this is where they're creating the soldiers for their war. I'm sure you planned to find it and destroy it, am I right?"

I held my sword tighter, but my eyes drifted away from the girl. "I know this is wrong, but they don't deserve this. What else is there? If they live, they could destroy everything in their path. I don't have the strength to stop them, nor could I even with all the supporters I have. They've been bred for war."

I moved the sword closer to the girl, who smiled as if nothing bad ever happened in the world.

"That's true. In a sense, they are monsters for war, but even monsters can be as beautiful as a rose."

I looked back and forth between the girl and Kilyon. "I hear you, but so many people could die because of this. I've been doing my best to save people, not kill them."

Kilyon walked forward, his appearance made of mist like before. "She's a beautiful girl. Maybe she might not have hopes and dreams. Maybe she doesn't even know what those are, but she could be of use. I know you want to be a great king to this world, but you have to give everyone the same treatment, even if they were created from experiments."

Lowering my head, I looked at her. She opened her eyes again to look at me, smiling. Sighing, I changed my grip on the sword and tapped the glass with the hilt. When it broke, goo splashed out. I sheathed my sword and caught her when she fell out, then I stood and looked at Kilyon.

"I have to take her through the Chaos Nation with me. I'll do my best to protect her and bring her home."

He bowed his head and disappeared. I shook my head and walked toward another entrance.

"You'll cause me more problems than solutions," I said, "though my master was correct to give you a chance."

She seemed asleep in my arms. Two doors waited for me. Both opened on hallways, but the right was my best bet, because it was burned to a crisp. I smiled and walked into the doorway. I was glad there were lights everywhere. Someone decided to keep the place well lit. It would be hard to summon flames with both my hands occupied.

I heard multiple footsteps and stopped to look around, but there was nowhere to hide. I would have to lay her down, then attack with all my power.

I prepared myself, as the footsteps drew closer. En came around the corner with Ruby. Ruby saw me and ran over to me. She was covered in bandages and was crying.

"You kept your promise," she sobbed.

"Of course I did. I was a little scared once you went underground, but we never gave up."

Ruby backed up to look at me with a smile. En walked over with the girl in her arms.

"Is that Felicity?" I asked.

En nodded.

"It'll be insanely hard to get out of here." I looked around. "Ruby, was there a way out you noticed?"

She shook her head.

I summoned chaos flames and make a focal point directly overhead. "I'm not sure how well this will work. You should stand close to me."

They came in as close as they could, and my flames grew hotter, until a purple beam shot up.

"All right," I said. "Both of you be safe. Follow as close as you can. I'm not sure how far this will go, so we need to be prepared for anything. En, make sure you protect Felicity. Ruby, stick close to me. I won't let you out of my sight for now."

She held tightly onto my side. "OK, My Lord. I won't leave."

I ignited my flames and shot upward. We burned holes through several floors. En followed as closely as she could.

As we shot up faster and faster, I smelled fresh air again. Smiling, I was glad to be out of that unbearable place.

We shot from the ground and rose into the sky, inhaling clean air and enjoying every second of it. En flew up beside me. We shared a look and headed toward our hotel.

Once we reached it, we moved close to our window and tapped it.

Razele ran over and opened the window. Once we were inside, I walked to the couch and set the girls down, while I sat on the coffee table. Looking at them, I rubbed my face wearily and felt Ruby still holding onto me.

"Lord, who's that girl?" she asked, pointing at the one we rescued.

"She's an experiment."

Ruby stared at her. "Experiment for whom?"

I shrugged. "Right now, I don't know, but I know we're in way more trouble than I thought. They're breeding some very powerful people below the Terra capital. I'm sure they planned to use you and Felicity as test subjects."

Felicity and Serina's faces were completely different. Serina wasn't much older, but they had the same marks on their faces and arms.

Serina awoke and saw me sitting on the table. With a gasp, she asked, "Did you...did you save my daughter?"

I nodded and indicated Felicity. Serina rushed to her daughter's side. When Felicity woke, she began crying softly.

"Mother, you're OK."

"Yes, my Dear. I'm fine thanks to Kit. I have you again, and we're both safe."

Felicity lowered her head. "Thank you, Sir, for saving me and my mother. What can I do to repay you?"

I wondered what to say. They needed to return with me, but if they did, it would cause even more problems for all of us. "There's nothing you have to do. I'm glad I was able to save you and your mother."

Serina shook her head and dropped to her knees in front of me. "No. I, Serina Castiliano, pledge myself and my life to the protection and safety of you and the nation you will create."

Felicity bowed her head, too.

Ruby came close to murmur, "Lord, is this a good idea?"

En smiled, and Razele nodded to me.

"It appears to be, Ruby," I said.

Raxel walked to my side. "I'm not against having them join us, but a larger group will attract even more attention."

She was right, but I knew how to fix that. It wouldn't be a big problem for the moment.

"We need to leave the city within a few hours," I said. "If not, we'll have to deal with many more enemies."

En asked, "So what's the plan? We don't have a large enough carriage."

I chuckled. "You're quite right, Sis. I need you to acquire a new one, preferably with some new gear."

En walked toward the door. "My dear older brother, what will you be doing while I gather all of that?"

I laughed. "Me? I'll make sure we have an exit." I asked Ruby, "Remember what I said? You can't leave my side, at least for a while longer."

She kissed my cheek softly. "That's fine. I want some payback. They were a little forceful, and I want to have some fun."

When I glanced at Razele, she seemed to know what I was about to ask.

"I'll make sure they're protected. We'll set out once everything is ready to go."

I bowed my head to her, thinking how amazing she was. "Raxel, I need you guard our new allies if you can."

She shook her head and smiled. "Well, I do owe you—you and your stupid plans."

When I stood, Ruby slowly released me.

"Sorry for leaving so quickly," I told them. "We'll have to get some sleep on the way to our destination."

No one even considered complaining.

En walked up and punched me. "Just make sure you don't cause another mass panic and die, Dear Brother."

I batted her forehead. "Don't cause me problems, and we'll see what happens."

I walked past them, with Ruby right behind. I stepped out the window and looked at Felicity, who was asleep again.

"Don't worry, Master," Valis said, checking the girl. "She's all right now. Make sure we can leave safely."

I looked out at the city, as Ruby grabbed my sleeve.

"Come, My Lord. We have chaos to spread."

I shook my head and jumped out after her. Ruby was slightly ahead of me, as we both fell toward the ground. Igniting my flames, I scooped her up and pulled her in close, then I shot down the city streets, sending flames out to strike the walls. Chaos fire spread quickly, enveloping the city. Panic set in. A platoon of Terra soldiers saw us and began firing arrows at us.

Ruby dropped alone and fell toward them. She did a backflip in midair and set yellow lightning bolts at the enemy. They struck hard, kicking up plenty of dust and debris. Screams spread throughout the city.

Ruby flew back and hovered beside me. "Lord, what else should we do?"

Part of the road opened up. "We make sure the enemies here never decide to attack this world."

Thunder cracked, and large flashes of lightning burst across the sky. "Should I aim for the underground part?" Ruby asked.

"Yes."

Two yellow dragons made of lightning circled overhead. They dived toward the opening and exploded upon impact, shaking the entire city. Buildings collapsed from the pressure.

Civilians ran around in panic. Ruby saw them, too, but I held up a hand.

"Don't harm them. They don't deserve it. We're here to distract. The only reason we're killing the soldiers is because they have it coming, all right?"

She looked away from the civilians. "I understand, My Lord. Won't this just add to the problem if we let them live? They might come after us later."

I said, "That's true, Ruby. There's always the chance a civilian might attack us later, but I believe no one in the city knows what's going on. If we let them live, they may come to realize that their true enemies came from their own country, not the invaders who exacted justice."

I looked down the street toward the bridge. "Anyway, we don't have time. We need to make sure the bridge is safe for them to cross in carriages. Let's go."

We quickly flew to the main gate and saw carriages racing toward the closed gates.

"How will we open up a hole for them?" Ruby asked.

"I might have an idea, but I don't know how well it will work."

I flew down to the street and looked at the city gates. Taking in a deep breath, I let my flames grow wild and surround me until even the ground underfoot was ignited. I heard carriages coming up behind me and raised both hands toward the city wall. Red flames sparkcd into a ball, and chaos rushed to fill it.

Ruby flew down and landed beside me. "Lord, won't that...?"

I tried to concentrate, though I understood her concern. If my plan backfired, I would accidentally level everything around me.

"Yes, Ruby. I need you to get back."

Her hand came down on mine. "I won't go anywhere, remember? This is where I belong."

Smiling, I felt a surge of power rush through my veins. Magic sparkled around the ball, completing it. I opened my palm, and a bright beam shoot from my hand to melt the gate away.

My jaw dropped. "That was awesome!" I nearly collapsed, as chaos flames continued burning around me.

Ruby caught me.

"Thanks, Ruby. That took more power than I thought."

She chuckled. "Well, you did just combine two different flames. I'm not sure how safe that is."

I shrugged. We watched from the side, as the first carriage flew past us toward the gate.

"Maybe," I admitted.

The second carriage was driven by Razele. "Get on, quick!" she shouted.

Ruby jumped and pulled me with her. We landed on the front bench.

"That was impressive, Kit," Razele said, driving us toward the open gate. "How'd you do that?"

My vision became blurry and faded. "I'm not sure. I'm just glad it work. Looks like...I'm going to black out. Protect the others until I can wake up."

My eyes closed.

21

"Tell me, Little Pup, what is love?"

I opened my eyes and found myself in a destroyed house, my back to a wall. Celnius lay on the floor in front of me.

"I don't know if there is a true way to explain it. Love is an emotion. You were human once. Didn't you ever feel it?"

She rolled onto her back and looked up at me. "When I was a little girl, I had a mother. At least, I believe she was my mother. She was slaughtered. As for my father, I never knew him. By the time I reached twenty, I was always on the move by myself. I had to kill, hunt, and slaughter to survive. I never had a friend or anyone I could say I loved."

I watched her stare up through the broken brick. A dark, gloomy sky radiated sadness like an ocean of sorrow washing over everything.

"I see," I said. "I never knew my real mother. As for my father, well, I didn't know him, either. Kilyon took me in and raised me like his son. The rest of the Icealis family treated me very well, but as for love, I know deep down that if Kilyon was in trouble, I would do anything to help him. If I lost one of the girls, I don't know what I'd do. I believe I would lose my mind and hurt those who harmed one of them."

She blinked and regarded me solemnly. "Why do you insist on taking over the world when you know you're only spreading fire even worse?"

Placing my hands in my lap, I looked at her confidently. "I know that the war I started will kill a lot of innocent people who don't deserve to die. I won't ever be able to find redemption for what I have done, nor will I ever have an excuse."

She sat up and scooted closer until we looked into each other's eyes. "Answer me this—why? What's the point, if you know all of this will be bad for other people? Why keep going?"

Sighing, I hung my head. "That's a difficult question. I can't say what we've done isn't good. I just know it could be better. Each nation is secluded from the others. Families and children are persecuted. At the heart of it all, we have a dictatorship standing over all the nations, making sure we do things that aren't right. What I've seen is sick. Take the girl I saved from that vat. She was created for war. After that, the only life she would have is to be tossed aside. That's not a life."

Celnius blinked and took my hand. "Then what's your plan for her? Can you truly say you have honest intentions for that girl?"

I shook my head, unable to lie to her. "I don't harbor any hatred for her or what she is, but either way, she's dangerous. I need to know what I'm fighting in this war. If I can get enough information, then giving her a normal life would be fine."

She shook her head. "She'll never be able to have a normal life. If she's bred for war, that means she'll always want to fight or kill. How can you stop that?"

Once she asked the question, I realized I didn't know how to reply. I couldn't take her life. There was no reason for that. "If she gets out of hand, I'll calm her down. If the worst comes, I'll be the one who stops her for good."

Celnius bowed her head and released my hand, as raindrops struck my face.

"All those who live aren't entitled to life. They can't be. They can earn it. That's what the god of chaos told me when he passed on, but I never truly understood until now."

I looked at her with confusion. Her words made little sense. "I don't follow you."

She giggled and looked at me, her hair dripping. "It's simple. Humans are absolutely disgusting creatures. They kill, rape, and commit atrocities just because they can. They're ignorant and blind to what's going on around them. They don't deserve an afterlife. For those who are worthy enough, though, they deserve to stand next to us.

"Your father was worthy. He knew what needed to be done and did it even at the cost of a whole family line. You, Kit, are his spitting image and are currently walking down the same path. I wonder, though, if you know where it will take you, or if you're just along for the ride."

She snapped her fingers.

I woke in the back of the carriage, with Ruby and Valis heads on my lap. En drove the carriage. Razele was talking to her, but I couldn't make out what they said.

I stopped from getting up to avoid disturbing Ruby and Valis, but when I looked up at Razele again, she immediately looked back.

"It's good to see you awake. How'd you sleep?" Her smile was like sunlight in a dark cavern. No matter what, I was always happy to see her, and I didn't know why.

"I did. Thank you. Where are we?"

She looked back at the road. "We're almost at the village where that man said he had a contact. It's weird. I haven't been able to see it. Raxel hasn't found it, either. She's just ahead of us with the rest of our group."

I nodded and felt Ruby stir. Her eyes opened slowly.

"Oh, My Lord, it's good to see you. Are you OK?"

I rubbed her head. "Of course I am. Why are you so worried?"

She blushed and laid her head back down. "I'm always worried about you. That's what happens when you care for someone a lot."

As I rubbed her head, she drifted back to sleep.

"Master?" Valis asked.

"Yes?"

"Do you love me?"

I lay my free hand on her shoulder. "I love all of you. I'm not very good with words, which is something I need to work on, but yes, I love you. I love you all."

She wrapped her arms around me. "Thank you so much." She began crying.

As she clung to me, Razele looked at me with tears in her eyes, too. I smiled and felt so happy to have them with me.

Wind picked up. I looked past Razele and saw we were coming over a grassy hill. At the top, we looked down at a small village in the midst of boulders. I saw a few houses with people walking around.

"Is that it, Kit?" Razele asked.

I nodded. We were very close to the wall around the Chaos Nation, and very few people would settle there. "Yeah, I believe so."

We rode for a while longer until we reached the outskirts of the village, where we attracted a lot of attention.

I moved to get up, waking Ruby.

"Lord, what's wrong?"

I patted her head. "We're here. I need to speak with them. Wait here. I'd like to get going as fast as possible."

She nodded.

I jumped out the back and landed on soft dirt. Walking past the carriage, I saw Raxel jump from the one in front and look in the back to check her sleeping passengers.

"What do you think, Kit?" Raxel asked.

"Be cautious. Do you know the man we're looking for?"

She shook her head. "No. He was a family friend, but I don't remember much about him."

That wouldn't help. I walked toward the villagers and saw an older man with a hunched back come through the group. He walked with a white birch cane.

"What can I do for our visitors?" he asked.

Raxel and I approached him and bowed.

"I'm looking for someone who served Galnius," I said.

He eyes lit up, and he dropped the cane before he disappeared. I summoned chaos flames to surround Raxel and myself, then heard a loud bang, as our shield shook under an impact.

"What was that about?" Raxel asked, holding my arm.

I wasn't sure how to reply. It didn't seem the man was willing to help us. Lightning crackled in the sky.

"This isn't good," I said, lowering my chaos flames.

The villagers lined up against us, and my party was behind me, ready to attack.

Standing in the middle of the two groups, I lifted both hands. "Everyone stand down! We aren't here to fight!"

Ruby was furious.

"Ruby, calm down. No one was hurt."

Her lips twitched. "He attacked you!"

I placed a hand on her shoulder. "Calm down. It's all right. I promise."

Thunder stopped rolling overhead, as she went to her knees.

"Good job," I told her.

A hand touched my arm.

"What do you want?"

The old man was back, his eyes pale white.

"The spirits in the land have nothing more than ears of the Dukslore."

Elscabar stared at me. "In an infinite universe, those will always be free."

I stared without comprehending. "Galnius asked us to talk to you. We need to get through the Chaos Nation, but most of my party would die by stepping in. I was hoping you could help. He even sent his daughter to speak to you about it."

He looked at Raxel, who was in a fighting stance. "That's the stance of your father's clan. No, it can't be! Raxel, is that really you?"

She calmed and stood up straight, nodding. "Yes it is. Kit, the man you're talking to, needs your help. We all do. Will you help us?"

Tears streamed down his face. He waved his hand, and two men and a woman came over. "Get ready," he told them. "We're making an expedition through the Chaos Nation. Don't dawdle."

They ran off.

"It's a ten-minute ride to the wall from the village," he said. "From there, it's a bit more difficult, but our village will be moving."

He turned to the rest of the villagers. "We're moving to a new nation. Pack only what needs to go."

They went back tot heir homes and began preparing. Elscabar turned to me. "We're coming with you. The code you gave me was the last order my brother-in-arms gave me. My village is now in your care."

I stared in shock. What had I just agreed to?

The villagers returned quickly carrying packs.

"I won't accompany you," I said. "Neither will one of my companions. I just need you to get the others through, then lead them to the Kai Nation. There, you'll be compensated, if that's all right."

Raxel looked surprised. "Where are you going?"

I looked down at her in sorrow. "I'm going home for a little bit. Once I'm done, I'll meet up with you at the Icealis family monastery. You'll be welcome there."

She began to protest, as Razele stepped forward. "It'll be fine Raxel. Kit will come home quickly."

Raxel hugged me. "Please be safe."

I held her close. "I will. Help the others. We have many who can't fight. Be mindful of that."

We parted ways, as a boy ran up with a long piece of cloth. "Father, I brought it, as you asked."

Raxel looked at it curiously.

"Raxel, my dear," Elscabar said, "your father gave this to me saying one day, you'd come to retrieve it. He was like a brother to me, and I owe him my life. Since I can no longer repay that deed to him, it now falls to you. This weapon was your father's."

The boy handed it to Raxel, who held it without moving. Elscabar, concerned at her actions, placed a hand on her shoulder.

"Make your father proud," he said.

She looked up at me with tears in her eyes. The cloth fell away to reveal a long silver sword with gold hilt. Two dragon hands reached down the sides, and a long, blue-and-red blade ran up double-sided etchings of a sun pouring down light. The hilt was engraved with the word *Telisteler*.

Raxel said the word softly.

"She will serve you well, My Dear. Please remember that as long as you say her name, she will always return to your hand." Happiness flowed from every word he spoke.

"Thank you so much." She hugged him.

"Of course, My Dear. Now we must hurry. I'm sure you're being pursued, aren't you?"

I glanced back but couldn't tell. "Ruby, scout behind us."

She flew off.

"We need to get them going," I said.

He bowed. "Thank you, Kit, for bringing her here to me."

I turned, and Razele held me tightly.

"I'll miss you," she said.

"I'll miss you, too. Please get everyone to safety."

We pulled away and looked into each other's eyes.

"Of course," she said. "I love them as much as I love you.'

She leaned close for a brief kiss. Happiness rushed through me, threatening to overflow.

"Thank you for saying it," I said.

Something trembled underfoot. When I looked back down the trail, a large stone carriage appeared with air tanks on the side, enough for all the villagers and my companions.

"This is the best way to get through," Elscabar said. "Everyone get in."

Ruby and Razele quietly went to wake the others.

Once all were inside, Razele carried the young girl. I saw her open her eyes and say softly, "Father."

She collapsed into Razele's arms, and I stared.

"Did she just say father?" Razele asked.

I turned. "Hurry! You have to go!"

All but Elscabar quickly got inside the contraption. En stood beside me.

"Are we really going home?" she asked.

I nodded. "We are. I have some unfinished business, just like you, Sis."

Ruby flew back and shouted, "They're coming, Lord! It's a large group." She landed beside us. "I can take them out. Let me stay."

I shook my head. "No. I need you in there right now. We'll hold them off and will see you soon, all right?"

She clutched my waist. "No. I won't leave you again. I don't want you to die."

I stroked her hair. "Even if I do, I'll always make my way back to you."

She began crying, but she let go. "You promise?"

I chuckled. "I promise. Now go."

Elscabar walked her to the back of one of the contraptions. They got in, and the stone doors closed, as it rolled away.

"You know we might not make it back," En said.

I smiled and watched them depart. "Yeah. We're going into an extremely toxic nation with an army after us. I'm sorry I dragged you into this."

She sighed. "Just don't let me die a bad death. That's all I ask."

I turned and ignited my flames. "Of course not. That wouldn't be any fun."

We flew back of the hills to the open plains and saw a force of at least 200 approaching. Eli led them.

"Looks like my brother is coming to play with us," I said.

En flew in close. "Isn't he one of our allies?"

I nodded. "He is, but this isn't his doing. My guess is the headmaster forced Eli's hand."

En looked back at the force. "What do we do? We can't take them with us, can we?"

I shook my head. "No, En. All our brothers and sisters in the order would be put to death if we did."

"That's not right!"

We knew it would happen, and I was sure Eli knew it, too.

En and I hovered in midair, letting the platoon approach until we were less than a quarter mile apart.

As I watched, Eli dismounted. "Kit, I've been asked to bring you in."

I flew down and landed a few feet from him. "Hello, Eli. I had a feeling this would happen."

His mask covered his face. "I'm sorry. I did what I could to buy you time."

I smiled. He crouched into a fighting stance. "You did a good job, Brother. Everything will be fine."

I heard a soft whistle of something flying through the air. From the corner of one eye, I saw a silver light coming toward us. It became a double-bladed staff that flew into Eli's arms.

"Her name is Crusader's Dance. She was won countless battles by herself. How do you think you will fare?"

I pulled Nebula from its sheath. "I'll manage."

He lunged, and I parried. He stomped on the ground, creating black flames. I jumped up and slashed down, as the staff came up to block. Eli forced me away, and we landed a few feet apart.

"That was good, Kit. Let's dance, Brother."

We dashed forward, both slashing at each other without success. We were locked in a deadly dance with neither of us faltering. Sparks flew, creating beautiful fireworks in the sky.

"That's good, Eli. Maybe you should have taught me how to fight against a spear."

He laughed. "That's quite a compliment. It's astounding how good you are with a sword. Kilyon trained you well."

I watched the spear break through my defenses on my right side. I leaned back and kicked his stomach, knocking him back.

We faced each other, both of us panting. We were evenly matched and running out of energy. The fight couldn't go on much longer, or both of us might fall.

Eli dropped his mask. "I will die a brother." He threw his staff. It flew toward his men, cutting them down in seconds. Blood flew everywhere, as they screamed.

A few moments later, the staff returned to his hands, covered in blood.

"Eli, I'm sorry." I charged.

He prepared himself with a smile, knowing death was near. Blood soaked his face. I was within a few feet when he lunged and stabbed my side. My own blade went through his chest.

We leaned on each other and stared at the ground.

"Thank you, Brother," he said. "It's been so long since I had a good fight. I'm glad to die for you and your cause. Please save our people."

He fell forward to the ground. I pulled the spear point from my side and sheathed my blade. Kneeling, I rolled him onto his back.

His labored breathing grew weaker. "I can save you. Hold on."

I took a knife from my waist.

"No, wait. I want to die like this."

His eyes locked on mine. "Why? You can live and fight again."

He shook his head. "No. Our brothers would be killed, and our sisters would be sold as sex slaves. I won't do that to our people."

I released my hand, as En flew down to land nearby.

"Entity," he said. "Such a beautiful girl. I'm glad I saw a sister before I died."

She knelt beside him, crying. "I'm sorry we met like this again. I couldn't fight you."

"That's all right. I am content. I want you to take my spear. It was forged by your grandfather. He's hard to control, but I know you can do it. Just be careful, all right?"

She smiled and took the weapon. Chaos flames came from her skin into the weapon.

"My master," a demonic voice growled.

"I'm glad he accepted you," Eli said.

She bowed her head.

"Can I ask you something?" I asked.

"What is it?"

There were so many things, but I asked, "Where do you want to be buried, Brother?"

He smiled. "Near the sea. I wish to overlook the water and the land. That's where I belong."

I nodded, knowing exactly where it should be. I vowed to make it happen.

His hand fell limp at his side. "Good night, my brother."

He was gone.

I felt a presence and looked behind me to see Celnius standing there.

"I can hold onto his body until you reach the destination you have in mind."

I stood. "Please do. Thank you, Celnius."

She waved a hand, and Eli's body disappeared, then she vanished.

"Now that it's over, are you ready?" En asked softly.

I looked up at the sky. "I am. We'll have to make camp at my village, if that's all right."

She nodded. We ignited our flames, while En attached the spear to her back.

"Crusader's Dance drains a lot of power," she said. "Does yours do that?"

We lifted off and moved toward the wall, increasing our height.

"Yeah, he does. If I'm in combat and aren't careful, he'll suck everything out of me. You'll have to practice a lot, but you'll be fine."

We reached the top of the wall. Sunlight beamed down upon the Chaos Nation. It was very eerie, filled with dead trees, the ground a mixture of black and brown, and purple fog hanging over it all.

En asked, "They'll be fine, won't they?"

I tried to spot them, but the fog blocked out everything. "Yes, they will. They're good fighters. They have a healer, too."

I flew down with En beside me, and we headed due east toward the village.

"Will we make it there before we have to land?" she asked.

"I'm not sure. If we could combine our speed, we should get there by nightfall."

En came close. "Let's try."

We held hands and shared power. The sudden increase in speed nearly pulled us apart, then we settled and raced over the interminable fog.

22

We flew for several hours in silence, occasionally glancing down, but everything was still covered in fog. When I saw the far wall coming into view, I slowed.

"We need to move toward the ocean." I changed course.

"How do you remember where you lived if you haven't been there?" she asked.

I scratched my head. "I've been there thanks to the goddess. She showed me a long time ago."

En's and my hands were no longer connected. "How was that?"

"It was awful. The house is destroyed. There were lots of dead bodies, with a lot of fear and depression around the place."

She looked away. "I'm sorry. I know your father did what he thought was right, but he was so wrong." She took a deep breath before looking at me again.

"This will sound bad, so don't take it that way. I'm glad he did it. He may have done some awful stuff, killing your family and cursing the whole nation, but if he didn't, then I would never have met you or the other people who came with us. I'm not saying he was right, because he wasn't. I'm just saying that because of him, I can have you and the others near me. I have a chance to change the world, even at the cost of everything else. The ones we've lost will always be in my memory. I'll do everything to make sure they didn't die in vain."

She flew close and wrapped her arms around me. "Thank you for saying that. I know how you meant it. I'm glad things happened this way. I'm still mad at your father for what he did, and I don't know if I'll ever get over that. I will follow you, Brother, until I can't walk anymore. Make sure to let me into your heart."

I nodded and looked down, knowing we were close. The village wasn't far. The sun sank, and dusk would fall soon. I knew the girls were far away, and that contraption wouldn't move very fast.

"We need to get lower," I said. "Cover your mouth. Don't breathe too deeply."

We covered our faces in our scarves and flew down into the fog. Once we broke through to ground level, we saw nothing but dead trees and gloom everywhere. Farther up ahead, I saw the village.

"Is that it?" En pointed at a house without a roof.

We landed softly outside the house, kicking up dust. The stench in the air was almost unbearable, leaving us little oxygen to breathe. En looked at the other houses. All were torn down, their bricks scattered or with missing walls and roofs.

She walked unto my house. Loud crunches came from under-foot. "I'm sorry. I didn't know these were your parents."

I looked down at two skeletons. "Don't worry. They aren't my family. Do me a favor, OK? Head back up above the fog. Where I'm about to go isn't somewhere you should be."

I walked to a hatch that led under the house.

"Is that where your father did his work?" she asked.

I opened the hatch, and the stench of rotting carcasses almost made me gag and throw up. "Yeah. It's in there. There's nothing but nightmares where I'm going."

Her footsteps came closer to me. "I will join you. If this is the only way, then it's what we have to do."

I stepped near the edge, wondering if I was ready for what I would find. Would I be able to put the Chaos Nation back together? I hoped so.

I jumped, my arms crossed on my chest, and En followed. The stench grew worse. *Father, what did you do to those people, for Celnius' sake?* I wondered.

I hit water and moved aside. A moment later En struck the water. The splash almost covered me in muck.

"That's disgusting," she said. "What are we standing on?"

Darkness surrounded us. "I could light a flame," I said, "but I have the feeling I would regret it the moment I did."

She laughed. "I'm one hundred percent sure you're right."

I raised my hand, as red flames circled above our heads, giving enough light to see by. A skeletal hand floated in red and black water.

"Yeah, you were right. I regret it. What if I turn it off, though?"

I walked through the muck, feeling bones break under my feet. Bodies floated along the cave walls.

"We can't watch our steps," I said. "We're walking on corpses."

En nearly jumped from the water. "Your father was really sick."

I peeked at her. "Technically, he's your father, too."

She turned red. "I don't accept that. I'll be your sister, not his daughter. No."

I followed the water. There was no other option. As we walked over multiple corpses, I felt increasingly guilty about what he did in the name of power. It didn't seem right.

"How is there so much water, Kit? This shouldn't be possible."

Looking ahead, I saw a wooden door torn from its hinges, floating before a doorway. "I'm not sure, but we'll find out."

We reached the door. I examined it carefully, but there was no sign of an enemy. Something brushed against my leg.

"If that's you, Kit, then welcome home."

I heard my father's voice and looked inside. His shadow hovered above the water.

"You have finally returned home," he said. "Now you can hear the truth. All in this room can lead you to power."

I didn't see anything other than what we went through out in the hallway.

"I'm sure you have figured out that your path needs to be lined with the same as mine if you want to gain true, unbelievable power. I was almost there. I was obsessed with the powers of dragons."

I stared at the shadow, knowing the headmaster was one.

"Dragons are the oldest creatures after vampires. They're incredibly powerful. I was able to grant you immortality at the cost of my best friend's family. I loved him and his family, but I was obsessed. I wanted more and more power, so I did the only thing I knew. I harvested their flames and sacrificed all but one of them. I couldn't bring myself to kill Entity, that sweet little girl."

I glanced at En and saw tears rolling down her cheeks. I never should have brought her with me.

"My son, to fulfill what I started, she needs to die. You need to sacrifice her here and now. Only that will give you the ultimate power to rule the world. There is no other way. I know you'll make the right choice."

The shadow vanished, and the water drained from the room. Looking down, I saw a magic circle with a blade lying in. We stood in the middle.

"Kit, what do we do?"

I stared at the knife. It grew hot enough to steam. I bent over slowly, every nerve in my body screaming that I should take it.

As my fingertips brushed over it, my memories of En began slipping away. "En, run!" I shouted.

When I didn't hear anything, I turned and saw her being held by shadows. Her arms and legs were bound. Tears ran down her face, and a hand covered her mouth.

I tried to stop my body from moving, but I took a step toward her. I fought with everything I had without any luck. I didn't want to kill her. *Stop!* I thought.

"I said stop!" I shouted.

My hand froze with the blade beside her stomach. Sweat poured off me. Shadows came from the walls and floating toward me, their arms wrapping around me.

"I thought you wanted power," one rasped in a mangled voice.

"I do, but this isn't the way. I'll find another way."

It laughed and flew over to En. "Come on. The power is right here. You can become the ultimate dragon. Just kill your sister. Take a life you love."

I shook my head ferociously. The shadow came back and grabbed my face.

"Do it!"

I pulled the dagger back. "No! I refuse."

It grabbed my hand, but my hand turned to ice and shattered, dropping the blade. It realized what it had done and said, "You insolent child!"

En looked at me. I still had one hand. I closed my eyes and let chaos flames erupt, flooding over both of us and destroying the shadows.

I slumped to the ground, gasping for breath. En collapsed, and I held her tightly.

"I'm sorry," she gasped. "I should have listened."

"I almost killed you for nothing."

She cried, as flames burned and destroyed the seal on the floor. The ground shook.

"We need to leave!" I took her hand, and we ran back into the hall. All the water was gone, and the corpses turned to dust when touched by the chaos flames.

We ran back to where the tunnel opened overhead. When I looked back, I saw the flames becoming more violent.

"You first." I watched her ignite her flames and rush upward. I followed immediately.

We shot out of the tunnel and zoomed from the house just as it began shaking. An explosion went off, destroying the house. Dirt and debris rained down everywhere.

When En and I were at a safe distance, we floated and looked back to see the earth open to reveal a cavern filled with black flames that purified the mess my father created.

"Do you think the dead can rest?"

I felt Celnius appear.

"Those who have lost their way to someone else can never truly rest, but that was a good way to relieve the pain that was brought upon them."

En and I turned to see Celnius floating behind us.

"I completed my job here," I said. "When will the nation return to normal?"

Her mood remained sad. "It can't."

"The whole reason I came back to my village was to fix what my father did and purify his sin."

She looked away. "His sin, as you say, was you, My Dear. You're the sin. The power you possess, your immortality, must be given up for this nation to heal."

En grabbed my arm. "You can't! The nation will be fine."

It all came down to my immortality. If I gave it up, that would be a bad thing, because I would be merely human. I looked at Celnius.

"I'll do it. I'll give up the power of immortality. I want to know that you'll take Razele and Valis' power, too."

She shook her head.

"Why?"

She looked at me sadly. "It was a gift from me. The power you possess wasn't a gift. It came from an evil deed."

I understood what she meant. Without my immortality, my task would be even harder than before. Saving my nation from my father's mistake was the least I could do. If the surviving people still wanted me to be their ruler, I would. If they wanted to put me to death, I would have to deal with it.

"OK. How do we do this? Is there a ritual? Do I have to die?"

She shook her head. "No. It's quite simple. Come closer, My Dear."

I floated to her. She placed her hand over my heart. It beat very fast. Shockwaves went through my head. Part of my soul being torn away. A silver silhouette left my body, and I lost my will to fight back. Once it was completely away from me, Celnius released it to the sky, and it dispersed into the air.

"It will take time for the nation to start healing," she said. "In a few days, the air should be breathable again. In a week, the lands will become pure. A month after that, it will be habitable again."

The purple fog began dissipating slightly. "Thank you, Celnius. Maybe my people can still be brought back from extinction."

She disappeared. En hovered beside me with arms crossed. "How do you plan to tell the others that you're human? How will you run the country if you can't fight on the front lines? What will you do?"

"That's easy. I'll do all of those things, anyway. I'll fight on the front lines, and I'll be king of this world even if I'm human. It's the only way. As for telling the others, I'm not going to, and neither are you."

She wasn't very happy with what happened, but there was no other way to make sure the nation could heal. "You're asking me to lie to them? You know they'll figure it out, right? They aren't stupid."

She was right, but if I told them the truth, they'd never let me fight, and I wouldn't let them fight alone. I'd want to die with them instead of leading from behind.

"Just promise me this will stay between us."

She sighed. "I promise not to tell them, but what happens if you're injured and don't heal?"

I looked around, trying to regain my bearings.

"Where's your home?" I asked.

She hung her head. "We don't have to go there. It's no big deal."

I shook my head. "If you don't want to, I won't make you, but I feel it would be good for you to return to your home."

She turned around. "OK. Follow me. It's not far." She flew off, and I followed.

We flew for a couple hours until we reached a monastery painted black. I flew down with En, and we circled the area. It looked like a big battle took place. Had my father killed them in their homes, too?

En led us to the square. All the walls surrounding it had holes of various sizes. My feet hit dirt, and I saw corpses decomposing everywhere.

En stared at the scene. Arrows lay everywhere.

"Are you OK?" I asked.

She took a deep breath and walked toward the front of the monastery. I followed, feeling her sadness grow, as we went up the stairs. Corpses lay around us, slaughtered without remorse. A small child stared vacantly up at the sky, her mother lying over her protectively. I closed the child's eyes.

Somehow, the bodies were still in nearly perfect condition. It was as if the curse stopped the aging process of the dead. Granted, they were decomposing, but very slowly.

En stood at the top of the stairs, staring at something. I stood and walked up the stairs to stand beside her.

The double doors were blown open. Men and women were impaled on the walls with swords. Blood pooled in circles under all of them. In the middle of the room, two people knelt holding onto each other inside a magic circle. Several swords were impaled into them to keep them in place.

En walked forward, and I let her go alone. Her footsteps echoed in the room. She knelt in front of the two, and black flames sprouted from her like a beautiful flower. Each flame followed the blood trails to the original person.

En lifted her hands and touched the two in the middle. Black flames submerged them. All the corpses quickly burned to dust. I bowed my head in remembrance of those who fought and died.

"I love you, Entity."

To my shock, I heard a voice and looked up. The room filled with silver ghosts surrounding En.

"My dear, Sweet Entity, such a beautiful girl you turned out to be. I'm so proud of you."

A man dressed in black stood there, his face shining in peace, as he stared at her.

"I'm sorry, Father. I never knew this was the result. I'm so sorry." She began crying, as he extended his arm.

"Our clan might be ruined, but you're alive, and you've given us the chance to move on. Thank you, my daughter."

She stared up at her father in sadness and grief.

"Don't cry, My Dear." A woman with scarlet hair and blue robes stood there, too. "It's OK. Nothing will change. We'll stay behind and watch the woman you become. We may be dead, but we'll always be at your side."

En reached out to hug her, but her arms simply passed through. "I'm sorry, Mother. I didn't mean for this to happen."

They smiled at her. "Please, don't. We're happy now. We have been in torment for so long. Now you're here, and we know you're alive."

Their gazes went to me. All the ghosts opened a path for me to enter the circle. With a gulp of fear, because I knew I wasn't a friend to this family, because my own family did this to them, I didn't know where to begin to apologize or attempt to make the situation right. There was nothing I could do to fix it.

I took my first step, feeling as if the entire world was on my shoulders. I pushed through it and kept walking, looking from side-to-side at the ghosts. They looked ready to gut me into pieces.

I reached the middle of the room and stood beside En, who lowered her head.

"My, you've grown into a lovely young man," the woman said.

"Thank you for your kind words, Miss."

She laughed and floated closer. "Call me Anastasia. I'm sure you know my husband."

I shook my head and looked at him.

"My name is Colbert. I was your father's best friend after Kilyon."

I bowed my head, feeling horribly out of place. I didn't belong there.

"Thank you for watching out for our daughter," she said, "and for giving her a new life. We can never repay you."

I looked up instantly. "No! I'm the reason your clan is dead. I'm the reason all of you suffered. Things are this way because of me."

She looked at me soberly.

Colbert leaned closer. "Did you slaughter my children?"

I shook my head.

"Did you gut everyone you met in here?"

I shook my head again.

"Did you butcher my wife and me and turn us all into unthinkable power?"

I kept shaking my head. "I didn't, but still, I'm the son of the man who did this just to give me immortality."

Anastasia waved her hand. The walls turned golden with black insignias on them, and a sense of peace and happiness filled the room. "This monastery was once a vibrant, happy place. No matter your status, you are welcome to dine and be with everyone else. Your father was like a brother to everyone here. He never hated nor envied us. He always wore a smile and became a brother.

"Our two clans lived in harmony. Whatever problem we faced, we did it together. I want a day like that to return. I want a day where I know my daughter and you will save this world and turn it into a happy place again. Kit, will you do this?"

I said solemnly, "I will do everything I can to make that a reality."

They smiled.

"Then think of that as your punishment. Make this world a better one. We await your results."

"My daughter," Colbert said, "please live, love, and remember that we love you."

All the ghosts floated toward the ceiling. They circled a few times and disappeared.

En and I were left alone in a darkened room like before.

"They were your parents?" I asked.

En didn't speak.

"They were amazing people. I'm glad I got to meet them, even if it was like this."

She remained quiet. I saw some wooden debris and piled it up to light a fire. I sat down beside it, as En remained where she was, staring at the swords on the ground. Watching sparks fly into the air, felt something unfamiliar.

Turning, I jumped aside just as a spear passed through where I'd been sitting. I saw En staring at me, crying violently.

"What are you doing? You could have killed me."

She threw the spear at me. It twirled in midair and came at me. I dodged and blocked the attacks with my sword, as the spear returned to her hands.

"Why did I have to lose all of them?" she demanded. "Why couldn't I die? Why did it have to be them?"

She rushed me, and the spear slid under my arm. I didn't want to hurt her, so I kicked her feet out from under her. She hit the floor hard, and I grabbed the spear to walk backward with it.

En lay there, crying, as the firelight cast shadows on the wall. The spear tried to escape, but I held a firm grip on it. Finally, I released it. It twirled and stuck into the ground beside En.

I dropped my sword and opened my arms wide. "You can kill me, En."

She looked up.

"I mean it. I've killed thousands. I have murdered them for the sake of the ones I loved. I'll continue to kill to make the world a safe place. Those deaths will create the same feeling you have right now in many more people. I won't fight you. I won't do anything. If you want to kill me to avenge your family, you have my permission."

She stared at the spear, then pulled it out with one hand and stood. Her legs shook, as she gripped her weapon in both hands and stared at me.

"If I were you, I'd do it. I haven't made anyone in the entire world happy. All I've done is used people and killed them in the name of peace. So do it."

She walked forward until she was less than ten feet away.

With each step, I knew I was about to die and prepared myself for it. It was the only way I could atone for everything I'd done. My life needed to end.

She stopped when her spear tip was only a foot away.

"I do love you, En. I never had a sister. I was a loner in my nation, and I'm happy I had you."

The spear tip touched my stomach. I felt a slight sting, then blood trickled down.

"It's just a flick of the wrist, Sister. Then it'll be over."

She didn't look at me the entire time, just stared at the spear, her legs still trembling.

"You know, Kit, I hate you so much right now. I hate you with every fiber of my being."

I smiled, unable to argue with that. "I know, Sister."

She took a deep breath. "But I love you so much, too. I couldn't have the life I have or the future my family wants for me. I may hate you, but you're still the best thing that ever happened to me."

She dropped the spear. I stepped toward her and hugged her.

"Hopefully, one day you won't hate me as much as that, but until that day, I'll do my best as a brother to keep you safe and fulfill the promise I made."

She nodded and stepped back. As she stepped back, the spear rammed through my stomach. Blood flew everywhere, hitting her face. Blood rose to my mouth, and I coughed.

"Kit! No!" She ran to me, as the spear dislodged from my chest. She caught me, as I fell. "Kit, it'll be OK. I can fix you."

I looked up at her, my body turning cold. "No. It's all right. You aren't a healer. This is far too bad to be healed. I'm not angry."

She lifted the spear with one hand and threw it across the room. "I didn't know it would do that, Kit. What should I do?"

She laid me gently on the floor. The heat from the fire no longer felt warm. I looked up when one of her tears struck my face.

"Do me a favor and destroy my body. Tell the girls I left. Don't tell them what happened. It wasn't your fault. Just tell them I had to do this alone, all right? Promise me."

She stared down at me. "I won't do it. Don't try to make me."

I smiled at her. "Do it as a dying wish, Sister. It's all right."

She shook her head and took my hand. "Fine, but it's not too late. I can still fix you."

I looked past her, as a dark, cloaked figure appeared with black wings that extended to the ground.

"Are you ready, Kit?" the figure asked, its voice booming throughout the room until it sounded like the depths of a chasm.

I nodded. Its fingers reached for me.

Suddenly, a bright light shone down and struck the cloaked figure, making it flail around and fly backward. Looking up, I saw figures appearing above me.

Celnius floated down in a black beam. The golden beam held a woman wearing a shawl. Lastly came Teralicion in a bright green beam.

En turned and saw the gods appearing in their beams of light. As Celnius and Teralicion walked over, the goddess with gold fought with the cloaked figure.

Celnius knelt beside me. "You aren't done yet, Kit."

I smiled. It was too late, so why even try to fight? "I am. There's nothing left to do."

Teralicion looked down at me. "The Church of Terra doesn't help those who don't help themselves, my boy. Now get up."

I looked at him, while Celnius moved En aside. Celnius held me and leaned over to kiss me with icy cold lips. Then she leaned back and looked into my eyes. "I know what love is now, Kit. Fight!"

They disappeared, and my body erupted in black flames, smothering everything. En flew away past the cloaked figure, which tried to claw its way toward me. The flames became more aggressive, burning through the walls and ceiling. Beams fell onto the cloaked figure.

I lay there staring up at the moonlight and stars twinkling beautifully.

"What a lovely night, and such a magnificent picture."

The rest of the ceiling collapsed on top of me.

23

Opening my eyes again, I saw beautiful stars overhead. "Am I dead?" Sitting up, I found myself floating on a lake, with ripples of water flowing away from me.

"No, you aren't dead. Well, not yet, that is. You know, through billions of years, I have watched over this world. I never met a human like you. It's the weirdest thing. You're stupid, compulsive, and short-minded, but your heart is in the right place. You constantly want what's best for the world no matter what. You always keep moving forward. It's almost comical to watch you."

I looked behind me and saw a woman in a light golden dress with a shawl over her face. "Who are you?"

She walked around me. "I'm the beginning and the end. I'm the reason the world continues and the reason it ends."

I knew who she had to be. "Are you the centurion?"

She kept walking around me, her eyes always on me. "Maybe I am, and maybe I'm nothing more than a boy's stupid dream. Maybe I don't even exist."

She snapped her fingers.

We stood on a mountainside, looking down into a valley, where a fierce battle raged. Dragons on both sides attacked each other, while ground forces clashed. Screams filled the air, even though we were far from the battle.

"Wars are fought over women," she said. "They're fought over politics. Some are even fought just because a few crave them. What drives you, my stupid child, to wage a war?"

I stared down at the carnage. "I just want this world to be at peace. I want to raise kids in a world that doesn't turn on itself, a world where all are welcome and no one has to fear persecution."

She laughed. "That's the stupidest thing I ever heard. Do you know what mankind is? They're creatures of war and selfishness. There aren't beings for peace. They certainly aren't beings who would ever want peace. The thought is disgusting to them."

Two dragons fell from the sky onto a group of soldiers.

"Then what should happen? I want to fix the world. I want people to be happy and see each other in a better light."

She shook her head. "Your dream is a child's dream. It's not viable for this race. Even if you hold peace for a hundred years, it would erupt in chaos and war. Do you really think you can stop that? Are you strong enough to change the world and all the views people hold?"

I shook my head. "I can't do it alone."

She nodded and turned to me. "Then what will you do? You know what you want isn't something that can be grasped. Will you quit?"

I shook my head again. "I won't quit. I'll make my dream a reality with or without your help. I can't let it die for those who lost their lives and who believe in me. I'll fight for it every day."

She giggled, catching me off guard. I turned toward her.

"What so funny?"

She shook her head. "You're so full of surprises and stupidity. Let's just say it all works out. In the end, your dreams come true. What would you do with all that peace?"

I smiled and stared down at the battle. "I'd build a house. All of my companions and the women I love will live there, raising kids and enjoying life until the end of time. I would relax and worry about myself for once."

She stood for a moment, then she snapped her fingers. "What a selfish ending. Is that the ending you'll receive? That's an answer I don't have. Deep down, I pray for your happiness and an ending where you can be in peace and live a happy life."

"What happens now?" I asked.

She walked away. "You'll fight for the future of your dream, and I'll watch from afar. I might help you occasionally, but I want to see you struggle, to bleed and fall, so I can see you rise up again like a phoenix and fight everything. I've enjoyed your story so far and wish to see more of it. Don't disappoint me, Kit, son of Tellium."

Her fingers snapped again.

I opened my eyes and found myself in a room. Looking around, I realized I was in Patrunice's home. En slept in a nearby chair with her head near me. On the side of the bed, I saw the girls sleeping with me.

How did they get there? How long was I unconscious? I shook my head and sat up.

En woke, saw me, and jumped up to hug me. "Kit, you're awake! I'm so happy. Thank the gods!"

I rubbed her back. "What's wrong? What happened?"

She sat back in her chair. "You've been like this for a month. You wouldn't wake up. Your body was badly hurt. Patrunice said it would be best if you were here. Razele and the others showed up last week and haven't left your side. They talked to you constantly and made sure you were never alone."

I smiled at the girls. I realized I wore cloth pants. Bandages covered my torso and arms. I sat up slowly.

"Was the damage that bad?" I asked, looking at myself.

She looked down. "You had a big hole in you. Then all that rubble fell on top of you, which didn't make it any better. I thought you weren't immortal. What happened?"

I stood. "I don't know. That's a good question, one I would like answered. I know I'm not immortal, because I was on the verge of death."

I grabbed a cloak on the side of the bed and pulled it on, walking toward the door.

"I'm going to get some sleep, Brother," En said. "Please be safe."

I nodded and walked down the hall. Patrunice and Kilyon sat at a table below, drinking and talking. I walked down the stairs, and Kilyon saw me.

He raised a hand in greeting. "Well, there's my son. What took you so long to heal?"

I shook my head. When I sat down next to him, a mug of ale appeared in front of me. Kilyon tossed my case of smokes and took one out to light for himself.

"I'm sure you already know, don't you?" I asked.

He nodded and looked at Patrunice.

"Yes, we both know. Why?"

I stared at the mug of ale, seeing yellow mead flow in a circle. "I saved the Chaos Nation. It will return to normal, as you know, but I had to give up my immortality to do it."

He slapped the table and laughed. "So the young pup becomes a hero and sacrifices everything to protect the land. I must say, I'm surprised that you had to give up that power."

I lit a smoke and inhaled. "Yeah, I am, too. I didn't want to, but it was the only way."

Patrunice was worried. "What happened?"

I recounted the whole story to them, which took awhile. She shook her head when I finished.

"You met not only the God of Black but the Goddess of Gold. Do you know how big that is?"

I shook my head. Kilyon was as confused as I was.

"Do either of you know who they are?" she asked.

We shook our heads.

"Imbeciles. I swear, Kilyon. Come now. You've heard stories of the Goddess of Gold, haven't you?"

I was still confused.

"Oh, I swear. OK, fine. I'll tell you. First, she's also known as the Mother of All Time. She's the reason the worlds in this universe exist. She's the reason life exists. The God of Black, more commonly known as the Reaper of Death, is the reason why planets die and why people grow old and die.

"He must've really wanted you, Kit. You were in his grasp, which meant he could finally kill the child who's been eluding him."

I asked, "Well, that's a bad thing, right? If he wants me dead, that means he'll be hunting for me, doesn't it?"

She shook her head. "No. He can't come after you unless you die or are very close to death."

I understood the situation a little better and flicked ash into the tray. "Then what happened? Why am I still alive?"

They shrugged, making me chuckle.

"You're saying I was just insanely lucky?"

Kilyon shook his head. "No. It looks like the gods of the natural laws of the universe happen to like you, or at least one of them does. It seems they're starting to come around to you. I still can't believe they came running to rescue you, especially the God of Terra. I've always heard he's an ass."

I thought for a moment. "Who's the goddess of the Kai Nation? Do you know her?"

Kilyon looked at Patrunice, then at me. "I'm afraid I've never met her, so I can't say. No one in the Kai Nation has seen her in a very long time."

I wondered what happened to her. Did she really leave, or maybe it was something else? I set the thought aside. "What's next for me, Kilyon. Should I return to the Kai Nation? It's been over a month. Should I go to the front lines?'

He smiled. "Actually, you have to return to the monastery. That's our next stop. I would tell you to take a break, but we don't have time. The Celestial Nation is pushing us hard. We haven't lost any ground yet, but they're really hitting us. We'll have to pull our forces back to regroup."

I nodded. I had the feeling all along we'd have to lose some ground, but I was worried about how much. "OK. That's our next stop. I hope Kelos doesn't try to kill me."

Kilyon chuckled. "That would be a fun fight, and you know it."

We chuckled, then we heard footsteps on the stairs. The girls came down with Ruby in the lead. They came to our table and stopped. I stood and walked over in front of Ruby, as she looked into my eyes.

"You promised everything would be all right," she said. "Why did you lie about that?"

I looked into her eyes. "I'm sorry. I didn't know what would happen. I shouldn't have said everything would be fine, when I didn't know it myself."

I bowed my head to her. A moment later, they surrounded me and gave me a big hug.

"I'm just happy you're back with us," Razele said. 'We've been so worried about you, not knowing what to do."

Ruby clutched me tightly.

"I'm sorry to all of you. I can't promise that I'll be fine, because I don't know what the future holds. I won't be upset if anyone wants to leave."

Someone slapped my back.

"I won't leave your side, Master. None of us will."

I asked Valis, "Are you sure about that?"

She nodded. All but Ruby had her face pressed against my chest, and they nodded.

"Thank you, all of you."

They backed up, all but Ruby.

"What is it, Ruby?"

She looked up with tears on her cheeks. "You aren't allowed to leave my side for a long time. That's my rule now."

I smiled. "That's fine. I'll follow that rule for now."

She backed up, although she still held onto the side of my garment.

Kilyon walked over. "You have to visit the girl from the vat. There's something we need to discuss, but before that...Entity?"

He walked past me to looked her up and down. "Entity, the Crimson Black Ghost."

She looked away.

"Your father was a true warrior, someone I would have loved to fight again."

She looked at him in surprise. "You knew my father?"

He laughed. "Oh, please. I knew him very well. Tellium, your father, and I were best friends. We sparred and trained together. We even fell in love with the same girl. Your father beat me to her heart, and I'm glad he did. You've been a big help to Kit and his friends. You're welcome to be part of this family, too. What do you say?"

En, bursting into tears, ran into his arms.

"It's all right," he said softly. "You have a family with us. It's the least I can do for you."

I smiled and leaned against the wall, as Ruby laid her head against me to watch them.

Patrunice walked up. "How is it, having a bigger family?"

I answered, "I'm not sure it's a good feeling. I just know I'll have to work ten times harder than before."

She laughed. "When I first met you, I didn't think much of you. You were just some stupid kid with an immeasurable power who could easily have destroyed this world. Now that I look at you and think of the things you've done, good and bad, I'm glad I didn't kill you that day. It was the right decision to keep you alive."

She blushed and looked away. "That may be true, but the real battle is far from over. I wonder how much we can take before everything tears itself apart."

Patrunice leaned against me. "Isn't that for heroes to figure out?"

I chuckled and felt Ruby tug on my cloak.

"She's right, My Lord. You're a hero, but you aren't alone. We'll figure it out together."

I smiled at her. "Thank you for saying that. You're right."

Patrunice lit her pipe and smoked it.

"I don't feel like a hero, though. When I look at my friends and family, I feel they're the real heroes. I'm just the one who's there to help."

En came over. "Thank you for everything, Kit."

I bowed my head to her. "It's the least I can do. I'm glad I saved your life. It was one of the best things I ever did."

She smiled, and Patrunice looked at her. "I'm sure you could use a bath, right? The other girls would love to see you. Shall I take you to them?'

En was immediately exited. "Oh, please! That would be wonderful. I feel like I haven't bathed in years."

Patrunice took her hand, and they walked toward the back of the building.

En looked back at Ruby. "You want to come with us?"

Ruby looked up at me.

"I'm not going anywhere dangerous," I said. "I'll be in the house. Go ahead and take a bath."

Ruby stood up taller and kissed my cheek. "Just be safe. I know how stupid you can be."

I laughed, as the girls all walked toward the baths.

"It's good to see you with so many loved ones. It's good for you. I like how you can turn anyone to your side." Kilyon reached into a pocket for his silver case.

"Care for another one?" He opened the case and offered it to me.

I took one out and handed the case back. Snapping my fingers, red flames appeared. He laughed and lit his smoke, then I lit mine.

"I missed having your power around," he said. "It was so helpful."

I shook my head. "Oh? I'm sure someone else would be willing to light your smokes."

"I missed you more than just for lighting my smokes. Anyway, on another note, the war is progressing. It seems the Celestial Nation is growing bolder. They've started a push to take over the school, but that received a quick response. Even then, though, the school is facing anarchy. It will institute martial law soon."

I inhaled smoked and blew it out. "I see. That is something I accepted. If the Terra Nation decides to join the war other than supplying the Celestial Nation, we'd have an even bigger problem. Hopefully, within a month, the Chaos Nation can stand on its own, and the people will rise with us."

He stubbed out his smoke, and we walked upstairs to the rooms.

"I see," he said. "On a separate matter, the girl from the vat—what do you think she is?"

I shrugged. "My guess is, they were breeding until they found a good match, then they continued."

He shook his head. "I wish that was the outcome."

He turned right and walked past a few doors before stopping at one.

"The girl is manufactured. She isn't using flames. They harvested flames from multiple high-ranking people, then cloned them into subjects they stole. What you'll see is an artificial magic in a sense. People like her can use all the flames and their variants at any time without warning. She was bred for war and nothing else, making her extremely dangerous."

As he opened the door, a cold breeze struck my face. The room was made of ice. Everything inside was completely frozen. I saw the little girl fully clothed on the bed.

She cocked her head to one side, as I walked in and knelt beside the bed. Her eyes filled with a rainbow of colors.

She touched my face with her hand. Her mouth opened, but no sound came out. When she began to panic, the ice melted, and the temperature in the room shot up. I shielded Kilyon with chaos flames and held onto the girl. Her flames died down quickly, as she clutched onto me.

"Please," she said so softly I almost didn't hear her. "I don't want to hurt anybody."

She fainted. I placed her back in the bed, as the room returned to normal. Slowly, I lowered the chaos flames.

"What happened?" Kilyon asked.

"She said, 'please,' then said she didn't want to hurt anyone. I think she's afraid of her own power. It doesn't help not being able to control them. What should we do?"

He bent over to touch her forehead. "She's normal right now, and she's asleep. That must be the natural point for her mind. The first thing is to train her to control her powers. Once she can do that, it'll be easier for her. The problem is, she has so many different powers, we'd need a master for each one."

I didn't think that sounded so bad. "That shouldn't be a problem, Master. We'll have to teach her every day. Can you handle her ice and water powers?"

"I can, if that's what you want."

I nodded. "I'd rather you did it. You're a good teacher, and she'll need someone like you."

He sighed and walked back to the door. "All right, but you need to find other teachers and have them brought to the monastery. This is the safest place for her."

I walked out and closed the door behind us. "What now? What's the plan?"

He punched my arm. "That's a surprise for when we reach the monastery."

I asked, "What kind of surprise?"

"Oh, you'll like it. Kelos is excited. Are you ready?'

We rounded a corner and saw Ruby and Razele standing at the bottom of the stairs looking up at us, their hair wrapped in towels.

"My Lord."

I went down the stairs to meet them with a hug.

Ruby looked up at me happily. "I'm glad we're all together again."

Razele giggled and kissed me quickly. "Sorry. I just wanted to kiss you."

I looked at the other girls, who seemed ready to pounce on her.

"I hope you're ready, Kit," Patrunice said, near the door.

When she opened the door, pink flower petals flew in, and I caught the scent of the ocean. Were we already at the monastery? I walked toward the door and heard applause and cheering. When I went outside, rows of soldiers stood on the walls, whistling and cheering, while civilians stood in the middle, waving and shouting.

As I walked out, Razele took my hand. "This is home, right?" she asked.

A tear came from my eyes. Ruby reached up to wipe it away.

"It's all right, My Lord," she said. "We're all home."

I walked out and saw Kelos fully dressed in his emperor's blue robe of the infinite dragon. It was made of golden fleece with a white dragon racing across the sky.

He opened his arms wide, as the door closed behind us, and we stood in a group, with Patrunice beside me.

"Welcome home, son of Kilyon, my dear and favorite nephew," Kelos said. "Please come to me."

Razele released my hand. As a group, we walked toward the stage. People stepped aside to let us through the crowd. They looked at me with such hope in their eyes. Kids stood in front of their parents, smiling up to me.

That was what it felt like to be loved by an entire nation, to be seen as something more than just another face. I walked over sandstone toward Kelos, then climbed the stairs when I reached them. My heart beat harder with each step.

Once we were on the platform, the girls formed a line beside me. I stepped toward Kelos.

"I'm proud of you and your companions," Kelos said quietly so no one else could hear, "even if it has led us into war. I will always stand with you."

He turned and raised his voice. "From henceforth, Kit Icealis, you are now the Emperor of the Kai Nation. I, Emperor Kelos Icealis, pronounce this before its people and its army. Do you, Kit Icealis, accept this honor and agree to always put the people of this nation first, no matter what?"

I looked at the assembled crowed. Kelos walked up behind me.

"I, Kit Icealis, will always protect the people and will always strive for peace."

He settled a robe on my shoulders. "Then Kit Icealis is now the emperor, but being emperor deserves a new name. Within that tradition, your father has created one for you."

Kilyon has always regarded me as a would-be proud father.

"You shall be known far and wide as the Immortal Emperor," Kilyon said. "Show us the way to the future and a new world filled with hope."

As I raised my hands, allowing chaos flames to surge above me and form a beautiful flower, the people cheered loud enough to shake the world.

24

Later in the day, Kelos and I went into the war room to discuss what happened recently. We walked to a table covered with a detailed map of the continent and studied it.

Kelos pointed. "Right now, the Celestial Nation has been pushing on the border. We moved our troops back, and they'll be camped on the outskirts of the capital, waiting for reinforcements. We have moved the residents of most of the towns in that area back here, so there shouldn't be too many civilian casualties.

"The capital is setting up defenses, but it could take awhile before they're ready for a defensive operation. The castle is still under construction from recent damage. With the improvements underway, rebuilding could take longer than we wish.

"I do have some good news, however. A lot of Kai warriors have escaped from the school and are returning to join the fight. Warriors from other nations are coming with them. They're currently being processed, but it'll take time to get accurate numbers."

I nodded. They were pushing us hard. "Why are they doing this?"

He smiled. "That's a good question. We want to lure them into the forest. Once they're inside is the best time for us to strike. They'll have to split into three different groups when they enter, and we can hit them separately, which works in our favor.

"Once we've killed them off, we can strip their armor and weapons. The civilians you brought from the Terra Nation have pledged themselves to you and have begun forging the armor we need. That will help us greatly in the attack.

"I also received a message from Hindoros addressed to you." He handed me an unopened letter.

Dear Kit,

I see that war has already started. I can't help with the war effort yet, so don't take this as a cowardly thing. We will join, but we're waiting for something to be finished before we can help.

Hindoros

I handed Kelos the message after I read it.

"What could they be working on that would take this long?" he asked.

I thought for a moment. "I'm not sure. Maybe they're outfitting their army, or doing last-minute training." I studied the map again. "Uncle, I want you and Kilyon as my top generals. I'll need both your help."

He laughed. "Did you think I'd leave? My dear nephew, I'll enjoy it. This war offers something to fight for."

I smiled and saw a smudge on the map. Looking more closely, I saw it sat between the Celestial and Kai Nations near the edge of the continent. "What's this, Uncle?"

He looked at it. "Oh, that. We had three hundred men stationed there, but the last report was really sketchy."

I asked, "What do you mean?'

He shuffled through a pile of paperwork and took one out to read to me. "Dear Leader, everything is fine. Nothing is up here."

Then he added, "The weird thing was, the soldier who brought this to us died a day later from exhaustion. We sent a squad to check out the situation two days ago, but we haven't heard back."

"What could wipe out an entire platoon and an élite squad? It must be demihumans, but I'm not sure which race."

Kelos shook his head. "That can't be right. There aren't that many left. The ones who remain are within the school seeking protection."

Kilyon came in and closed the door behind him. "Well, if it isn't the emperor. How goes the new job, Son?"

I chuckled. "It's great, but call me Kit. That's better than emperor."

He laughed and walked closer. "What are we discussing?"

I pointed at the smudge on the map.

"I see. I've been wondering about that, too. I was planning to check it myself, but I wasn't sure what I might run into."

I crossed my arms. "It's a good idea, but you'll have to take someone with you."

Kilyon raised a finger. "I'll take only one. What about Razele? It would be good for her to get away."

I nodded. "That would be good. She also has a stone, so she can contact me immediately."

Kilyon looked at me in confusion, so I took out my white stone and brought it to my mouth. "Razele, could you come to the war room?"

I put the stone away, and she came in a minute later.

Kilyon laughed. "Now that's amazing!"

She came up to the table.

"I'd like it if you went with Kilyon," I said, "to help with an assignment."

She looked at me intently. "I don't want to leave your side again."

I sighed. "I know, but you're one of the best warriors in the world. We have a problem, and you could help us with it."

"All right. I'll accompany you." She bowed her head.

Kilyon laughed. "It's fine. I'll bring you back to your boy-friend in no time."

She blushed and left the room.

Kilyon looked at me and asked, "What titles will you give the girls?"

"They'll be commanders of their own forces when the time comes. With their help, I know the jobs I send them to do will get done."

Kelos sat down. "Indeed. They'll be able to reach farther than our people, but remember they love you, so don't use them harshly."

I nodded. I loved them in return, but it seemed like the best way to get things done. "Kilyon, when will you leave?"

"Tomorrow morning. We'll have to go soon. We don't need any more problems. Hopefully, we'll be finished by nightfall and on our way back. If it's demihumans, what are your orders?"

"We need them. As long as they're willing to talk and meet with me, that seems best, don't you think?"

"It would," Kelos said quickly, "but remember, there's tension between our races. We caused them a lot of trouble. How can we make up for that?"

I looked at the map. "We'll give them the land they hold right now and set up a trade. In return, they fight with us. Hopefully, we can establish good ties with them and work toward becoming friends."

Kelos nodded. "That's a good way to do it. The more allies, no matter how small, the more benefit to us. All right. I can draw up some paperwork about it. Then we'll have it ready."

I looked out the window at the setting sun. "I have to go do something. If there's anything else we need to discuss, send a messenger. I'll be behind the monastery."

As I walked out, Kilyon asked, "Saying good-bye to your brother?"

I nodded.

Kelos asked, "Who died?"

Kilyon chuckled. "The stupid kid who helped our dumb emperor."

I smiled, as I left the room. He might have been stupid, but Eli was also a good man to have at one's side.

I sneaked away from the monastery and walked down the beach until I found a cliff overlooking the ocean. I heard someone and turned to see En behind me.

"I see the emperor is very busy," she said.

I laughed and walked toward her. "Just Kit is sufficient. Just because I have power doesn't mean I'll use it to make myself higher than those who are my equals."

She hugged me. "You'll change the world. I can't wait, Brother."

She backed away, as a breeze washed over both of us.

"Hello, Emperor."

I turned and saw Celnius standing there, smiling.

"I see you completed the first part of your mission, but there's still something missing, isn't there?" she asked.

"Yeah, there is. He wanted to be buried near the sea, where he could overlook both land and sea. This is the best place. My aunt and I watched the waves from here. This is our home for now, until the rest of the world becomes our home."

She smiled. I waved my hand, and chaos flames burned a hole in the ground. Eli's body appeared and floated into the hole, his mask clutched in his hands on his chest.

"Sorry, Brother," I said. "I wish you were with us right now."

Celnius motioned with her hand again, and sand began dripping in to fill the hole. I took a piece of wood and stuck it into the ground for a headstone, then we stood there until the grave was finished.

En stepped forward. "I didn't know you that well, but I know you were a brother from the Chaos Nation. You helped Kit and fought like a true warrior. You deserve a peaceful afterlife." She fought to control her voice, as she began crying.

I placed a hand on her shoulder and looked at the grave. "You won't be forgotten, Brother. Everything you did helped me with the first part of my journey. Soon, the world will be at peace, and it's because of you and the help you gave."

When I looked at Celnius, she regarded the grave with a tear in her eye. "I'm sorry that this is your life now, my dear little Eli. You completed your mission. You may have saved the entire world. I hope I can see you in the afterlife one more time. Rest in peace."

She lowered her head.

"What happened to the Kai goddess?" I asked her.

She answered, "She fell in love with a human and gave everything she had to make sure he would live on. There is no Kai god or goddess right now. The land is without one. I've heard it won't stay that way much longer."

I was immediately filled with more questions. "Is that possible? Can a god and a human have a relationship?"

She drifted closer to me. "It's not accepted, but no one in the universe can stop love. I want to thank you, though. You were the one who showed me what true love is, and I'm very thankful."

Before I could say anything, she continued. "Kit, may I give you a gift?"

I was confused. What did she want to give me?

She held my face in her hands softly, pulling me in quickly. As our lips touched, a cold feeling came over me. Her tongue explored my mouth, and a round object was transferred to me. She helped me swallow it.

When I pulled away, I asked, "What was that?"

En was disgusted by what she saw.

"It will be apparent in time, my dear little hero. I've been wanting to do that for so long. Thank you for everything."

She turned to dark smoke and disappeared, as En and I stared at the sunset.

"That was disturbing, Brother."

I laughed. "How do you think I feel? I was just fed an orb."

En gagged. "No more talking. I need you never to speak of this again, Brother. Hush."

I laughed. "Oh, come on."

She gagged again and bent over, trying not to vomit. "That was awful! My god. I'll have nightmares about it for the rest of my life."

She finally straightened and looked at the sea. I placed an arm around her shoulders.

"Ready for what's next?" I asked.

She nodded. "I am. I'm ready for anything the world can throw at us."

We stared at the water, as flower petals blew across our view. I was ready, too. It would be an amazing journey, and I couldn't wait to see what happened next.